For our great-grandmother, Martha Ann Ashworth,
may you finally have peace.

Love, your great-granddaughters, Cynthia, Carol, Jane, and Jeanette.

Cynn Chadwick

THE INCORRIGIBLE ROGUE

AUSTIN MACAULEY PUBLISHERS™

LONDON * CAMBRIDGE * NEW YORK * SHARJAH

Ordering Information
Quantity sales: Special discounts are available on quantity purchases by corporations, associations, and others. For details, contact the publisher at the address below.

Publisher's Cataloging-in-Publication data
Chadwick, Cynn
The Incorrigible Rogue

ISBN 9798886930795 (Paperback)
ISBN 9798886930818 (ePub e-book)
ISBN 9798886930801 (Audiobook)

Library of Congress Control Number: 2023906383

www.austinmacauley.com/us

First Published 2023
Austin Macauley Publishers LLC
40 Wall Street, 33rd Floor, Suite 3302
New York, NY 10005
USA

mail-usa@austinmacauley.com
+1 (646) 5125767

In each of my past novels, I've found the acknowledgements' page to be a heavy lift, as there are always so many to thank with the writing of a book. While we may write in solitude, alone, we are always indebted to the kindness, expertise, and interest of generous friends who become integral early readers, dedicated editing professionals, and those whose worth's unknown until the unexpected need.

This story's heavy lift page is of an even greater density as it is historical fiction, a family story, and one that is settled in a place and time I've never lived, and so there are many more to add here.

Acknowledgements begin with the Chadwick family: The US and UK, Lancashire and Yorkshire, branches. My father, Harry Chadwick, Jr. and his UK cousin Frank Chadwick met through genealogical discovery in 1987; soon, after swabbing spit, they discovered they shared a grandfather, Samuel Chadwick, who was once married to my great-grandmother, Martha Ann Ashworth, the star of this novel. And, so began a twenty-odd year journey to the writing of this story. The bonus of this process has been that my family has multiplied, and I have been quite blessed to be embraced by Chadwicks of both The Red and White Roses.

In February, 2020, just before the pandemic, I travelled to Rochdale, UK, to begin my search for this story. I'd planned my stay in a beautiful converted English manor house, The Moss Lodge, where I was treated like family by Samantha and Polly. Sadly, the lodge no longer has accommodations, but for the "Brigadoon" time I was there, it was magical and close to many of the old terraced houses, frequented pubs, and the mill where my family had lived and worked, and has found its way into this novel.

Most of my UK family thought I was crazy for coming to the North in the miserable month of February, but I needed to feel what it might have been like in the bleak Edwardian times, and so I went in the bleakest of months. I was chilled to the bone, it rained, sleeted, snowed, I slipped on wet slate and cobblestones, and somehow felt exhilarated to be standing in front of the same fireplace at The Flying Horse Hotel where my ancestors had also warmed themselves. I am most grateful for the experience, although, I'm sure it wasn't even close to the real feeling of the era.

A grateful thanks to my Yorkshire cousin Frank Chadwick who chauffeured me around, showed me family hotspots, and arranged for a private tour of Helmshore Mill Museum with Curator Suzanne Rothwell. The two wonderful young docents who answered every question, provided small details, and were full of such great enthusiasm for their subject, and they even turned on the machines so we could hear how loud it was back then.

It was a treat to spend this time with Frank and his wife Val, sons Mark and Michael, and his boyhood friend The Rev Nev, who sadly most recently passed, as they each filled in small gaps of this story. During this time, a trip to Lyme Hall (to see how the other half lived) and high tea provided by and with cousins Sheena, Iain, and Tallulah Chadwick Owens, all teachers, who shared their resources regarding school and education history, and the possible crimes of an Incorrigible Rogue.

Even before I'd made my trip over to the UK, I'd been in touch with and received much helpful information from Ms Jenny Driver at Touchstones Rochdale, part of the Royal Trust. Jenny and I had been in touch for months before I made my trip over, and she provided historical information, census data, newspaper articles, and photographs without which I would have missed so much. In addition, thanks to a Mr Owens for guiding me through the cavern that is St Chad's and for the ride through the rain to St Mary's in the Baum, where I sought family marriage, death, and baptismal records.

It wasn't until I was sitting in an Italian restaurant somewhere in Lancashire, going over family photos and sharing family stories with my two cousins, Jane Allen and Carol Pindar did the true reason for my visit emerge. You see, the stories about our great grandmother, Martha Ann were not flattering. She was known to be a drunkard, a fishwife, a brawler and a whore, and yet there amongst the photos was a large black and white in which she was surrounded by her family, her husband, her children and grandchildren and even great grandchildren.

It was my answer to my cousin Jane's question: 'Why do you want to write about Martha Ann?' That was a surprise even to me.

—'I think I've come to redeem her.'

And so it began. In addition to Carol and Jane, we'd dragged Jane's sister, Jeanette Walrath, into our Sunday Zoom chats where they helped create this story about our great grandmother. This was a true collaboration. They checked the dialect, rid England of the chipmunk I'd given her, and warned that Yorkshire pudding, Toad in the Hole, and Bubble and squeak could not be picked up at the market, and would not be eaten together!

Once the telling of the story was complete, I was fortunate enough to find an editor in Rogena Mitchell-Jones at Two Red Pens Editing, whose expertise in dialect and historical fiction was a boon for the book and for me, as my confidence in both was a bit shaky. She put my mind at ease and combed through the manuscript with the finest of teeth. Writing about another culture, place, and time is a risk and Rogena was the net that let me take it.

There is always a place on any acknowledgements' page reserved for those dear ones who I entrust and they kindly subject themselves to a first reading. I'm not sure I could go forward without their counted on cheering. Shirley Chadwick, Martha Vanderwolk, Barb Tirrell, and Carol Colon—you are always my trusted first readers.

Here is a special thanks that I must extend to two very special groups of women in my life. My UK (Zoom) book club and my US (in person) book club. Each of these fabulous groups of women came to me via invitations to talk to their clubs about my last novel *Things That Women Do* and then lucky me, I was invited to join each, and have been profoundly engaged by their insights and interests.

Because they are savvy readers all, a few talented writers among them, I had the idea to ask if they might participate in an early reading of The Incorrigible Rogue with the purpose of generating a Book Club Q&A for future readers. With the graciousness they each possess, they were eager and serious about the task. These very busy women were exceptionally generous with their time and patience to and for this project, and there are few words to describe how humbling their good will and support touches me deeply.

And so, I'd like to first thank both Anne-Marie Dany (US) and Natalie Holland (UK) for facilitating the book club meetings. They each composed, gathered, compiled and organised the questions, which was a burdensome task and one I most appreciate. (Always helpful to have writers/editors in one's book club). An additional shout-out to Anne-Marie Dany, Freelance Editor extraordinaire, for conducting the Author Interview included at the back, which compliments the Q&A nicely. And was fun.

Thanks to my UK book club friends for sending notes, making comments, taking time to keep me honest and true, and for your thoughtfulness and considerations during our Zoom meeting—you were all up so late: Carol Pindar, Liz Quigley, Julie Slack, Cath Whitrow, Deirdre Stables, Lorna Young, and Julie Johnson.

For my US book club friends, what a time it was! Adding flavour to the evening with an appearance by my British cousins Jeanette, and her sister Jane whose short reading of a piece in her very Lanky accent gave me a lump in my throat. Thank you Jean Roberts for your thoughtful and composed questions, Niki Ogg and Trish Hord-Heathery always appreciate your keen insights, and last but not least Ann Hord-Heathery, you were good.

Table of Contents

Part I
Martha Anne Ashworth

Chapter One

1885

Martha Anne peered around the door frame into her father's darkened study. With only the light from the fire and a low candle on his desk, she couldn't help but wonder how he could even work his numbers in such gloom. She'd been in trouble—again—in school, that wicked place where they sent children to be tortured by barren, spinster teachers hating each student for being some other mother's child.

Today, Martha Anne had turned around and mimicked the ugly horse-faced hag to the children seated behind her. She'd wiggled her tongue and ears, crossed her eyes, and dared to whisper a little whinny. Her classmates had been stifling giggles until their smiles and eyes simultaneously rounded to Os and fixed on the looming figure behind her.

She felt the heat of her presence as the musty scent of Miss Royds settled on Martha Anne's sweaty neck. Before she could right herself, the woman grabbed her left plait and yanked her off her seat. Martha Anne fell to the ground and was dragged up the skinny aisle by a hank of hair, held in the teacher's tight fist, to the front of the class. She was on her side facing her peers. Martha Anne squeezed her eyes shut and attempted to disappear.

Miss Royds let go of her plait, and Martha Anne's skull crashed to the stone floor, immediately raising an egg. She could feel it. She knew how much that would hurt tonight when her sister Alice was tasked with brushing out her tangles. Alice would be mad.

'You'll stay just like that.' Miss Royds pointed at her, frowning. She looked over her class, satisfactorily noting the fear in the eyes of each of them, not one sure whether to hold their teacher's gaze or to stare at their classmate hunched into a fist of herself. Instead, most chins dropped, and each child became devoted to picking lint off jumper sleeves.

Martha Anne's usually generous grin slid sideways, a string of drool dripping, and her bottom lip fighting against its quivering. She'd wrapped her arms around her knees and pulled them to her chest. Her usually shiny hair, a luxurious mix of chestnut, strawberry, and gold strands woven through her plaits, was now a dull tangled mess webbing across her face.

When Martha Anne attempted to rise, Miss Royds shoved her back down with her foot. Then, as Miss Royds placed her boot on Martha Anne's shoulder and dug its hobnailed sole into her flesh, a girl called Sophia, in the front row, began to cry as she saw the speckles of blood burst onto Martha Anne's white blouse.

At that moment, the new headmaster, a young Scotsman named Malcolm Bruce passed by the classroom door. He slowed as he witnessed a child on the floor trying to get up and the teacher shoving her down with her boot. He rushed in, pushing Miss Royds aside and quickly helped Martha Anne to her feet. He saw the blood blooms on her shirt and looked over at Miss Royds, now busying herself at the slate board. He knew the child to be the daughter of John Ashworth, a well-respected businessman, educated, a buyer for the mill. He served as a town councillor and, more importantly, he was a warden in the parish church. This was a child to be treated with kid gloves, not kicked with a boot.

'There now,' he said, brushing the sweaty hair from Martha Anne's face. He reached into his pocket, pulled out a handkerchief, wiped her mouth, and handed it to her. 'Keep it,' he said. 'And get your belongings.' He pointed in the direction of the coat closet at the back of the room.

'Oh, she's fine,' Miss Royds said, striding towards them. 'She's always playing the fool.' She made to lift Martha Anne by her armpit. 'Thanks for your help,' she said, 'I'll take it from here. Get to your seat.' She pointed to the empty desk from which she'd yanked the girl by the hair and dragged her across the room earlier.

'I think not, Miss Royds.' Mr Bruce added a stern note to his words. 'I'd like a nurse to have a look at her.' He did not lower his gaze from hers, reminding her who the headmaster was in the room. No matter his youth or short time in the position, he was her superior on the job and of a certain aristocratic class. This was most evident at this moment by a child being pulled by the elbows like a wishbone between them. Emma Royds knew who would win this snap, so she released Martha Anne to this impudent pup.

For Miss Royds, this was painfully humiliating. She was typically treated by children and adults alike with certain deference and respect for her higher education and persuasive position. Over two decades of teaching the children of Rochdale, she'd been given a sure and steadfast elevated stature. This, combined with her self-sacrificing spinsterhood, added a sort of martyred dignity to her claim that she'd sacrificed love and babies for teaching. And here she was, publicly humiliated by both this incorrigible child and this, this…this arrogant Scot.

Martha Anne sat beside Mr Bruce's desk with tea and a biscuit, waiting for the nurse to arrive. Mr Bruce asked, 'Now, Martha Anne, Miss Royds said you were distracting the class from their studies. Would that be true?'

'Not really.'

He looked surprised. 'What do you mean by not really? Either you were or you weren't.'

'I weren't because the studies were so borin' that a fly on the wall could've just as easily been a distraction for them.'

Mr Bruce couldn't stop a slight twitch from tugging at the side of a smile. 'Well, that may be so, but it does not exonerate your actions. Is it true you were making faces?'

'Not when she turned around.'

Such a literal child, Mr Bruce thought. Do you think you might apologise to Miss Royds for being disrespectful?

Martha Anne took a sip of her tea and then looked into Mr Bruce's dark brown eyes and said, 'Do you think Miss Royds might apologise to me for pullin' me down the row by me plaits and diggin' 'er boot into me shoulder?' She tugged on the edge of her bloodied blouse.

'I'd like to think she would,' he said, looking away from the child's evidence of abuse. 'She did have cause, so perhaps you could go first.' He dipped a pen into a nearby inkwell and scratched something on a piece of school letterhead.

'I don't think I will, then.'

He paused in his scribbling and looked up. 'Why not?'

She set her teacup on his desk, got up, and began wandering around his office. She stopped beside a shelf and picked up a small knife in a decorative leather scabbard. 'Why do you 'ave this?'

'That's my sgian-dubh,' he said, thickening his brogue, and smiled. 'Go on, pull it out, but be careful. It's sharp.'

'What's it called?'

This time, he sounded it out slowly, 'Skee-en-doo. It's Gaelic,' he said. 'Some know it as a dirk.'

Martha Anne slid the shiny blade from the leather scabbard ornately adorned with silver at its tip and top. 'I like skee-en-doo,' she said, marvelling at its precise sharpness. 'Why do you 'ave it?' She turned it over in her hands.

'I wear it with me kilt and sporran. That's the little purse there on the shelf.' He pointed to the pouch with a fringe of deer hide on its flap.

She looked up at him. 'So, do all Scotsmen wear skirts and carry purses?'

'We do.' He nodded and grinned.

'No wonder you need a knife,' she said, sliding the steel back into its sheath and returning it to the shelf.

'Yes, well…' He cleared his throat and felt a tad chastised but wasn't sure why. Goodness, she couldn't have been more than ten, now could she? Just as an emboldened adult might capture his attention, Martha Anne had distracted him from his task. He was beginning to have a bit of sympathy for Miss Royds. 'Please, sit back down, over here,' he said and pointed to the chair she'd abandoned. 'I'm writing a letter to your father telling him of the bother you've caused today.'

'The bother I caused?' She narrowed her gaze at him. 'I don't see anybody else wi' a bloody shoulder and patches of hair yanked from 'er head.' She grabbed his hand and pressed it to her skull. 'Feel that egg? That lump there?'

She was a cheeky one, he thought as he felt the lump.

'It'll be our Alice who'll be most angry, you know. She has to brush me hair, and when she feels this lump, she'll be tellin' me dad all about it.' She leaned back against the seat, appearing as if she'd just settled a legal case.

That dawning expression adults got after talking with Martha Anne and suddenly remembering that she was but a child was the look on Mr Bruce's face. He'd tilted his head and seemed to be studying her with one eye squinted.

Martha Anne was no ordinary child, her father claimed. She was gifted. And since her dad was the smartest man in the world, she believed him.

Interrupting their analysis of one another, the opening of the outer door let in a burst of cold air over the shoulders of a large brusque woman. She carried a big satchel and attempted to tie a too-small white cap onto the top of her head with one hand. Mr Bruce stood and made his way around the desk, offering to take the woman's bag and proffering a seat opposite Martha Anne, both of which she refused. Instead, she settled the satchel on the chair. Then, she ripped off the white cap and tossed it on top of the bag in a swift irritated move.

'Ah, thank you, nurse. Thank you for coming on such short notice,' he said as he remained standing. 'Is there anything I can get you? A cuppa?'

'No, 'aven't time to linger. Got me deliveries comin' this afternoon.' She placed her hands on her ample hips and squinted at Martha Anne. 'We best get to it, then,' she said to Mr Bruce as she kept the girl in her sights.

He strode back to his desk. 'Martha Anne, I want to give you this letter to your father before you leave today.' He retrieved the paper from his desk.

She didn't respond. Well, not with words nor a nod of her head. She just stared at him.

'Do you understand?' he pressed.

She said slowly, 'You want to give me a letter to me dad.'

'Yes, good. Good.' He'd turned the doorknob but stopped and turned back. 'I want you to give this letter to your father.' He stressed the tiny preposition, making the pinch between his brows meet. 'Do you understand?' He waved the white sheet in his hand. 'You're to give this letter *to* your father.'

Martha Anne nodded once, and he closed the door behind him. Then, turning, she looked at the woman now staring at her. 'You're a nurse?' she asked. 'You don't look like a nurse.'

'Is that so?' the woman said as she opened her satchel, releasing a flowery plume of an herb garden into the stale-book smelling room. 'And what, exactly, does a nurse look like?'

'Well, not like you. With or wi'out that silly bonnet, you don't look like a nurse.'

'What do I look like, then?' She rummaged to the bottom of the case and pulled out a green bottle with a cork in its mouth and a dark liquid swishing inside.

Martha Anne tiptoed closer to the open satchel, her eyes darting from a magical pile of colourful bags with drawstrings to tiny, corked bottles filled with liquids, pottery bowls containing medicinal smelling pastes and poultices, and some flowery scented balms and rubs. She watched the older woman deftly uncork and unravel items and set them on a tray.

19

'Well, you look like a gypsy wi' your peasant dress, long plait, and mucky boots.' She pointed to the older woman's feet. 'Are you a gypsy?'

'A gypsy? What an idea.' She unrolled a damp white rag revealing a large shimmering dark green leaf.

'What's that?' Martha Anne leaned close and pointed but did not touch the slimy sheaf.

'That's seaweed that grows in the ocean. It's good to heal sores and whatnot.'

Martha Anne plucked a small shimmery bag from the case and held it to her nose to smell—nothing. Before she could work the string loose, though, the woman gently took it from her and placed it back.

'I'll let you see any what you like, but you 'ave to ask first.'

'What's in that one?' Martha Anne pointed to a light blue pouch and quickly put her hands behind her back and clasped them together—she didn't trust herself not to touch one.

The nurse lifted the blue bag from the chest, opened it, and pinched from it. 'Let me 'ave your 'and,' she said and turned Martha Anne's little palm up and sprinkled the shimmering blue dust into it. Martha Anne watched the woman's rough finger swirl the dust into a paste as it warmed her palm. She smiled as her eyes widened.

'It's warm,' she near whispered.

'Good for a hobbled knuckle joint.'

'What's in it?' Martha Anne asked, now swirling the paste herself.

'Now, that's a gypsy secret I daren't share,' she teased.

'So, you are a gypsy!'

'What if I were? What would you think of that?' The woman sprinkled whatever liquid was in the green bottle onto a white rag and bunched it in her fingers.

The girl seemed to take a moment before answering. 'Well, I'd wanna know if you live in a caravan, if you can tell fortunes, read tea leaves, and cast spells, for starters.'

'And that would do it for you? If I could read the leaves in your cuppa, I'd be a gypsy?'

'Well, no, not just that…' She hesitated.

'What then?'

'Then, before you leave, I'd check your pockets to make sure you 'aven't stolen anythin' from Mr Bruce's office.' Martha Anne said, matter-of-factly.

'Well, you've certainly made up your mind about gypsies, now 'aven't you?'

Martha Anne replied, 'Not all of me mind.' Martha stroked a small silver flask with unusual etchings of forest animals engraved on it. She quickly remembered not to touch and swung her arm behind her back. 'What's your name, then?' She asked.

'It's Betty. Betty Nuppy.'

'From Betty Nuppy Lane?' Martha Anne asked, trying to remember why this was familiar to her. She recalled eavesdropping on a private conversation between her older sister, Lizbeth, and their mother, and so she'd paused at the threshold to the bedroom to have a listen.

Tomorrow, Mum, Lizbeth had implored. *Up Betty Nuppy Lane. Go see Nell. She'll put you right*, she'd said low and urgent as she sat on the edge of their mother's bed. It was their mother's response that had clutched the memory in Martha Anne's mind—*No! She's a witch!*

Martha Anne had filed away the words, even though she did not fully understand their meaning. But she knew what a witch was, and she suddenly felt frightened that she might be standing right next to one. So she took a few casual steps back and away from the gypsy-witch and her smelly satchel.

'I am that same Betty Nuppy. Do we know each other?' she asked.

The girl shook her head and slid a bit further away. She eyed Mr Bruce's Skee-en-doo and wondered if she should slowly sneak it off the shelf or quickly grab it before it was too late.

'What is it, child? Cat got your tongue?'

'Are you also called Nell?' she asked.

Betty frowned and tutted between her teeth. She brought the tray of medicines to a small square writing table. Betty cleared the paper to the side and beckoned Martha Anne to sit in the nearby chair. 'Let's 'ave a look at you.'

Martha Anne stood equal distances between the small knife, the office door, and the gypsy-witch possibly known as Nell. Betty approached Martha Anne and gently guided her to the seat. She tapped her collar. 'Will you undo the buttons, lass? Let me 'ave a peek at that shoulder, eh?'

Martha Anne didn't think Betty sounded like a witch—or a gypsy for that matter. In fact, she sounded a bit like the nice nurse who came to tend her sick mum.

Martha Anne pulled back a bit as Betty slipped the top button from its hole. 'Dearie, I can't look at your shoulder if you don't loosen your collar. Just the collar, I promise.'

Martha Anne worked the last few buttons.

Betty gently pulled back the girl's shirt, slipping it, carefully, over the angry red punctures. She couldn't help the grimace tightening across her face, shock and anger mixing.

Oh, she could strangle that evil woman herself, Betty considered. Unfortunately, this was not the first time she'd had to mend a child whom that so-called teacher had abused. Why they'd let her continue working with children, she did not know but had hoped this new headmaster might put an end to her career, except he hadn't.

Before entering Mr Bruce's office, Betty had stopped by the desk of his secretary, Miss Lake, who shared a detailed description of Miss Royds's abuse of Martha Anne. Then, with a particular bit of shame, Miss Lake slid the thick envelope across the desk to Betty.

'Here's for your services today.' And then, leaning closer, she said under her breath, 'There's an extra bit from Mr Bruce who hopes you understand the delicacy of the matter,' she'd whispered.

Betty had come to understand by delicacy that the extra bit was meant to keep her gob shut. She didn't answer but slid the envelope into her satchel.

Betty examined the raised red wounds, three of them neatly clustered in a triangle pattern. It made her regret taking the hush-money stowed in her satchel. No one should be able to get away with this kind of treatment—not of a child, or an animal, for that matter.

'This next might sting a wee bit.' Betty held up the little green bottle, sensing the girl would be more curious than afraid of what was happening to her. Betty soaked a small ball of cotton. 'This is iodine. It'll clean this up proper. All reet?'

Martha Anne stuck out her jaw and nodded.

'Ready to howl like a hound?' Betty asked genially, trying to distract the child. Not only did Martha Anne not howl, but she also did not even flinch. She just kept a steady stare at something in the corner. The only show of pain appeared in the pricks of tears in the corners of her eyes. When Betty finished cleaning the wounds, she lifted the slimy green sheet of seaweed from its dampened rug and spread it over the three fiery sores.

'Ahhh…' Martha Anne seemed unable to prevent this response when her brows rested, and she closed her eyes. 'That's nice and cold,' she said, seeming to enjoy the treatment.

Betty proceeded to wrap Martha Anne's shoulder in a soft, clean rag, tying it neatly beneath her armpit. Then, carefully, she pulled the shirt back over the gauzing and buttoned her up.

The big woman stood back, admiring her handiwork. 'Anythin' else botherin' ye?' She turned Martha Anne towards her.

'Just this egg on me 'ead.' She cupped her little palm over the bulge.

Betty felt it too. It wasn't just raised, it was hot, and that wasn't good. 'Here, let me see what I've got in me bag o' tricks.' She untied a pretty purple pouch, dipped a cloth into the cool water in the basin and sprinkled some dust from the pouch.

'Lavender!' Martha Anne said, smelling the familiar scent rise.

'It is. It'll soothe that goose egg. Here, 'old it there.' She placed the rag in Martha Anne's palm and settled it on her head.

As Betty was closing the satchel, Martha Anne quietly, almost reverently, asked, 'So, are you called Nell, too?'

Betty turned around and looked down at the child. 'Why are you askin', lass?'

'Me mum says there's a witch called Nell up Betty Nuppy Lane, and seein' you're some sort of gypsy, I just wondered how many witches could be up one little lane, is all.'

'Is all, ye say? Do ye know what they do to witches in these parts?'

Martha Anne shook her head, her eyes wide.

'You should ask yer dad. He'll know. Ask him about the Pendle Witches. He'll tell you.'

'Are you a Pendle Witch?'

The child was not petulant, Betty could see, but in fact, quite serious.

Betty closed her satchel, placed it on the floor and sat in the chair where it had been. 'No. I am not a Pendle Witch, nor a gypsy, though some'd say I were both.'

'Why?' Martha Anne picked up a pencil from the writing table and began scratching on a small square of paper. 'Why do they say that about you?'

'Because I know flowers an' 'erbs and how they 'elp ailments. I know when to plant and when to harvest. I know which combinations of which herbs can cure a cold or stop an achin' tooth. Ye see, Martha Anne, it were me mother who were called Nell, and she were a wise woman, a bit of a gypsy even, sure.' She smiled in response to the memory of her mother. 'Me mum taught me all I know about the healin' power of a garden, the sea, the sun and of the creatures all about us.'

'So…you're not a witch?' Martha Anne asked, her pencil darting here and there on the paper.

'Not as far as I know. I live in me little cottage in a big garden right at the end of me lane. I've got some chickens, sheep, and goats, and I make soap and poultices. I sell 'erbs and seeds, and now and then, I read a tea leaf or two…' She grinned now, revealing bright blue eyes that Martha Anne had not noticed before.

'So…you're not a witch, you're not a gypsy, and you're not a nurse?'

'Not that I am aware.'

'Then, what are you? Just some old wise woman?'

'Seems so…' Betty said, watching the little girl scratch away with the pencil. 'What you drawin' there?' She asked her own question this time.

Martha Anne held up the paper to reveal the very scene Betty had just described: a flower garden by the sea under the sun overseen by a little grey squirrel, a chubby sparrow, and what appeared to be a sheep.

'Why, Martha Anne!' Betty exclaimed as the child handed it to her. Betty held it up and away and took in the little scene. 'It's lovely!' She peered at the page. 'You're quite a talent, do you know?'

'That's what me dad says. Says this here school is wasted on me, on me talents. He wants to send me to a school for lady artists, but Mum won't 'ave it. She won't let me go far away. She's not well. Dad says schools like this one are for average children, and I am not average.'

Betty stood and handed the paper to Martha Anne. 'I'll agree wi' him on that for sure.'

Martha Anne didn't take the picture but instead asked, 'Would you like it? You can 'ave it if you'd like.'

Betty looked down at the beautiful little black and white sketch. Everything she loved was in this one little fold of paper. 'Thank you. I'll frame it and put it in me shop for all the world to see!'

'You've a shop?' Martha Anne said, now more curious about this gypsy-witch wise woman than ever.

'I do. It's next to me cottage, in me garden. It's quite lovely, and I know exactly where I'll hang this. Will you sign it?' She handed it over and watched as Martha Anne very carefully printed her name at the right bottom.

'Can I come to your shop?'

Betty lifted her suitcase and herself in the same motion and began heading for the door. 'Come to me shop? What for?'

Martha Anne now looked about as if searching for an answer. Finally, she said hesitantly, 'I dunno, I guess to see your flowers?' More a question than an excuse. 'I'll come to see me drawin' hangin' there!' She seemed relieved to have found a real reason.

'If you like, bring yer dad round,' Betty said.

'Do ye know me dad?' Martha Anne looked surprised.

'You'll have to ask 'im,' Betty said and swiftly exited the office.

***

When he cleared his throat, Martha Anne's father did not lift his eyes from his figuring as he said, 'I understand there was trouble at school today.'

'There was,' she admitted readily, not about to speak of her own. 'Mr Bruce rescued me after Miss Royds tried to stomp me to death.'

Her father looked up and gently removed the wire-rimmed glasses from his face. Then, setting them down on the desk, he rubbed his eyes and the bridge of his nose with a certain vigour. 'Is that so?'

''Tis.'

'Martha Anne, come.' He gestured with a wave. 'Sit and tell me what 'appened.'

'Well, first…' she began as if warming to her story, 'there I were, mindin' me own bored business, when, suddenly, I were yanked from me chair by me hair, dragged up the row, and stomped by that old horse-faced hag. I'm sure I would've been kicked to death had Headmaster not come to the rescue.'

Her father peered down at his desk and lifted the letter from Mr Bruce.

25

Martha Anne had given it to her sister Alice, not her father, hoping Alice might read it and decide to keep it a secret, or at least break the news in her favour.

'Mr Bruce writes that you'd been a distraction to the class, and this is the reason Miss Royds punished you. Is that true?'

'I don't think so. I think I was an entertainment to the class, and this is the reason Miss Royds attacked me.'

Her father sighed and gave a nearly imperceptible shake of his head.

Earlier, when he'd arrived home, his wife had given him the letter that Alice had shared with her mother in hopes of an intervention on the girl's behalf, but Ellen was ill and could not deal with such things as they caused her head to throb and her body to drop to her bed like an exhausted air balloon. And so, she'd called for her husband, handed him the letter, and said, 'You created the little bugger, you deal wi' 'er.'

And so, here they were. His wife may have held some truth in her words, but she did not understand their youngest child. She was unique in her intelligence, especially for a girl. Not a dullard like her brother James, away at an apprenticeship. A shipbuilder, of all things, he wanted to become. Stupid boy. His son was a disappointment. His elder daughters, Alice and Lizbeth, met the usual expectations for girls, but Martha Anne was extraordinary. He'd seen from her birth when she'd latched onto his finger, her bright eyes opening before due, and she'd held his gaze as if saying—I'm countin' on you, Dad.

Now he looked into those bright eyes as if daring him to contradict her, and he knew if he did, there would be a lengthy discussion on the semantics between distraction and entertainment, and he was too tired for all that, so he read from Mr Bruce's letter:

It was reported that Martha Anne was clowning to her classmates, making faces and disturbing noises, creating a distraction, impeding learning...

'Well, is Mr Bruce wrong? Is 'e lyin'?' her father asked sternly.

She thought about this for a moment, considering all the words: "distraction", "impeding", "learning". Nevertheless, she believed that Mr Bruce wasn't exactly lying, as the operative word "learning" was what should have been happening in the class. So, in his estimation, she supposed, it might appear to be true, but it wasn't. So she couldn't rightly agree that she'd either "distracted" or "impeded" her classmates from any "learning". So she said, 'I think Mr Bruce were misinformed about what happened.'

'She's at it again, Dad!' Lizbeth said, rounding the corner and entering the room with a tea tray. She set it down on the side table and turned to glare at her younger sister. 'She's a devil, Dad, and you've got to put a stop to it!' Lizbeth was a plump, unattractive girl, face full of pox-marks and a nose hooking her chin.

'Shut your cake 'ole,' Martha Anne said to her sister. 'What do you know of it, Lizbeth? You weren't even there.'

'I didn't have to be there! Everyone were talkin' about ye. Everyone describin' the spectacle ye made of yourself, shamin' a teacher like that, actin' the fool as always. It's humiliatin' is what it is, Dad. Do you know what it is to be Martha Anne's sister? It's no wonder the lads won't even look at me with that girl for a relative.'

Martha Anne laughed. 'You think I am the reason the lads won't look at cha? Have you looked at yourself in the mirror? Because your answer's there.'

'Dad!' Lizbeth stomped her foot and swung a look at her father.

'Enough. Both of you.' John Ashworth had just about had enough of them. All these women tugging away at him. He'd had enough of their bickering, their costs to his pocket and his sanity.

'It's none of your concern, Lizbeth. Thanks for the tea. You may leave,' her father said. In his estimation, Martha Anne was probably right. With Lizbeth's weak chin, hawking nose, and puny ways, his eldest daughter would probably never attract a lad unless he were compensated greatly, well beyond John Ashworth's means. He supposed he'd be saddled with this one the rest of his life.

'What's goin' on?' Alice asked as she, too, entered her father's study, a worried line across her brow.

'It's 'er. It's that gormless git, always after me.' Martha Anne pointed at Lizbeth and threw her arms around Alice. 'She's always tryin' to get me into a bother.'

'You need no help with that, now do ye?' Lizbeth spat.

Alice turned to Lizbeth. 'She's a child, for goodness' sake. Have you no heart? Didja not see what was done to 'er today?' Gently, she eased Martha Anne away and lowered the neck of her nightgown, exposing a soft, pale shoulder and three fiery red weeping holes.

'Dad? Didja see?' Alice turned her sister to face their father. 'And didja feel this?' She pushed Martha Anne around the desk, took her father's hand

and placed it on the hot lump on her sister's head. 'All this in one day! How often does that evil witch get to 'arm this child before you put a stop to it, Dad?'

He'd lost control. He'd meant to have a talk with Martha Anne, alone. Try to help her see how her behaviour wasn't appropriate, that it was unacceptable. These were his intentions, all the while knowing, even if he got her to agree out loud, she would harbour her own considerations about her behaviour, and these would not align with his own.

'Do you know why, Dad?' Lizbeth interjected. 'She was acting the goat, all chuffed with 'erself, makin' fun behind poor Miss Royds's back. I 'ad Miss Royds, back in the day, and she was a lovely teacher.'

'Dad?' Martha Anne piped up from the fray that she often was between her sisters. She knew Lizbeth did not like her one bit, and Alice, maybe a bit too much. Ever since their mum got ill and couldn't manage the house, the laundry, the meals, never mind Martha Anne, Lizbeth had been tasked to take over the chores. The sicker their mother got, the more Lizbeth hated Martha Anne, and the more Alice loved her. Since she was little, her mother had been sickly. She'd never known a mum as anyone who did much of anything but lie about in the bed.

'Dad?' Martha Anne said again as he was amid trying to mediate between the two elder sisters. 'Do you know Betty Nuppy?' she asked, seeming to shut down the noise of their negotiations immediately. They each turned their gaze to her as if she'd asked after the devil himself.

'What?' Lizbeth said. 'Why you askin' about Betty Nuppy?'

'How'd ye know Betty, luv?' Alice repeated more gently.

But it was her father's narrowed gaze and rising from his chair that caught Martha Anne's attention, as he seemed to turn a fairer shade than he'd been whilst seated.

'She's the one who fixed me up today, in Mr Bruce's office.' She turned to Lizbeth now, noticing that her father hadn't answered her question but was still looking at her. 'And when I asked if she was also called Nell and did she know me dad, she said she wasn't called Nell but to ask me dad if he knows 'er.'

Now Lizbeth and Alice exchanged what could only be described as worried glances.

'Why did you ask if she were called Nell?' Alice near whispered.

Martha Anne hesitated, suddenly realising her mistake. She'd have to admit to eavesdropping on Lizbeth and their mother's conversation. 'Dunno.' She shrugged. 'I heard a woman called Nell lived up Betty Nuppy Lane, and I was just wonderin' if they were the same.'

'What'd she tell you?' Lizbeth demanded.

'She said she wasn't called Nell. She said she wasn't a gypsy or a witch, as far as she knew, and all she'd learnt about potions and herbs she'd got off 'er mum, who must be dead by now because Betty Nuppy is old.'

Finally, their father seemed to recover from his sudden muteness and said, '*All reet*, daughters, it's time for bed. Leave me.' He sat down hard in his chair, and both Lizbeth and Alice turned to go. When Martha Anne didn't follow, Alice turned back and beckoned her.

'I'm goin' out the back,' Alice said. 'It's dark. Come now, or go on your own.'

Martha Anne shook her head and sat back down in the chair beside her father's desk. Alice shrugged and followed Lizbeth out of the room.

Martha Anne thought that her father hadn't noticed she'd remained, but eventually, he poured tea into a cup and then a bit into the saucer, which he passed over to her. She blew across the steamy puddle and slurped a bit from the saucer's edge. She wanted to lap it up, like she'd seen the neighbour's cat would do, drinking milk from a saucer, but she knew now would be no time to agitate her father any further.

'Dad?'

'Yes?'

'Do you know Betty Nuppy?'

He nodded. 'I do.'

'She 'as a shop, do you know?'

'I do.'

'Can we go one day? To 'er shop? To visit?'

He set his cup before him. 'Why?'

'I want to see 'er chickens and 'er goat. She's got a sheep, and she makes potions. I want to see how she makes 'er potions.'

'What for, lass?'

'Maybe I could learn a potion to make Mum better again.'

She was a curious child, thoughtful and mostly kind, but determined to her own will. These traits would be admirable in a boy, but in a girl, it was troublesome. Sometimes he thought he should send her to Paris to the Sorbonne. He wished they'd accept women scholars at Oxford, where he'd send her to become a scientist of some sort. He'd even once, just once, thought to send her up north to his sister Belle's farm, but Ellen, even as sick as she was, would have none of it. Letting James go off nearly killed her. He could not have insisted they send Martha Anne anywhere. As much as he favoured the company of his most brilliant child, he would let her go away from this ever-grey, rainy landscape before it dimmed and dulled her bright little spirit.

He couldn't blame Ellen for wanting to keep her girls around. Especially Martha Anne. For all that bothered her mother, Martha Anne was also the one who could make her laugh, who would rush into her room each afternoon to tell her all she'd learned in school. Be it spelling or gossip, the telling was equally entertaining. Martha Anne brought news of the outside world. Sometimes she'd sing a new song she'd learned or demonstrate her improving whistle. Even if Ellen had said it weren't lady-like, Ellen seemed quite pleased by it. Martha Anne would bring pictures she'd drawn, sweets she'd share, stories she'd heard or made up, and would eagerly read aloud for hours, long after Ellen had fallen asleep.

Martha Anne could also be a trial on Ellen's frayed nerves, John thought sadly. On good days, she welcomed the little sprite of a girl bounding into her room with news and thoughts escaping before she even said hello. But when Ellen was having a bad day, a day when the laudanum was wearing off or John had held back on the dosage, trying to conserve, or a rainy day might spiral her into an inexplicable melancholy sending her to her bed, drapes closed, the room dark, no visitors, not even or perhaps especially not the rambunctious Martha Anne. However, as she'd grown older, Martha Anne learned to temper her moods to match her mother's mood. On those bad days, she'd tiptoe in with something to read, as she knew her mother would not want to chat but listen—only listen.

His youngest daughter's arrival into the world was the worst delivery of the seven his wife had born, leaving just the four alive. It took its toll, the deaths of babies, but not just on the mother. Although, how everyone went on about it, you'd think only mothers suffered the premature deaths of the lives of many lost babies.

It was no wonder no seasoned parent would allow themselves much early affection for their newborns as they may or may not make it through the night.

They'd had to keep their love at a distance until they were sure the child would survive its birth. It's how he'd braced himself after the death of their firstborn son, Robert, and the deaths of the following, Stephen and then Daniel, until finally, James came screaming into the world.

By then, he'd conditioned himself to view his baby's mewling as he might a kitten struggling to find its mother's teat. He prayed for the boy, but he didn't have much hope for his son's survival. He remembered now that he hadn't taken much interest in the child until one afternoon, he passed the boy sitting up in his pram, fat cheeks, smiling, gnawing on a whisky-soaked rag, and noticed his son had two bright white teeth at the bottom, shining in his baby slobber, and making talkative undiscernible baby sounds.

James's survival seemed to have signalled the all-clear for Lizbeth and Alice, who arrived and thrived in the next three consecutive years. When Ellen had not gotten pregnant again after nearly six years, they'd both believed that the Lord had finished blessing them with three healthy, pleasant children. When Ellen's late in life pregnancy was evident, they were each equally worried for different reasons. Ellen had confessed she hadn't wanted any more children at her age, that the three they'd had were enough. And then, she became disinterested in her very own condition. But for him, this pregnancy and birth of his third daughter was the one that had captivated him. He wasn't sure why or how, but Martha Anne's energy, her soul, had surged through him as she held his finger tightly and locked his eyes the very day she was born. They'd bonded in a way that he'd never connected with another soul, ever, and it humbled him.

He paused to see if there was any underlying mischief in his daughter's eyes, but she was, as always, earnest, even in this new interest in potions and Betty Nuppy. 'We'll have to talk about that again. We've got to talk about what 'appened at school today.'

'Told you, Miss 'emmor Royds—' She giggled.

'Martha Anne!'

'Fine. Miss Royds pulled out me hair, smashed me head, and kicked me wi' a boot. That's it. That's what 'appened.'

'They've suspended you. They 'ave.' Her father scowled and shook his head.

'Suspended? Does that mean I don't have to go back?'

'No, it means you can go back when you've changed your attitude.'

'Changed it to what?'

'Changed it to a better one.'

'And where'll I find a better one?' she asked.

'Well, that's up to you. You'll need to search your soul for it.'

'I'm not sure I've got a soul. What if it's not there? Or what if it's there, but it's the same attitude found, then what do I do?'

'Then you'll just need to promise you'll stop being a distraction in class.'

'I don't believe I'll be able to keep a promise like that, Dad. I'm afraid I will always be a distraction for Miss Royds, as she 'ates me.'

'Well, then, perhaps you'll find a way to make Miss Royds like you.'

Martha wrinkled her nose. 'I don't want Miss Royds to like me. I just don't want 'er to kick me again.'

'There are ways, Martha Anne, smart ways, to get what you want without causing others' bother.'

'Like what?'

'Like what would it take for you to behave at school?'

She thought about this, leaned over, and nearly whispered in her father's ear, although there was no one around to hear. 'I want to go to Betty Nuppy's shop.'

He looked surprised—yet he'd nearly fed her the prompt, so why should she ever surprise him. 'You'll behave at school if I take you to Betty's shop?'

'I can promise if we go to the shop on Sat'day that I'll try to behave as best I can.'

Chapter Two

It'd been hard for Martha Anne to stay out of Lizbeth's way for the entire week of her suspension from school. *Actually,* Martha Anne thought, *it's been hard being especially good and staying out of Lizbeth's way.* She'd been promised a trip to Betty Nuppy's shop on Saturday, but only if she were a help and not a bother to her eldest sister, her father had warned. And at every turn, Lizbeth would threaten her with a broom, a poker, a pan—whatever she had in her hand at the time. She'd swear to the devil that she'd beat Martha Anne with it. Or she'd threaten to tell their father some horrible lie that was not said or done, only to put Martha Anne in a bad way with him as soon as he came home from work. The worst Lizbeth promised was to sell Martha Anne to the mill: 'With all the other unwanted buggers in town,' she'd hissed in Martha Anne's ear just this morning when they'd passed in the hall.

Martha Anne felt her scalp tingle and a genuine shiver slither down her spine as she imagined it. She'd heard of it happening—the selling of children. She knew it to be true. She'd seen the poster signs: "Wanted: 250 Orphans. Apprenticeships at Helmshore, Moss, ERA Mills. £3 each". She'd even witnessed it. There'd been children in her classes, those dirtier than dirty, hungrier than hungry, poorer than poor, whose eyes grew big when they eyed your dinner box, and whose names neither you nor the teacher ever bothered to remember. After all, these were the same children always at home sick or taking care of a new baby. Some were truant, off in search of discarded food behind bakeries and butchers. They could be seen following the rag and bone man, the coal wagon, the black pea man, chasing bits and pieces that sometimes fell and sometimes were thrown at the bony lads and their scrawny sisters. These were also the pickpockets and thieves down at the market, those who'd risk it all to nick a potato or a gold watch, each having their value.

And then, yes, sadly, Martha Anne knew of a boy down the row whose Dad had died, and there were too many little ones, so his mum sold him and three brothers to a mill. It was said to be a good thing, as the boys would get a roof over their heads, food in their bellies and training for a lifelong trade.

Then one day, as Martha Anne passed by the Moss Mill, her grandfather's mill, she noticed the dirty wee workers, some bare-footed, traipsing across the lot carrying big pelts of weave, pushing carts of bale cotton, and hauling buckets of water. They seemed somehow dazed, staring straight ahead with their tasks, moving through the thick fog of smoke huffing from the chimneys like ghosts. She'd looked up at the tallest of the dingy brick buildings, across the cobbled quadrangle, to a long row of squat windows at the top, where the orphaned children were said to be kept. At one window, she saw a small face peering down at her. Encircled by a speckled kerchief, the face nearly glowed in the black backdrop behind him—or her. She thought her. Ghost-like, she met the girl's round black eyes and watched the slit of her mouth turn up at each edge. When Martha Anne smiled back, the girl raised her hand and waved. She recalled waving a hesitant hand and fluttering her fingers up towards the waif, but she also remembered how quickly she'd hurried along as if befriending the child from afar was somehow a betrayal of her family. Martha Anne didn't understand her own figuring, but shame was attached to it, and shame she understood just fine.

Oh, she knew Lizbeth's threat to sell her to the mill was real. *She didn't think Dad would go along with it, but Mum might,* she thought. That frightened her even more.

She'd been sitting on the stone steps leading to the manor house, waiting for her father. It was a beautiful house that came with his job at her grandfather's mill. It was really Mum's house since Grandfather had given it to her as a wedding present. It was a sore spot between her parents, she knew. Dad hated that it didn't belong to him, but he belonged to it with his twenty-odd years of sweat investment. Sadly, Mum liked to remind him of his place in her world—at least it seemed this way to Martha Anne. She admitted she always sided with Dad on it. She didn't like seeing him beaten down.

The house was a two-story with three bedrooms above, a kitchen, Dad's study, and Mum's bedroom below, then a lovely garden out the back door with a swing in a big tree. But even with all that, it was here in this tiny sunspot on the front step that she liked best for privacy. No one ever looked for her out here. Why would they? They searched the garden, of course, even ventured to spy over the back wall to see if she'd jumped and was playing in the lane, but they never seemed to think that a nice warm sunspot on the front step would be a place she'd be, and so she was mostly left alone until a visitor or the post came round. Here, she'd bring her sketchbooks and pencils and draw the ivy-covered wall, iron gates, cobbled street, and woods beyond. She'd study the tiny creatures—the squirrels, mice, and toads. She'd try to capture crows on the posts, robins in their nests, and swifts in flight. But what she liked best to draw were buildings, rooftops and chimneys, gunnels and gardens, steeples and viaducts, and the village-scapes in between.

She slid the large thin picture book from beneath her sketch pad—"Etchings of Edinburgh". The cover alone made her heart beat faster. It was a colourful drawing of Edinburgh Castle, high up on the hill with the bustling city below. Carefully flipping through the large pages, she'd attempted to memorise each one. There were sketches, paintings, and photographs of Scotland's Edinburgh, views from the Highlands, the vast lakes, small villages, and the isles in the mist. She felt a small stab of guilt as she traced each detail into her brain.

Mr Bruce had been so busy that she was sure he wouldn't even notice she'd nicked it from his shelf. She couldn't seem to help herself. Her father had instructed Miss Royds to gather lessons and readings for Martha Anne to complete whilst in confinement to avoid falling behind. He'd walked with her on the way to the mill and left her at the school gates to pick up the package Miss Royd's had decided for her. Martha Anne had been relieved when Miss Lake, the secretary, sent her to Mr Bruce's office rather than down to her classroom where she was sure Miss Royd's waited with a hot poker.

While she'd waited, she wandered around. *It was not a cheery room, nor was it depressing, but very masculine,* she thought. Behind his big desk was a small black and white photograph of Mr Bruce dressed in his scholarly robes, standing next to an older couple, a man and woman who must've been his parents. Martha Anne decided that Mr Bruce was very handsome as she stared into his large eyes, noticing his straight nose, full lips, and tousled black hair. She'd not thought it of him before, but here in this picture, a bit younger, a bit jollier, she could see why her sister Alice seemed quite interested whenever anyone mentioned his name. But his gentler brighter demeanour was not reflected in the paintings and pictures on the walls.

These were dark oil paintings of rugged men hunting, men riding muscular horses, fishing in rushing streams, and men in kilts playing the bagpipes on a

Highland cliff. She considered that this wasn't exactly the kind of man Mr Bruce seemed, either. She couldn't really picture him hunting or riding a big horse. However, she could imagine him fishing, somehow. His taste in the books that lined his shelves also did not reflect those rugged men doing rugged men things the pictures suggested. No, Martha Anne could see right away that Mr Bruce's taste in literature reflected a curious young man with wanderlust and a craving for knowledge beyond the classroom. There were travel books, poetry and history books, books about plants and gardens, stars and oceans, medieval bards, minstrels, castles, and dragons. There were journals specific to medicine, science, sporting, and food from around the world. A woman even wrote a story! Martha Anne picked it up and turned to its back cover, where a small paragraph described the contents. Her name was Amelia Edwards, and she'd travelled to Egypt and back and wrote all about it. Imagine that, Martha Anne considered, a woman all on her own in a big desert—riding a camel, no less.

Nearby was a story by a politician called Disraeli. She'd heard of him through her father, who had disdain for his conservative politics. According to Dad, this Disraeli was some sort of lazy-lord-so-and-so sucklin' off the gov'ment writin' luv stories whilst the rest of us sorry lot work for a livin'. So she was surprised to see his book on Bruce's shelf. He must be a "Tory", she thought disappointedly, but not surprisingly, as most Scots were contrarian', her father had once warned.

There was also a journal featuring a group of smiling young women, captioned "The Glasgow Girls" and seemed a society of sorts for "lady artists". Beside it, with no seeming regard for order, lay a small catalogue of sketches of medicinal plants and herbs, the kind Betty Nuppy must grow and use. *Betty would love this little book,* Martha Anne thought. And so she quickly tucked both beneath her skirts and slid them up under her blouse in hopes they were smooth enough around her middle not to be noticed.

Finally, on Mr Bruce's writing table, she came across an envelope with her name scrawled in black ink and set on a stack of papers and books. As she was about to pick up the pile, she saw a big colourful book on a low shelf next to the table. She'd allowed her fingers to flutter through the glossy pages of "The Etchings of Edinburgh", where drawings of castles and shops, villages and farms, barns, alehouses, and tiny stone houses with peat roofs, squat chimneys, and windblown gardens were too much for her heart. It seemed she had fallen in love with Scotland and this book. It was too hard to part with, and so she slid it into the stack of books and lessons.

She'd spun quickly around when Mr Bruce entered the office and clutched the stack close to her chest as if it might fly away. She was sure he'd seen her pinch the book, but he appeared more surprised by her presence than by what she'd been doing with the papers.

'Martha Anne!' he chirped as he scooted behind his desk. She neared the door with her cache but smiled his way. 'Miss Lake was away from her desk. She didn't warn me you were here!'

'Well, 'ere I am,' she said, 'came to get me homework from the old hag, I mean horse-face, I mean teacher...' she said, waiting to see the rise she'd get from the headmaster. There...*Just a small smile,* she thought, *but then he'd composed himself and became serious.* She saw his dark hair needed a cut and thought the springing curl that sometimes fell across his forehead and bounced in front of his eye made him seem more boy than man. He had freckles, she saw for the first time. Why, he looked Irish more than Scot, she thought as she studied him.

'Did you find your lessons?' he asked, distracted by something at his desk. 'They're over on my writing table.' He pointed dismissively.

'I've got them.' She lifted the stack in her arms as proof.

'Oh, good.' He looked up at her and smiled. 'Sorry,' he chided himself. 'I haven't meant to be so abrupt. It's been a harrowing morning.' He did not know why he was explaining himself to this girl, this child, who always seemed to be able to put him at something of a disadvantage, he felt but was unsure how or why. Whenever she appeared, he felt thrust back into those awkward moments when at university, and he would encounter an inspiring professor outside the classroom and found himself unable to form a question or mount praise until the professor was well beyond hearing distance.

'Why do you 'ave all those pictures?' She pointed to the paintings of the adventurous men on the walls.

He followed her finger as it traced around, pausing at the paintings. 'Why do you ask?'

'They don't seem like you.'

He raised his eyebrows and then frowned. 'What do you mean "don't seem like me"? What do I seem like?'

'Well, you don't seem the kind to be off roamin' the hills huntin' stag or playin' the pipes. Do you play the bagpipes?' She turned to him, suddenly curious about the answer to her question.

'No, no,' he shook his head, 'I don't, but my dad does.'

'Why don't you, then? He could've taught you.'

'True. But I'm not full of the same hot air as he,' Malcolm said, indulging himself, and then added, 'I'm not much of an ear for music, I'm afraid.'

'Do you hunt then?'

Again, he shook his head.

'Fish?'

'No, no, I'm afraid I don't do any of those things.'

'Then why do you 'ave these dark-awful paintin's? They don't suit you.'

He laughed. Oh, she was keen. She saw details most adults wouldn't see if they tripped over one. He nodded his head and made for the smallest of them. It was a foxhound hunt, and the rider in the red jacket was blowing a trumpet.

'Can you keep a secret?' he asked.

She followed him, her eyes wide with intrigue. Finally, she nodded and stood back from him as he lifted the small painting from its nail.

'See, back when I took over this study from the previous headmaster, a Mr Donald, I believe.' Then he asked. 'Did you know him?'

She said, 'I knew who 'e was by 'is smelly bum when 'e passed in the hallway. It came right to here.' She saluted her nose, indicating where the man's buttocks must've measured to her height. 'I was shorter then. I'm sure I would be up to 'is big belly now.' He noticed she did not smile while relating either of these observations, realising she was not trying to shock or shame him. She was just telling her truth.

'Yes, well then,' he said, stumbling to compose himself. He faked a slight cough into his fist. 'Well, Mr Donald, it appears, was fond of all these outdoor activities, and after he died, no one came to collect the paintings.'

'Why do you keep 'em?' she asked.

Having already lifted the small painting from its hook, he stood away from the wall. Martha Anne's smile revealed her immediate understanding as she saw the white square where the painting hung. It was the room's original colour, now a dingy grey. 'All of them'—he gestured to the other paintings—'are hiding the same white squares and rectangles all around.'

'Why don't you just paint the room over?' She looked about, now seeing the grime. 'Or why not replace them with paintings of your own fancy?'

He nodded and placed the painting back in its spot. 'I suppose my only answer to both is laziness,' he said and stood back and looked at the painting. 'Just haven't the time or inclination, to be honest.'

'Can't you hire a painter? Me dad hired a lad called Roddy to paint the upstairs rooms of our house.'

Mr Bruce leaned back against his desk and folded his arms, looking at the paintings. 'I could, I suppose. I just don't like spending too much time in here, though. Seems a waste to cover up or replace, for a few hours spent.' He looked at her. She'd begun to make her way to the door again, and somehow, he didn't really want her to leave. Before he could stop her, though, she turned back again as if something had occurred to her.

'How long you gonna be here?'

'What do you mean? Be where?'

'Here. At school? As Headmaster? What's the plan? Two years? Twenty?'

He shrugged. 'I hadn't really thought.'

'If it were me, I'd get rid of them.' She gestured to the paintings.

'Would you? Why?'

'Because the longer you're here, and the longer they're there, the more you're gonna feel like you might need to start ridin' horses and playin' the pipes. Paintings like that ask a lot of a person.'

He wasn't sure what to say or if he understood what she meant, but he didn't think either of those things was at all what he wanted to do. He stared for a moment and tried to imagine himself standing in waders in the middle of a stream catching a giant salmon, which he had once, with his dad, up in the Highlands on a father-son outing, which they'd both enjoyed but promised never to do again, lifting their pints in a warm pub later that day. She was right, he thought over the paintings. He could see how they might settle on him. Seep into him, making him feel like a caricature of himself. These paintings did not seem like him, not in any way, because they were nothing like him. Martha Anne's quick observation about his length of time in this position lent a sort of foreshadowing of his future he did not want to imagine. It felt foreboding, damp, and grey, the way this North Lancashire countryside seemed to be every single day of the week, month, and year. He thought Scotland was cold and damp. It was, but not like this, not in the way that there was no hope of a day or even a ray of sunshine. No, there were plenty of sunny days in Scotland, whereas here, there were just small glimpses and pockets of it, every now and again, if you could capture one.

'Is there anythin' else?' she asked, now wanting to fly out the door with her robber's loot but kept her voice steady, as if she hadn't just stolen books from his shelves.

He moved back to his desk, being startled from his meditations, trying to shake off the nagging burden she'd somehow laid across his shoulders, which now felt somehow heavy, but again, he did not know why.

Finally, he asked, 'Did you have a look at the lessons? Do you need my help understanding them?'

She backed away from him, nearer the door. 'No, don't think so. Our Alice always helps with me studies. I'm sure we'll be able to figure it all out.'

He was messing about his desk now, looking for something. 'All right then,' he mumbled.

'Can I go?'

He looked up and asked, 'You didn't happen to see a fountain pen here?' And he began to come from behind his desk as if he wanted to check her apron. She backed up more, now ready to fling the pile of books and papers into the air and flee right out the door. But then she looked over to the writing desk where a beautiful gold and ivory pen hovered just at the table's edge, ready to fall.

'Is that it?' She pointed. 'On your table? Near the back edge?'

He went to the desk and plucked the pen from its certain calamity. He held it up. 'Ah! Yes!' he said, pleased. 'Thank you! My dad gave it to me when I graduated college. I don't know what I'd do if I lost it.'

'You should put it up then,' she suggested, inching her way to the door.

'Put it up?' He looked at her, frowning.

'Yes, put it away. Don't use it. Save it for your memory box.'

'Why would I do that?'

Now she shook her head. Was he dense or just playing her? 'I dunno. You said you'd hate to lose it, so don't use it, put it up for safekeepin'.'

'But a pen's made to be used.' He admired it, turning it like a delicate instrument between his fingers.

She visibly rolled her eyes at him, exasperated. 'Honestly, don't ask for advice if you don't want to take it then.' And with that, she turned and left his office.

She tucked the "Etchings of Scotland" book back under her sketchpad when she saw her father sauntering down the lane. He seemed tired. No, he seemed sad. They were different on him. Tired had him at a dragging but steady pace, just anxious to get home, but this…this…sad bent his shoulders and furrowed his brow. It didn't just drag his step but made it hesitant, as if he weren't sure whether to take another or not. She imagined he was anxious about her mother. She'd been coughing and sleeping more lately and had heard the nurse mention "consumption", but she hadn't quite worked the worry out of that word yet. She also thought her dad was anxious about work and money. This, too, was a complexity as she didn't fully grasp concepts about buggy cotton, black markets, or company furloughs, but she was smart enough to feel the worry in the hush that came after conversations that her father had been confiding in her sister Lizbeth. Martha Anne had overheard these quiet conversations between her sister and their father, at odd hours, after everyone else had gone to bed.

These talks often centred on both the state of her mother's health and the state of her grandfather's recent downturn of mind. Her grandfather was a very old man who mostly scared Martha Anne whenever she was forced to be in his presence. He had a bald head and a giant grey moustache. His red eyes were often runny, and he never quite looked at her, but above or to her side, and so she was never sure if he were speaking to her or not. To be honest, she didn't like him, so she pretended not to hear him whenever he did talk to her. He'd had something called a stroke, and according to Lizbeth, 'He can't tie 'is own bloody shoe, never mind run a mill, Dad. So you've got to do somethin'.' To which their father nodded solemnly, knowingly, but unwilling to do more than nod.

Martha Anne also considered that she herself might be a bit of weight holding down her father's shoulders as he trudged up to the garden gate. He stopped before pushing through. Looking up at the manor, squinting, as if he were assessing its worth or burden, it wasn't clear, but his study was that of someone not sure of what to make of its place on the street. Finally, he turned the latch. Martha Anne heard the familiar iron squeal of the gate and waited as he approached. His smile slowly came as he saw his youngest daughter perched on the step, sketch pad settled on her knees, pencil in hand, a smear of graphite across her nose. What had she done now? was his first thought, but his second was softer: What couldn't she do?

'Ello, luv.'

'Ello, Dad. How was it out there in the workin' world today?'

He laughed. Out loud, even. And this made her happy. It was few and far between times when she heard her father laugh, and this was a nostalgic, if not melancholy, reminder of his younger, more carefree self. He set his case down on the step and settled himself beside her.

'Are ye out here gettin' away from our Lizbeth?' he asked, knowing that this was Martha Anne's special hiding spot, and he couldn't blame her. It was warm and cosy, behind the big bushes, and a perfect place to escape, even though it was right here in the front of the manor just behind the stone wall and gates.

'I am,' she started, 'but I'm mostly waitin' on you, cos Lizbeth is gonna tell you I've been a terror today. She's gonna say I shouldn't be taken to Betty Nuppy's shop tomorrow and that you should sell me to the mill!' Her tears pricked as her voice rose, and even she hadn't been aware of how potent a threat that had been until this very moment.

Her father sighed. It was never easy, this…this…thing of girl children, this constant female bother. They were mean, these smaller versions of women. Sons. If he'd only had sons, they'd just fight it out between them. He'd never know about their rows till they were grown men sharing lies about the broken nose, black eye, or missing tooth one had knocked out of the other and laugh. But he didn't have sons—just one spoiled child who was a worse bother than his older daughters.

'What 'appened?' he asked and leaned against the house. He fixed his eyes on a tiny wren hopping along a nearby branch in the big oak. He took out his pipe and pouch, pinched a bit of tobacco and stuffed it into the bowl. Then, striking a match against the stone, he sucked the flame until he saw the bright ember and set the burned matchstick on the step. He watched as his daughter picked it up and began shading the roof of the mill that she'd sketched off in the distance. She was a marvel, he considered. Her mind never still. *Like his own,* he thought. A blessing and a curse.

'Well, it all had to do with the berry pie I'd been makin' with our Alice. It were an accident. Lizbeth will say I'd done it on purpose, but it were an accident, I swear, Dad.' She pleaded her case without stating her case.

'What 'appened?' he asked again, puffing away on his pipe. *He could sit out here in the sun all day long,* he thought. No wonder Martha Anne found refuge here. It was like being in a secret garden with only the birdsong and his daughter's chatter filling the air. A mild breeze somewhat cleared away the usual smog of the many mills' chugging smokestacks across Lancashire.

'It were as much 'er fault as it were mine!'

He looked over, meeting his daughter's eyes. 'What…'appened?'

She took a deep breath, and in one long carrying-on sentence, she said:

'I cut a piece of pie to take to Mum, not knowin' it were still a bit warm, and just as I was roundin' the corner to 'er room, our Lizbeth comes barrelin' down the hallway and slams right into me—flippin' the plate and pie right onto 'er…'—Martha Anne swiped at the front of her frock—''er bosom,' she said boldly, 'and it melted right through 'er blouse, to 'er…undershirt…onto 'er…bosom,' she said more self-consciously, 'and our Alice, who helped clean 'er up, says Lizbeth's bosom is now stained a purplish red…' She exhaled the finale and turned her gaze to her father.

On her first try at the word bosom, he'd held in a startled cough, but when she'd said it over and over, as she described what happened to Lizbeth, he could not help but smile, then stifle a small giggle, and finally, as Martha Anne described her sister's purple bosom, he let loose a long smoke-filled laugh which devolved into a choking fit, as his eyes filled with tears, and his daughter patted his back.

'Oh, Martha Anne,' he tried and had to take some breaths to continue. 'You do make me laugh.' He hugged her to him.

'Not mad?' she asked, worried.

'No, but I do see what's comin' when I open that door.' He thumbed over his shoulder. 'You know, don'tcha?'

'She's gonna make you punish me. Sell me to the mill is 'er plan.'

'Well, we won't get enough for you to make it worth our while, so what other punishment can we bear on you that'll satisfy Lizbeth's wrath?'

'You could send me to me auntie Bell's farm for the week!' she suggested, hopefully, but knowing that a trip to the Lake District to visit her favourite aunt, her father's youngest sister, wasn't going to happen. Mainly because getting there would be expensive and impossible and because Mum hated Auntie Bell and wouldn't allow it, even though she'd never even know Martha Anne was gone, for all she cared.

'That's not a punishment, an' ye know it,' her father said. 'Have you had your tea yet?'

'No.'

'Are you 'ungry?'

'Not really. I ate a lot of pie today.'

'Then we'll settle on an early bedtime with no tea tonight. How does that sound?'

'You mean we can still go to Betty Nuppy's in the mornin'?'

'Of course. We'll go, but do me a good turn and make a fuss in front of our Lizbeth when I send you to bed without your tea. All reet?'

Chapter Three

Martha Anne had been awake long before the sun had even begun its rise. She was completely dressed for her outing to Betty Nuppy's shop. She lay on her back on top of the quilts on top of her bed, letting her clogs hang over the edge so as not to soil the bedclothes. She'd tucked her sketching tablet into her coat pocket along with a pencil and a little penknife her brother, James, had given her before he left home. It was for sharpening her pencil, he'd told her, 'And for slaying dragons,' he'd said as he waved the little folding knife. She patted her pocket and counted the seconds along with the grandfather clock in the hallway.

One-one thousand, two-one thousand, three-one thousand—until that made her anxious. So she sat up and waited. She was ready. She was prepared. She wasn't going to waste a minute once her dad awoke. When the knocker-upper went past, she leapt from her spot and hurried down the stairs. Starting the coal fire on the hob, she filled the kettle and set it at the back. She cut two pieces of bread from the thick loaf and placed each piece carefully on the stove. It wasn't long before the kettle whistled and the toast light brown. She poured the tea in her cup and smeared each piece of bread with butter, listening for her father's footfalls as he finished his morning washing up and made his way to the kitchen.

'Well, look who's up and ready for 'er big day!' he said cheerfully. He realised he did feel cheerful and was nearly as eager for their morning outing as Martha Anne was herself. So he sat across from her, and they were quiet as they finished their tea and toast.

'Come 'ere,' he said as he'd set their empty cups on the sideboard. He handed her the long knife and told her to cut two pieces of brown bread. Then he brought a large chunk of cheese from the larder, along with some boiled ham left from the night before. He wrapped both in a rag and placed them alongside a jug of water into a basket. Then, quietly, they put on their jackets and hats and near tiptoed out the front door so as not to wake the household, almost skipping down the steps into the dewy fall morning. Puffs of breath hung in their wake as they hurried to the gate, now giggling as if they were in on a secret prank.

Once through the gates, they lifted their faces to the warm sun, and her father said, 'I think we're off to have a good day. What 'bout you?'

'I've not been this excited since me birthday!' she admitted.

Martha Anne skipped along beside her father as they headed around the corner of the manor house, away from the main thoroughfare, leaving the sounds of the wagon wheels, horse hooves, and clogs all tapping and sparking against the cobblestones behind them. They'd wound their way down little dirt lanes and into the countryside. The brick row houses became fewer and farther between, and shops and cottages gave way to low stone walls squaring off fields and farms. Sheep dotted the hillsides, and animal noises replaced people noises: songbirds, bleating goats, mooing cows, roosters crowing, sheep baaing and dogs barking. All the sounds seemed to change with the landscape as if they were walking into another world.

She recognised they were heading to the tiny village of Milnrow. She'd been with her dad before, as there was an alehouse where he liked to meet up with some old men he knew. She liked to stand by his side, listening to their banter while he passed her sips of beer from his pint. Milnrow was home to the Lancashire poet, Tim Bobbin, who lived a hundred years before, but people remembered him and even named this pub for him. So she was not surprised as they rounded the corner and the pub came into view, that her father began reciting his favourite Bobbin poem "The Battle of the Flying Dragon":

'Our hero's courage none can doubt;
Nor love or fame was he without;
For when this glorious feat was done;
And such a vic'try fairly won
Ambitious Oamfry in a crack
Put kersey coat on sweating back
And then with cautious stare he view'd'

Here, Martha Anne chimed in her favourite line. She growled slow and low.

'The Dragon…which 'e…hacked…and…hewed…'

Her father finished out the tale.

'But still it proved above his ken
As it might do to wiser men.'

He laughed and squeezed her hand. 'Did you know his real name wasn't Tim Bobbin?'

'What?' She was surprised. 'Then why was he called it?'

'His real name was John Collier, and by that name, his Christian name, he was known for his art, his drawings, more than his poetry.'

She thought about this for a moment. What a thing to be, she wondered. *A man of two lives,* she thought. One, a famous dead poet. Another, a renowned dead artist. And to think that women were hardly ever allowed "one" famous life, never mind "two" famous dead ones. She planned to change all that. She might even have "three" famous lives and "four" dead ones. She'd be an artist, like Rembrandt, maybe a pirate, like Mary Wolverston, and an architect, like Gustav Eiffel, who was building a great statue called Lady Liberty to be sent to America to honour the freed slaves. She and her dad had read about them all in "Tit-Bits", which he picked up every Tuesday on his way home from work. Lady Liberty was just one of many stories from around the world that her dad would read aloud to her. Before her mum got too sick to join them, everyone would gather around the fire, and he'd read to the whole family.

'Have you seen 'is paintin's, Dad?'

'I 'ave. Would you…? Here, come along,' he said as if something had just occurred to him, and he picked up his pace a bit, making Martha Anne double-time her little legs.

They came to the old Tim Bobbin Ale House, and her father pushed his way into the darkened chamber. She noticed it smelled like sour beer and burned oil lamps. *The old creaky floors announced their presence more than their actual presence,* she thought. It was quite dark inside, a stark contrast from the bright sunshine they'd just come in from. She was surprised that the room was crowded, and the low murmuring was the din over them.

Men were drinking, even early on a Saturday morning. She heard the barkeep ask her dad for his pleasure, and she sidestepped to a wall near the

47

smudged front windows. Covering the plaster were pictures, posters, and newspaper cut-outs. They were dark scenes of angry gargoyle-ish looking men and witchy old women with bulging eyes, hag's moles, and hooked noses. They were horrible reflections of angry people who probably didn't look quite so hideous in real life. The men were of the upper class. She could tell not only by their dress but also by their gouty jowls and bloated bellies—tell-tale signs of wealth. Some were screaming with wide mouths and eyebrows shooting into frowns. In one, a horrid figure was hoarding bags of money whilst a homely baby screamed in a poor woman's arms. She was crying too. Another showed a clergyman screaming at a lord waving what appeared to be a bible.

Martha Anne slid her notebook and pencil from her pocket and began scratching. There were others. The worst showed a fat man with his hand on the bosom of a frightened woman. It was clear the artist did not think kindly of his subjects.

Then, finally, her father joined her and handed over his glass, letting her take as long a sip as she liked, and she admitted, she'd come to like beer. She passed it back but let the foam tingle along the edge of her upper lip, popping tiny bubbles, and then, with one swipe of her tongue, they were gone.

Gesturing with the pint glass, her father swept across the frames of pictures. 'Well, what do you think of old John Collier's art?'

'Nowt.'

'What? Haven't got an opinion?' He took a sip from his glass. 'That'd be a first! Everyone, attention, please! Martha Anne Ashworth's got no opinion! Send it up the flagpole, lads!' He lifted his glass in the air to a crowd that was not there.

'You told me if you don't have anythin' nice to say, best to say nowt.'

'Since when do you do what you're told?' He laughed. 'What is it you don't like?'

She spoke as she sketched, looking up from her pad and back again. 'First off, they're dark, like he might've even drawn them in the dark. As if he didn't even try to show some light. That's me off-the-mark impression.'

'Can't disagree with you on that one, for sure. What about that one?' He gestured to an old-man-looking baby squalling in a pram. He had on a torn bonnet and was waving a whisky bottle. The woman standing nearby, maybe his mum, was laughing with a man whose moustache was thick and black and dastardly.

'They're dark scenes of life, don'tcha think?' She took another sip from the glass. 'I mean, the whole sad story's right there. The babe is hungry, teethin' maybe. So 'e should 'ave a whisky rag, but not a whole bottle. And that's 'is mum, not a very good one, I don't think. She's ignorin' 'er babe and laughin' with a bad man. You can tell by 'is black moustache and eyebrows 'e's no good.'

'They're called "caricatures", and that is what they're showin'…the dark side of life.'

'Why would 'e want to show that? I don't like seein' that. So why not show the bright side? Especially here in Lancashire when even a sunny day is covered in chimney smoke or darkened by damp clouds that come over the moors just to pour down rain on us like we're plants needin' waterin'.'

He took her hand and led her out of the pub and onto the sunny lane. They both squinted, their eyes pierced by the brightness of the day, leaving the dark room and Colliers' caricatures.

They stood, getting their bearings. Her father smiled and stretched out his hand. 'Can I see your sketch?'

She'd closed the book and had nearly slid it into her pocket when the request came, and so she handed it to him. He removed the pencil clenched in the page and opened to Martha Anne's quick sketch inside the pub. It was not what he'd expected. He'd expected, he guessed, that she was copying Collier's work, as a study, perhaps, but instead, her etching was of the smudged leaded windows and the brightness beyond the wavy glass. Through a small pane, she'd drawn a cat sitting beside the lamppost across the street and a pretty berry bush behind it. John looked up towards the corner, where the grey cat was licking itself in the shade of the berry bush, just beyond the gaslight. He handed her the book.

'That's the bright side, Dad. Do you see now?'

'I do.' Her father then stepped off the curb and crossed the cobbled street to a little lane, walled on each side by stone fences harbouring sheep within its checkered pastures. Overhead, a gauntlet of giant Sycamore trees with leaves the size of a grown man's hand, intermittently, shaded them from the warmth of the sun.

'But we can't always be lookin' to the bright side, Martha Anne. Sometimes there isn't one. Sometimes there is no window or light beyond it. We just have to feel our way along, even if only by inches every day.

49

Sometimes, the hardest part is pickin' and choosin' which dark or bright spots to be in. Do you see?' He pointed down the shadows of the big Sycamore leaves as they danced beneath their feet. 'Bright and sunny dark and shady spots, there?' He watched as the mild breeze cast the leaves every which way, wiping away sunny spots, darkening them, and in the next instance, like magic, the sunny spot would reappear.

She looked down to the moving shadows cast across the muddy lane and began hopscotch from sunny spot to sunny spot, sometimes racing from one brightness to the next. Finally, she skittered around her father. 'Me? I'm not goin' to ever draw dark sides. I'm only ever goin' to draw the next bright side.' And with that, she let go of her father's hand and skipped ahead.

They'd walked quite a distance, Martha Anne a bit farther along, as she could barely contain herself. Then she realised she'd left her dad quite a ways behind her, and so she retraced her steps to find him around the bend, leaning on a fence post, smoking his pipe, and seeming to be staring off into space.

'Dad!' she shouted and ran to his side. 'What are doin'? I thought I'd lost you!'

He startled and then waved her over. 'Are you 'ungry?' he asked and lifted the towel covering the basket, unwrapped the cheese and ham, and put the slices between the bread, handing half the butty to Martha Anne. Somehow, everything tasted better outside, she decided. Her father was staring across the road from where they were seated on the stone wall.

She turned to follow his gaze, and hers landed on a squat whitewashed farmhouse with a peat roof and a fat chimney. Behind it was a stone barn with a tin roof. All around the yard, loose chickens chased one another. There were cows and sheep in the nearby pasture and pumpkins getting ready to turn in a far field. There was an abandoned wagon in the lane and a pony tethered to a post not far off.

'What are you lookin' at?' she asked, not seeing much of anything interesting.

'When I were a boy, I fancied I'd grow up and buy this farm one day.'

'What? You? A farmer?'

Her tone was incredulous, and this made him tug his gaze away from the farmland to his daughter's face. 'Is that so strange?' he asked. 'Could I not be a farmer?'

She shook her head slowly. 'I think it is strange. I'd never take you for a farmer. No offence, but you've got soft hands and tidy shoes. Do you even have any muckin' boots?' She looked to his black shoes, shined up.

'Well, if I were a farmer, I'd 'ave muckin' boots, and I'd 'ave hard hands, too.'

'Why would you want to be a farmer?'

He took a deep breath and lifted his nose to the wind as if he were a hound dog sniffing out his territory.

'Smell that? That's the sweet smell of the country. Imagine bein' out in that lovely fresh air every day? Imagine days spent takin' care of animals, tendin' crops, makin' your own rules, your own schedules, your own…livin'.' He stopped. 'That would've been some life,' he said more to the breeze blowing by than to his daughter, or even to himself. He popped the rest of his butty into his mouth, handed Martha Anne the water bottle, and put their remainders back into the basket.

Martha Anne swallowed her own last bite, finished off the last of the water, and they hopped off the wall. She dusted crumbs from her coat and imagined the delight of the mouse or hedgehog that might come upon such an unexpected feast.

She asked, 'Why didn't you then? Become a farmer and all?'

He smiled, shrugged, and turned to continue their walk up the lane. 'Dunno. Met your mum, 'er dad gave me a good job, we moved about a bit, then the babies came, Mum got sick. Dunno, just never thought I could've done it back then.'

'What about now? Could we be farmers now?' The idea had sparked excitement in her. Tending baby chicks and lambs had suddenly become a joy she could nearly reach out and touch. 'I'd love to live on a farm. And wouldn't it be lovely for Mum? She could breathe easier out here in the fresh air, don'tcha think?'

He nodded and even gave a smile as if he tried to imagine it along with his daughter for that one moment. He glimpsed his wife wrapped in a light blanket sitting in a rocker in the yard tossing chicken feed at the brood and smiling in the sun. He saw her face tinged pink, not the deathly pallor she wore now, but the rosy cheeks of her youth. He wanted to reach out and touch the glossy shine of her hair, and he could almost hear her girlish laughter. It made him think for one quick moment that maybe they could do something different. Leave the manor house in the heart of the dirty mill city for a lovely clean little farmstead out here, in the foothills of the Pennines, with the River Beal running along the boundaries. *What an idyllic life they might've had,* he sadly thought.

'Well, we're too late,' he said jovially. 'I don't believe the farm's for sale. And I believe we might be makin' ourselves a bit of a bother to the current occupants if we just decided to move in one day. Now come on. We've a ways to go.'

As they strolled along, Martha Anne chattered, imagining them all moving into the farmhouse. She said, 'I do think the farmer's wife might not be keen on us moving in, especially if she saw our grumpy Lizbeth comin'. She'd set a ram on her if she did!' And she burst out into giggles at her own wishes.

'Awe, now, Martha Anne. You've got to give Lizbeth some slack. You can't always be a bother to her. She's got a lot of responsibility these days. Aside from her job at the mill at night and taken care of your mum, now more than ever, it'd be good if you could show a wee bit o' sympathy for her.'

'What if I 'aven't any?' Martha Anne bent to pick up a stone, and she tossed it into a puddle to watch it splash.

She was so honest, he thought, *and it worried him.* As if she did not understand that in a world full of good and bad people, even if you didn't have sympathy or compassion for another, you right better pretend to have it because that's what good people had or at least pretended to have. Martha Anne never quite understood that voicing her lack in these benevolent emotions made her seem cruel, which she really was not, but just more free-spoken and frank to a fault.

'Why, she's your sister. You'd think you'd want to help 'er, or at least wish 'er well. She's carryin' quite a load, a lot of worry with not much payback.'

'She doesn't have to be mean while doin' what she does. I don't know why she 'ates me so.'

'She doesn't 'ate you. She's just bein' put upon, and that's me own fault. I put too much on 'er. She's a good daughter to your mum.'

'She's just like Miss Royds, she might be a good teacher, but she's a mean person, deep down. I could see Mr Collier drawing a *Cra-Ca-Ter* of both of 'em. They've both a dark side.'

'*Cari-ca-ture,*' her father corrected.

'Caricature,' she said. 'They would be right perfect subjects in Mr Collier's mean dark drawins.'

He couldn't really argue with her. She was right. They were each in their own way perfect subjects for the dead poet-artist. He was glad not to have to answer because, as they rounded the bend, just a pasture or two up ahead, was Betty Nuppy's little shop and home.

He smiled and tapped Martha Anne on the shoulder, pointing ahead. 'There it is,' he said and watched her expression as she turned to gaze upon the little cottage up the lane.

Her eyes grew wide, and a smile appeared. 'Is that it? Is that Betty Nuppy's shop?' she asked in a near whisper. Her father caught a certain reverence in her words.

'That's her shop and cottage,' her father said.

Surrounded by rock walls, the two-story cottage stood tall with a stone façade of warm yellow rock hunched under a slate roof with matching square windows on either side of the vast wooden door. A chimney chugged grey clouds into the sky as Martha Anne held her breath as she neared. She saw gardens of herbs and flowers of every colour flower, late summer vegetables laying in low rows in a long patch, and apples turning in the orchard behind a stone shed with a Dutch door whose top half was open.

'That's Betty's shop over there.' Her father pointed to the shed with the halved door. She looked down to see a slate path leading from the gate where they stood, through the garden, and up a step into the shop.

'Do you think she's up and about, then?' Martha Anne asked, feeling suddenly shy.

'Why, I don't know if Betty Nuppy ever sleeps, to be honest with you,' her father said and unlatched the wooden gate, letting it swing wide before them. 'After you, luv,' he said and ushered her with the wave of his hand.

There was a small carved faery with wings fastened to the wall, and threading through the faerie's hands was a lace of leather.

'Go on, pull it,' her father said, jostling her shoulder while pointing to the little figure.

Tentatively, Martha Anne pulled on the chord and soon heard a bell tinkling beyond the split door inside the shop. There was a bustling from the back, some clomping around, shifting of things. Then, as the blustering came closer, Martha Anne heard the familiar voice.

'Oh, for crime's sake.' The sound of something being shoved, or maybe kicked, could be heard, and then 'I'm comin', I'm comin'. I'm gettin' there…'

Then, with one quick movement, the top half of the big door was pulled back and there stood Betty Nuppy in its frame. Hair flying, cheeks flushed, she looked first at John and then swept her gaze down to Martha Anne.

'Well, what do you know,' she said, slowly smiling. 'You got His Lordship John Ashworth 'ere'—she thumbed at him, but her gaze didn't leave Martha Anne's upturned eyes—'to bring you all the way to lowly Newhey and Betty Nuppy's shop, on a Sat'day, no less!' She placed her hand on her hip. 'You must be a bit of a witch yourself, Martha Anne, to get Mr Too Big for 'is Britches, to come all the way 'ome for a visit.'

'Home?' Martha Anne frowned and looked at her father.

He nodded, smiling shyly, somehow. 'True. Grew up just over that little rise. The 'ouse is gone now. Burned to the ground. What is it, Betty, nigh fifteen years or more?'

'Twenty, now. You've been gone more 'n 'alf your life, ducky, don'tcha know?' she corrected him and swung the door inward, inviting them inside.

The first thing that struck Martha Anne, even before her eyes adjusted to the dim light, was the smell. It was of flowers, herbs, dirt, dust, pine, acorns, worms, and mulchy forest bottoms all at once. She closed her eyes and took a deep breath, and her brain seemed to catalogue each scent and its accompanying association, filing them away in some corner of her mind.

When she opened her eyes, she could see it was not as dark as she'd thought. There was just the little window beside the door, but a whole section of the roof and room was missing at the back, replaced by a giant glass greenhouse that lit up the entire shop. As she peered about tried not to stare, Martha Anne could see this was a magical place stuffed to the brim with magical things. She thought that perhaps Betty Nuppy was more witch or gypsy than she was letting on. One other notice she made was that this place was also a mess.

'Well, shut your gob, luv, or you're liable to swallow a spider with your mouth hangin' open like that.'

Martha Anne's mouth closed, but her eyes grew wider.

'You see anythin' you like, lass?' Betty asked. 'There's quite a bit to take in, I know.'

'Yes, it's a bit of a mess, I'd say.'

'Martha Anne!' her father snapped. 'That's rude.' But he saw the amusement on Betty's face and added. 'Even if it is true.'

'Says the boy who washed up under a rain spout most of his life.'

'Well, no longer. I've got a right proper tub I soak in twice a week, I'll have you know.'

'And it's turned you into right proper gentry, has it? Do you get your shave at the barber, too?'

'Now and again,' he said, proud that he could say now and again.

'No harm meant, Betty Nuppy,' Martha Anne interrupted, 'but have you been ill?' Martha Anne picked up a dirty rag between two fingers and threw it to the back of the table.

'No, why?'

'Well, I can see no other excuse for lettin' a place go to pot like this unless you're very ill.'

John stifled a laugh but managed. 'Now, Martha Anne, that's no way to talk. You must apologise immediately.'

'Oh, leave her be, John. She's just sayin' what you're thinkin'. Don't lie. I can see it in your eyes.'

He turned away from her as if this would deny her accusation, but she was right. The place got worse and worse each time he visited.

'Dad, you can see it yourself.' She tapped on a filthy countertop and kicked a sack of seeds. 'This shop is all higgledy-piggledy. And where's me little picture I drew for you?' She twirled around. 'You said you'd hang it in your shop. So where could it possibly be?'

She felt the urge to pull the notebook from her coat pocket to sketch a realistic version of the imagined idyllic gardens she'd drawn in Mr Bruce's office while Betty Nuppy was cleaning her up. That was her bright-side view of Betty Nuppy's shop and farm. This, this mess of a place here, the reality of this shop was John Collier's dark-side view of it. All out of place, helter-skelter, confused and confounding. The dust alone veiled the truth of what might have been, could have been, and should have been a most magical gleaming bright farm, like the one in her sketch.

'Why, it's right over here.' Betty gestured towards the counter where the till was set, and sure enough, there on the wall just eye level above it was Martha Anne's sketch. She saw, to her delight, that someone had braided supple birch twigs and fashioned a frame around her picture.

'Oh…' Martha Anne took a moment to marvel at the transition to greatness her drawing made while surrounded by such a frame. 'That's quite pretty there. Did you make it?' she quietly asked.

'I did. I didn't want it to get lost or ruined, so I wove that out of some birch sticks and braided those bits. I quite like both, don't you?'

'I do.' Martha Anne seemed to be studying the piece. She then turned quickly in a circle and said, 'I'm glad it didn't get lost in all this!' Her arms outstretched, taking in the whole of the shop. 'I mean, just look at the danger over there.' She pointed to three opened sacks. 'You've got lye, flour, and…cinnamon, I'd guess, all slumped together. Somebody's like to be poisoned if the lye gets into the flour or the cinnamon and into the pie!'

Betty frowned at John, who shrugged and said, 'She's got a point.'

'You mind your own, John Ashworth!' Betty said sternly but swatted at him as if he were a schoolboy caught in mischief.

'You've always been a bit of a disaster when it came to keeping up a house, now haven't you, Bets?' her father teased. 'But you've always taken care of everybody who walked through your split door, so there's that part, too,' he said more gently.

She shook her head. 'I've got loads more things to be worryin' about than whether I've swept up me floors.'

'Do you not have any help?' Martha Anne asked, tying up the flour sack and setting it away from the lye.

'Don't need help. It's just me. Havin' folks about will just mess things up,' Betty said defensively.

'I could come help if you'd like. I could keep things tidy.'

'Could you now? And do what? You're just a little thing.'

Martha Anne finished tying up the next sack, this of lye, so she was careful when she moved it to the outer rock foundation in the greenhouse. 'I could do that, for one. And a lot more, by the looks of it.' She gestured around the chaotic room as proof. 'Tell 'er, Dad, tell 'er how good I am at tidying around the house. No matter what that hateful Lizbeth says.'

'She is right helpful,' her father agreed, 'if you were ever looking for a lass. I'm sure Martha Anne would make a good charwoman for your shop.'

'Well, I'll keep that in mind if I ever find the need, but I'm doin' just fine, thank you both very much.' Her words were defensive, but her tone was playful, and she brushed Martha Anne's hair back and said, 'Now, go have a look about while I catch up with your dad.'

Martha Anne began a slow wandering, tentatively, fully aware that at any moment, either of the adults behind her could reel her back to them like a fish on a hook. But she kept going towards the light of the greenhouse and all the plants cosy in its warmth.

There were shovels, trowels, rakes, and clippers scattered everywhere. Piles of dirt in corners, bird feeders hanging from rafters, pots, urns, vases, and buckets seemed to be on every surface, and wherever one looked, everything was covered with decades of grey dust and seasons of silvery cobwebs.

There was a certain familiarity in their tones, but she could not quite hear their words. She heard little endearments: "luv", "lass", "chuck", the sort of words grown-up friends and family used with one another. She watched this unspoken dance their hushed tones were orchestrating:

'How's she been since the last time?'
'What can I say? Never better, only bitter…'

Martha Anne's curiosity drove her farther away from them, but as she paused to smooth a fuzzy lamb's ear between her fingers, her ears perked. Not because her father and Betty's conversation had become loud, but because it had become quiet.

'I'm sorry, John. I know it's hard…'
'It's not hard, Bets. Hard is doable. This…this wasting away is draining the life from us all…'

On tiptoes, Martha Anne peered over a high chest to see settled pestles and mortars of varying materials: polished stone, brass, ivory, and a dark shiny wood, each containing colourful ground bits of this and that, was all she could tell.

'I know. I dunno what to say, John, but…I know.'
'Have you got more of the elixir? The one for the pain?'

Martha Anne pinched a green leaf between her fingers and popped the scent of peppermint into the air. Then, plucking it, she chewed the mint between her teeth.

'Already need more? It's just been a fortnight since the last.'
'I know, but it's unbearable at times.'

They reminded her of siblings with a childhood history but separated by distance in time and space, and sadly, a chasm of lonely heartaches, as well.

'I've told you, John, it's deadly. You can't use it often, and you can't use too much.'

As she stood as still as she could, becoming a statue in the shadows, she felt more than heard a slight tension between them, made taught by their hushed voices, which became even softer the more they…argued? Not exactly. *Discussed?* And she wondered…a shared secret? She almost said *secret aloud* as the word came into her mind. She pulled her sketch pad out of her pocket and began to search for a subject of interest.

'Five drops. Right? That's what you said.'
'Five and no more, John. More will stop her heart.'

Then, her father's voice became throaty—almost as if he'd let out a sob, as if he might be crying. 'Thank you, Betty. Thank you.' Martha Anne heard him, his voice no longer a whisper, and so she turned her body quickly, so they could not see her watching.

As they walked to the counter by the door, John and Betty leaned into one another, their heads nearly touching, shoulders hugging. They appeared suddenly younger, like children, together. *Her father's smile was somehow that of an adoring brother,* she thought. The way James sometimes smiled at her when he lived at home. She was her brother's favourite sister. She knew this for a fact because he told her outright and often. She even had written proof.

Every one of his letters began, "To Martha Anne, my favourite sister!"
Yes, her father and Betty reminded her of herself and James.

Then, as he stood on the far side of the counter, watching as Betty measured out a green liquid tincture into a small vial, she saw her father stand upright, take a deep breath, wiping his eyes with the sleeve of his jacket, an act very unlike him. Then, as she handed him the package, Betty reminded him.

'John, I don't have any more in me shop right now. I can't get certain ingredients for this tincture very easily. I have to send to Manchester, sometimes London, for them, so be sparing in your use.'

'I will, Bets,' he pleaded, using her childhood pet name. 'I promise,' he said, but they both knew he'd be back in a month needing more.

Betty started to say something more as she was becoming concerned by how much both John and Ellen seemed dependent on the tincture, but she saw that Martha Anne was sketching in her notebook, pretending not to listen, but Betty thought she was very intently doing just the opposite. Posed in the sunny corner, Martha Anne was serious and scratching away.

Soon, though, Martha Anne saw her father making the purchase, handing over pennies and taking the wrapped package tied with string from Betty's hand.

'Betty Nuppy?' Martha Anne called from a spot in the greenhouse where small decorative plants were growing in clay pots. She was admiring a little spikey fern with green and white stripe leaves. 'What do you call this one?' She held it up, bringing Betty from behind the counter, squinting.

'Oh, of course, you'd pick that one. It's called Dracaena, derived from the Greek, also known as the "female dragon",' She watched the little girl's eyes grow wide. 'Some even know it as dragon's blood because it's got a red sap that can heal.'

'So, it's not true dragon's blood,' Martha Anne asked, a bit worriedly, as she peered at the plant.

'Not that I know of,' Betty said. 'Do you like it?'

Martha Anne nodded.

'Would you like to take it home with you?' she asked.

'You mean to keep it?'

'Can you take care of a plant? First, you'll need to water it. And keep it in a sunny window. Have you got one of those?'

Martha Anne nodded, not taking her eyes from the plant. She stroked its leaves. 'I've got a sunny window.' She looked to her father. 'Can I keep it, Dad?' she asked.

'I'm not sure. Will you remember to take care of it?'

'I will, and I'll even recite "The Flying Dragon" to it at night!' She saw her father smile at the mention of his favourite poem.

'Well, you've manipulated me, haven't you? So how can I say no now?'

'Thank you, Dad!'

A walk through the outside garden included a stop to pet the fluffy sheep, but they only watched the goats who threatened to butt those who came near. Martha Anne chased a few chickens, chatted with a donkey called Robert, and enjoyed the schooling from Betty, who had plucked fruits to taste, leaves to smell, and balms to feel, explaining the medicinal, herbal, and nutritional qualities of each. Martha Anne was glad she had her notebook as she began taking notes on everything. All the while, she had carried the little Dragon Blood plant in her coat pocket. As they neared the shop entrance, her father said it was time to go, and these words had broken Martha Anne's heart.

Betty saw the disappointment in the little girl and said, 'You'll just have to come back.'

Martha Anne brightened. 'Can I, Dad? Can I come back to Betty Nuppy's?'

He seemed a bit awkward. A moment of discomfort fell over him, but then he said, 'One day. We'll visit again, one day.'

And Martha Anne nodded but knowing that she'd be back a lot sooner than one day. She'd come on her own and clean up Betty Nuppy's shop. Then Betty will beg her to come around every day. And she won't have to go to school, but instead, she'd get a job with Betty Nuppy.

Betty watched them trot down the lane. Her dear old pal and his littlest daughter. What a smart one she was, chattering away as she skipped along beside her dad, Martha Anne, careful with her little fern, John with his pipe. They'd be a good pair were it just the two of them. But that poor man married to that…She bit her tongue.

Ellen Moss Ashworth was not now nor ever was a nice or good person for what it was worth. No, she was a demanding girl, an only child spoiled by her rich father. John was an accommodating fellow, and Ellen only married him to make sure she'd be able to orchestrate her comfy life. Betty suspected it was also to bother Ellen's father. He'd been against Ellen marrying John Ashworth and pushed for the idiot-son of another mill owner. But Ellen wouldn't have it and put her foot down. *She'd married John out of some personal spite,* Betty thought.

Before his marriage, John Ashworth had been a mill worker—a weaver. He was rough around every edge. He went to work in the dark, came home in the dark. Most of the time, his otherwise handsome face and homespun clothes held the same grimy pallor. What only Betty knew at the time was that he was trying to better himself. He was getting a secret education. He'd burn a candle low each night teaching himself about business, numbers, accounting, and such. He saved his pennies to buy a nice shirt, good shoes, and a pair of trousers. He had odd jobs at the weekend in hopes of learning a business and making successful acquaintances. He swept floors, counted inventory, pitched hay, stocked shelves, and even cleared rubbish bins.

As his best friend, Betty, had initially been supportive of all his ambitions. But, she admitted, it was easy to support him when his early ambitions of buying Emerson's falling-down farm and making it right had kept him nearby, right down the lane. She knew these dreams because when they were children, they'd make their way to the river's edge to lie on their backs and share their hopes and dreams. Betty remembered whispering secrets to each other and believing in them. Except it didn't happen that way.

Instead, Ellen Ogden Moss ran after the handsome John Ashworth, seeing him as one who would be forever grateful to her for pulling him out of his poverty. Instead, what she'd done was to position him in lifelong servitude to her and her father. It was this new reality that blindsided John shortly after the wedding when he'd walked in the door after a long day's work, and Ellen told him to remove his hat and shoes, slide into waiting slippers, and seat himself at the dinner table. What he'd wanted to do was sit in his comfy chair, read the paper, doze a bit, and then get up to fill his belly in an hour or two. That dream, like all the rest, would never become a reality.

Sad, Betty considered as the twosome disappeared over the hillock. She turned and made her way back into the shop. As she was tidying up the counter—who was she kidding, she wasn't tidying up a thing, just moving messes from one place to another—she saw a small book near the till. It was a catalogue of medicinal plants, seeds, and flowers she could see as she flipped through it. There were the Latin names, the common names, and black-and-white drawings of the species themselves.

A torn piece of paper was marking a page, and Betty slid it from inside. It was a sketch of the little Dragon Blood plant with its striped leaves. Emerging from its centre was the tiny snout of a fire breathing dragon. Smoke and flames shot from its nostrils, and its spikey head and neck blended into the body of the fern. She looked back to the catalogue and saw Malcolm Bruce, Headmaster, written in ink at the top of the page. She turned the little book over in her palm and smiled, shaking her head. What a cheeky little thief she was, that Martha Anne Ashworth.

Chapter Four

Martha Anne had been sitting on the hard bench outside Mr Bruce's office for nearly an hour, and while she could hear the low murmuring going on behind the door, she could not make out the words or exactly who all was in there. She was in trouble, again. But, this time, it was big trouble. Behind that door, she knew, was Mr Bruce, her father, and at least three maybe four other voices, but she could not tell who they were or guess how there could be so many people interested in her. She'd suspected one would be Miss Royds, no surprise. But the others, they were mostly quiet but for a word or two, here and there. She sat on her hands to stop herself from picking away at her nails. It was a narrow look from Miss Lake, sitting across from her, that warned her also to stop jumping her leg, as the jiggling had rocked both a pencil and book to the floor.

She knew why she was in trouble, but she really didn't see it as trouble at all. On the contrary, she saw it as reasonable, smart, and best for everyone involved. But those behind the door discussing her fate, right now, did not see it this way at all. Her decision to skip school was for her own good and the good of everyone, she surmised. No one, not herself, her classmates, nor Miss Royds, wanted her back in class. And Lizbeth certainly did not want her home.

It was Betty Nuppy and Martha Anne who'd gained tremendously from these recent absences. She'd keep Betty out of it, she decided, and she'd just defend the matter at hand—"Self-Directed-Learning" was the term, and it was a way of learning by which the student would pursue genuine interests and their related sub-cultures, rather than an imposed curricula. She'd read about this new way of thinking in an education journal she'd found in Mr Bruce's office. A place she had been visiting, invited or not, as he was rarely there. It was quite easy to get in. Miss Lake was a poor sentry and quite remiss in her duties. She was something of a gossip and spent a good bit of time away from her desk chatting up errand boys, delivery men, and the teachers who wandered by to hear the latest from the rumour mill.

Miss Lake's distractions made slipping into Mr Bruce's office quite easy, actually. If he had ever been there, she'd make an excuse for her visit, but so far, she'd managed to avoid him. When he was not there, she'd return the latest book she'd borrowed during the previous visit and search for another to take home. She was curious about his things. Pictures and mementoes were the things he surrounded himself with, and she could see they somehow defined him. The books he loved demonstrated his broad interests. A small silver trophy determined a win on a grammar school football team. A letter of commendation was framed thanking Mr Bruce for his volunteerism during a flood in Scotland. A heavy glass was etched with an award for a performance in a university play. There was a small black-and-white photo of a young woman, pretty enough, leaning against a seemingly younger Mr Bruce, taken on a high ledge overlooking the sea.

She wondered if this was Mr Bruce's…"paramour" was the word she chose. It was a French word she'd recently learned and had decided it was "sophisticated", another word she'd also just come to know and was using both with utmost frequency. Upon opening his desk drawers, she'd revealed a square tin box of small round…"mints"…she'd decided after licking one. She picked up a bottle of hair ointment that promised to tame "unruly locks", which, in her opinion, was a particular waste on Mr Bruce's rebellious curls. He kept several handkerchiefs stacked neatly, probably for all the crying children, like herself, to whom he'd given them away. The most enthralling thing she'd found was a jar full of colourful glass marbles, of kinds she'd never seen before. Clear round balls of vibrant blues, greens, reds, and yellows winked at her. Others were of a thick white milk-glass laced with streaks of pink, lavender, and orange, colours she'd only seen in the trees during autumn. Some marbles were as large as her palm, others so tiny nearly too small to spot. She unscrewed the lid and lifted a large orb to the light as if it were a fragile egg. Even though she hadn't meant to, she wound up borrowing the beautiful blue marble with green veins that reminded her of a map of England, and which she quickly pocketed before returning the jar to its rightful place in the drawer.

After her suspension, when she'd returned to class nearly a month ago now, her seat had been moved to the very back of the room into the darkest of all corners. She could barely see the lines in her reader, never mind the ones on the chalkboard. As Miss Royds ignored her, Martha Anne passed the time sketching in her notebook and daydreaming out the window to the grey skies hanging over the distant moors.

It was during one of these flights of daydreaming that she'd not heard Miss Royds call on her, especially since it was a rarity for the teacher even to acknowledge she was in attendance, never mind that she should participate. Her apparent awakening from her imagination sparked a smattering of giggles from the class before Miss Royds demanded they cease and stood tapping her finger on her desk, staring at Martha Anne.

'Well? Do you have the answer? Or shall I ask those who are here to actually learn?'

'Sorry, I didn't hear the question. Would you repeat it…please,' Martha Anne offered the courtesy, as her father's advice had suggested she try not to agitate but instead ingratiate herself to Miss Royds. The roll of the teacher's eyes and her quick turn to the slate board told Martha Anne that she had succeeded in the former rather than the latter despite her plea.

After Miss Royd's gave the class a lecture on the evils of lying and laziness, featuring Martha Anne's faking deafness to excuse her daydreaming, she'd been made to go to the chalkboard and write "I will not lie away my laziness", one hundred times. She remained long after school had dismissed, and the sun had begun to dip.

As she was stepping over a muddy puddle, making her way home, Mr Bruce, who was leaving for his tea, caught up with her as she crossed the cobbled street.

'Ah, Martha Anne, you're late leaving school this evenin'?' he said, two-stepping to catch up with her. 'Did you stay to help Miss Royds with somethin'?'

Martha Anne gave him a dark sideways glance and quickened her pace.

'Oh, did somethin' happen then?' he asked.

She stopped. 'Mr Bruce, no disrespect meant, but you've left me to 'er whims, so why not just leave it?'

'Well, I…well, I just want to help. I want you to be happy in school. You're quite bright, you know.'

She looked up at his deep brown eyes and saw the sincerity, rather misplaced she'd decided, and heard the genuine concern in his voice. She wanted to help him, permit him to leave her alone, but she knew that would be for now.

She answered, 'I am quite bright, and I, too, would like to be happy in school.'

'Good then—' he began but she interrupted.

'But I am not 'appy, nor do I expect to be unless or until Miss Royds is no longer my "teacher"—and I use that "term" lightly.' And she quickened her step, leaving him paces behind.

'Is there anything I can do?' he asked, trotting to catch up with her pivot as she hurried down the lane.

Having rounded the corner, he saw she'd stopped before a big iron gate in the stone wall. She was a bit startled to see Mr Bruce had followed her and was suspicious of how he was staring up at the manor house. A slight fear pricked within her middle, and she knew this to be a feeling to be noticed. Her sister Alice had warned her of strangers and had said not to speak to them.

'Especially men, men of any age cannot be fully trusted, Martha Anne,' she'd said.

'Except Dad, right?'

'Except Dad…for now.'

'Is this where you live, then?' Mr Bruce asked, approaching in great strides.

She suddenly felt like a rabbit on alert. Her body stilled as her heart raced. She took hold of the gate-latch, readying to throw it open in case Mr Bruce tried to grab her, or choke her, or even kidnap her, and so she was ready to dart inside and slam the gate in his face, leaving him unconscious and bleeding, she imagined.

Martha Anne squinted at him suspiciously. 'Who wants to know?'

His hand went straight to his coat pocket, and he blushed. 'Why, me…' he quietly said.

'I might,' she said. 'I might not.' She lifted the latch from the notch. 'What's it to you?'

'It's just that I've read about Moss Manor. It's historical, as I'm sure you know.'

She actually didn't know but said, 'Sure I do, but how do you know?'

'I've read an article from "Tit-Bits", I believe. A few years back now. Would you like to see it?'

Her curiosity took hold, and she could not stop her guard from sinking. 'Yes!' She couldn't help herself from blurting, 'I'd like that very much.'

'Good. Come by my office next week. I'll leave it with Miss Lake.'

'Thanks,' she said and began to push open the gate but stopped when Mr Bruce asked.

'And…your sister, Alice, is it? Is this where she lives as well?'

'Why are you askin' after our Alice?'

His white cheeks bloomed red roses, and a bright pink splashed to his hairline and blazed down his neck. *Had his collar been loose,* Martha Anne thought, *his entire bosom would probably be as red as Lizbeth's bosom got when the berry pie landed there.* She giggled.

He started, hesitantly, 'I…I, well, I…met your Alice…at the sweet shop…we were both gawkin' at the window.' He grinned like a shy schoolboy. 'I was goin' to buy some humbugs…She's quite pretty, your Alice, and so I thought to ask what she fancied, and well—'

'You only thought to ask her a question because she's pretty?'

He was caught off guard and attempted to clarify, but Martha Anne's contemptuous eye roll told him it would be no good and probably make it worse.

'Anyway,' he continued, 'she was deciding between pear drops and pastilles—'

'Wot?' Martha Anne interrupted. 'Our Alice had pear drops and didn't share?' She pushed at the gate. 'I'm gonna see about this! How selfish of 'er!'

Mr Bruce attempted an intervention to the trouble he'd just caused and grabbed the top of the gate, halting its swing. 'Please, Martha Anne, I'm sorry! I didn't mean to cause a riff with your sister, truly!'

'Oh, no riff, 'ere, Mr Bruce! Not yet, anyhow. How dare she sneak my favourite sweetie into the 'ouse without telling me? She knows I love a pear drop!'

'I'm not sure she even bought any, Martha Anne, is what I'm trying to say. We only just shared which sort of sweets we fancy, that's all.'

She squinted, giving him a suspicious look. 'And you? Deciding on humbugs? I wouldn't have taken you for a humbug fella.'

'No? What would you have taken me for?'

'Barley sugar, I think.'

'Oh, I do like a Barley Sugar to tuck in me cheek.'

'Evertons? Do you like Evertons?' she asked, closing her eyes and tasting the striped hard shell with its soft toffee middle. 'They look like humbugs, but so much better.'

'I do like them,' he said, reaching in his pocket and pulling out a little cloth pouch tied with a string.

'As it turns out, I've got all three, right here! An Everton, a humbug, and yes, I do love a barley sugar.' He splayed his palm, revealing one of each sweet, and held them out to Martha Anne. 'Would you like them?'

She hesitated. 'All three?'

'All three.'

There was resistance within her, fighting the mouth-watering desire of a sweetie in her own cheek. 'So, you don't think our Alice was keeping a pear drop from me after all?'

He shrugged. 'I dunno, but even if she were, would these make up for it?'

She nodded and carefully lifted each piece and dropped them in her coat pocket. *Then, without warning or word, she turned and swiftly trotted through the iron gate, up the steps and into the house, leaving Mr Malcolm Bruce on the walk, staring at the manor, in much the same way her father did,* she thought, spying from the window, as he stood looking at each story. He finally turned and made his way up the cobbled street and turned down a muddy lane. And that was the first she'd learned that their Alice and Mr Bruce had met and talked of sweets.

Not long after this, she began skipping school and making her way to Betty Nuppy's shop in Newhey. The first solo journey turned out to be a bit of a horror. She'd been caught in a torrential downpour that had soaked through to her skin. That not being bad enough, she'd slipped and slid until she'd splashed into a big puddle. By the time she'd rung Betty's little bell, she was covered head to toe in brown mud.

When Betty opened the top half of the door and saw her, she shooed her away with the wave of her hand. Then, she began to close the door. 'I've no time for urchins! I've nowt for you. Get!'

But Martha Anne wedged her arm between the door and its frame and squeaked out, 'It's me, Betty Nuppy! It's me, Martha Anne Ashworth!'

That first day, she'd stripped off her clothes and rinsed out her hair in Betty Nuppy's big tin sink. Then she'd slipped into the soft cotton nightdress that belonged to the old woman and returned to the kitchen where Betty had wrung out her clothes and hung them on a line draped in front of the big fireplace. A kettle was starting its whistle, and Betty gestured that she sit in the little wooden chair by the fire. Before Betty settled herself in the chair opposite, she handed Martha Anne a thick mug of tea and carried one of her own.

'Would you like to tell me what you're doin' 'ere, lass?'

'I, uh, I've been suspended, again,' she said, trying to sound remorseful. 'And so me dad said that rather bein' a bother to our Lizbeth, that's me awful sister what 'ates me, he thought maybe I could come by 'ere and be a 'elp around your shop.'

'He did, did 'e?'

Martha Anne nodded, bobbing her head just a bit too enthusiastically.

'Well, then.' Betty seemed to consider the proposal, blowing across her cup and sipping loudly before asking, 'What are the terms of this help I'm about to receive whether I want it or not?'

This put Martha Anne on alert. She wanted to help Betty more than anything in the world and calculated the pros and cons of all her calibrations, but she did not want to ruin her chances by asking for too much. On the other hand, she did not want to insult Betty by offering too little. She could tell Betty was a proud woman and would not accept anything that felt like charity.

So in a more measured tone than her quick-beating heart let on, Martha Anne suggested, 'Me dad said it would be a fair trade and right lesson for me if I straightened up your shop, catalogue seeds, organised spices, make it so you can walk a straight line from the greenhouse to the till without winding through the maze of clutter you've got around now.'

'Is that all?' Betty asked.

'No. Sweepin' and dustin'. Those were on 'is list too. And anythin' else you need done.' Martha Anne looked hopefully over the rim of her cup and tried to appear just mildly interested.

'How much is all that tidyin' gonna set me back? I don't have much in the way of pennies, you know.'

Martha Anne cleared her throat and said gently, coaxingly, 'Dad said it might be fair if you'd give me supper and…and…"liniment"…for me mum— to help her with the pain.' Martha Anne crossed her arms and waited to see if she'd pushed it too far by adding the liniment. After giving the offer a bit of scrutiny, Betty agreed, and so the trade agreement had become their way of life. Martha Anne worked for Betty Nuppy in exchange for liniments, oils, spices, fruits, vegetables—and supper.

That first day of chores, after Martha Anne had cleared pathways of boxes, crates, barrels, pots, stacks of newspapers, and deliveries that were never put away, she swept until the slate floor was grey instead of brown. Following visits entailed straightening the potting shed, and clearing out the greenhouse. Next, she spent time staking small posts with the names of plants written on them, placing them with their similar species, and arranging a long table full of seedlings. She'd impressed Betty when she'd also devised a clever irrigation system involving three watering cans strung on a clothesline made to rain down on the plants using a pulley system she had also rigged out.

Pots, buckets, crates, and vases were shelved together according to size and purpose, tools in duplicate were set conveniently around the shop in different areas, others found spots high up on the wood shelf along the back wall and in a closet with cubby holes for just such a purpose.

Just yesterday, Martha Anne had begun to separate seeds into small envelopes, neatly identified and labelled in her own hand: salt, pepper, dill, rosemary, thyme, lemon zest…and so many more. She'd actually grown weary and fallen asleep on the bench beside the worktable, and Betty Nuppy had shaken her awake as it was nearing dark, knowing Martha Anne had a good distance to get herself home.

'Go on, luv. It'll be dark before you get to Milnrow, so hurry and run like the wind!' Betty had pushed her out the door, looking worriedly up at the darkening sky.

But Martha Anne was surprisingly quick on her feet and ran so fast that she'd been home and back at the manor house before anyone knew she'd been gone—before Lizbeth could get mad or Alice could worry or her dad could become suspicious.

And that's why she was sitting outside Mr Bruce's door for an hour now, awaiting her punishment.

It was Mr Bruce who finally opened the door and gestured for Martha Anne. Catching a wink off Miss Lake, she felt that slight tightness in her throat that often precipitated tears.

She stepped across the threshold, taking two steps into the office, and came to a full stop, causing Mr Bruce behind her to bump into her. There before her, she faced not only her previously predicted suspects: her father and Miss Royds, but there was Alice, a bald man in a black suit wearing spectacles, whom she did not know, and…Betty Nuppy, looking none too happy. Worse, looking forlorn, even.

'I've done nowt wrong,' Martha Anne blurted.

'You've done nowt right, Martha Anne, by the looks of it,' Alice was the first to speak, having stood and turned upon her sister's entrance. Alice's eyes couldn't help darting from her troubled sibling to the handsome headmaster, seeming to gauge his response to her outrage. Finally, it was her father who placed his hand on Alice's arm, urging her to sit back down.

Mr Bruce instructed Martha Anne to take the seat next to his desk. She noticed he did not offer tea this time. She tried to catch Betty Nuppy's eye, but each time, the old woman cast hers down and studied her fingernails.

Mr Bruce cleared his throat and took his desk chair, swivelling it towards her. 'As we all know'—he paused and gestured about the room—'you've been skipping school on more than one occasion.' He slid his finger along a line in his ledger, 'Actually, twenty-eight occasions, if the attendance book Miss Royds keeps is correct, which I am sure it is. Now, I'm not going to sit here and ask why you've done what you've done. I'll leave that to your dad here.'

'But I've done nowt—'

'This is not the time for argument, Martha Anne. You'll be quiet and listen for a change.' Her father's serious tone matched his serious face, and so she sat back and waited to hear the accusations and the verdict—guilty or not.

'Fine. Do your worst, but it won't make anythin' right. Let me just say that before you start your monkey trial against me—'

'You see!' Miss Royds pointed at her. 'THIS is what I've got to put up with day in and day out. She's got a cheeky tongue.'

'Yes, thank you, Miss,' Mr Bruce said quietly. 'We've been informed about the injustices served upon you by this child.'

'At least, I'm not tryin' to bore a whole class to death…'

'Martha Anne!' Her father now slapped the arm of the chair. 'You will be quiet and listen to what's to become of you, and if you're wise—which seems a near impossibility at this moment—you will stay quiet until the end.'

She'd not heard such a harsh tone in her dad's voice, and for the first time since arriving, she felt, perhaps, that this trouble may very well be worse than she'd thought. She wished Betty would look at her, but Betty was now staring out the nearby window wishing she was anywhere else.

Mr Bruce continued. 'In England, it is against the law for children under thirteen to be out of school without their Certificate of Proficiency—'

'Or a Dunces' Certificate if I had my way,' Miss Royds interrupted.

'In an instance where a child continues to flout the law, as you have, even though you've had many warnings from me and Miss Royds, more severe measures must be taken. The first is, unfortunately'—he looked away from her father and set his eyes on her—your dad will pay a fine for your truancy—'

'That's not fair!' Martha Anne stood and stomped her foot. 'It's not me dad who's been truant. It's been me!'

'Well, then, maybe your dad will find a way for you to pay him back, but that's the way it's done here. It's the law.'

'It's a stupid law.' She frowned and gave them each a dark look.

'Sit down, Martha Anne. You're doin' yourself no favours,' Alice chimed in, and Martha Anne settled down, but not before flicking her tongue at her older sister.

'Now, you'll begin attending school every day, and you'll refrain from visiting Miss Nuppy's shop.'

At these words, Martha jumped from her seat once more and shouting to Betty across the room, 'Don't let them do this, Betty. You know 'ow much you need me.' Her voice caught in that tightness in her throat, and she felt the first sting of a tear at the corner of her eyes. Betty looked down and attended to a loose thread on her blouse cuff.

'Don't do this, Dad.' Martha Anne now pleaded with her father. 'You know it's all I love. Don't take Betty away from me! Don't make me sit in that dark corner with that…that…gormless—' she raised her chin to Miss Royds.

'Martha Anne!' Her father stood. 'You will sit down and be quiet until it is time for us to leave. Do…you…understand…me?' His words were measured, and his face was flushed. He pulled a handkerchief from his pocket and mopped the glistening beads of sweat from his brow.

She sank slowly to her seat and slid her hands beneath her thighs to stop fidgeting.

'In addition,' Mr Bruce said, and turned to the bald man standing beside the far bookcase, 'I would like you to meet Mr Bloome. He is our school attendance officer, and he will be monitoring your situation until the end of the term. Only if you are sick and on death's doorstep shall you miss any more classes. Do you understand?' He waited.

She looked to her father and back to Mr Bruce.

'Well? Do you understand, Martha Anne?'

When she looked back to her dad, he shook his head in exasperation and said, 'Oh, fine. Speak. Go ahead and answer the man, do you understand?'

She looked at Mr Bloome, Miss Royds, Betty, back to Mr Bruce, and asked, 'Or what?'

'Oh, my dear sweet Jesus,' Alice said as she shook her head. 'Or what?'

'Or what happens if I'm not on death's doorstep and I miss a class? I mean, what if I'm hit by a cart? You know it happens all the time. I know a lad up Kathleen Street got knocked over by a cart and broke three ribs. Am I to come to class with three broken ribs? What if I'm not on death's door but have the cramps and am spewin' me tea all around? Do I come then? How about if a band of gypsies has kidnapped me—'

'Martha Anne! Enough!'

'I need to know, Dad.' She turned on her father. 'I need to know. I need to know what I'm allowed and what the punishment will be because even if I understand what's bein' said to me right now, it still won't mean I agree with it.'

'I'll tell you what the consequences will be if you keep up these incorrigible behaviours.' Miss Royds rose from her seat and waved a stack of papers in the air. 'There are places for the likes of you. We've got you ready to go to an industrial school where you can learn a trade, a skill, and your Labour Certification. You'll be out and working the day you turn twelve.'

The thought of it horrified Martha Anne, but she swallowed hard to stay steady and turned an evil eye to the teacher, saying, 'Anythin' to get away from you.'

'How about a ragged school, then? Eh? That too can be arranged.' Miss Royds waved her papers and sat down before she attempted to choke the wicked girl.

'Before any of that happens,' Mr Bruce interjected, 'we're going to give you a chance to earn your certificate of "Due Attendance", in the hopes that you'll also earn your "Certificate of Proficiency". Mr Bloome here will be keeping an eye on you. You're now on notice.'

She didn't look at anyone or say anything. Instead, she got up, lifted her chin, and slowly headed for the door, but Mr Bruce's words stopped her.

'There's one more thing,' he said.

She turned to see that he had a long thin cane in his hand. Her eyes grew big, and she looked to her father. She could not speak. She'd only had the cane once, and that was on her left hand, even though it was her dominant, and it had been the rule to only cane the non-dominant hand—Miss Royds had told her it was the devil's doin' that she was cack-handed, and it be best to use her right hand like the rest of the world. It hurt very badly, she recalled, and she couldn't draw for weeks. She glared at Miss Royds and then looked to her sister.

'Oh, Alice, don't let 'im do this to me. Remember I couldn't use me hand last time.'

Alice adjusted her skirt and kept her eyes to the floor.

'Dad? Dad? Are you really goin' to let this…this…stranger' was the only word she could come up with as if it should somehow matter, '*cane* me?'

Her father stood, as did Alice, but neither said a word to stop the caning. Martha Anne realised that anything other than submission, at this point, was only going to prolong the already too-long situation.

So she held out her hands to Mr Bruce and upheld her palms. But instead of giving her the expected six or seven smacks, he said, 'No. Turn round.'

She froze. Her eyes landed on each pair of eyes in the room, looking for some friend to rescue her, but each turned away.

'You heard me, Martha Anne,' Mr Bruce said solemnly like a priest on Easter morning. 'Turn around and bend over.'

She did as she was told and placed her hands on her knees. She felt the first stinging slap of the cane on the back of her bare thighs, and then another, and another, each hatching thin red lines across her soft pale skin. She turned her head to see Betty Nuppy fleeing to the door. Just before she slipped through, she turned back, and Martha Anne could see the stream of tears running down Betty's pink cheeks.

***

'Where's your sister?' John Ashworth asked his daughter Alice, looking down at his pocket watch and up at the grandfather clock in the entryway. It was half seven, and Martha Anne had not returned home from school.

Alice looked up from peeling potatoes and out the window. 'I'm not sure. I only just got 'ome a little bit before you. To be honest, I 'adn't noticed she weren't here.'

He hadn't begun to worry until the sun began its dip. Since her probation period at school for the last few months, she'd become as model a student as possible. She'd not missed a day. She'd kept her cheeky tongue tucked into her cheek, and she'd surpassed every child in class in her studies. He'd felt for her, he really had, because it was as if it had been her spirit that had left her body after that caning. Everything she did now was just mechanical. There was little joy, never mind life, in her pursuits. He closed his eyes as he could not bring himself to relive that awful day in Mr Bruce's office. He counted it as one of the worst days of his life. Right up there with all the babies he'd lost over the years. That's how he'd felt—like he'd somehow lost her that day. 'You let a stranger cane your own daughter…"Father"…' is what she'd called him. Not "Dad". And never "Dad" again since. He could not get her words out of his head, even if he could sometimes block the images from entering.

With all her good behaviour modifications, she had not complied with one condition: to come home directly after school. She more often didn't and wouldn't, and it was the one action he didn't seem able to control, as he was at work during this time. And so he chose to ignore her tardiness without question. Sometimes she'd come flying in the door just as the sun went down over the moors. Sometimes it was only an hour or so late, or just before tea. But no matter when it was, Martha Anne would only speak to him or Alice if spoken to and would only answer in monosyllables. She'd completely ignored Lizbeth as if she were not even there. Martha Anne had withdrawn inside herself, and only Lizbeth was happy about the quiet. Even their mother, bedridden and rarely conscious long enough to notice what day it was, worried aloud that she hadn't had a visit from her youngest daughter in days. As Ellen was given more to complaints than compliments about Martha Anne, she surprised everyone by her sudden admittance that the little girl made her laugh even when all the world seemed primarily grim.

These days, since her confinement, Martha Anne only paused by her mum's bedroom door, only to stare in at her. She no longer popped in to show off her latest sketch or try to cheer her mother with a story or a funny joke. She used to bring a flower, a piece of soft flint, or a bird feather she'd found. During those times, Ellen would close her eyes and let her daughter's chatter give white noise to the magical potions John brought home from Betty's shop that soothed the pain in her bones. She'd fall asleep to Martha Anne's prattling stories. Now Ellen longed for them as they were the space between the here and there, the now and then, and the light and dark. Now when she saw Martha Anne pass by her bedroom door, she thought to call out, ask her to come back to tell a story or sing a song, but Martha Anne seemed to know when this request was about to come and would hurry quickly past the door, down the hall, and away from having to comply.

Since her suspension, John Ashworth considered Martha Anne had grown sullen and seemed at a loss with the world. What he knew and what he could accept were two different things. He knew it was Betty Nuppy who Martha Anne was at a loss for and what he could not accept was allowing the cure for it. Martha Anne had been banned from Betty's, and even Betty made sure she'd stayed away. When Martha Anne had shown up on her doorstep just days after her caning, Betty would not open the door for her, no matter how mournful her crying. No matter how long she sat out there on the step, in the rain, into the dark, until it was John's lantern that she saw swinging as he'd come to fetch his youngest. When Betty had invited him in to warm up before the fire, he just shook his head and pulled Martha Anne off the step and held her hand until they'd gone through Betty's gate and down the muddy lane.

Now he moved to the window and stared into the darkening night as it was now nearly eight o'clock and not a sign of her. Then, finally, he went straight to the hallway and pulled on his overcoat.

'Where you goin', Dad?' Alice asked, wiping her hands on her apron and heading for her own coat on the hanger.

'I thought I'd go around to the school, see if maybe she'd been held over. Maybe Mr Bruce will know.'

'I'll go with you, then.'

'What about tea?' he asked, pointing to the boiling pot and peeled potatoes.

'Lizbeth can tend to them,' she said and caught Lizbeth's eye as she'd come out from their mother's room.

'Lizbeth will do no such thing,' Lizbeth said, 'I've got me own chores to finish up. You'll stay and cook tea. I'm sure Dad can handle Mr Bruce without you, Alice,' she said with every implication balanced at the tip of her sharp tongue.

Alice threw the peeled potatoes into the pot of boiling beef, onions, and carrots, turned the flame to low, and slid the lid on top. 'I'm goin' with Dad. This'll cook while I'm gone. If you don't want burned tea, Lizbeth, you'll keep an eye on it.'

They'd hurried down the dimly lit street, mostly empty but for those coming home late from the mills or early from the pubs. Neither she nor her dad said much while they kept a fast pace, but each had the world of worry in their hearts and were trying to keep their imaginations from conjuring up the worst.

They approached the broad brick building with its small rectangular windows lining across two stories, all black as the night within. At the far end of the school building, across a patch of soft grass, was a carriage house where Mr Bruce lived in a flat above and where the soft glow of candlelight filled a front window.

They both caught their breaths as they stood at the top of the staircase in front of Mr Bruce's door, and John smoothed his wind-worn hair and moustache while Alice bit on her lips to plump them up—beauty advice she'd read in a woman's weekly, to which she'd subscribed. It was her father who'd rapped against the wooden door, and only moments before Malcolm had swung it wide.

'Mr Ashworth!' He nodded, surprised, and then 'and Miss Alice!' He scrutinised his own attire, embarrassed by his stockinged feet. He'd been warming them by the fire, sipping brandy, and reading a sea-faring story by an American author named Melville when the knock came to his door. He did not think to change from his robe but merely tied it in place as he reached for the door handle and pulled it back. 'Come in,' he gestured and stepped aside, 'what can I do for you at this time of night?'

'It's Martha Anne. She's not come home from school today,' John said, worrying his cap in his hands.

'Not come home?' Malcolm looked to the clock on the mantel and out into the darkness.

'She's done this before,' Alice said, beginning an explanation that immediately sounded defensive. 'But never so late. She's always home for tea, and surely by dark, but this is the latest she's ever been out.'

Malcolm looked out into the night again and felt his stomach lurch. It was cold and damp and not a safe place for young girls. 'Do you have any idea where she might've got to?'

'I thought'—John looked down and shook his head slowly—'well, maybe she's gone to Betty's, but we've decided to start here first. Betty's is a long way off. I hate to bother her at this time of night unless it were an emergency.'

Malcolm was gesturing to the couch and chair beside the fire. 'Here, please, sit while I change into my day clothes. Can I get you tea?'

'Not for me,' John said.

'Nor me,' Alice's eyes followed Malcolm until he disappeared around the corner and closed a door beyond the wall. She imagined him undressing only just feet away from her and had to fan her face to stop the flush from rising.

'You hot?' her father asked. 'Step away from the fire, then, if you're hot.'

And so she did, giving herself a moment alone with her thoughts of Malcolm Bruce and (almost) alone in his flat where she was noting his books and paintings and whatnots, souvenirs of sorts scattered about. A small rough blue stone had a place of its own on the mantelpiece. Then, a bit further down, a brass elephant with its trunk raised was carved in great detail and appeared to be foreign, perhaps from India, she imagined, and wondered if he'd been, and then imagined that he had, and imagined the market where he'd haggled for the little trinket.

She saw he must've been reading the book beside the chair and opened it up to its first page. "Call me Ishmael…" she read and saw by the cover art that the story was about a fish. A whale, she supposed and put it down where she'd found it just as Malcolm was coming back into the room, now dressed in his day clothes and with shoes on his feet.

'Shall we just have a look in the classroom?' he suggested hopefully. 'Perhaps she's fallen asleep at her desk?' He began to embellish his hope.

He'd given both John and Alice a lantern, and they followed him across the courtyard, into the cold building. The classroom was very dark and very empty. All chairs were upended on the desks, floors had been swept, the slate board washed, and there was not a soul in sight. Shadows cast by the lanterns were a bit frightening, and Alice found herself standing closer to Malcolm than she imagined proper. And when a broom fell over in the corner, smacking the floor, she jumped and even more inappropriately grabbed his arm. She noticed that he did not pull away but pulled her closer, instead, despite her dad being just on the other side of her.

John lifted his lantern high, did one last sweep of the room and said, 'Well, she's not here, that's for certain.'

They left, and Malcolm suggested they go around the corner to the small cottage where Miss Royds lived, hoping that she might shed some light on Martha Anne's whereabouts.

John said, 'I doubt Miss Royds would know, given Martha Anne has made a point to avoid 'er at all costs. However, I'll come, just in case. If not, I'll make me way to Betty's and hope she's disobeyed me.'

Malcolm looked at the older man and felt his fears. He had a lot on his plate. Not many knew that John Ashworth was struggling for money, but Malcolm knew because Malcolm had been ignoring John's late, partial, and missed tuition payments for months. He admitted he'd had his own reasons for overlooking these delinquencies, and that was because of Alice. He'd become smitten, he admitted. And it was good timing as he'd been in search of a wife, in fact.

Up until a year ago, ever since he'd lost Jeanie, the love of his life, he'd thought he'd be a bachelor for the rest of it. But it was a sit-down with his father, "the Laird", during his last visit home that forced him to reconsider a new reality. The father-to-son talk took place in the book-lined study, beside the fire, drinking whisky together.

His father began by laying out his side of the argument, actually the only side that mattered. The lecture opened with a brief history of their landholdings (Malcolm already knew). Then, upon his fingers, his father listed the previous Lairds and Ladies who'd held the family title, his ancestors (Malcolm knew and counted along) with responsibilities to the land, the family, the title. These were the important matters of life that the Laird, Sir Douglas Bruce, had laid out for his son, and now it was his duty to return home with a wife and begin to take on his ancestral responsibilities.

Claiming that his love of teaching, learning, and travel were his only true passions, he went so far as to determinedly tell his father: 'I don't want the land, the money, or your ridiculous title. I canna give up me loves for your dreams instead of me own, Da.'

That was a year ago, and Malcolm finally admitted to himself that being a poor schoolteacher, no matter whether he was headmaster or not, his once bright dreams had been dampened by the surrounding landscape. The intellect of the Northern people was limited to pub jokes and mill woes, and he could not relate to either. He hadn't met a person of interest since he'd arrive—well, except Martha Anne—and was longing for the sounds of a Scottish tongue, the intensity of the raucous discussions in the Scottish alehouses, and the breeze and fresh air of the Highlands of his home. He needed a wife, and he needed one soon. He had to get out of Lancashire before he became the image of those dark pictures hanging in his office at school.

So, when he'd met Alice Ashworth, a pleasant enough young woman, compliant and kind, pretty in that very safe way, he imagined bringing her home, and he suddenly felt a longing for family and making one of his own with a woman who would make a good wife. This would be his first serious chance to get himself out of this grey hell-hole and back into refined society. Alice would adapt well to the aristocracy but would never really become part of it—this he knew. In some way, he was glad of that, as it meant he could continue his private life, and she wouldn't be any the wiser. She would acquiesce to both the bounties and the oddities of a life of leisure. All that said, he was sure Alice would be content.

Malcolm's thoughts turned to the task at hand, and his concern registered, admitting he indeed was worried for Martha Anne. He was concerned about her even before she'd been caught truant. He was worried that she was languishing in this school whose limited education she'd surpassed years before. She could teach the classes, he smiled, thinking of her sketching out fun lessons on the chalkboard. She was a wonder, he caught himself musing. She challenged his intellect and made him want to share his knowledge, readings, art, and interests with her in ways he did not even consider sharing with Alice as she was a wifely woman. She was pretty and witty and listened to him in earnest, prattling on about simple bits of nothings with little need for attention beyond a bob of the head. He felt content in that, a good life's companion who'd bring him babies and a kind of freedom he enjoyed now. He couldn't imagine Alice questioning, never mind arguing, one decision he would ever make. Not like her sister, for sure.

He smiled to himself, thinking of that headstrong, feisty girl who would someday be a feisty, headstrong woman. God help the lad that winds up with her. But then, as he thought of Martha Anne, his desires shifted, became pronounced, he could feel as his thoughts lingered too long there, shaming

himself. As these fatal imaginings floated by, so too did the alarm race in—
Martha Anne is but a child—and its entrance into his mind shocked him, rattled
him, and he shut his eyes tight to extinguish it. He shook his head as if to make
sure it was gone. *Don't think about it, Mac*, he warned himself.

Instead, he'd convinced himself that without his help, Martha Anne would
lose her way. As her family's money and health will someday run out, he was
committed to making sure that Martha Anne Ashworth and her big, beautiful
brain would not be lost to the mills or the drudgery of housewifery. He thought
now, as his heart was racing to find her, that when they did, he would do all in
his power to help her get beyond the sooty dank air of Rochdale. He'd send for
the applications to Cheltenham Ladies College and the Roedean School, both
fine academies for young women.

The windows at Miss Royds' little cottage were all darkened, and even her
chimney was dormant of smoke. It was cold out tonight, and John shivered to
think how cold it would be inside without a fire on the hob. But then, it
wouldn't be a far stretch from Miss Royds cold heart, as far as he was
concerned. He wouldn't say it out loud to another soul, but as far as he was
concerned, the problem at the school was not Martha Anne, but Emma Royds.

Malcolm knocked on the door, gently at first and then harder, as it appeared
Miss Royds slept like the dead. Not until he went around to the back of the
building and tapped on a window did a light come on. The three then waited
for the glow of the candle to reach the front door. Miss Royds stood with her
hair in rags, a long night dressing gown, and the stump of a burning candle
held above her head. She squinted at them. It was evident that they'd awakened
her.

'What is it?' she asked without addressing any of them. 'I've been asleep.
What time is it?'

'It's half nine, Miss Royds,' Malcolm said. 'We're sorry to wake you at
such a late hour, but you see, we're quite worried about Martha Anne—'

'Martha Anne?' she repeated and stepped back away from them.

'Yes, Martha Anne Ashworth. You know Mr Ashworth here and Miss
Alice.' He gestured to each. 'They came to see me this evening. It seems
Martha Anne did not come home after school today—and—we were hoping
you might remember her leaving school this afternoon.'

Miss Royd's eyes grew wide, and her hand went to her trembling lips. 'Oh,
dear. Oh, dear, what've I done?'

'What is it, Miss Royds?' Malcolm went to the older woman's side and helped her sit down on a small settee, placing the candle beside her on the table. She appeared pale in the light but for her neck and ears, which were of a bright red. She began to shake.

Malcolm asked gently, 'Please, Miss Royds, do you know where Martha Anne is?'

She could not seem to form words. She looked out the window to see the pitch of night and thought of how many hours it had been since she'd locked the child in the cubby at the back of the coat closet. Before noon, she determined, counting on her fingers. A near ten hours. She looked up to see Mr Bruce and Mr Ashworth staring down upon her. Both faces held the same grim expression.

John Ashworth now spoke, a bit more forcefully than Malcolm had, and using her familiar. 'Dammit, Emma! Do you know where me daughter is? If you do, speak, woman! Time's wasted on your muteness.'

She flinched at his demand, and a tear escaped her eye. She let it roll down her cheek. She attempted to answer, but his impatience interrupted her effort when he pounded his fist, knocking a picture from the wall. They watched it clatter to the floor, but no attempt was made to retrieve it. John toed it aside, and Alice placed her hands on her father's shoulder, 'Now, Dad, let's not lose our temper here.'

He leaned close to Emma Royds' face and hissed, 'Tell me where me daughter is, you daft old witch, or I'll throttle you!' Alice pulled him aside as Emma burst into sobs.

'I've left 'er…in the…the coat cubby,' she managed.

The three looked at one another, each more horrified than the other.

'You what?' Malcolm asked.

'She were…misbehavin' again. She's a handful, I'll give you that.' Miss Royds pushed back her shoulders and lifted her chin. 'And, well, I'd had enough, and so I locked her in the cubby at that back of the coat closet.' Emma had composed herself as she'd justified her side of the mishap.

'You locked my little girl in a coat closet nearly half a day ago and left her there?' John's face had gone near purple. Alice made to stop his advance on the teacher, but he shrugged her off. Then, pulling back his hand as if he were about to lay a slap across the teacher's face, he instead turned his palm up to

Malcolm. 'Give me the keys to the school, now!' He seemed to rise in size and stature, his barrel chest boasting.

Malcolm pulled the ring from his pocket. 'This one opens both the outer door and the classroom door. Miss Royds, where is the coat closet key?'

'In me desk. Top right drawer. It's the littlest key of the lot.' She slumped in her chair and wiped her nose with the handkerchief she pulled from her sleeve.

Before John was out the door, he pointed at the schoolteacher and looked at Malcolm. 'I want that one gone.'

John tapped on the closet and called out her name, but there was silence. Unlocking the small door with the smallest key, it swung wide with the weight of her propped against it. He'd pulled her out of the dank space set at the back of the closet. She was sleeping or passed out, he couldn't quite tell, but she didn't open her eyes when he shook her. She didn't open them when he yelled her name. She hung in his arms like wet laundry on a line. And so he ran with her, out of the school, through dark empty streets, tears streaming down his face, holding her close as her body was limp...and lifeless. NO! Not lifeless...Tired, exhausted, weak, but not lifeless—but barely alive. He held his ear to her mouth. He could feel her tiny warm breaths.

He cut through gunnels and gardens and got a bit turned about before he found Toad Lane, and not quite sure which way to go, he trusted his instincts and went right. It was a matter of remembering which of the big homes set back from the street belonged to Dr Stevens. When he thought he'd found it, he was thankful the lights in the windows downstairs were still on, and he rang the bell with his daughter in his arms.

They brought her into the house and placed her on the settee in the parlour. Mrs Stevens left them to make tea and sent her eldest daughter back with glasses of whisky. John stood back as Dr Stevens waved smelling salts under Martha Anne's nose, and they watched the little girl struggled to revive. Her eyes fluttered open, and she choked on the pungent ammonia in her nostrils. Squinting, she looked around, unsure of where she was.

Finally, she found her father's worried face and sat up. She took a sip of water and said, 'I'm never goin' back to that school ever again.'

Chapter Five

After the incident, as it was referred to, she wouldn't get out of bed for days— no—she couldn't get out of bed. She'd been having nightmares, easy to identify, even for a ten (almost eleven) year old, because they all involved being trapped in a small box. Sometimes, it was the dark cubby, sometimes a dank trunk, and sometimes a scary coffin, but each time, it was terrifying. And as she'd done whilst trapped in the cubby, even in her sleep, she bloodied her fingers scratching at the wall beside her bed, trying to get out of her dreams.

She'd cried a lot in that dark hole and screamed until her throat was raw and she could scream no more. Then, finally, in her right mind (when she caught a piece of it), she knew that her dad would come looking for her. She just wasn't sure he'd know where to look. This frightened her even more as it was Friday, and she started to panic when she thought about three days being locked in the closet, half sitting and half lying in the tiny, confined space.

And so she refused to go to school until, one day, Mr Bruce sent Mr Bloome, the school attendance officer she'd been assigned, and he came to their door and ordered Lizbeth to get her out of her bed and back to the classroom. There was only one bright side—Miss Royds had been relieved of her duties, and Mr Bruce was teaching the class until a replacement could be found.

While the distraction of a real teacher made the boredom of the classroom a bit less tedious, she found that she was restless. She wanted nothing more than to be out and about with her sketch pad. If she wasn't to be allowed at Betty Nuppy's, at least being outdoors was better than listening to the droning of children reciting the ABCs she learned years ago or practicing cursive, which she could write with her eyes closed. Moreover, she knew her addition and subtraction tables by heart. So there was little to do but listen to Mr Bruce's lovely Scottish brogue, stare out the window, and sketch in her tablet.

School was tolerable for a few weeks until the new teacher had come along. He was a very old man, maybe older than her dad, and called Mr Holt. He was quite deaf and hard to understand as he mostly mumbled. He didn't seem to mind or even notice the hijinks the children were pulling behind his back. The class was becoming out of control, Martha Anne could see from her dark spot at the back, but she no longer led the rebellion or participated in it. Instead, she'd buried her head in a book or sketchpad as tiny pebbles and wadded balls of paper flew around the room, plaits were pulled, clogs were sparked, seats exchanged whenever the teacher turned his back to scribble nonsense on the board. Mr Holt had them read aloud for hours while he sat at his desk with his feet propped on the bottom drawer he'd pulled out for such comfort. He drank a lot of tea. Once, when asking a question that required she leave her seat and speak loudly to Mr Holt as she stood beside his desk, she'd sniffed the distinct scent of whisky wafting from his cup.

For his part, determined to keep her interest, Mr Bruce brought books from his office, slipping them onto Martha Anne's seat each morning before classes began. He felt a certain comfort knowing that she was at least reading, even if she weren't participating in the class. Unfortunately, it was not long before she once again began skipping school, coming in on rainy and cold days, just enough to keep her absenteeism in check, but if the sun were out and the sky blue, she'd stow her books and dinner pail in the bushes outside the manor house and fly down the hill towards Milnrow and Newhey. At the start, she was almost always determined to visit Betty on these truant days, but she never followed through, knowing the bother this would be for both. She'd go anyway just to sit on the stone wall and sketch the cottage, the shed, and the shop with the split door. She'd fill in the plants, herbs, fruits, and vegetables. When she'd once spotted him, she'd added Betty's goat to her picture. She missed the shop more than she missed anything. A few times, she'd seen Betty at the split door or watering her flowers, and a few times, she thought Betty had seen her, but she never let on, just kept at her chores. This was as close as she would get to Betty, though, as Mr Bloome was always just hours, sometimes minutes, behind her, so she didn't take unnecessary chances.

When she wasn't sketching Betty's cottage, she'd wander the moors, explore the villages, cross under and over viaducts, sometimes daring to go as far as Hollingworth Lake where she'd bring a picnic, lay out a blanket, and sketch beside the water. Her current fascination, especially of late, was the

Rochdale Market off Toad Lane. She'd been before with Dad and Alice, but never alone. On this day of aimless wandering, she'd more happened upon the market rather than sought it out. She passed stalls of potato, carrot, and onion merchants all in a row. The potatoes were piled in near over-flowing barrels. She tripped over one, just stopping herself from falling. For her troubles (and almost broken ankle), she picked it up and stuffed it into her coat pocket. Nobody seemed to notice her, never mind notice that she'd borrowed a potato. The sounds and smells of the market blended together. One without the other would not be as melodious. Along with the buyers' bustling and the sellers' hustling, the market was a symphony of sights, sounds, smells, tastes and newly inspired imaginings, and quickly became a favourite place to while away her day.

Today, she'd been dodging Mr Bloome all over town, through the backs of terrace houses, until eventually she'd made her way into the market where she hoped to lose him among the crowds. Instead, she'd decided to go see a new friend. About her age, he was a lad called Tom, who didn't have to go to school because he worked in his dad's shoe-repair stall. Tom had dreams of going to America, and he read all about it. He liked to tell stories of it, and she wanted to hear them. And he always had a sweetie for her. With its busy patrons and busier sellers in side-by-side stalls, the market was a whole new world to Martha Anne. There were merchants selling everything from tripe to black pudding, to lung tablets, loose teas, fish, mince pies, fruits and veggies, all sorts of household goods, boot polish and moustache wax, hats, kerchiefs, every sort of sewing bob: cloth, thread, needles, scissors, buttons and the like, and best of all, in a stall at the back, there were children's books, toys, and trinkets, which she liked to look at and occasionally borrow.

She'd made herself useful to the shopkeepers, though. She swept up for the ladies selling soaps, dusted for the tobacco seller, helped unload parcels for the butcher, and would count out bits of this and that for the ironmonger. She was often given a penny or a newspaper-cone of fish and chips or a hot mince pie for her time. Whenever she kept watch over Mick's big pot of black peas (so he could go off and place his bets), she always came away with a cup for herself. So she was well fed around the market, and the shopkeepers thought her helpful and quite amusing.

When they'd learned that a school attendance officer was after her, in keeping with their distaste for authority, they helped hide her, warn her, and lie for her whenever Mr Bloome came around looking for her. Today he seemed quite determined and was turning up his nose sniffing for her, even after the shopkeepers along the row shrugged at his questions. She'd kept him in her sights and scurried in and out of the backs of stalls until he finally seemed to give up and left down the lane.

After waiting a little while, she re-emerged and was cheered by the merchants who helped her elude Mr Bloome. Someone threw her an apple glazed with sugar, and she squealed with delight. But Mr Bloome seemed to have caught on to her shenanigans because he'd reappeared just then, and caught her wrist with an iron claw, and would not let go.

'Oh, go on!' Tom had yelled, attempting to interfere. 'You really goin' to use the claw on a little lass?'

She'd turned eleven years old just weeks before and felt some resentment about being called little, but her littleness worked in her favour as she was able to twist her tiny hand out of the contraption meant to capture her.

As soon as he saw that she'd freed herself, Tom yelled, 'Run!' and she scurried between Mr Bloome's knees, while Tom and a few other lads pushed a fruit cart in his way, tripping him up and allowing her to escape.

As she hid behind a barrel full of potatoes, she saw Mr Bloome's red face and bulging eyes searching up and down the stalls for her. He whipped around when he heard the lot behind him laughing. As much as Martha Anne was enjoying this lark, she could see by the look in Mr Bloome's eyes that he was as determined as ever to find her and bring her to justice—his sort of justice was what frightened her, and so, after heart-pounding days like this, she would make her way to her dark little desk at the back of the class, where she'd read the books Mr Bruce had left for her. Sometimes she would borrow them and hide them on her own bookshelves in her room. Sometimes she'd bring them to the market to trade for books or sketch pads, pencils, charcoal, and sometimes, she'd sell them outright for pocket change.

Not all the merchants were as kindly towards her as others. She accidentally borrowed an apple and wedge of cheese from Babbit's grocer, but she hadn't got a bite of either, as Mr Babbit grabbed her, pulled the food from her apron, and thrashed her about the head with a wet rag, snapping like a whip, raising welts on her cheeks. He'd warned he'd beat her bloody next time if he caught her at it again.

'I'll not wait on the likes of some truancy officer to take care of a thief like you!'

And so she stayed away from Mr Babbit's stall. Afterward, Tom had warned her that it wasn't just Mr Babbit she needed to worry about, but other merchants who did not like the loiterers, the truants, the thieves, or ragamuffins looking for scraps. Those merchants took rewards for helping a truancy officer catch one.

Martha Anne had come to learn that she was not the only truant schoolgirl in the market. She'd met a few older girls who neither worked in the mill nor went to school. These big girls had to be thirteen or fourteen, almost women. Even though they were a little rough, they were mostly nice to her. She thought they were all pretty and made even prettier by the rouge on their cheeks and red on their lips. They were always ready with a joke or a tease. They were nice unless they were leavin' with a lad to 'go around the corner' (is how they put it), as she'd learned early on.

She'd mistakenly followed Dolly going around the corner with a lad, only to be smacked across the face by the girl just before they turned the corner. Martha Anne held her bloodied lip and did not follow, did not even peek. Instead, she turned and ran all the way home with tears stinging her eyes. She didn't go back again for quite a while, but when she did, Dolly had given her a big hug and a pretty blue and white scarf as an apology for punching her, and then said, 'Never follow any of us when we leave with a lad, you understand?' Martha Anne nodded and wrapped the scarf around her neck. After that, she accepted the hugs and sips of whisky she'd been offered from the lasses' flasks and liked smoking the little cutties they gave her.

Unlike the girls at school who thought she was a snob for her smarts and forthright curiosities, these market girls seemed to enjoy her prattling on about everything under the sun. They encouraged her chattering, impressed and envious of her extensive vocabulary, vast knowledge, and keen curiosity. They were amused by her boldness, as she was inclined to make straightforward statements and ask questions with the same surety.

'Maude, is your bosom not cold, 'angin' out of y' stay like that? And 'You know, Kathleen, the lads will see your bum if you keep your skirts hiked up so high!'

And the women would burst into uproarious laughter, which sometimes confused Martha Anne as she wasn't ever trying for a joke. They'd offer her cutties to smoke and beer to drink and include her in their secret gossip, which they'd huddle together to share. Even though she mostly did not understand what they were saying, she liked to be in their nest because they all smelled so good. Flowery and musky perfumes mingled, and she liked to pretend she was in the centre of a fragrant rose when they had their arms around her.

She'd lecture them on the evils of swearing, the goodness of herbs, and the importance of history after one had proclaimed: 'Ev'rybody knows England weren't a country till the baby Jesus were born in the Tower of London.' One called Meg, good-naturedly dubbed Martha Anne the "Tiny Teacher", and it stuck. Sometimes they would quiz her about their own curiosities:

How does the moon stay up in the sky? Is there a sea monster in Hollingworth Lake? What is twelve plus three minus eleven plus two? Had she ever been to London? Is there a God? After smoke rises from the stacks, where does it go?

And after they'd seen her sketches, they all wondered in collective awe: 'Tiny Teacher, where'd you learn to draw?'

After some time, the market and her people had become Martha Anne's haven and family. She was happy enough being away from school and home but sad that she could not go to Betty's. Apparently, Mr Bloome had reported that she'd been seen at the shop, even though she'd not gone beyond the wooden gate. That had made no difference. She was warned off, and fines were threatened, not just against her father, but large sums would be levied against Betty for 'employing' a truant. Even though this was a lie, as Betty hadn't let her near the cottage since her caning, but it was enough of a deterrent for Martha Anne to keep far away from her beloved Betty and her sweet little shop.

When she'd first rebelled against the whisky-drinking dolt of a teacher, she'd not been sneaky about her intentions. Instead, she'd gone right to her father and told him that the new teacher was an old drunk, and she wasn't going back, no matter the punishment. And then she flopped into the chair beside his desk, folded her arms across her chest, held her breath and waited.

John Ashworth, also, sat back in his chair and looked at her. He reckoned that any punishment he thought up would be more welcome to Martha Anne than going back to school. He looked long and hard at his near twelve-year-old daughter, whose mind and body were both beginning their shifts into adulthood. He honestly did not know what to do with or about her, so he sent her to bed without deciding either way.

Later that evening, having sent all three of his daughters to bed early, he poured a whisky and quietly sat in a chair beside his sleeping wife's bed. He was tired. He was growing wearier by his circumstances, and his daughters were part of those circumstances. He wished he could talk to Ellen. He wished she'd been able to be a mother to her three daughters. Wished she'd taught them about running a household, raising children, and what it means to be a woman during their most private times. But she hadn't been capable of any of these things for years. Instead, it'd been he who'd ruined his girls, and he just didn't know how to fix them.

He looked at his wife's peaceful face. She knew nothing of the havoc being wreaked on their family. She knew nothing of her own father's declining mind, his inability even to dress himself, and his unwillingness to hand over the reins of the mill to his son-in-law, making every decision a fight to the bottom. She knew nothing of the trouble the mill was in and the many sleepless nights he'd had wrestling its salvation. She knew nothing of Lizbeth's intentions to abandon her, to abandon him, to escape this gritty drab place, this gritty drab family, because deep in his heart, he knew that anything outside of Rochdale and the Ashworth family would be a life improvement for the likes of Lizbeth.

He reached out and held Ellen's limp hand. 'Luv…I've a heavy 'eart and a heavier mind…' His voice cracked as he tried it out on his wife for the first time in weeks. Ellen was so deep in her opium-induced stupor that even his voice and the reach of his hand did not cause her to stir. 'Our Lizbeth…she's leavin' us,' he said, waiting to see if his words had landed in any part of Ellen's consciousness, but her forehead remained smooth, eyes closed, breathing steady. He continued, anyway, as it felt good to say the words aloud, even upon deafened ears.

He fortified himself with a long sip of his whisky and settled into his story. 'Lizbeth, she found a position. A nanny's position. Up north. Near our Bell's farm, she says. It's pretty there in the Lakes. She'll be happy there, so I'm gonna let her go.' He smiled and shook his head. 'Though, by the sounds of it, she's goin' whether I like it or not.' He suddenly realised that the daughter whose future he'd been fretting over most was, in fact, the most independent of all his daughters. Lizbeth could take care of herself, he knew, and this made him proud.

But, unfortunately, this feeling was quickly replaced by a dread that immediately followed.

'But, you see, luv, I was just coming to rely on Lizbeth at the mill. She's got a head for figures, our Lizbeth has. She's like her dad that way, she is...' He watched the candlelight flicker shadows across his wife's pale face. She was no longer the beauty she'd been when they'd met, but even after so many years of debilitating illness, she remained a handsome woman. He never could understand why a girl of Ellen's looks and class had ever taken a second glance at him, a lowly mill worker.

But she hadn't just glanced. Instead, she'd set her sights on him. She had focused her intentions so determinedly that he couldn't help wondering if she'd got him all wrong, confused him with another John Ashworth. After all, it was a common name. Perhaps, when they first met, she believed he was a John Ashworth born to a higher station with a pocketful of money and a path through life already carved and laid out for him.

He was sure, at their first meeting, that Miss Ellen Moss did not suspect the handsome young lad she'd walked with on Whit Sunday was a John Ashworth raised in a one-room hovel at the end of a muddy lane. The shack where he'd lived as a child had dirt floors, crates for table and chairs, and two pallets on either side of the fireplace where he'd slept head to toe with two brothers whilst his ma lay on the other side with his baby sister. For most of his growing up, there'd been no father, money, food, clothes, shoes, or education. He stole coal for the fire and potatoes for their soup and spent many days down at the market picking the pockets of men in suits.

Luckily for him, there had been a small shining light in his young life that had saved him from an otherwise starved childhood and led him to a future he would never have imagined on his own. That light had been Nell Nuppy and her daughter Betty. These were their closest neighbours—although his mother never said or did one neighbourly thing whilst they lived there.

Nell, on the other hand, was neighbour to even the passing stranger. She always had enough to share, always traded fairly, and from the day she'd set eyes on the ragged ten-year-old John Ashworth, Nell Nuppy was determined to save him from his lot. She put him to work on her farm at their first meeting so she could feed him. Instead of paying him in pennies (as she suspected his mum might take off him), she settled in food, sewed him shirts and trousers, knitted socks and gloves, gave him haircuts, baths, and showed him how to clean his ears and nails. When she found out he couldn't read, she put her daughter, the then twelve-year-old Betty, to the task of teaching him to read and how to write and figure numbers. Had Nell not taken him into her heart and her home, he would not know today a worry beyond a grumbling tummy and a chill that never left the marrow of his bones, he was sure.

Nell Nuppy had been a wise-woman, an herbalist, healer, and midwife, a widow with gypsy in her blood. This last bit made some whisper that she was a witch. John knew for himself that was not true, not in the way they meant it. She did, however, read his palms and tea leaves with certain accuracy, he had to admit. Nell saw signs in the stars, the skies, the flights of birds, and in each tiny snowflake. She drew tarot cards for ladies and charwomen alike, each paying handsomely for the information. She was known to make potions to clear a chest, calm a nerve, shrivel a mole, soothe a toothache, and dry up a weepy eye. Folks came from everywhere for her predictions and advice, eggs and butter, herbs and flowers, potions, powders, and ointments. Women called for her when a baby was coming. They called for her potions to help a life begin when all the fucking in the world didn't work. They called for her to stop the bleeding when the babe died within. And they called for her to take away one more mouth to feed before it could release its first hungry scream.

He felt some need to justify, to explain, to defend Lizbeth's leaving. To help Ellen see all the reasons that it was good. He sipped his whisky, let go of his wife's hand, settled back into his chair, and continued his confessional confiding.

'After all, we both know Lizbeth will never marry. It isn't so much her plain-ness. It's her demeanour. As our Martha Anne says, she's just mean about the world. And I'd 'ave to agree with her.' He shook his head and felt his throat tighten, surprised by his own emotion. 'But, Ellen, it's because she's so burdened.' He felt the weight of his own complicity in her unhappiness. 'At this point in her life, I don't think our Lizbeth could summon a good word for the baby Jesus. Can't say as I blame her.'

Ellen shifted and moaned but did not awaken to her husband's bedside confessions.

'And so, I'm glad for the girl, and to be candid, I'm a bit relieved to have one less daughter to worry about. But, that said, Lizbeth's leavin' brings a new bother…' He took out his pipe and packed in a thumb of tobacco. As he stoked the tinder, watching the smoke rise from the glowing nest of chopped leafy embers, he closed his eyes, imagining the near and far futures for himself, his wife, and his two remaining daughters. He no longer had to worry for his son, and, in only these last few days, he could honestly say he was finally able to be proud of him.

A most recent letter from James had changed John's mind and feelings about his eldest. It was curiously postmarked Scotland. James had written to let them know that he'd joined a shipbuilding firm in Glasgow. He sent hugs and well wishes to his sisters, Alice and Lizbeth, love and apologies to Mum for not seeing her before he left, and, near the end, there was a humbling paragraph of gratitude to his father for 'Givin' me the boot so's I could be me own man…' The packet included a small trinket, a silver thistle on a chain, for Martha Anne from 'Your favourite brother, Jamie'.

James's letter did not ask for the usual sums of spending money nor if his boarding stipend was coming, as John had not had the funds for months. Instead, as John read along, he could almost feel it coming—his son's declaration of independence. And he was right, as it began at the top of the second page, just above his final salutations.

'Never again will I ever set foot on that cold black north ground the sun left behind, the clouds smother, and the rain always, always, always pisses on no matter the pleasantness of the day…'

John did not share this sentiment with his wife or daughters as he read the letter aloud to them. But later, after he'd read it over again and before he folded it away, he considered his son.

'Good for you, lad. You've finally straightened your spine.'

John leaned forward, elbows on knees, smoking his pipe, and staring at his wife. He wondered if, had she not been ill and drugged, she would view this dilemma facing them differently than the way he viewed it, as women often will have different perspectives on things. Mostly inferior perspectives, he'd admit, because a woman's brain could not comprehend complex thought. And while he believed this of most women, he also believed that women sometimes had a keener sense of how to manage the emotional aspects of situations. Such as this current one involving their daughter Alice.

He supposed he could imagine some of what a healthy, thoughtful, mothering Ellen might say: *Our Alice isn't a problem, John! For goodness' sake, the girl works in a sweet shop and appears to be heading to marriage*

93

with the headmaster of a day school, and a very handsome one at that! Imagine how pretty those grandbabies will be!

He imagined her impish grin and flirty smile as she reassured him that our Alice was right on track to claiming her own next life, leaving them, him, with just Martha Anne. *And here we are, dear God. Help us.* He threw back the rest of the whisky in his glass and wiped his mouth with the back of his hand. Tears pricked the corners of his eyes, whether from the whisky or the ache in his heart for his daughter, it mattered not. They flowed over his eyelashes and damped his beard.

'You're right, luv,' he said to his wife, who was still peacefully sleeping without a worry in the world.

Alice will be taken care of. There was no real worry there. No, the worry begins and ends with Martha Anne and the running of a household without a mother to guide the way. He could no more afford to have a charwoman come in than he could afford to imagine Martha Anne handling the cooking, laundry, cleaning, shopping and on and on…Oh lord, what was he to do? There came no answer from his wife, not in real life and not in his imagination.

'She's gone wild, our Martha Anne,' he said quietly now, near whispering in Ellen's ear. 'She won't go to school, and every day she's got a truant officer after her. She roams the countryside, loiters in shops, spends time down by the canal with a gang of rough ones.' He'd heard but didn't say it aloud to his wife that the truant officer, Mr Bloome, had been following Martha Anne around the market nearly every other day. Mr Bruce had come by to share he'd heard that Martha Anne had been cleaning and running errands for the stall owners, and her payment was usually in food. He also said that other merchants had pegged her for a thief and kept an eye out for her for Mr Bloome. But, most disturbing, Mr Bruce had whispered, she'd become quite friendly with the painted women of the back alleys.

'I'm worried, Ellen,' he now said aloud. 'I feel I've made a terrible mistake with Martha Anne. I should never have allowed the authorities to be involved. She's not like other children. She does not respond to discipline with submission but with rebellion. Ever since we gave her that caning, she's been out of control. I'm afraid it isn't going to just be the taint of truancy upon her, but a real chance for arrest!'

That's ridiculous. She's just a little girl. He imagined his wife's disbelief.

'It's not up to me anymore, Ellen,' John said, looking down at his peacefully sleeping wife. He stood, stretched his back, and picked up his glass. 'It's the law. She's got to stay in school until she's twelve, and she's got to complete her "Certificate of Proficiency". That's what she's got to do.' He sighed. 'And I've got to find someone to take care of this house.'

***

The pounding on the door roused the entire household. It was the middle of the night—the night before Lizbeth was to leave for the north. They'd been up late with a small going away party that included Mr Bruce. Alice had helped with the packing, and Martha Anne had readied a basket of cheeses, breads, ham, black pudding, and cakes from the shops. Not long after they'd finished, John had brought out some sherry, and they'd gathered in Ellen's room so she could toast Lizbeth's leaving. John had gone to bed thinking it had been a right good night, considering everything. Lizbeth was happier than he'd ever seen her. Mr Bruce gave her a mapping book of Glasgow, and even Martha Anne gave Lizbeth a framed sketch of Moss Manor as a parting gift. Alice seemed most upset by Lizbeth's leaving, which didn't surprise John at all. His middle daughter had a heart of gold and loved everyone right past their failings. She'd been a good friend to Lizbeth, a good sister. And he saw Lizbeth wipe a tear as she hugged Alice one last time before bed. Lizbeth—she'd miss Alice just as much. He comforted himself to think, especially after tonight, that it would be none too soon before Malcolm Bruce would be coming around to ask for Alice's hand.

As he slipped into his robe, John knew that this late-night disruption was probably not that visit. This pounding on the door was more urgent.

Alice and Lizbeth had joined him at the foot of the stairs with lamps lighted and robes tightened.

Alice jumped and clung to her sister as the pounding thumped three more times, and on the third, the voice belonging to the fist was low, angry, and urgent.

'Open up and getcher little wretch!'

The three looked at each other, and John waved them down the hall as he made his way to the door and opened it.

There before him was a red-faced Mr Bloome. He was sweating and huffing, breathing ragged as if he'd run a race. By her wrist in an iron claw, Bloome held Martha Anne, now slumped over the terrace railing, and…John looked over the attendance officer's shoulder…and saw his daughter heaving into the hedges.

'What's all this?' he demanded of Mr Bloome, now attempting to catch his breath, bending over his knees to do it.

The man stood and yanked Martha Anne back from the rail, and John stepped across the threshold and caught her like a rag doll. She smelled of whisky, and she was laughing. 'Why Daddy, it's you! You've a lovely robe!' she said, smoothing a hand over his arm. 'It's soft.' She smiled. 'Soft like a bunny's bum!' She threw her head back and let out a laugh and a belch at the same time. She appeared to have startled herself.

Mr Bloome looked from the child to John and said, 'Drunk as a whore on payday, she is!'

Martha Anne lifted her clamped wrist and pointed at Mr Bloome. 'Ello, Ducky, you still 'ere?' she asked, allowing him to twist the brass ring on the claw, releasing her wrist. At the same time, her knees buckled out from under her, and John let her slip to the ground.

'Oooh, look, he's lettin' me loose! So sad after a fine walk 'ome, weren't it, Mr Bloooo oome…?' Martha Anne pursed her lips like a fish as she extended his name and pawed at his coat. 'Used that claw so's 'e could cop a little feel of me bosom along the way, didn'tcha MIS-TER Blooooomeeeee…'

He pushed her away now and stepped down onto the garden path. 'She's trouble, John,' was all he managed as he wiped his upper lip with a handkerchief. 'Bad trouble.'

'Dad! It's not me that's the trouble. It's this 'ere dirty owd man, right 'ere!' She then toppled over, but it didn't stop her complaints. 'This 'ere Mr Blooooomeeeee's been chasin' me all over t' market an' moors'—hiccup—'for days!' She swayed and laid down on her side. 'Bloody 'ell, 'e's been chasin' me roun' the whole town for weeks…months, don'tcha know!'

John looked down at his daughter. Her hair was a fright, and she'd a black streak of something across her cheek. Not only was she disheveled, but loose belts and bows were askew, torn, ripped, and missing. She had mud on her hems and stains down her front and indeed smelled as badly as she appeared.

Finally, he saw that she'd only one clog on her left foot, and her right was also bare of a stocking.

She sang out, 'I think Mr Blooomeeee'—she giggled as she attempted to lift herself up—'owd Blooomeeee 'ere wants a piece o' me bosom and me cunny—'

'Martha Anne!' Alice started, but her father put his hand up.

Winking at her father, she slurred, 'If y' get me-meanin', Dad.'

'Let's get her inside,' John said quickly, as much to himself as to Mr Bloome. He suddenly knew what he'd been ignoring about his youngest daughter's misbehaviour. He looked to the sky and figured they were just hours from Lizbeth's departure, leaving him to finally face what he'd been avoiding, right there, drunk on the ground before him—his beloved daughter. He could feel his heart tearing as he peered at his precious girl. The weight of certain guilt landed heavily as he attempted to lift his shoulders, but he knew then that it could not be so easily shrugged off.

Martha Anne was on all fours now but could not figure out how to rise from them, so she didn't. Instead, she remained like a small rodent, a mouse, she decided, and swung her head upward and sideways towards Mr Bloome, twitching her mouse-nose whiskers, and said, 'But Dad,...me pals down on Towd Lane says I'm to keep away from Blooomee, 'ere, cos 'e's an owd perv...perverver...perververt...' and right then, she leaned over the rail and heaved once more.

'Martha Anne? Are you all reet, luv?' Alice asked, pushing past her father to reach her sister, now lying prone between the bushes and the doorway.

'No, she's not all right, Alice. She's drunk, for God's sakes!' Lizbeth snapped.

'Well, 'elp me lift her, then.' Alice yanked under Martha Anne's arms, but it was like lifting a sack of sand.

Before he was asked for help lifting the little bugger into the house, Mr Bloome pulled a packet of papers from his pocket and nearly shouted at John, 'Here!' He waved the envelope above his head. 'It's official...this, this...brat of yours has been arrested and charged as an incorrigible rogue!'

'A what?' John took the packet and patted himself down for his glasses. 'Me glasses!' He snapped his fingers. 'Lizbeth, now!' he ordered. She returned quickly and raised her lantern so he could see the official-looking documents. John folded back the papers. They were stamped and sealed court renderings determining that Martha Anne Ashworth had been charged as an "incorrigible rogue" with many counts of disruption. In addition, there was truancy, loitering, pickpocketing, public displays of drunkenness, and evading both the truant officer and the police.

'I found her down by the canal with the…uh…ladies of the night.' He'd lowered his voice as he eyed both Alice and Lizbeth with embarrassment. He attempted to temper his version of the actual story he would've shared with John had it been just the two men.

'He's lyin'. I were at the Flyin' 'orse havin' a luverly round with me mates.' He continued, 'She were drinkin' whisky and smokin' a cutty when I caught her.'

'Another lie! I were pissin' in the ginnel when he nabbed me!'

Again, he eyed the women 'I, um, I don't believe she's been off with any lads.' He lowered his gaze to the floor, but not before he saw John's eyes go wide with shock. And so, he studied his boots when he tried to assure. 'I think I'd know if she had been off with any of them lads. I, uh, been keepin' a pretty close eye on her…not always, no, but enough…' He now searched John's eyes to see what sort of impact his words were having on him. The father's pain was visible in the cross-hatched lines on his forehead. John's eyes seemed to be imploring Bloome to deliver some good news, some hope, and so he said, softening his voice as one father to another. 'The Canal girls…the ladies…down at the market seem to have taken a liking to her. He pointed to Martha Anne. 'They're…protective of her—'

'Protective?!' Lizbeth now spoke, charging across the threshold to reach her father's side. No matter her personal feelings for her wretched little sister, Martha Anne was blood, no less. 'They've plied 'er with whisky! They've given 'er smokes! They've hidden 'er away from authorities, encouraged 'er truancy, and you 'ave the nerve to say they've protected 'er?'

Bloome lowered both his eyes and shoulders in a gesture of defeat. Then, shaking his head, he said, 'Look, I can't explain it to you. Sure, they egged on her bad behaviours, that's true, but they didn't let others—bad-others, men-others—take advantage. That's all I can say for now. Take what you will from it.'

'What's this all mean?' John asked, interrupting the conversation, finally looking up from the charges.

'It means you pay a fine, and she's done with school. I've already spoken to Mr Bruce, and 'e knows we're done 'ere. She's not to go back, and I'm off her case. She's your responsibility now, not mine, not Mr Bruce's, and not the bloody Crown's, either.'

'But she's not yet twelve. The law says she can't leave until she's twelve.' John said this knowing its argument even sounded weak as he said it. 'That's months away.'

'The law also says she's got to attend school to stay in it. She hasn't done that, and I should know. As far as I see it, it's the mill for that one. Bloody bugger. And with that, he retreated and headed for the gate.'

John turned to see that Alice and Lizbeth had pulled Martha Anne into the house. They'd lain her down on the rug in the hallway. She appeared to have passed out and was snoring. He looked sadly at Alice. 'Go on to bed, luv. I'll take care of 'er. You too, Lizbeth. You've got a big day ahead of you. You'll need some rest.'

'As if that were possible,' she said, begrudgingly. For a minute, the contemptuous look in her eye made John think she would kick Martha Anne before stepping over her, but she did not. She did, however, hold her nose.

'Are you sure, Dad?' Alice asked. 'I'll help you get her into the sitting room. Put her in a chair at least.'

He shook his head. 'No, go on. You've got your sweet shop job in the mornin'. You'll need your rest for your workday.'

After his elder daughters had left him, John stood for a long time in the vestibule. Finally, he settled his lamp on the sideboard and reread the charges, ticking up the fines, working out the punishments Martha Anne had inspired for herself.

He went into his study and brought out a quilted throw, and as he placed it over her, he noticed something shiny peeking out of her coat pocket. He pulled out the silver flask. Uncorking its top, he lifted it to his nose—whisky.

As if he could no longer bear the weight of it all any longer, he slid down the wall, hunkering near his daughter's feet, one shod and one bare, and took a long draught from the flask. He finally closed his eyes and fell asleep.

Part Two
The Incorrigible Rogue

Chapter Six

1890

It'd been nearly two years since she'd been arrested as an incorrigible rogue, Martha Anne thought, then smiled. As drunk as she'd been, as awful as that night had been, she believed it was the best thing to have ever happened to her. She laughed, right out loud, as she was slowly meandering towards Newhey and Betty Nuppy's shop. She'd been 'spared the mill' despite those last threatening words of that boorish truancy officer…Mr Broome? No *Bloome. Bloomeee,* she'd called him when he'd clawed and dragged her home. She'd been having a right fine time with her new pals down at the Flying Horse when he'd caught her outside taking a piss in the ginnel. He'd clamped on his iron claw even before she'd had a chance to pull her skirt down.

To the police station, he'd dragged her, kicking and screaming, adding another charge of "resisting arrest" to the already long list: "truancy, loitering, stealing, running numbers" for a bookie and more, all to the disgrace of herself and the entire family. Most hurtful was to her father's shame. She recalled the pained disappointment in his eyes after he'd watched her heaving in the bushes. As drunk as she'd been, his look had registered, and she still felt that familiar lump of shame settle in her middle.

It was her sister Lizbeth's parting words that had scraped against her cold bones that same early morning as they'd lined up in the chilly dawn to see Lizbeth off to her new life. The carriage had arrived on time, and it was with haste that they'd loaded her trunk. Lizbeth had briefly hugged both her father and Alice, but when she turned to Martha Anne, she did not reach out her arms. Instead, Lizbeth hissed between her teeth, 'I told ye. I warned ye. And now it's the mill for ye!' She climbed up into the rig, but before she closed the door, she pointed at Martha Anne. 'Ye truly are an "incorrigible rogue", and ye deserve whatever ye get!'

Martha Anne had begged her dad not to send her to the mill. She knew she'd die there—she just would. So when her father came home and told her there was an opening for a spinner at Moss Mill, her imagination overtook, and she'd laid out the situation for him as if it were happening before their very eyes:

'There I'll be sittin' spinnin' me life away, gettin' drowsy with the boredom of it all, me eyes close, I lean a bit too close, and one of me plaits gets caught in the bobbin, wrappin' round 'n round, until the machines seize-up, but it's too late. By then, I'm bloodied and bald and need draggin' out by me clogs! Can you see how that'll look on you, Dad?' She included him in her concoction in hopes of shaming his slavish demand to force her into this sort of servitude.

She'd pleaded, cried, stormed about, and recruited Alice, who'd had enough of her. Swallowing her pride, she'd even gone to Mr Bruce to see if he might intervene on her behalf. He wouldn't even look at her. He appeared equally as disappointed in her as her father was and sent her away without much of a hearing. He was done with trying to help her, she could tell.

He wasn't done with Alice, however. She knew this because she'd followed the couple many a time and spied them kissing and cuddling in corners and ginnels. She once caught Alice disheveled and nearly tripping down the stairs from Mr Bruce's flat, adjusting herself as she did, and when Martha Anne confronted her—

'What you been doin' up there?'

Alice had huffed away and wouldn't speak to her for the rest of the week. This sort of personal ostracism from Alice was her way of punishing Martha Anne. She knew it crushed her younger sister to be ignored. Usually, up until now, it most always worked, as Martha Anne strived for Alice's approval and wanted—no, needed her on her side. Now, though, now that she saw how Alice was misbehaving with Mr Bruce, Martha Anne felt a certain contempt for her sister's holier-than-thou attitudes, considering her improper behaviour. After all, Alice was always made out to be such a "saint", an "angel", and "the purest soul on earth", as a group of gossipy church ladies had described her.

But Martha Anne knew that pure Alice was no better than the horny bawds down at the market. And this made her feel disgusted. She was also feeling something else towards Alice and Malcolm, something that confused her because it was the same something she'd felt when she first saw her friend

Sally's new kitten. It was all Martha Anne could do not to borrow Sally's new pet. It was so soft and cuddly. She knew she was easily given to borrowing things she liked, but Sally was so in love with her little joy that the thought of making her friend sad was unbearable, and so she didn't take the kitty. Jealousy was never very strong within her, and if raised, she was often able to negotiate it—albeit on her own terms. This jealousy was new. There was an intensity to it that she'd never felt before. And it always began and ended with Alice and Malcolm Bruce.

She found herself wanting the prize of Malcolm Bruce a hundred times more urgently, more desperately, more determinedly than she'd ever felt for Sally's kitten. And, despite their sisterhood, Martha Anne did not feel the same concern for Alice's potential heartbreak as she'd had for Sally's. No, Martha Anne felt none of that kindness towards Alice when she imagined borrowing her sister's fiancé. In all honesty, she hadn't really been thinking about taking Malcolm or even borrowing him. She'd more just wanted to feel him. She wanted to touch his hair, eyes, and lips to feel him in the ways of men and women. She had no intentions of breaking her sister's heart. It wasn't like she wanted to court him or marry him, good lord, no…no, she just wanted to…feel him.

As she often did on her way to Betty's, she scanned the countryside looking for a glimpse of him, as he would sometimes take the long walk to town while she was on her way to her own job. He'd walk beside her and ask all sorts of questions about working for Betty. She'd begun to wonder if he'd been following her out here to Betty's shop on purpose.

After the incident, she thought back. Her father had decided that if she wouldn't go into the mill, she would be tasked with taking care of her mother, as Lizzie had. Anything was better than the mill, she knew, and she was grateful. Back then, she'd seen a good bit of Mr Bruce who came around often calling for Alice. He'd been entirely dismissive of her presence, and that cut to her core more than she'd reckoned. His attention and support for her smarts, for her creativity, curiosity, and education had been unfailing up until then. When she was younger, she recognised she didn't need his encouragement to satiate her deep curiosities, but with all that had happened this last year, his withdrawal of these approvals also seemed to quash her early interests. Especially so since her pretty but vapid sister seemed only to bat an eyelash to gain Malcolm's full-on adoration. Maybe she was a little jealous, she'd admitted only to herself, but she guessed that Alice knew her deeper feelings, and for this, Martha Anne had begun to stoke an unreasonable contempt for her elder sister.

Unfortunately, Martha Anne wasn't very good at taking care of her mother. She was good at telling stories and making her laugh. She was good to bring tea, brush hair, and rub her always cold feet and hands. These were the easy parts of caring for her mother. But Martha Anne wasn't good at remembering her mother's personal needs and would let hours pass before remembering to check on her. Or be called by the incessant ringing of the little silver bell on the bedside table. Emptying the stinky chamber pot made her gag, and so she too often avoided it. At those times, its already over-flowing contents would splash everywhere, and she was often left mopping up the mess that she'd only herself to blame. The list went on. She wasn't good at helping her mother in and out of the tub she'd drag by the fire to help her bathe. Inevitably, her mother would slip, or the water would be too hot, or too cold, or the towels too rough, or on and on, the sick woman complained. And if she missed the potions from Betty Nuppy, well, Ellen Moss Ashworth would turn into a violently vile patient, Martha Anne learned when Ellen lifted a teapot and hurled it across the room because the tea was tepid.

And so, when she turned fourteen, behind her father's back, she'd gone to Betty and had begged, cajoled, argued, and eventually wore her down to let Martha Anne work in the shop. She took the same measures with her father, who finally acquiesced after she'd left her mother unattended, and they'd found Ellen in the back garden in nothing but her undergarments. It was then that John could see how the arrangement would not work for either him, Ellen, or Martha Anne.

She'd expected to see much less of Malcolm after she'd begun working for Betty, as she was away more than when she was home, but it was soon after she'd started her job that she'd coincidentally run into Malcolm on the way to or from Betty's. She thought it odd, and she said as much one afternoon when he'd suddenly appeared from behind a large tree, frightening her a bit.

She asked, annoyed by the fright. 'How is it I see you more since I been workin' for Betty than I ever saw you at school or, for that matter, at home with all your sniffin' around our Alice?'

He never answered this question, just kept pace with her, walking to or from the shop, chatting her up. She realised, soon enough, though, that he never came inside for a cup of tea at either destination after these walks. And she noticed he hadn't been interested in either Alice or Betty knowing he'd been accompanying her. Instead, he'd laughed, told stories, sometimes stopping in the middle of the road to act out or demonstrate his experiences.

However, of late, Martha Anne sometimes caught him watching her, looking at her in that way the blokes looked at the ladies down at the market before they went around the corner with them. This look of Malcolm's, this studying of her developing womanly body, revealed a longing in his eyes as they rested on her bosom, traced the contours of her curves, and sculpting the softness of her lengthy hair, all the while believing others were unaware of his imaginings.

When Martha Anne had dared a look in return, the meeting of their eyes had awoken new and startling desires in her, as well. She'd dreamt of his lips seeking hers, gazing into the deep pools of his dark eyes, his hands tangling in her hair, undoing the buttons of her frock. When these episodes of fantasy took hold, making her so weak inside that she thought she might explode, she'd often race out the front door and run all the way to Betty's shop where she'd throw herself into a pile of hay and lay there until the unsettling needs, she felt inside had worn out of her.

A donkey pulling a wagon ambled past, and she was startled by the animal, which seemed to have just sneaked up on her, although she didn't know how since the creaks and groans of the old wooden wagon were loud enough to wake the dead.

'Ello, luv, fancy a ride?' The old farmer tipped his cap as he made pace with her. 'Off to Betty's, I am. You?'

'Ah, Ernie, it's you!' She grinned and gave a pat to the donkey. 'And you, Rollo!'

Ernie stopped the rig, and Martha Anne climbed up in the seat next to him.

She gave a backward glance to the parcels in his wagon. 'Is it our order from London, then?'

He snapped the reins and gave a click with his tongue, jerking the wagon as Rollo moved at a snail's pace. ''Tis. One of 'em, at least. Picked up a load from the rail station in Manchester yesterday. Parcels, letters, packages from London, Manchester, Liverpool, all just waitin' for delivery.'

'What 'appened to the Royal Post?' Martha Anne asked.

'Oh, did you not 'ear? Another post-boy robbed at knifepoint! Regular bands of Robin Hoods out there in the countryside between the towns and villages. Those poor lads, unarmed, all dressed like peacocks in their fancy red uniforms. Just askin' to be robbed.'

'So, you're the Royal Post now?'

'Nah, just had a run to the city and back. I offered to pick it all up and deliver. Puts a bit of coin in me pockets, you see.'

She smiled. 'I do,' she said as they rounded the corner to Betty's cottage bright spot of sun shone through the grey of the heavens and the smog of the chimneys, right onto the little cottage. *Like an angel's little dwelling all lighted up,* she thought. As it was market-day, Betty was dressed for town in a bulky wool coat, grey felt hat, and thick lace-up clogs that reached above her ankles. Slung over her shoulder was a large burlap sack that appeared already full, but Martha Anne knew that in addition to her own wares that she would sell and barter, she also stuffed a good number of smaller sacks to separate the goods she'd be hauling home.

Martha Anne tilted her head and placed her hand on her hip. 'You'll bring me back a Cornish pasty, eh?'

'You're a cheeky bugger.'

'But you love me.' Martha Anne helped Betty up into the wagon and pecked Betty on the lips.

'Aye, that I do, against me will, but that I do…'

Ernie slapped the reins and clicked his tongue, and the wagon made its turn and headed up the lane. As they left the gate, Martha Anne shouted, 'From Fat Joe! In the potato market!' she called through her cupped hands. She saw Betty's hand raise and wave.

It was just shy of noon. Martha Anne had finished cataloguing the new arrivals and was taking a break in the warm dryness of the greenhouse, having a cup of tea, when she heard the bell at the front door jingle. She reluctantly made her way to the front of the shop to see that the door hung open, but there did not appear to be anyone about. She stepped outside looking for a delivery or patron waiting politely, but there was no one. She checked in the pigsty, chicken coop, and barn to discover nowt out of sorts and closed the door firmly behind her. She walked about the sheep paddock, gardens and even peered into the privy out back, just to be sure. She'd done a full investigation, which traced her steps back to the split door, and still, no one about, near or far for that matter.

Turning, she was about to step back into the shop when there appeared the darkened silhouette of a man standing behind the counter. She wasn't sure if she should run and hide until Betty returned or stride inside and demand that the scoundrel leave. Before she had a chance to make a move in either direction, she'd been frozen to her spot when she heard her name called out from within.

'Martha Anne? Is that you?' The figure emerged from the darkness of the building and out into the yard. To her surprise, it was Malcolm.

'Mr Bruce?'

He stepped into the yard and joined her. 'Oh, come now, call me Malcolm.' He smiled. 'After all, we're nearly family.'

'Is there something wrong with me mum?' she asked, ignoring his directive. 'Dad? Our Alice?'

He shook his head, interrupting her next guess, and said, 'No, nothing. Everyone is fine. Well, as far as I know. I haven't been to the manor house since Sunday. It's been a busy week.' He bent to smell a bouquet of herbs. 'I did see Alice at the sweet shop this morning. She is well,' he said as if he needed to insert her sister into the conversation to shield himself from being alone with her, somehow.

Martha Anne made her way past him and up into the shop. She moved behind a potting bench, where she started to fill small pots with dirt. Randomly counting out seeds from packets whose contents she was barely paying attention to and would have a hard time remembering which was which by the time she'd finished. She pretended to be quite intent upon her task as she watched Malcolm make his way through the shop, poking about shelves, uncorking bottles, smelling them. Frowning or nodding determined his reactions.

Finally, she turned to face him and asked, 'Is there something I can 'elp ye with?'

He turned and came across the room in just two long strides. 'I was hoping to see Miss Nuppy,' he said, now standing very close and looking up to a shelf just above her head.

'She's not here.' Martha Anne could smell the musky scent of him as his sleeve brushed her cheek, something, apparently only she noticed.

'Not here?' He reached above her, his chest just inches from her face. She was pressed against a cupboard and could not extract herself graciously, so she closed her eyes. After he'd retrieved whatever he'd been leaning for, he stepped. 'Will she be back soon?'

'Doubt that. She's gone to market.'

He was burying his nose in the sack of herbs he'd pulled from the shelf.

'You goin' to buy that or just sniff it?' she asked, jerking her chin at the small pouch.

He pulled his nose from the satchel and smiled, 'Smells like a grand feast in one little bag.'

'We charge for sniffin', you know,' she said.

He grinned. 'Is that right?'

''Tis. Thruppance a sniff that'll cost ye.' Sliding past him, she went to the cash box. She put out her hand, palm up.

He laughed and reached into his pocket. Gently taking her wrist, he placed the little silver coin into her palm. Meeting her eyes, he pressed down, just a bit, and then smiled. When she made to pull away, he tightened his grip, and with a mischievous look, he placed a shilling in her palm as well. She looked surprised.

'What's that for? That's more than the price of two sniffs and a bag of tea!' She grinned.

He carefully pulled her closer, not letting go, and brought her hand to his cheek. She could feel the bristles of his beard as the hot breath from his lips touched her skin. She stilled, holding her own breath. She could not exhale as she watched him close his eyes. Then, pressing his nose to her soft damp wrist, he inhaled deeply. Her heart sped and urged her feet to do the same, but she could not move. There was a tingling in her newly bloomed bosom and between her legs, and she leaned close enough for a soft curl of his dark hair to touch her cheek. And then, suddenly, he took one long and loud sniff up her arm and released her with a flourish as if she, too, were some fragrant bouquet.

'For that!' He laughed. 'A shilling for a sniff of you!'

Now she did pull away and moved across the room, angered by his frivolousness, angered by the passion he'd roused in her, angered by the fact that she'd let him and angered by the knowledge that she liked it.

'Awe, now, Martha Anne, ye canna be angry over a wee bit o' a lark, can ye?' His brogue was as thick as his voice had become, and she could see that he was attempting to recover from his small mischief.

'You'll need to leave,' she said, not smiling. 'It's not right you're here alone w' me. It's…it's…'

Quickly, he strode around the counter and clasped her to him, whispering in her ear, his hot breath making her weak, making her tremble. 'It's what? Tell me what it is…' He grazed his lips against her soft earlobe.

'It's…improper…' she managed but did not move. She dared a look into his eyes and saw a longing there as ferocious as her own. She could feel his need against her, matching her own throbbing. He reached for her breast and stroked her nipple with his thumb, causing her to moan as she closed her eyes. His lips met hers, and she felt his tongue push between her teeth as if searching. Clutching a hank of his hair, she gripped tightly, pulling with every tremble.

Suddenly, there was the distinct sound of a wagon outside and Betty's voice calling her. Martha Anne pushed away from Malcolm, nearly toppling him onto a sack of grain. Then, he caught himself, and their eyes met, each filled with a certain immediate shame, regret, guilt. She could tell the feelings within her were also within him.

'Out the back!' She pointed to the small side door. 'You'll have to go over walls and through the brambles down there to pick up the road below. Hurry!'

She watched him run as she re-tied her apron and straightened her skirt, and then she ran to the greenhouse, all the while hoping and praying that the gypsy in Betty wouldn't immediately detect the deceit in which Martha Anne was now firmly ensconced.

She made it back at the table, pretending to sip the tepid tea, attempting to catch her breath.

Betty marched in, hat askew, face red, one hand on her hips, and pointed. 'What's up wi' that one?'

'What do you mean?' Martha Anne looked to where Betty was pointing out the glass panes of the greenhouse where, in full view, they watched Malcolm running through the pasture, over the rock wall, and disappearing down into the dale.

'Were 'e here? In me shop? Alone w' ye?' Betty held Martha Anne's gaze and would not let go. 'Tell me the truth, lass, or I'll tell yer dad.'

Martha Anne broke down. She could not lie to Betty, so she admitted to her feelings for Malcolm. She tried to explain that these emotions were not all that new or sudden but went back to that very first time she'd been in trouble at school with that horse-faced hag, Miss Royds. She told of wandering around his office, peeking into his life, gleaning his interests, his curiosities, his devotions, and she'd made them her own.

'I've been in some kind of love with 'im since back then, Betty, can't ye' see?'

Betty shook her head and scoffed. 'In love? What do you know about love, child?'

'I know…I know…enough to know how I feel when I'm around him. Everything inside me spins me out of me head.'

'That's not love, lass. That's lust. And that's a very dangerous feeling to be 'avin', girl. Your Alice is about to marry that man.'

'I know. I do know that, Betty, but I can't 'elp my feelins.'

'You can and you best!'

'He's got the same for me. He does, I know it!'

Betty whipped around the table, pushed aside a nearby chair and poked her nose just inches from Martha Anne's, making her drop her teacup into the saucer with a clatter. Poking Martha Anne in the chest, she spat. 'Now, you listen to me, girl. And you 'ear me. You need to keep yer knickers up around that haggis shaggin' scoundrel.' Betty scowled when Martha Anne grinned.

Betty slapped the table. 'If you're that horny, if yer that hard up, find yerself a lad of yer own, a husband of yer own! Not right to take your Alice's, for God's sake!'

'Oh, I weren't thinkin' of takin' 'im, I was just thinkin' about borrowin' 'im for a bit of a roll, is all,' she said, mocking up the cheekiness in her tone, knowing it would infuriate Betty.

'That's enough! No way to talk! You've spent too much time with those whores down at the market.'

'Yes, well, at least those ladies understand that all's fair in love and war…and'—Martha Anne's tone shifted from teasing to serious when she slid a look to Betty, catching her eyes 'and…Betty, I think 'e's in love wi' me, too…'

Betty shook her head.

Martha Anne could feel the disappointment in the gesture and defended, 'It's not just me fancyin' 'im, Betty!'

Betty puttered around the tool bin.

Growing exasperated, Martha Anne went to the small cubby where she kept her things and rummaged through her satchel, pulling out a small book. 'He slipped this into me book of poetry. I'd left it bookmarked in the parlour last weekend.'

'Poetry?' Betty blew a dismissive whistle.

'Yes, poetry. Browning, Shelley, Shakespeare…'

'Ooh, Shakespeare, La Di Da!'

Martha Anne ignored her contempt. 'After he'd come calling for Alice, and they'd left for a walk, I opened to the marker, and I found this.' She handed the book to Betty.

Scrawled beside a poem that began "How do I Love Thee"…was a crudely drawn heart encircling the initials "MAA + MRB" in its centre. Martha Anne tapped the paper twice. 'That's me, "MAA", and that's 'im: Malcolm Robert Bruce, "MRB".' Martha Anne crossed her arms in a sort of final satisfaction of proof.

Betty slapped down the book. 'Never did like that one,' she muttered. 'Too 'andsome for 'is own good. Too big for 'is own britches. And too rich for this poor mill town.' Betty shook her head. 'To think I'd been right all along.'

'What d'ye mean?' Martha Anne asked, now following Betty as she'd grabbed a broom and began ferociously sweeping the stone slab.

Betty stopped for a breath, her bosom quickly rising and falling, either from the exertion or this worrying situation, or both. 'Wot I mean is, I always thought Lord Thistle-Banger paid too much attention to you ever since you were little. I took 'im for danger, then, just as I do now.'

'Betty!'

'What? Do you not know the unnatural affection of a sheep fucker when you see it? Why'd ye think Scotsmen wear kilts, eh?'

Martha Anne couldn't help but giggle at Betty's bawdy descriptions despite her feelings for Malcolm. 'He wears breeches, not a kilt.'

Betty ignored her. 'I thought it odd and wrong back then, but now that you've turned woman'—Betty paused to give Martha Anne a long slow up and down look and then lifted her palms to the whole of her—'and more than a beautiful one at that.' Then, sighing, she wiped a tear, took a deep breath, and again began sweeping with less anger.

'It's a dangerous game that blasted bugger is playin' with you Ashworth sisters—'e's no good, Martha Anne. So keep away from 'im.'

After such a direct warning, Martha Anne had done her best to heed Betty's words. Whenever Malcolm would be expected at the manor, or if he'd arrived without notice, she'd hide in her room until he was gone. This fortitude, however, did not stop her from creeping to the top of the stairs so she could listen to his beautiful soft brogue or catch a glimpse of his curly brown hair, and when she'd heard the door close upon his departure, she'd run to her bedroom window and watch as he—or he and Alice—headed down the street. Only once had he turned back to see her staring down at him, and his smile nearly made her swoon.

After that, she'd had to fight off her feelings and would often take to running along the moors, the river, forests, and dells. She'd run until she could feel no more, and then it would be safe to return to the land of proper people and pretend to be one of them too.

It was on one of these escapes from herself when she'd found herself lost. She'd wound along the moors, through sheep fields, over stone walls, and under a garden fence. She'd crawled until she found herself on a hidden path whose view at the end was Hollingworth Lake itself. She'd discovered a tight grove of silver birches in a mossy patch away from the footpath and sat down beneath the largest, resting her head and closing her eyes.

She must've fallen asleep as it was the nearby sound of footfalls and the darkening of the sky that let her know it was getting late. She stood and emerged from the bushes when suddenly she was pushed aside, back into the grove by a dark figure barreling down the cut towards the lane. She landed on her bum, and her teeth smacked together, sending stars before her eyes.

'What the bloody 'ell!' she'd yelled. Her molars clamped her tongue.

'Martha Anne?' It was Malcolm. 'What on earth are you doin' out here at this hour?' He offered a hand to help her up, but she refused.

She stood and rubbed her jaw, the metallic taste of blood filling her mouth. 'I could ask you the same, and in such a hurry, at that!' She peered around him. 'Somebody chasin' ye?'

He dusted down his coat front as if he were the one who'd taken the spill. His face was flushed, and he was sweating. 'No, no one is chasin' me, 'cept me demons…' He looked away as if he regretted his words as soon as they'd left his mouth.

'Demons, have ye?' She squinted at him. 'What sort o' demons could a fella like ye 'ave? You've got everythin' in the world. Good job, nice clothes…' She gestured up and down his physique. She noticed the neat cut of his trousers, the easy sway of his jacket, his shined boots, and while he'd no cap on his head nor tie at his collar, he appeared ready for just about any event from church to a garden party.

He looked to the sky as if searching or beseeching and took a deep breath and shook his head.

Martha Anne continued her evaluation of his life. 'You've got me sister in your pocket, a marriage on the horizon, and I'm sure a dozen babes to follow. Demons, my arse.'

He frowned, staring at her as she teased him. Her hair had loosened from its bow, and thick dark waves draped her shoulders. She'd grown from an unremarkable child, careless about her appearance, often disheveled by her curiosity-driven exploring, something that had only improved a bit over time, but what had changed dramatically was that she'd matured into something of exotic beauty, unlike her sister Alice, who was safely pretty in the most acceptable ways: fair, blue-eyed, soft blond curls, and rosebud lips Martha Anne was the polar opposite. No safety in that dark beauty. Those eyes, shadowed by thick lashes—hiding, flirting, and gripping—were a warm brown but would go black if in attack or retreat and were forever watchful. He couldn't help noticing the voluptuous curves of her womanhood moulded by her damp skirt and blouse—damp from the dew of the evening—clinging to her skin. He could see through to her bosom, to her nipples taut against the white cotton. He reached for her and pulled her to him.

Between his clenched teeth, almost angrily, he hissed, 'You! You, Martha Anne, are my demon!' He pressed his mouth on hers, searching with his tongue, running his hands along her bosom, down her spine, between her legs, and he could feel her tremble and gasp, leaning harder against him. He pressed his nose to her hair, kissed along her neck, and felt her hands inside his shirt, against his skin, touching his chest, sliding down his middle, past his navel, to the top of his trousers.

He quickly pushed her back into the grove of birches, off the path, into the darkness of the clearing's edge. He found a wide oak and pushed her up against the tree as she began to unbutton his breeches. Then, hiking up her skirt, he lifted her onto his thighs, slid inside her, and they rode the moment until Martha Anne let out such a scream that Malcolm covered her mouth. They rolled to the soft mossy floor of the clearing, where they burst into a string of uproarious laughter. She pulled down her skirts and then slid up against him, stroking him, making him hard all over again. She mischievously grinned as she saw his eyes roll back in his head.

'Nah. Lass. I canna go again…Not again.' He heaved each word with a deep breath.

She stroked harder and began kissing him, down his middle, placing her lips on him, watching his ecstasy with upturned eyes, and it was his turn to scream aloud until she climbed onto his chest and covered his mouth with her own. She wanted to explore him with her tongue, her eyes, her hands. Feel him. Every bit of him. She wanted him on her and in her all at the same time. She writhed against him. Feeling him as she had wanted to feel him all along.

She laid her head on his shoulder, and he wrapped his arm around her, his hand stroking her hair. He hugged her tightly as their breaths met in sync, and there, in the silver birch grove, as the sun set over the Pennines, they fell asleep in each other's arms.

Chapter Seven

Martha Anne unpacked three Cornish pasties from her sack, along with a thick hunk of cheese, crusty bread, and cold lamb. She set it out on the potting table and sat on the high stool. Tucking a tea towel down her collar and closing her eyes, she took a bite of the still warm pasty and sighed.

'You've been stuffin' yer face for days!' Betty said. 'Beware, you might 'ave worms.'

'I don't 'ave worms. I just 'ave a cravin' for a pasty, is all,' Martha Anne defended.

'Is all. Yesterday ye' finished off me Bubble and Squeak after ye' made a dent in me Toad-n-the-Hole. Good lord, girl.'

'I'm 'avin' a growth spurt, is what me dad says. Would you like one?' She handed Betty a pasty.

She took it and settled on a stool across from Martha Anne. Looking the girl over, Betty thought there'd been something different about her lately. She'd been like a wild hare all summer, hopping around the moors, running from home to shop to market to the lake, splashing bare-foot in rivers, forgetting her shawl, careless with her laces, leaving her hair bows untidy, daydreaming through tasks, Martha Anne was a bit of a mess, Betty decided. If she didn't know better, she might think that lout of a schoolmaster was hangin' bout, but Martha Anne promised she'd given him the boot after his advances in the shop. She said she'd dumped him like "the pile of shite 'e is", were her exact words, Betty recalled.

But Betty knew besotted when she saw it. She knew it because she'd once been besotted with John Ashworth. She remembered that summer when they'd run over the moors, splashed in rivers, slept in crofts, kissed, touched, and tumbled together—just a few times, but enough to last Betty's heart a lifetime. Then, soon after they'd explored each other's bodies, made promises of a future, without so much as a warning, John had up and married Ellen, and that was the end of it. It'd been a blow. She'd been angry. It took her years to speak to him again, but Betty got over him after a while. Her passions for him had waned as his backbone bent to the will of his new family. She saw how soft he was, how weak he'd become under the knee of his father-in-law and the thumb of his wife. And when he'd once confessed that he would be "nowt w'out 'em", Betty thought him pitiful, as she believed John was nowt because of 'em.

Of course, she'd never said any of these feelings aloud. No, instead, after his visits and attempts to make things right between them, she'd given in and had become his best friend, his sister, his mother. She attentively listened as he'd shared his woes. She nodded approvals, tutted sympathies, shook her head in allegiance with his grievances, and if asked for advice, she would never tell him the truth. She would always tell him what he wanted to hear. She barely recognised this pathetic grown-up John Ashworth. He was not the boy with whom she'd shared a childhood of brave exploring and adventuring. It meant nowt now in the grand scheme of things. John had chosen convenience, money, status, and power over love and happiness, perhaps giving up the last, first.

Oh, Betty knew besotted, all right, and as she watched the young woman gazing out the window, miles away with the fairies, Betty knew Martha Anne knew it too.

'Who is 'e?' She decided to come right out with it.

'Who is who?' Martha Anne frowned.

'Whoever 'e is that's got you all goo-eyed in case you think nobody's noticed.'

'I 'aven't a clue what yer on about. I'm not goo-eyed, no matter what ye think ye've noticed.'

Betty shifted on the stool and took a bite of the pasty. 'Oh, ye got a fella all reet. The question is who? Who is this lad that's got ye tangled up in twists?'

Martha Anne broke off a chunk of cheese but had suddenly lost her appetite. 'It's no one, and none of ye mind if I 'ad, but I don't.' Her hands had begun a slight tremble, and she slipped them to her lap.

'Ye know, I were smitten once.' Betty picked crumbs from the table and nibbled them. 'I were like you—daft w' 'im, couldn't concentrate, couldn't think, could barely do a thing when we were apart, and then could barely do a thing when we were together. It was a wild fling, and I learnt from it. No matter 'ow much of a tizzy you might be in now, it won't last. It never does. Especially if y' tumble with 'im and get wi' a babe. In the end, all those butter-churnin' feelings won't last. Only the hungry cries of a baby will be keepin' you up at night. Remember that…'

Betty was right about one thing—they'd tumbled all reet. Martha Anne heard Betty's words resounding in her head as she made her way slowly homeward. She and Malcolm had tumbled everywhere: in the birch glade, in Betty's own shop, the croft, on the moors, in ginnels and around corners, Malcolm's office after dark and his bed before dawn—a whole summer of secretive shagging like sheep in season. Martha Anne thought Betty too keen, and it made her nervous. It was as if she could see all the pictures and words running through Martha Anne's mind. She was sure Betty could hear the hidden truths in Martha Anne's bald-faced lies. She tried to block Betty's view of her mind and heart and veiled the images of Malcolm kissing her, touching her, inside her. The more she tried to hide these thoughts and pictures, the more exposed they felt.

If there was anything to heed in Betty's admonitions of this afternoon, Martha Anne did understand that if anyone found them out, it would be the end of Alice's wedding, never mind their sisterly relationship. It would probably be the end of Malcolm's career. And then what would they do? Betty had put it to her, somehow knowing that she'd not given Malcolm the boot as she'd promised. But she didn't give in. She wouldn't betray their love. And since Malcolm had never mentioned any of these cautions, she had never thought of the dangers she posed to him. This worried her now and furthered her belief that they should flee Lancashire together, perhaps head to Edinburgh where he'd surely be able to gain a teaching position. Until then, she wouldn't utter a word to anyone. She'd shield him as she had because…she was in love with him, and she would not be his downfall.

A cloud made a pass across her path, darkening her way and her spirits. She hadn't seen him in days nor heard from him, which worried her more. Whenever Malcolm called for Alice, he would wait in the parlour. Martha Anne would leave her latest reading material on the side table, and he would slide notes between pages. After his last two visits, though, she'd been disappointed to find none. So she reasoned that, perhaps, Alice had given him no time to wait and rushed him off to the next shop where she was buying up all sorts of clothing and linens to fill her trousseau.

That morning, before light, Martha Anne pulled the loose brick from beside Malcolm's door, placing a small note in the hole, and then turned the brick from its red to its grey side—her sign for him. She'd taken the side road home to see if the brick had been flipped, signalling he'd gotten her note and inviting her up. As the sky was darkening and splatters of rain began to fall, she rounded the corner and saw that lights were on and smoke was billowing from his chimney. She smiled and took the steps two at a time, but she suddenly stopped when she reached the door to see that he had not flipped the brick, nor had he pulled it out and taken her note. And it was just then that she heard her sister Alice's laughter coming from within, and she fled down the steps and up through the ginnel, her tears and the rain washing down her face.

She'd gotten home to see that her mother was asleep, and her father was nowhere to be found. Probably down the pub, his latest distraction. She put the kettle on and took a towel from the rack, rubbing her dripping hair. She poured the tea and crept up to her room quietly, as she did not want to awaken her mother and must attend to whatever needs she might have at the moment. Slipping into a soft cotton nightgown, she slid her feet into dry stockings. Her father must've stoked the little stove before he left, and so she stirred the coals and placed a large round stone on the hob, warming it for her bed. She wrapped her hands around her cup. *Tea always seemed to fix everything,* she thought, smiling—and then not smiling because tea wasn't going to fix this.

Was it any wonder that she'd missed her time again? She almost couldn't remember the last time she'd used a rag. Was it any wonder that she'd been ravenously eating all day and sick each morning? Was it any wonder that her nipples were big and bright and tender? Was it any wonder that when she lay quite still in her bed, she could crown her palms over the small slight mound of her belly? Was it any wonder that whilst lying so very still, holding her breath, closing her eyes that she could hear two hearts inside her body, a second heartbeat thumping beside her own?

***

She waited for him inside his flat. She'd noted that after he'd seen Alice home, he sat in the parlour sharing a whisky with her father, and she'd dashed out the back and ran towards the school. She knew where he'd kept a key under the mat, and she let herself inside. She lit the lamps, stoked the fire, put the kettle on, like a right proper wife, she thought, smiling at the little spread of biscuits and tea she'd put out on the table. She was soon to be the mother of the schoolmaster's child, his wife sooner than that, she hoped. So she thought she should get some practice at it. Martha Anne had waited beside the table for him to arrive and anticipated his delighted surprise to find her making herself at home. But when he'd flung open the door to the cosy domestic scene, his face shifted from confusion to disappointment to what she thought she saw— a flash of anger that darkened his brow. His face flamed at his cheeks, and his eyes darted from the fire to the teapot and finally landing on her.

'Martha Anne, what are you doing here?' He slammed the door harder than he'd meant to, and they both flinched. 'How'd you get in?' He pulled off his boots and hung his coat. 'You need to leave. You can't be seen here, and you know that.' He now stood in the middle of the room, turned towards her, and stared.

'I 'aven't heard from you. I 'aven't seen you. You 'aven't left notes in me book, and you've been by, I know you 'ave. I've seen you 'ave…' Her words trailed off, seeing the distance in his eyes, and then his gaze dropped to the flames of the fire.

It was beginning to dawn on her that he had not immediately taken her in his arms. He had not covered her mouth with his, stroked her breasts, whispered in her ear. Instead, he was just standing there, as if she were, once again, a petulant child needing his attention.

'I've been, I've…been busy,' he stuttered. 'School's back in session. There are things to do.' He picked a pipe up off the mantel. 'Look, I'm sorry. But, well, summer's gone. We've had our fun.' He looked over to her. 'I'm not sure what you expect of me?'

'Well, not…not…this…' She waved her hands at him as if to explain this. 'Not this send-off. Not we've had our fun, now run along. Is that what this is?'

He stuffed a thumb of tobacco in his pipe. 'Now Martha Anne,' his voice calm. 'You know Alice and I are to be married. You had to know that our times together would end. You're a bright lass, you are. You've had to know better than to think we could continue with our merrymaking.' He managed a slight mischievous grin with the lift of his eyebrow. Then, lighting a match, he touched it to his pipe and made a clicking sound with his tongue as he sucked. It made her stomach roil.

She saw him now, just as Betty saw him, just as Betty had said—he's had his way. He was done with her. She could tell it was just a matter of words before her whole world would come crashing down, and when it did, she'd have to believe it, accept it, and get on with it. Perhaps it was this urgency that made her blurt out her own words because if her words could get in the way of his words, block them, she would only have to believe and accept her own truth.

'I'm pregnant.'

The air stilled. Malcolm seemed caught in a pose with his match in the air burning towards his fingers. Then, when it got close, he tossed it in the fire.

'What?' he managed. He loosened his collar, warm from the heat from the fire, his throat burning from his pipe smoke, and this news having a combusting effect on him. He felt a trickle of sweat run down his cheek, but he dared not wipe it.

'You heard me.'

'But…how…'

'Really. That's your response? How?'

'I mean…' He frowned and shook his head as he hadn't heard. Finally, almost to himself, he asked, 'Is it even mine?'

It took less than two strides to cross the room, but when she'd got to him, it only took one swing to slap the clay pipe from Malcolm's teeth, shattering it on the hearth. He tripped backward into the mantel and caught himself. The metallic taste of blood filled his mouth.

'How dare ye.' She spat between his feet and made for the door. Before leaving, she threatened, 'We'll see how our Alice feels about raisin' your bastard, eh?'

She fled down the steps out into the street. Instead of heading home and having a chance run-in with Alice, she turned towards the village. Heading for Toad Lane, where her lady friends from the market would be found at any nearby pubs, and she could surely use some cheering tonight.

***

It'd been days since she'd left Malcolm's flat, and the events of such were still fuzzy in her mind as she lay in her bed trying to make some sense of the week: where she'd been, who she'd been with, but worse, what she'd done. As far as she could remember, she'd roamed pubs, went up the ginnel with this fella and that one, slept in the beds of her mates from the market and others, strangers, men and women both, all who were generous with their blankets and their roaming hands. But she gave it no mind. She'd mostly blacked out through the invasions of her intimate places.

She'd no idea how she made it home, especially since her clogs were missing from her belongings. The stinking dirty lump of a mess in the corner was reeking of whisky, piss, shit, and vomit. She'd gone through it earlier, looking for her money pouch and her whisky flask, both gone. But she did find the remains of a little cutty and smoked the rest of it beside the fire before crawling back into bed. Oh, her head banged. She squeezed her eyes shut tight against the small light making its way under the curtain.

And then, she remembered she'd been carrying a baby. The reality of it washed over her. She suddenly felt the heat of fear travel the length of her torso as she slid her hands over her belly. She closed her eyes and became still, listening inside herself for a very long time. She heard her heartbeat and pressed fingers against her throat to be sure. She counted along until she got tripped up by an extra beat, and another, and another, the extra beats of a second heart right there thumping alongside her own. The fear did not subside but grew. What was she to do with a baby and no father?

***

The sun had sunk, and Martha Anne lit the lamp beside her bed and managed to stir the fire. Then, finally, she felt better and slipped into a pair of slippers to make her way to the kitchen for some tea when there was a slight tap on the bedroom door.

'Yes?'

Alice peered around. Seeing Martha Anne up and seated beside the fireplace, Alice pushed her way in with a tray of toast and tea. 'Hello, luv…Thought you might be 'ungry,' she said, her voice kind and gentle as it always was. She set the tray on the table between them and took a seat on the edge of the bed. 'How are you feelin'?'

Martha Anne poured the welcome tea into the cup and lifted it with two shaky hands. Then, after she'd sipped and settled back against the chair, she finally said, 'Thanks, I needed this. Was just coming down for it.'

'Good. Good timin' then.' Alice looked to her hands and fidgeted with a string on her cuff. 'Glad you're up. I was worried about ye. Especially when we couldn't find ye…for days…'

Martha Anne felt the guilt and shame collide, her face hot with both, and she turned to the fire to hide them from her sister.

'I'm sorry...' she managed. 'Honestly, I 'aven't an idea what I were thinkin', or doin', for that matter…Sometimes the drink gets hold of me.'

'I know…you and Dad both.' Alice felt the darkening of her spirit as she recalled her father and sister both stumbling into the house, blind drunk, singing at the top of their lungs. John stood on the landing shouting jumbled lines from an old Tim Bobbin poem, Martha Anne joining him. When she couldn't remember a verse, she made up a new one, bawdy as can be, to which her father doubled over in loud, raucous guffaws, laughing right along with his drunkest youngest. Then, just before he'd passed out on the floor in the parlour, he announced that he'd found the best drinkin' mate in all of Rochdale, and it had been his little girl all along!

'So, that's how I got home?' Martha Anne remembered none of it. She couldn't recall seeing her father in the last few days. Especially not in a pub, especially not drunk, but who was she to argue with Alice. It must've been true because here she was, all in one piece. 'How'd I get up here to me bed?'

'Malcolm carried—'

'Malcolm?' Martha Anne stood. 'Malcolm! What the hell was Malcolm doin' 'ere?'

Alice sat quite still and said in an even tone, 'Well, Martha Anne, we were worried 'bout you. We didn't know where you'd got to. Of course, I'd told Malcolm. Of course, he was beside himself with worry, too. Like everyone else, he was out searching for y'. He was here wi' me when you got home wi' Dad. He carried you up to bed.'

Martha Anne looked at the pile of clothing in the corner. She could smell it from this distance. So he'd seen it all. Seen her drunk, blacked out, and carried her in his arms, covered in piss and shit, up the stairs and into the bed…

Martha Anne was suddenly mortified. 'He didn't…he wasn't here when… when you… when I…' She looked to her nightgown and back to the soiled pile of clothing. She could not find the words to speak of the horror of her possible exposure to Malcolm in front of Alice.

Alice's frown smoothed with understanding. 'Oh, no, luv, no. He left before I got ye' changed and washed up. It were only me that saw your pretties.' She smiled, and Martha Anne sat back down.

124

'How's me dad?' Martha Anne asked, trying to distract Alice and gather her thoughts.

'Good. A wee bit of a throbbing head, but he's been sober and back to work the week now.'

'It's been a week? I've been laid up a week?' She couldn't fathom it. An entire week of her life that she was missing. Good lord, what had she done? 'What about Betty? She must be wonderin' what 'appened to me.' Now she did rise and went to the wardrobe and began pulling her work clothes off hangers. 'What time is it?'

Alice opened the watch pinned to the ribbon around her waist. 'It's on seven.'

Martha Anne stared at her, turned to the window, and looked back at her sister.

'In the mornin'. Seven in the mornin'. It's Friday.' Alice helped settle Martha Anne's world.

Slipping into her shift, she pulled on stockings and grabbed an old pair of leather boots she'd found in her brother James' closet. They fit her fine once she jammed a rag in the toes. 'If I leave now, hurry, I'll be to Betty's by eight and will be finishing my apologies and amends by nine. Back to it,' she said, distractedly looking for her hairbrush on her side table.

Alice stood, 'Martha Anne, I've somethin' to tell you, something important that can't wait,' she said. 'It won't take long.' She patted the seat by the fire Martha had earlier occupied. 'Here, luv, have your toast and finish your tea before it gets cold.'

Martha Anne stopped her busying and made her way to the fireplace. She frowned, seeing her sister in the soft light. Her face was serious, and there were lines across her brow.

'What is it? Is it Mum?'

Alice shook her head. 'No, no. She's fine. She's actually in good spirits, even been up and about a little bit. She's found a word game in the ladies' journal she gets and has been puzzlin' through 'em.' She was stalling. They were both stalling.

'What…then?' Martha Anne sat back and waited.

Alice took a deep breath. 'I'm not sure what to say first…'

'Well, just say it. I'm not sure what could be so hard. Y' 'aven't murdered anyone, 'ave ye?'

Alice smiled and shook her head, but a tiny tear pricked at the corner of her eye. 'No, not murder, yet.' She grinned. 'We'll see 'ow Mr Bruce behaves before I promise anythin'.'

At the mention of Mr Bruce, something tugged inside Martha Anne, and she sipped her tea to soothe it away.

'You see, luv, I'm leavin' today…We're leavin' today—me and Malcolm. We've got tickets to Scotland. We're goin' to be married in Edinburgh…'

Martha Anne wondered if Alice could hear the drumbeat pounding against her ribs, as it was thrumming in her ears, and she wondered if a skull could actually explode and then imagined her pink brains splattering the walls and then tried to pull her eyes away from the mess of her mind as it slid to spreading puddles along the floor until Alice called her name twice, bringing her back.

Finally, she managed to ask, 'You're goin' now? I thought it weren't till May? But why?'

Alice's worried expression smoothed, her smile widened, and her eyes filled again with tears. She let out a small laugh and knelt beside Martha Anne's chair, where she wrapped her arms around her sister and whispered, 'I'm pregnant.'

***

She'd run all the way to Betty's. She couldn't remember the journey, but she rushed through the door and dashed through the shop, the croft, and finally found Betty in her kitchen making a pot of tea.

Martha Anne had stopped at the threshold, hanging onto the doorframe, bending to catch her breath, when Betty said, 'Look wot the cat dragged in…'

'SHUT UP!' Martha Anne flung her head back. Hair loose and flying wild everywhere, she appeared like a banshee heralding in the dead. Her face was red and blotchy from the run, from the baby, from the blow. 'I can't hear your judgements today, Betty. I can't. I know I've fucked up. I know it in so many ways you can't know how badly, sadly, terribly I know it. It's more than a mess. It's the worst mess in the world.'

Betty brought the cups to the table and sat down next to the girl. She wrapped her in her arms and pulled her into a tight hug. Martha Anne's sobs were loud and long. Betty stroked her wet hair, shushed and rocked her until she was worn out and whimpering.

'Here now. Ye 'ave some tea. It'll make things right.'

Martha Anne sat up and gratefully held the warm cup in her cold hands. She sipped and could feel the shivering begin to subside. She was grateful for the comfort of both the tea and Betty's soft words.

'What's got ye so wound up, lass?'

'Alice…' she started and then felt the tears well, so she took a deep breath. 'Alice and Malcolm left for Scotland today…'

'Aye, yes, I heard.' Betty patted Martha Anne's arm. 'Well, they're off to a new life, then, eh? That's good. I know you'll miss your Alice, but maybe you can visit her in Scotland?' Betty consoled, although she knew good and well what the real bother was all about, but she'd just let Martha Anne get it out in her own way, in her own time. 'Somethin' to look forward to, lass.'

'She's preg…nant,' Martha Anne said, the word cracking in two in the break of her sob.'

'Ah, yes…' Betty sipped her tea. 'I did know. Your Alice came by to let me know you'd come 'ome, and she told me 'erself. Seemed quite 'appy, lass, and why not, why shouldn't she be thrilled? And you, you're 'er sister, you should be 'appy for 'er…'

Martha Anne could not stop the onslaught of tears, but their hot tracks down her face stung more than salve, and she wiped with a bit of ferocity. Taking a deep breath, she turned to Betty and said quite carefully. 'Well, I'm not 'appy for 'er, Betty. I'm not 'appy one bit.'

With certain resolve Betty met her eyes and asked quietly, 'And why is that, lass? If you can't tell me the truth, I can't hear the lie. Why is it ye canna be 'appy fer your own sister?'

The silence between them stretched, but Betty would not let go of Martha Anne's gaze, and as silent tears spilt, the young woman, who suddenly looked years and lifetimes old, said in a most hushed voice, 'Because I am pregnant with Malcolm's baby, too.'

Betty already knew. She had that way about her, just like her mum. She'd known from the minute she'd spied that rotten sod running out of her shop with his trousers loose. She had known. She'd prayed, she'd asked the cards, the tea leaves, and even read their charts, and each time, each bit of evidence, each blank page filled and turned over, and here they were. And, sadly, Betty knew what was coming next, and it broke her heart.

Martha Anne stood and moved away from Betty. She wiped her nose and eyes and made a half attempt to smooth down her hair and apron. Then, with the same fortitude, she straightened her spine, threw back her shoulders and said, 'I need you to help me get rid of it, Betty.'

She wouldn't. She couldn't. She said as much. She tried to explain. She was not her mother. She was not Nell who took care of these things for women. She'd never taken up the knife, wouldn't even know how because she'd refused to learn how. She told her mother when she was just a lass, after a bad go in the infirmary when something got botched. They'd taken the bother away, as her mother had called it, but something inside the woman got nicked, and there was blood everywhere, so much blood. Betty cringed at the recollection. And the woman barely made it home to her bed where she'd bled to death.

After that, Betty would have no part of it. It were an accident, her mother had pleaded, and the first and only in all her years of helping women in need. Betty was immovable on this. She told her mother to find another helper because she would flee as soon as she saw that look on a woman's face as she came hobbling down the lane.

At first, Nell was angry with her, but she had come to respect Betty's convictions after some time. And when Betty did agree to learn the concoction of herbs, roots, bark, and some magic that could do the same for a woman if she'd caught herself quick enough, they'd patched up their differences. Betty's potions had been perfected over the years and worked well for many, but there was one catch. They had to be taken early in the pregnancy, within weeks. Otherwise, they lost potency, and many women didn't pay close attention to their missed times. At least not enough to count the calendar days.

Betty's refusal to do the abortion or to send Martha Anne to a "real Wise Woman" or to make a potion that would rid her of this bother had enraged the young woman. She ran from Betty's kitchen to the shop where she found Betty's book of medicinal plants and potions. She found names of the herbs and roots that, when appropriately concocted, would do the job Betty refused. Martha Anne began going through powders and pastes, lifting pot lids, reading tags, running from one end of the shop to the other while Betty looked on from the doorway with her arms folded.

'You need to help me!' Martha Anne glared at her. 'I mean it, Betty! I want rid of it!'

'So you say now—'

'NO!' She threw a pot across the room, smashing it against the stone wall. 'NO!' This time, she threw a bottle containing special rose water at the glass panes of the greenhouse, cracking a spidery web through one.

Betty stepped inside, hearing the glass break. She made for Martha Anne, tried to get her to sit on the stool. 'Take some breaths, lass. Sip some water.' She handed the cup to Martha Anne, who promptly threw it across the room. She was out of control, out of her mind, red faced, huffing, her eyes wild, searching everywhere. She jumped from the stool and moved like a twitchy caged cat.

'Leave me BE, Betty!' She pushed past the older woman. 'Tell me where the potion is!' She began ransacking the very shelves she herself had organised neatly. She pulled off boxes, untied bags, dumped dusty ingredients, wasted seeds, and stomped through it all.

Betty'd had enough. She grabbed Martha Anne by the shoulders and spun her around. 'You'll be leavin' now,' she said and grabbed her wrist.

'Let go of me, you cunt!' Martha Anne twisted this way and that. 'You old witch, leave me be!'

Betty pulled her along a row of tall shelves heading towards the door.

'NO! Give me the potion first, and I'll go!'

'You'll go now, you will!' Betty shouted.

'I hate you!' Martha Anne screamed and bit Betty's hand. Then, with a strength born of rage, she wrenched her wrist free and pushed Betty aside, fleeing out the door and into the night.

Martha Anne did not see Betty hit the tall shelves. She did not see the clay pots come crashing down on Betty's head or the blood spurt from her cheek, sliced open by a broken shard. Martha Anne did not see Betty slide down the wall like a rag doll as the shelf collapsed across her legs, the weight of it pinning her, cracking her leg bone, crushing her ankle, snapping some ribs just before she passed out.

Chapter Eight

Of course, it was John who'd found her. It was John who'd torn off his coat and wrapped it around Betty, who lay shivering and very pale on the damp stone floor. He couldn't lift the shelves by himself. He couldn't imagine how they'd come down. Never in all his years visiting this cottage had they budged. Yet here they were crushing Betty's lower half. He brought a glass of water to Betty's parched lips, but she couldn't even take a sip. She just shivered. Her cheek was also bloodied from a deep gash.

Suddenly, her eyes rolled in her head. John knew he had to get help and knew he'd have to leave her to do it. He propped Betty up as best he could, then rolled up an empty seed sack and pillowed her head. After a too-long search, he found a blanket to cover her and began a quick trot down the lane. Then, just up ahead, he saw two figures coming towards him. It was early, just on dawn, and they seemed to be on a mission. He could tell by their determined strides. Each carrying empty sacks, limp for now, but would be full on their trek home. As he got closer, he was sure he recognised the woman and her daughter from the mill.

'Is that you, Mary Halkyard?' he called out.

''Tis, and me daughter Sophia,' she shouted. 'What is it, Mr Ashworth?' She was a bit breathless as she'd run the last bit to meet him. He too was winded but turned on his heel, gesturing for them to follow. 'Come, come, quick. It's Betty. There's been an accident.'

Together, the three were able to lift the shelves from Betty's legs. They slid her free and could see right away that the bones were smashed. Trying not to move her much, as she cried out with every small wrench, they got her to the near corner, on a soft bed of hay, and propped her leg up with a seed sack. John stood and turned to Sophia, who, he thought, would be about Martha Anne's age.

'Sophia? Can y' run, lass?' he asked.

She turned away from the horror of Betty's bloodied face, nodding her head vigorously at John.

'Good. Good. I need you to run to Doctor Michaels. Do you ye know 'im?'

Again, nodding.

'Now, if he's not there, go straight to Doc Munro's.'

Sophia frowned. 'The animal doctor? Up Healy Dell?'

He smiled. 'The very one. He'll know how to set a bone, and she needs that straight away.' He pulled coins from his pocket and made to give them to Sophia, who protested. 'Oh, no need, sir,' she said, pullling her hand away.

'No, please, Sophia, take them. I've a favour to ask.' He pressed the coins into her palm.

'Yes, sir?' The girl slipped them into a fold in the sleeve of her frock, looking at him expectantly.

'Do you know where I live?' he asked.

'You mean Moss Manor?'

'Yes, do you know where it is?'

'Yes, sir.'

'Do you know me daughter Martha Anne? You might've been in school w' her?'

Sophia's eyes widened at the mention of Martha Anne's name, and a wave of eager trepidation furrowed her brow. 'Um, I…I…do. We were in third year together. I dunno, after that, she stopped comin', I think. 'I 'aven't seen her since…'

'I'd like you to run to the manor and fetch 'er. Bring 'er 'ere. Tell 'er what 'appened and that she's needed. Can you do that?'

Sophia didn't answer but headed for the door.

***

It was just by chance, as she rounded the sloping corner, Sophia saw a figure on a dappled horse trotting out the lane from Rob Lily's farm. He was turning towards town. She was almost sure it was the veterinarian Dr Munro, and so she called out his name. At first, she didn't think he'd heard, but he pulled on the reins and spun his horse around. He shaded his eyes as the sun rose behind her.

131

'Doctor Munro!' She waved her hands above her head, and he trotted towards her. 'Oh, good! Tis you.' In one long gasp, she managed, 'There's been an accident! It's Betty Nuppy. Her legs are broken. Mr Ashworth is up there w' her 'n me mum. He sent me to find you or Dr Michaels. Well, Dr Michaels first, and then you if I couldn't find 'im. But 'ere y' are, and so y' should I go to 'im.'

He looked up the hill. 'Need a lift?'

He put out his hand to help her up, but she had an errand to run, she told him, and then asked, 'Should I bring Dr Michaels back w' me?'

The cocky young vet shook his head. 'Not yet. We won't bother 'im. If we do need 'im, we'll send for 'im later. Go on w' your errand. I'll head up.'

Sophia took off for the Moss Manor, her heart thumping from both the sprint and her nerves. She hadn't seen Martha Anne Ashworth in years. She didn't know the girl very well, but she'd had equal amounts of admiration and intimidation for her. Martha Anne had easily been the brightest student in Miss Royds's class. She could read and write whole paragraphs in cursive and knew all about animals and flowers, but what Sophia remembered most were Martha Anne's drawings. They were very realistic. She sketched houses and sheep and mountains and lakes, and these were wonderful, but it was the drawings of Miss Royds with buck teeth, witches' moles, and buggy eyes that Martha Anne would pass to her when the teacher wasn't looking, that made her giggle out loud. Sophia had been in awe of the brave-hearted, big-brained girl, funny girl, but not enough to be a friend, only enough to admire from afar.

It was all coming back to her now as she stood at the front gate of the big stone manor house. She remembered all those school days, when the girl with the giant bow set clumsily to the side, with beautiful thick ringlets of brown and gold hair draping her shoulders, and long dark lashes framing her eyes had sat next to her. Martha Anne was never cruel or mean. She'd lash a bully in a minute and was quite generous with a sweet, but Martha Anne had few friends and mostly kept her nose in a book. It wasn't that some hadn't tried to befriend her. It was just that she had little use for any of them—those her own age. None were as smart or interesting or relevant, Sophia supposed, as the adults in Martha Anne's world, who'd fawned over her intelligence and were bemused by her quick wit. Many had even remarked on her dark beauty back then, for one still a child.

Martha Anne had just quit coming to school and ran wild over the moors from what Sophia had heard. As she opened the iron gate, her heartbeat quickened, just a little bit. She made it to the front door and knocked.

There was no mistaking the young woman who yanked open the heavy door. It was Martha Anne, all right. Despite the mess of wild hair flying around her head and the hardness of her dark eyes as they searched Sophia up and down, Sophia thought Martha Anne Ashworth was the real beauty everyone suspected she'd become. Her features were strong and sharp, unlike the ruddy complexions of most Lankies, Martha Anne's skin was warm, sun-kissed, and her womanly shape was evident beneath her frock.

So when Sophia had finally worked up the courage, she managed in her most timid voice, 'Martha Anne?'

Martha Anne came outside, closing the door behind her, forcing Sophia to take a step back.

'Who wants to know?' Martha Anne crossed her arms and stuck out her chin. The crease of her brow made her appear angry, but she was only just curious.

'I'm Sophia Halkyard. We, you and me, we were in school together—'

'Don't remember much about school. Sorry. What y' want wi' me?'

Sophia backed down the steps to the gravel pathway and peered around the garden as if the answer might be hanging in the air somewhere. She looked up at Martha Anne, now taller by steps but farther away and less intimidating, somehow. 'I've come from your dad. He sent me. He's up at Betty Nuppy's. She's had a terrible accident…'

'An accident?' Martha Anne took steps forward, grabbing the rail. 'What sort of accident?'

Sophia shrugged. 'Dunno, really. Found her on the floor, one of the big shelves fell and crushed her legs. Your dad says I'm to fetch you back to Betty's.'

Martha Anne could feel it draining from the tip of her skull to the pads of her heels. The blood was rushing down, down, down through her body and into her boots. Her nose, mouth, lips, even her ears were burning, as if a wintery gust had whipped by, leaving icicles where fingertips and toes had been. She'd frozen in place, watching Sophia's mouth open and close. Like a fish, she was underwater and could hear nothing, only watching as bubbles flew from Sophia's lips, floating up into the sky. But that couldn't be right. That couldn't

133

be happening, except the ground was spinning, and the trees were swaying, and so she'd managed to carefully lower herself to the stone steps. She rested her head between her knees, afraid she was about to heave, when she felt the soothing touch of Sophia's cool fingers reaching out to her hot neck. She was saying kind things in a kind tone, and the sickness passed. Breathing in and out, steadier now, so when Sophia offered to help her indoors, she agreed but left her at the door, promising to follow as soon as she'd readied.

'Tell me dad I'm on me way,' she called after the young woman.

Martha Anne arrived at Betty's cottage to see a clump of villagers milling about. She went past them, into the shop, which looked like an army had marched through, destroying everything in the way. She hung her head, knowing she'd been the one-woman-battalion the night before. What stopped her immediately, though, was realising what kind of Herculean strength it must have taken her to topple the giant shelf lying on its side. Everything that had been stored on it was strewn across the shop in ruin. She had been mad. Out of her head. Wild. Unleashed. Good God, what had she done?

Betty was in the parlour, propped up on the day bed. They'd pulled it close to the fire, and someone had built a good hot one, as the room was nearly stifling. Both Dr Michaels and Munro was hovering over the old woman. Even though her eyes were closed, she was moaning with each breath.

Martha Anne had sidled in beside Sophia, who leaned close and whispered, 'They're setting her leg. It was badly broken. Poor thing. Nearly done.'

'Is she awake? Didn't they give her anythin'?'

'Did enough laudanum to bring down a cow, but both legs are shattered, and Dr Michaels said he thinks it'd been hours that they'd been sittin', so Dr Munro had to do a lot of wrenchin' to get the bones right. Good thing you weren't here. Betty's screamin' nearly woke the dead. Poor dear.'

Martha Anne's eyes swept the room, and she saw her father and Mrs Halkyard standing together in the corner. When she caught her father's eye, she noticed he did not smile or even nod. His eyes were dull and looked through her like she was rubbish to be tossed. She thought, *He knows.* Nobody else knows, but he knows.

Both doctors packed up their cases and walked outside with John, Martha Anne, Mary and Sophia Halkyard. The small crowd of neighbours, patrons, and friends of Betty had gathered around, waiting for the verdict. It was Dr Michaels who told them that Betty had had quite the blow. The shelving had crushed her ankle, broken her tibia, and they believed cracked a few ribs. He patted Dr Munro on the shoulder and gave much credit to the young veterinarian's bone setting prowess. Both doctors agreed and believed that Betty would once again be able to walk on her own with much care and good luck, but, in the meanwhile, she'd need a good deal of help. And upon this declaration, the men mounted their horses and trotted down the lane.

It was just a bit past dusk. John and Martha Anne had been sitting in silence at the foot of Betty's bed. John was cross with his daughter for the mess she'd created over the last few weeks. Betty had told him, days before, that she wouldn't have Martha Anne back after this latest bender she'd been on. Betty had been a godsend, so he couldn't blame his old friend for her anger and frustration. But now, now that she was laid up, it was only fitting that Martha Anne should make up for her delinquencies and disappointments. She'd work off all this bother by moving in and caring for Betty. It was a done deal in his mind.

In a low whisper, he spoke to his daughter. 'You'll stay the night here. I'll bring your things in the mornin',' he said with a dead calm that made Martha Anne flinch.

'What do y' mean?' she asked, now unsure if he did know what she'd done the night before.

John leaned forward and looked his daughter in the eye. 'You let her down. You disappeared on her for a week wi'out a word. If you'd been doin' your job instead of bein' out gettin' pissed and whatever else you were doin' this'—he gestured to the now deeply resting Betty—'this would never 'ave 'appened.'

He didn't know, she realised.

'It's your fault, it is, and so you'll be takin' care of Betty until she gets better.'

Just then, Betty awoke. Looking confused, she searched the corners of the room, passing over John, until she landed on Martha Anne. She met the young woman's wary eyes and held them for a long time.

Martha Anne thought it was as if Betty were deciding. She didn't dare to break the spell under which Betty held her. Instead, Martha Anne steadied her gaze, silently pleading with her. She reached deep down inside herself, all the way to the bean of her baby, and prayed Betty would have mercy.

Without breaking their hold, Betty asked, 'What's she doin' 'ere?'

John looked over to his daughter. 'She's come to take care of y', Betty. You've had a blow. An accident.'

Martha Anne could tell by the look in Betty's eyes that the decision was firming up in her mind.

In hopes of hurrying it along in her favour, Martha Anne said, 'I'm here to help—'

'GET OUT!' Betty belted out the two words as best as her broken ribs would allow, and she sunk back into her pillow as if she'd been punched.

Martha Anne jumped and looked at her father, unsure what to do.

Mary and Sophia entered the room with a tray of tea and were stalled at the doorway, unsure of what to do.

'Now,' Betty said breathlessly. 'Out.'

'What d'ye mean, Betty?' John asked. 'I know you're upset about her missin' work, but she's going to make it up while you're in need. All right, luv?' he asked, his voice softening.

Betty's eyes fluttered. In a near whisper with strangled breath, she managed, 'She didn't tell ye it were 'er, did she?'

'Tell me what, Betty?'

'She didn't tell you it were 'er who ransacked me shop, did she?'

John looked to his daughter. The look on her face told him she was about to bolt.

'She didn't tell ye why she trashed me whole life, did she?'

'Betty, maybe now is not the time…' John began but saw that familiar determined look on Betty's face as she continued to lock eyes and horns with his daughter.

'She didn't tell ye she's with child, did she?'

John's head whipped from Betty to Martha Anne, who met his eyes and appeared somewhere between fear and defiance. He opened his mouth to speak, but he dropped his eyes as he could not look at her. Who had done this? She was but a lass. Not just turned fourteen. Who was it? He'd kill him, John decided, but Betty interrupted his murderous thoughts.

'Tell 'im why y' did it, girl,' Betty said.

'Martha Anne?' John managed, although it came out more query than question.

Martha Anne did not answer but looked to her hands clasped at her waist.

Betty was able to pull herself up, 'It were because I wouldn't 'elp her get rid of it and she went mad.' Then, leaning forward, in small gasps aimed at Martha Anne, she hissed, 'It were 'er what pulled that shelf over, leavin' me for dead.'

John deflated against the chair like a burst balloon.

But…Martha Anne did not know the shelf had come down. She did not know Betty had been in the line of destruction. She had not, could not, have known that Betty had nearly been killed, certainly crushed by the massive shelving as it landed on her. Of course, Martha Anne had been out the gate and down the lane by the time it had toppled, but that didn't seem to matter in the here and now.

'No, Betty, no, I didn't know—' Martha Anne began, but Betty cut her off.

'Get out. I never want to see y' again.'

Just one small look passed between the disappointed father and his shamed daughter as the double-sided dagger pierced each of their hearts.

As Martha Anne fled the room, John's face crumpled into his hands.

Despite her pain, Betty reached over and pulled him to her, letting him sob against her as she stroked his damp hair, whispering, 'Shh, shh, there, there…'

***

They were angry strangers living in the same house. After Martha Anne wouldn't give up the name of the father, except to say, "It might've been one of the lads down Toad Lane", landing like a slap across John's face, he hadn't spoken to his daughter but once since.

He hadn't slept since that dreadful night with Betty. In the end, she'd banished both him and Martha Anne, telling them they were no longer welcome. He'd arranged for Sophia Halkyard to move into the cottage to care for Betty, doubling the wages that she'd earned at the mill. While it made up for nothing, it eased John's mind.

But now, taking care of two invalid women was costly, both financially and emotionally. He felt he'd aged years in these past few days. His hair had whitened at the temples, as had his moustache at the tips. He saw lines, like tram-tracks across his forehead, a fan at the corners of his eyes, and were he to shave off his moustache, he'd reveal taught stitching around his mouth. He was as unsure of the future as he'd ever been in his entire life. Even as a lad, when his tummy rumbled for lack of food with none in sight, had he never been so scared.

What options did he have with Martha Anne? For her baby? His firstborn grandchild. He was tempted to save a few shillings and put the care of his wife into her daughter's hands, but he did not think that would be healthy for any of them. Send both Martha Anne and her baby to the workhouse? That would never happen, not by him, at least. Put the babe in fostering or give it to the Rochdale Children's Home? Send it to Alice and Malcolm in Scotland and beg them to adopt it? He had all the questions and none of the answers. He imagined that given his daughter's temperament, he may or may not have any say in the matter at all.

It'd taken him a week to compose himself enough to come to some decisions about all their futures. Then, finally, he'd called Martha Anne into his study, gestured for her to sit, and poured them each a cup of tea.

Her face was a bit swollen, red, and blotchy. He'd heard her crying in her room well into the night. Beneath her dark eyes and lashes were dark circles, evidence of her sleeplessness. He imagined if the two of them stood side by side at the parlour mirror, each would appear the same kind of tired, bedraggled, and wrung out.

Before he began this conversation with his daughter, he recalled the one he'd had with Mary Halkyard as they departed Betty's cottage that morning. While he'd dozed throughout the night at the foot of Betty's bed, Mary and Sophia had stoked the fires, swept the floors, and cooked a giant pot of stew from the leg of lamb brought earlier by Farmer Lily.

Then, after they'd made a soft pallet in the corner by the fire, Mary told Sophia to have a lie-down, 'You'll need yer rest, luv. T'morrow will be 'ere soon enough.'

The following morning, John and Mary had just gone through the gate when a dozen of Betty's neighbours carrying buckets, mops, scrub brushes, brooms, and a variety of tools ascended upon the cottage. John stepped to the side and held the gate until the last Good Samaritan had made it inside. He jogged a bit to catch up with Mary as he wanted to thank her for her time and give her a bit of silver. And to, hopefully, he prayed, illicit a certain discretion when it came to speaking of the events of the evening, witnessed by the Halkyard women. John cleared his throat to speak and again before he actually could.

'Mary, I dunno what would've 'appened if you an' Sophia 'adn't come along,' he began. 'I wanted to thank you and make it right.'

He stopped her stride, took her hand, and pressed silver into her palm. Unlike her more polite and humble daughter, without hesitation, guilt, or shame, she closed her fingers tightly over the coins and dropped them into the pocket of her sleeve.

Stuttering at first, he was trying to find the words to ask that she keep the sordid details she'd witnessed from the public view.

He was pleading. He could hear it in his own shaking voice. 'Mary, please. I'm just askin' for some privacy here. I'll make your silence worth it.'

She felt for him, surely. Were the whole bother to get out, there'd be ruination. She could see it all plain as day.

His voice became hopeful. 'I'll make it worth Sophia's time. I'll pay her double what she gets at the mill.' He could see Mary Halkyard mulling her options.

'Well, that'd take care of our Sophia's silence, I would think…' She let the sentence end and looked away across the moors.

John wasn't stupid. He saw the trade. He could hardly blame her. What woman wouldn't use the opportunity for a bit of power if it fell right into her lap as this had? She'd be a fool not to negotiate. He had to admire her just a bit and decided to be straight up with her.

'And you, Mrs Halkyard? What would the same silence on this matter be worth to you?'

'I'll take the same rise in pay at the mill. Double what I'm earnin' now.'

John nodded and said, 'Right then. It's done.'

They'd come to the crossroads where they would part ways. With the business transaction behind them, no hard feelings, John tipped his cap and made to cross the cobbles when Mary stopped him.

'John, wait.' She pulled him to the side, off the path, away from the few passing villagers.

He leaned close, waiting to hear what he thought might be another condition of their arrangement, but instead, the woman put her hand on his arm and said in a very kind voice.

'A word if I might,' she asked but did not wait for permission. 'What's done is done. There's no changin' it. There's no goin' back. There's only movin' ahead. You can't undo any of it. Martha Anne can't undo any of it. And believe me, John, that's her worst punishment, for her whole life.'

***

There's no changin' it. There's no goin' back. There's only movin' ahead, John repeated to himself before clearing his throat and addressing his daughter.

'I've got me own ideas about the future,' he said, taking a sip of tea. 'But I thought I'd hear what plans you've been makin' for yourself before I'll be sayin' me own.'

Martha Anne was both surprised and confused. She'd been bracing for the punishment, the ultimatum, the dressing down, the lecture doused with disappointment at well-made points, and yet, here they were as they'd always been, since she was little lass, face to face, across this desk, in this room, sharing tea and stories, she and her dad, as always, as usual—as never before.

What plans had she been makin,' her father had asked. 'Plans?' she considered. She'd not been making any plans. She'd no idea what was to become of her or the babe. She was terrified. She'd no husband, no job, and no home to call her own. If her father were to boot her to the workhouse, he'd have every right to do it. Were those his plans? Dear God. She hadn't given even a thought to the next day, never mind the next…What? Month? Year? Decades…"down the road, across the bridge, all the way to Devon"…Where did that come from? She could not stop the rhyme in her head. She wanted to complete it, but she'd never been to Devon and didn't know a thing about it.

She was going mad. She'd decided earlier as she lay on her back in bed, resting her hands on her raised belly, feeling the flurry of feet or fists, elbows or knees. She didn't know and thought it too early to feel a babe in there, but she was restless, and so was he…she knew it'd be he, and she could see him. He had Malcolm's brown eyes, dark hair, and curls. Ever since the horrible night at Betty's, while laying here with only him, she'd found a spot in her heart for him and the idea of them. She and her babe, her son. She would be a real mum to him. Not like her own worthless mum. He would be her constant as the rest of the world abandoned her. She was glad she didn't get rid of him, glad that Betty had refused her. She was especially pleased that, as far as she knew, Betty had not told anyone who the father was, and Martha Anne knew Betty wouldn't. It would be their secret to the grave.

'Well?' John looked over his teacup at her. 'Cat got your tongue?'

She shook her head. 'I dunno. I 'adn't really thought of a plan. I 'adn't really thought of anythin' these days.'

'Do you think you might start thinkin' of a plan?'

'I could care for Mum, would that 'elp? You could let Millie go, and I could take over…' Her voice trailed at the end, knowing as well as her father that this plan would never work. And she had to admit that finding and keeping Millie had been a godsend after Alice left. Her mother was a handful, and Martha Anne knew that the idea was a bad one, even as the words were coming out of her mouth.

'That won't do. Millie's an angel sent from heaven.'

'Do you think they'd hire me on at the sweet shop where our Alice used to work?'

Without meaning to, John's eyes swept over his daughter's middle and then down into his tea as if shining his shame into the cup.

He said, carefully, 'I don't think they will, lass.'

'Why not?'

He wondered if she really could not connect her condition to that work situation, so he didn't answer but waited for her to come to it.

She pointed to her stomach. 'What? You mean because of this? They won't 'ire me because I'm pregnant?'

'I would be surprised. I'm not saying you shouldn't try, but you asked what I thought. That's what I think.'

She flopped back against the chair and threw her hands up. 'I'm not sure why it should matter…Who are they to judge, anyway? Lousy buggers…' A dark cloud had crossed her brow as she pursed her lips to a small tight bud.

John kept quiet, knowing the brewing storm that was happening within her. She was looking for a fight, looking to take a swing at anything or anyone within reach. He knew the look, he could hear the tone, and he felt her anger rising as it tapped out on the floor beneath her jiggling knees. He knew the way his daughter's frustrated emotions would take over, and the hysteria would begin. She'd rail against everything, she'd scream, she'd cry, kick a door, punch a wall, throw a glass across the room. She'd wear herself out. She'd blame a nearby lamp or chair, hoping her shame would shed off her and stick to it. He'd seen the tantrums before. From toddler to child to a woman bearing a child, she'd acted out the same, and he saw it coming now. He wouldn't have it. Enough was enough. She'd been old enough to get herself into this situation—she'd better damn well start acting like an adult to get herself out of it.

'Stop!' He slammed his fist on the desk, making his teacup and his daughter jump, rattling them both.

Martha Anne sat up, startled. Her father rarely raised his voice never mind, slam a fist. She began to shake and then burst into a tsunami of heaving choking sobs. The teacup left her fingers and crashed to the floor. She grabbed hanks of hair, wrapping them around her fists, pulling her head to her lap, folding nearly in half, and she began rocking.

John's heart cracked, he was sure. He'd heard a tiny piece shattering as he watched his beloved, his favourite, his most gifted child, devolve into a puddle of sadness. He wanted to be strong and stern, he wanted her to manage her own pain, but he could not. So he arose, and as he rounded the desk, he sank to his knees, like a younger man might have done with ease, and wrapped his arms around his daughter, rocking along with her.

Tears, drool, and snot soaked her father's shirt. As soon as he'd embraced her, she relinquished the twin twines of hair tightly fisted and grabbed onto him as if she were drowning and he a floating branch. She did not let go until she was utterly wrung out. When she finally pulled away, she saw that hers were not the only tears that had drenched her father's shirt, but his own had washed his neck and collar. *This,* she thought, *may have been the saddest thing she'd ever done to him.* If for only this moment, she was so very, very, sorry about it all.

But she didn't say this, couldn't say it, because when all the bother is mostly not your doin', when it's mostly not your fault, there's little to be sorry about, she reckoned. So she took a deep breath and pushed out her chin, lifted her chest, and dug in her heels. In her mind, she ticked up the wrongs against her, from her mum being primarily out of her mind, Lizbeth's full-on hatred, Jamie's leaving, Miss Royd's bashing, Malcolm's betrayal, and Betty's abandonment…It all adds up.

At that moment, watching her poor dad slowly rise from his knees, tears streaking his lined face, making him appear much older than his years, she saw that all this bother needed to stop before it made him ill, or leave, or boot her, or worse, kill him. She saw him carefully lower into the chair, wiping his face with a soft handkerchief. He blew his nose and tucked the cloth back into his pocket, then poured tea into his cup and more into the saucer. Then, as he'd done through her childhood, he passed it over and set it before her. She smiled and raised it to her lips, blowing across the small sea of tea, and took a sip. It calmed her nearly immediately, as it had him. She could see his brow smooth and his eyes soften.

She knew then that he didn't just want her or expect her to make a plan, but he needed her to make one. He needed her to decide this for herself. He loved her too much to decide it for her. He was the only one who had not abandoned her, betrayed her, left her, not even when he could've, should've, maybe even someday might. For now, he needed her to be strong, make a decision, and have a plan.

'Do you think they'd 'ave me at the mill, Dad?'

The relief that washed over him was the surest sign she'd said the right thing. He was surprised, she could tell, but he didn't seem to want to jinx it, so he remained thoughtfully reserved in his response but did not attempt to talk her out of it.

'I'm sure we can find a place for you.'

Chapter Nine

1891

The babe had come like a lamb in the night. Gently, quiet, and without much fuss, the midwife had said, as she'd only just arrived as he crowned. She'd peeked under the sheets, reached inside Martha Anne, slipping a finger beneath his soft chin, easing just a little, and he'd slid effortlessly into her waiting lap.

The midwife was awakened when Millie Swanson had come banging on her door, saying Martha Anne Ashworth was about to have a baby. They'd run down the lane and went in through the back garden, where John Ashworth was standing outside holding the door open, allowing both women through the entry. He pointed to the stairs.

'She's in her room, Millie,' he shouted.

As he was locking up, his wife called out, asking about the commotion. In response, along with reassuring words and loving caresses, he tipped drops of laudanum from the tiny bottle, not once but twice, into her tea. It was not a night to have Ellen wandering the house or even her own tragic mind.

There was little to do, decided the midwife, except check the baby boy's parts (he had them). His lungs were clear, and while his wailing was robust and healthy, she considered, he appeared less demanding than most babies. Instead, he seemed more accepting of the assault on his wee wet body. His cries simmered down as soon as he was placed in his mother's arms. The bond between Martha Anne and the babe was immediate, the midwife could see. Unlike most mothers and babies who appear shy with one another, getting to know one another, this first meeting was not so with Martha Anne and her babe. Instead, the midwife saw a different sort of bond—an old one, an ancient one.

The Midwife professed, ''Tis a bond bound long before either mother or child were here on earth…' and as she was leaving, she put her hand on John's arm and said, 'God help the wee lass who marries that wee lad. She'll never get between them two…'

They watched as the babe reached out and tugged his mother's loose strands, pulling her face closer to his own, and John thought the midwife right. Perhaps this babe would bring a settling down to his daughter, to his household, maybe even to him.

***

She'd placed the babe in her father's arms and stepped back to see his struggle to stay neutral. When he finally looked up, she saw that in addition to his smile, which was soft, his eyes were glistening.

'What'd Mum say?' he asked hopefully, knowing his daughter had brought the babe to meet his granny while John was away at work.

'It went well. He was very quiet and still, as if he knew to be, and she even held him.'

'Did she?' This surprised John, as Ellen rarely engaged in the lives or interests of others.

'She did, and she asked that I bring him around to visit.'

'What's he called, then?' John asked.

She'd named him Francis James Ashworth.

'Francis?' he'd asked. 'What sort of name is that for a lad?'

'For the explorer, Sir Francis Drake.' She'd been reading about him.

Her father looked to the placid baby resting in his arms. He didn't see him as much of an explorer.

She continued her defence. 'He was a favourite of Queen Elizabeth, sailed all the way around the earth, and staved off the Spanish Armada.'

'He was a pirate and a slave-trader,' her father said.

'It was long ago. If he was good enough for 'er majesty to knight 'im, then that's reason enough to honour his name.'

'It's a lot to live up to, don't you think? For such a little one.'

'It'll give him a measure,' Martha Anne said, undeterred.

Her father smiled and then noted, 'He's a bit more of a Sir Francis Bacon if you ask me,' John said.

'Who's that?'

145

'Well, he was also a favourite of Queen Elizabeth, around the same time as Drake. He was a scientist, a philosopher, a lover of books and an advocate for libraries.'

Martha Anne tipped her chin and leaned over her babe. He had hold of her dad's finger and was drawing it to his mouth, sucking it, pulling away, screwing up his face, and doing it all over again.

'See, right there,' her dad said, '"Baconian Empiricism" at work.'

'What's that?'

'Bacon believed that knowledge comes from experience. Through the senses, like taste. Right here, the boy is proving me right, as we speak!'

'Fine, think what you will, but I'm naming him for Sir Francis Drake, the "Brave Sea-Faring Adventurer".'

'He's goin' to get beat up with a name like Francis,' her father became serious. 'It's also a name for a girl.'

'It's also a name for a boy.'

'Call him James, for your brother, then.'

'No, James is James.' She held out her arms, and the baby had begun to mew. 'Give him back. You're workin' him up.'

'I'm not workin' 'im up. He just doesn't want to be called Francis, is all. That's what's workin' 'im up.'

'Oh, for goodness' sake, he 'asn't a notion what you're goin' on about.' She twirled a tiny baby curl around her finger and let it bounce just above his eyes.

'Then call him Frank,' John said.

'Frank?'

'He'll be both Drake and Bacon if you call him Frank.'

'I don't know how you figured all that out,' she said and grinned at her father.

'It's a proper nickname for Francis and not a bad quality in a man. To be frank,' he said. And now he grinned.

She could see the delight her son had sparked in her father's eyes, and this joy, rare in her dad, had pushed her over. 'Would that make you 'appy? If we called 'im Frank?'

'It would.'

***

It was the night before Martha Anne was to go to the mill for her first shift since having the baby. She'd washed up Frank and wrapped him in a clean nappy and a soft white gown. She gently pulled a cap over his crown, and after she'd fed him, she walked him about the room, humming a little tune, until he fell asleep. Rather than put him in the wooden box made up as a cradle, she held him closer. She took a long-drawn breath at his neck to smell him and then tasted his skin as she kissed him, then smoothing her cheek against his little one until he'd grown heavy in her arms. Only then did she set him down. Millie had agreed to look after him for a few extra shillings a week, in addition to taking care of Mum. The plan was that Martha Anne would return at tea to feed him, and with any luck, he'd be a cooperative baby and sleep most of the afternoon so that Millie could get the work of the house done and a meal ready. Tomorrow would be the first time Martha Anne would leave Frank with anyone, and even though she trusted Millie, she was heartbroken about it.

Before she went to her bed, she sat in front of the small vanity and mirror in the corner of her room. She'd brought a candle and set it down in front of her. Its flame seemed to set the room on fire, lighting up the three-sided mirror.

She'd been made a Doffer at the spinning mill. It was the lowliest of jobs. She'd be working with boys and girls younger than herself, but she was small, compact, and seeing it was the only work offered, she took it. Her job was to run up and down the rows changing out the spools on the mule before they emptied or knotted, all without the machines shutting down. She knew it could be dangerous. There were stories of lads catching a sleeve or shirttail and losing a hand or even an arm. There were also stories of lasses getting their hair caught and scalped, losing an eye, fingers, or worse.

She opened the side drawer to find her brush and took long strokes through her thick chestnut hair. It passed her shoulders and came to a stop somewhere around the middle of her back. She was counting, remembering when Alice would patiently brush her hair, carefully untangling the tangles, snipping the ends when they deadened, and always counting to one hundred, each night. Martha Anne had lost count now, as she worked the brush around her head until she pulled the entire hank of hair at her neck over her shoulder and held it in her fist. Then, reaching back into the drawer, she withdrew a long kitchen knife. She held it still in her lap. Her hair, she knew, had been her crowning glory. The strands of gold, copper, and bronze were the envy of all the girls at school. She had heard the whispers. Everyone said it. Everyone loved her hair, touched it, and petted it like a kitten. She recalled how Malcolm would reach up and into its folds, press his mouth against it, breathing in, closing his eyes, and he would kiss her through the veil of it across her mouth, and she, too, closed her eyes to remember, and remember once more.

She now looked into the mirror, into her own eyes, dark black spots in her angry face staring back at her, daring her to…what? Smile? Laugh? Cry? Not if she could help it. This mess of hair would do her no good in the mill. With that, she began to saw through the thick rope of it, allowing long strings and short tufts to fall from her fist like straw loosed by a scythe until there was no more in her palm but a few stragglers. She nearly ripped them away but instead drew the knife across them, too, as if playing the violin.

***

The days had turned to weeks, and the job at the mill, while all the dangerous things that were said of it, was turning out not to be as horrible as she'd imagined, it was difficult at first. You could not hear yourself think or speak, never mind hear anyone else. And the air inside was so thick with cotton lint floating like snowflakes all around that you could barely see two feet in front of you, never mind across the looms. Nevertheless, keeping your eyes on the spools was the best way to stay on top of the job, and at present, all she wanted to do was finish her shifts and get home to Frank.

Most workers had the distinct sound of cotton cough, but this condition could only be heard outside the mills as workers made their way to and from the mills. It was also impossible to speak to one another or be heard even if you yelled, as the machines echoed a hum so loud that it not only deafened the ears but buzzed through blood and bones, leaving the entire body shaky by the end of the day, making the walk home a most welcome quieting time for her, when air and ears were equally clear, even in the rain. She'd quickly learned the routine of her job, the hierarchy of positions, the women who could help or harm you, and the men who couldn't keep their eyes or hands off your bosoms or bottoms.

She'd quickly learned the unique *Me-Maw* language of the Moss Mill. It was most important to be able to understand this form of communication in any mill job. Throughout the north, each mill had its own unofficial but distinct language that was made up of signs, hand signals, miming and *Me-Mawing,* or lip-reading, to communicate across the vast spinning rooms with their thick air and loud machines. She was a quick study and could make out what others were acting out, even if she didn't quite know how to do it herself. The mill hadn't been as awful as she'd feared, and even though she was exhausted when she'd arrive home, it was the kind of tired that made her feel grateful for the food, the babe, and the bed all waiting for her after a long but satisfying day of work.

She'd even made a couple of friends, as these mill girls were a happy lot, friendly and curious. There were a couple of winders she'd come to enjoy. Val and Mags, who at first, treated the boss's daughter with a bit of sceptical wariness until they pushed her into a cotton cart, arse over tea kettle, and sent it flying across the spinning room. It landed with a loud bang up against the foreman's office door. When he jerked it open, red-faced and looking for a fight, Martha Anne righted herself and poked her head up through the pillowy fibres, her short hair covered in white cotton balls.

She looked at the boss, pulled down her bottom lip to show a gap, and asked, yelling loudly, ''Ave ye' seen me tooth, guvnor?'

And the whole place broke out in guffaws, including the boss, and from then on, she'd been treated like the rest of them. They were an *all reet lot*, she'd told her dad.

***

It was an awful dark and rainy morning when the knocker-upper came by. She'd fed Frank and had taken him to the kitchen where her dad had started the fire in the stove, and then she poured herself a cup from the kettle.

'Where's Millie?' she asked.

'Dunno. She's usually here by now,' John said, looking out the window. 'Maybe the rain's held her up.'

'It's not like her to be this late, is it?'

John shook his head and slipped into his raincoat. 'It's not. Maybe I'll pop around on me way, see if she's in need.' His face turned to the dark sky to see black clouds had hunkered low and appeared to be settling in for the day. He looked at the baby playing with his own toes as he lay in the basket on the chair. 'I'll go on ahead. You wait here for Millie. I'll let them know on the floor that you'll be late.'

'Thanks, Dad. I'll be quick as soon as Millie arrives.'

'Look in on your mum then, would you? She might like a cuppa.'

The sky only lightened from pitch dark to dark grey as the sun struggled to push into the thick morning gloaming. Martha Anne brought her mother both a cup of tea and the baby Frank, who seemed to adore his granny, somehow finding sweet contentment in her arms—and she in his, Martha Anne suspected. Ellen was in good humour and more alert than usual. Martha Anne was happy to see this and often hoped that the baby was bringing her mother just a wee bit back to life in his own small way.

As she jiggled her bracelet for the baby, she asked Martha Anne about his teething and was impressed by his early sleeping through the night.

'You don't 'ave to worry, you know,' Ellen said, pinching a tuft of Martha Anne's short hair. 'It looks like a mop now, but it'll grow back.'

Martha Anne tried to be mad, but as she gripped her forelock in her hands, she instead laughed and said, 'In the meanwhile, I'd like to be called Matthew, if you don't mind.' She grinned.

'Oh, it's not that bad.'

'I look like a boy.'

'Not with that bosom and those hips, and this baby, you don't!' Ellen smiled.

Martha Anne could almost pretend that her mother was normal, finally getting better. Maybe even that her mother was being motherly in ways she'd always meant to be but couldn't because of the laudanum. The dosage was something Martha Anne had convinced her dad to cut back on, which he must have because each day, her mum sounded less exhausted and more engaged and more interested in the world than ever—in Martha Anne's recollections of her mother, at least. The babe had quieted in the crook of Ellen's arm and was making a funny little snore as he began to doze off. The women smiled at him and then at each other.

'He's a joy,' Ellen said. 'He reminds me of Jamie when he was a babe. So calm and pleasant. Rarely did he fuss and always ready with a giggle.' She kissed the top of his head.

'He is a joy, all reet,' Martha Anne agreed distractedly as she watched the hands of the clock round out another few minutes.

'Did you read the letter from our Alice?'

Martha Anne felt the heat rise to her face. 'Letter?'

'Dad didn't give it to you?'

'No, he never mentioned it. When did it come?'

'Just a few days ago, I think.' Her mother seemed to become a bit flustered. 'He probably just forgot. I'm sure he'll show it to you. He'll want you to read the news.'

'And what news is that?' Martha Anne braced herself, but she wasn't sure if it was in anticipation of good news, like Malcolm leaving Alice and coming to bring her and Frank to Scotland instead, or bad news like—

'Alice had the baby!' her mother blurted out. 'He came a bit early, but he's fine!' Her mother smiled, looking from her to Frank and back again. 'Oh, I should've let you read the letter, but I'm just too chuffed about it!'

Martha Anne felt the thrum of her heart pounding within the hollow of her ribcage, muffling the words her mother spoke next. Something about his lovely curls, and Alice's strong constitution, and naming him for Malcolm, but calling him Robbie, and Malcolm being over the moon…

*Malcolm over the moon…Malcolm over…over…over…*Malcolm—over.

She leapt up from her mother's bedside and rushed to the window, peeling back the curtain, seeing her streaming tears reflecting on the glass pane, racing raindrops.

'Are you all right, luv?' Ellen called from the bed, forcing Martha Anne to wipe her face with the cuffs of her jumper and take a large breath before turning around with a smile on her face.

'I'm fine, Mum. Happy for our Alice, I truly am. She'll be a good mum,' she managed.

'Yes, she will. And now I've two grandsons to spoil, don't I?' She had more asked the baby than Martha Anne.

Then, in a voice so laced with concern, so out of character, Ellen asked in a way that made Martha Anne almost believe her mother was interested in her, 'Is anythin' botherin' you, lass? You can talk to me, you know. I am your mum.'

She smiled and shook her head. 'Thanks. I know, Mum. I'm good— everythin's good. No, I'm only worryin' about Millie. She should've been here ages ago, and there's no sign of 'er.'

'Oh, I'm sure she'll be along any time now. It's a lasher of a storm goin' on out there. I bet she's just havin' another cuppa, waitin' for a break in the clouds.'

Martha Anne looked to the grandfather clock in the hall to see that she was already twenty minutes late, and no matter that her dad was her boss or maybe even because he was the boss, coming in late to work is not a good look on the new girl, never mind the boss's daughter.

Ellen, sensing her daughter's quandary, offered, 'Go on, then. Go to work. Leave Frank here wi' me,' she cooed at her sleeping grandson.

Martha Anne looked at the pair, cuddled like a couple of bugs in a rug. If she didn't have to go to work herself, she'd like to huddle in there with them. 'I can't, Mum. You can't care for 'im by yourself.'

'It'll just be till Millie gets 'ere, any minute now.'

The rain was not letting up. She'd be drenched by the time she got to the mill. It would take longer to get there in this weather. Never mind trying to avoid the puddles and whipping rain, the cobbles would be slick, and the mud would be thick. She'd have to go slow whether she wanted to or not.

'I don't know, Mum. You're not well.'

'I feel well enough to lay here cuddlin' me own grandson for a little bit while the storm rails out the windows. Stir up the fire, luv, and leave us be. We'll be fine.'

'But what if Millie doesn't come?'

Her mother seemed to consider this for just a moment and then reassured. 'Look, even if that 'appened, even if she doesn't come, for whatever reason, you'll be soon back for your tea in a few hours. We can surely manage till then, eh?'

Martha Anne was torn, looking from the miserable weather with no sign of relief or Millie coming from any direction. Over her shoulder, she saw her mum all cozied up with her babe. What harm could come? It would be for just a little bit. She'd be back in no time, and when she did, she was sure she'd find Millie holding down the fort and apologising for whatever it was that held her up.

When she got to the mill, she'd not been able to find her dad to see if he'd found Millie, so she'd wrung out her stockings, changed into dry ones that she'd thought to bring along with her, rubbed down her hair, and got to her workstation as fast as she could. She was a solid hour late, and while no one said a word, it was clear that her tardiness was not approved by any of them. After all, they'd all made it through the wind and the rain. They'd all left babes, husbands, and breakfasts to work themselves out. They'd punched the clock on time that morning, as they'd done every morning. No matter the rain, sleet, snow or even the occasional sunshine would cause them to stroll in an hour late like they were the Queen herself.

A mark against her, Martha Anne knew. The next mark would be checked off when she left to go home to feed Frank. They'd expect her to stay, to skip her meal, and make up the time she'd missed. But she wouldn't and didn't. She didn't explain herself to any of them. None of anyone's business, anyway. Before leaving the yard, she crossed the quadrangle to her dad's office to see how he made out with Millie. She knocked and popped her head inside.

He was at his desk and speaking to a young man who was seated before him. Hat in hand, she noticed, and he rose as she entered. He was dressed in a suit, with a proper vest and tie.

'Sorry to interrupt,' she said, nodding at each of them.

John waved her in, 'You're fine. Come in, luv. I'd like you to meet Mr Chadwick.' He gestured to the young man, whose smile grew wide beneath his formidable moustache. His blue eyes twinkled, and his whole face joined in on his grin as it creased across his cheekbones.

He took a slight bow. 'Samuel, please, miss,' he said, his voice quite deep, making him seem taller somehow, she thought, oddly.

'And this is my daughter, Martha Anne.'

She nodded. 'Nice to meet you,' she said somewhat dismissively and turned back to her father. 'Dad, I can't stay. I'm off to see to Frank and Mum. Did you find Millie?'

He frowned. 'Frank and Mum? What d'ye mean by Frank and Mum?'

She looked nervously from her father to the young man, now seemingly trapped in the middle of a family situation.

'Maybe we can talk about this later,' she said and glanced at the man, who was doing his best to pretend to be scrutinising a small etching on the wall. 'Dad, I've got to get 'ome and back. I'm in enough bother w' everybody on the floor as it is for bein' late. I can't afford anymore. Did you find Millie?'

John felt a need to carry on his interrogation, but he saw Mr Chadwick in the corner, appearing trapped as he was now examining his fingernails, having nowhere else to look.

He finally took a breath and answered his daughter. 'No. Millie weren't there. At least, she didn't answer the door. Windows were black.' he said, now beginning his own worry.

'All right then. I'll be off,' she said and pulled up the hood of her Mac and was about to open the door when the man in the corner turned around and addressed them both.

'I don't mean to intrude, but I've hired a horse and carriage for the day.' He looked out the window and pointed. 'It's out there, under the eaves.'

Sure enough, there was a horse and covered carriage cosily nestled under an awning, keeping both dry. They turned back to look at him.

'I could give you a lift, Miss Ashworth, if it would be helpful?' he offered. 'You could keep dry if nothing else.'

She looked to her father, who nodded. Now a certain relief crossed his brow as his worry about Ellen and Millie were taking over.

'Yes. Thanks. Let's go, then,' she said without taking time for politeness, and she turned and left through the door with Mr Chadwick quick to catch up from behind.

They'd made no small talk on the way. The rain pounded the roof of the carriage, and it was impossible to hear or talk. When they pulled up to the manor house, Martha Anne leapt from the stage and right into a puddle, but she didn't care. She turned to close the door when Samuel touched her hand and stopped her. Startled, she looked up into his blue eyes, sharp and keen. She found fortitude in them. She found this somehow calming in this near panicking moment.

'I'll wait,' he said.

'No, you don't 'ave to. I'll be fine. I'm sure Millie's wi' me mum,' she said and stepped to the stone. 'Thanks, though.'

She pushed open the big door, and when she turned to close it, she saw that the carriage was still there. Samuel leaned forward and waved to her. She gave a slight lift of her hand and closed the door. What on earth was he doing? she wondered. And who was he, anyway? But this thought left her as she felt the cold of the dark house.

And then all thought left as the stillness of the house enveloped her like a tight grip from behind. She removed her jacket and shoes, dropping the first on top of the second onto the floor. There was no warmth from the hearths in the front parlour or Dad's study, no smell of savoury stew that should have been simmering on the stove. There was no light from a lamp or candle burning.

She called out, 'Millie?' and hurried down the corridor past dark rooms. The damp had seeped in through the thick blocks of stone that were the manor's walls and had already winnowed through her jumper, under her skin, and into her bones.

'Mum?' She now ran to the silence that was the last room at the back of the house and near skidded to a stop at its threshold. Turning, she looked to the fireplace, embers only, but the room was still warm, thankfully. The candle had doused its quick, and the same grey cloud shrouding the lodge was filling the room. She was relieved to see her mother asleep, and Frank was only just beginning small mewling noises that were his hungry stirrings. Seeing them safe together was a relief. She was worried about Millie, though, and would send someone around to check on her again. But, for now, she'd tend to the fire, the baby, and her mum, in that order. She'd already decided not to return to the mill today. The day's final mark against her would steer the rest of her week, if not the rest of her time at the mill, and she knew it would not be pleasant. She'd seen the harassment of lazy or careless workmates, and she wouldn't wish the treatment on anyone, but she didn't care. She wasn't long for the mill, anyway, not if she could help it.

Placing coal on the glowing cinders, she stoked the fire, blowing until a bright flame burst, and as she added bits to it, she was grateful for its warmth. The room warmed, the babe settled, and she thought to take the opportunity to get the fire on the hob in the kitchen going, so she could start some food cooking. As she went to lift Frank from her mother's side, she thought she heard a noise coming from the front of the house. The baby seemed content in his warm spot, and so she tiptoed to the doorway and listened. Again, hearing sounds. This time she could make out the clanking of pots and lids in the kitchen.

She didn't want to wake her mother or the baby, and so she sidled down the hallway and quietly called out, 'Millie?'

No answer.

'Dad?' she tried as she got closer to the threshold of the kitchen.

No answer.

Wishing now that she'd grabbed a poker from the hearth as the distinct sound of the kettle rattling could be heard. She felt a burst of warmth coming from the kitchen, and fully expecting to see Millie making tea, she was brought up short by the presence of that Chadwick chap.

'What are you doin' 'ere?' she demanded. 'I thought I said I'd be fine.'

'You did.' He grinned that same clever grin. He had kept his wool vest buttoned, and the scarf wrapping his neck had tucked into it.

'Then what's all this, then?' She looked around the kitchen, now warming with the heat of the stove, lighted lanterns and candles, and a pot of water beginning to boil next to the whistling kettle on the hob. She could see he'd piled peeled potatoes, and he was cutting them into cubes, as it appeared he was about to add them to the water. She hadn't been inside for long. He must have rushed right in and got to work. She frowned, not knowing whether to be pleased or affronted by his brazenness.

'You're making…soup?' she asked, incredulous.

'I found this'—he held up a platter of cold meat—leftover beef and lamb— 'in the spring room. Thought I'd add it if that's all reet?'

She didn't answer. She just stood with there, gob-stopped, she had to admit. She couldn't be more surprised if the Queen herself were doin' up her kitchen.

'I just thought you might need some help,' he said, rather innocently as he saw her confusion and wariness.

She looked longingly to the tea kettle wishing for a hot cup in her cold hands.

'You left the door unlatched, and the wind blew it open. I only meant to close it, but I heard you calling for Millie, so I settled the carriage under your archway.' He pointed to the covered structure at the side of the house. 'And…well, then, I thought it might be helpful if I made some tea.' He gestured to the cups he'd lined up on the counter.

She gave him a side glance. 'You sure can run your gob, can't you?'

He let out a loud laugh. 'So, you'll have a cuppa?'

At that moment, the baby started crying, and she looked from the hallway to Samuel. She could see the eagerness in his bright blue eyes.

'Let me get Frank,' she said. 'And add a cup for me mum. She'll be wantin' one too.'

Martha Anne smiled, leaning over Frank, she whispered, 'There, there, Mummy's here.' She slid her hands beneath his squirming body, his tiny face reddening, his impatience for his position almost became a scream, but she swooped him up on her shoulder, where he put his thumb in his mouth and began to suck. Through the darkness, she could barely see her mum but was glad that she and Frank hadn't awakened her.

As Martha Anne made to leave the room, something tugged her back inside. Something felt wrong. Her heartbeat quickened as her eyes darted around dark corners, to the flames of the fire in the hearth and the flicker of the newly lighted candle. 'What is wrong?' she whispered into the room. Holding Frank close, she stood still, taking breaths in from her nose and out her mouth, stopping the panic that was unreasonably rising inside her. And then it lured her eyes to the stillness of her mother in the bed. As Martha Anne's eyes peered through the dimness of the room, she homed in on her mother's form beneath the covers. No movement. Nothing.

Martha Anne dropped to her knees, the weight of Frank in her arms too much to hold, and so she set him on the floor. At first, she attempted to pull the covers up, but Ellen's hand was gripping the blanket.

'Mum, here, let me…' She tugged and saw her mother's fist was tight and white in colour. Martha Anne slid her hands over her mother's stiff arms, legs, feet. Her skin was cold. There was no breath, no heartbeat, no life left in the body of the woman who had once been her mum. Martha Anne reached down and picked up Frank. Then, hauling up his and her own weight to her feet, she stepped away from the bed, gripping Frank tighter to her. She made to open her mouth, to call for the stranger in the kitchen, but there was no sound. There was only the baby whimpering against her ear.

Somehow, in just a few hours, her mother had died. "Died". "Died in the bed" with her grandson in her arms. Just like that. Dead.

Chapter Ten

When Martha Anne did not return to the warmth of the kitchen for some time, Samuel loaded up a tray with tea and toast and made his way down the dark hallway to the yellow glow of the room at its end. At the threshold, he peered inside to see a woman, Mrs Ashworth, he presumed, lying on the bed, but he did not see her daughter or the baby. It wasn't until he took a step within that a sound to his left turned his head, and he saw Martha Anne standing in the dark corner, clutching her baby to her breast, staring at the bed.

Quickly, he settled the tray on a dresser, and followed the young woman's gaze, and immediately understood. He knelt beside the bed. Mrs Ashworth was not sleeping, as he'd first assumed. Her face was grey, her lips blue and pulled away from her gums. One eye was closed, but the other had peeled open, and she seemed in pain as if she were stopped mid-anguish, or so he considered. He thought to check her pulse, but the cold stiffness of her arm told him there would be none to find. He rose and carefully reached for the quilt at the foot of the bed and pulled it up and over Ellen Ogden Ashworth's head. He turned to the young woman in the corner, more like a little girl who just lost her mum, and put his arm across her shoulders, guiding her and the baby out of the room.

He settled them at the table near the fire in the kitchen. The babe was hungry, and so Martha Anne covered herself to feed him. Samuel retrieved the tea tray, poured a cup, then left to give her privacy. She quietly wept as Frank suckled. Somehow, both acts seemed tied to one another. A nursing mum loses her sick mum whilst her babe lies in the dead grand-mum's arms. *It were a riddle!* she thought. *Answer? Where was the father? Wrong? I give up!* She snorted a laugh, then stifled it, knowing the creeping madness was upon her again.

Frank being the easy-going chap that he was, had finished his meal and was already fast asleep. She carefully lowered him to his little wooden cradle, covered him with a downy blanket, and made her way out of the kitchen. She heard Samuel rattling in one of the rooms. Lamps had been lighted down the hallway, and there was a fire in her father's study. She came upon him in the sitting room, lighting the fireplace. When he heard her, he turned and stood.

'I'm sorry 'bout your mum,' he managed.

She was angry at herself when tears welled at his words. She could not speak past the tightening of her throat, and so she nodded.

'I've finished up the soup. It's boiling on the hob. I've lighted the hearths.' He pointed to rooms on the other sides of the walls and to a lamp on the table. 'And lamps.'

She nodded again. This time, she made her way into the room and sat on the sofa by the fire. He lowered himself to the chair opposite. 'I found this in a puddle by the front door. I was able to dry it out.' He handed her the crackled piece of paper. In Millie's rudimentary and smeared hand, Martha Anne read the note letting them know she'd been called away to her daughter's in Bury, in the middle of the night, and wouldn't be back till the morrow.

She looked up to the young man whose charming smile was replaced with grave concern in his eyes. The pale blue seemed to have darkened with the mood of the day, the moment, the situation.

'I'll go back to the mill to fetch your dad,' he said hesitantly as if he weren't sure that was the next course of action.

She nodded and remembered to thank him. Before he made it through the doorway, she stopped him, 'Mr Chadwick?'

'Yes?'

'Who are you?'

'I'm sorry?' His forehead furrowed in confusion.

'I mean, who are you to me dad? We've never met, and you're being very kind.'

His face cleared, and a smile appeared. 'Why, I'm the new accountant. For the mill,' he said. 'I was just settling my affairs with your dad when…' He looked away and out through the window to the rain, which seemed as if it would never end.

'When I barged in, and the Ashworth family swallowed you whole,' she said.

'I don't see it like that, miss. I'm glad to be of service. However I might help your family, it would be an honour.'

'Do you live here? In Rochdale?'

He smiled. 'I do now. Or I will soon when me things arrive. I've the end terrace house on Prince Street. Number One, it is, which I took for a good sign.'

'Well, I am thankful for your kindness. After all, you are but a stranger, and we've burdened you beyond your accounting duties, I'm afraid.' She was somehow feeling guilty for bringing this lad into their family's crisis.

'Please, say no more. I am happy to help. I hope one day not to be a stranger but a friend to you and your father. As for now, I will fetch him. Is there anything else I can do for you before I go?'

She stood as he did. 'No. No. We'll be fine. I'll get the funerary trunk and lay out our clothes…I suppose.'

He nodded but did not respond as it seemed she was more talking to herself than to him. As he reached for the doorknob, he paused to see she was still standing in the middle of the kitchen, staring at seemingly nothing. Her short-cropped hair was thick and had dried spikey around her head as if she didn't care at all what she looked like. He suspected she didn't. But she was a beauty. A dark horse beauty, he mused. She was the type he liked to bet on, a bit unpredictable, a little wild and surprising, but tameable, he'd decided. He noticed that while she could've been any young age, her bosom was not well hidden by the shawl she'd wrapped around her shoulders, and the baby that had suckled there revealed she was older than he first thought. And yet, even in this most vulnerable moment, he could see that she was a strong woman, no matter her age. And intelligent. He had seen it immediately in her eyes. Looking around the shabby manor house, he thought that perhaps he'd been called to Rochdale to do more than right the mill's accounts, but maybe even John's personal ones. He saw a nearly imperceptible straightening of Martha Anne's shoulders and spine as if she were demanding of herself to buck up, and he knew he was about to make a bet on her.

***

Samuel and John had arrived at the manor as the rain began to let up, and the clouds broke apart, leaving the blackest of them all gathering for one last lashing, but the hint of pale sky beyond the grey was giving hope. Martha Anne had tended the soup, made a Yorkshire pudding, and the kettle was poised to fill the teapot ready for her dad's arrival. She saw them drive into the courtyard, wiped her hands on her apron, and went to the front door where Samuel had stopped the carriage so John could get out. Granted, it was still dim and rainy, but she nearly did not recognise her father as he slowly, nearly painfully it seemed, descended. His back was bent, and his shoulders hunched as he climbed the steps. He did not turn to close the carriage door, nor did he pause as he passed his daughter at the door. He did not even look at her, speak to her, or pause to hug her. Instead, without removing his muddy boots or wet Macintosh, he slogged down the hallway as if he were a man making his way up a steep hill taking every breath and step with near exhaustion. She followed and reached for his shoulders.

'Dad, stop…here…let me…' She pulled the wet coat off and hung it on its proper hook, then grabbed his hat. She gave him a little nudge when he remained in place and followed him to her mother's room. She'd kept the fire going but would not look down at the bedstead when she passed it. Her mind was already playing tricks, whispers of "dead-in-the-bed" repeated in her head. They grew louder when she was in the room with her "dead-in-the-bed" mum, under the quilt Samuel had pulled over her mum's "dead-in-the-bed" head.

'Stop!' She unwittingly said aloud and grabbed the sides of her head, pressing her palms against her temples and closing her eyes tightly. This caused her father to halt, mid-stride, and she bumped into him. Her eyes flew open, and she reached out to steady him. 'Sorry, Dad. Sorry, not you. Go on. I'm goin' to wait 'ere, though.'

She paused and leaned back against the wall. She couldn't bear it—the stifling heat of the room, the chill of her "dead-in-the-bed" mother, and the abject sorrow flowing from her father were too much. She took long breaths in through her nose and whistled them out through pursed lips. She closed her eyes and wished for Alice, Betty, or Lizbeth—for any of them to come to take over, help with their dad whilst they bury their mum or help bury their mum whilst she dealt with their dad. Either way, because he seemed as near to dead as their mother. His eyes were dead. He did not speak, the weight of the world had pressed down on his shoulders, and he could no longer hold it up. She heard the crash come from the room, and she rushed in to see her father on the floor, blood coming from somewhere.

'Dad!' She attempted to roll her father onto his back. Then, instinctively, she called out, 'Samuel!'

The young man rushed into the room and helped John to a sitting position against the bed. Blood trickled from his nose, and he looked from Samuel to

Martha Anne with a dazed expression. She'd grabbed a rag from the small table and pressed it up against her father's nose.

'Dad, you all right?' She knelt and placed her palm against his cheek. 'What 'appened? Did you fall?'

He did not speak but leaned into her shoulder, where, suddenly, tears burst, and his mighty sobs shook them both.

***

It seemed to Martha Anne that Samuel had taken care of it all, watching from the kitchen as he graciously welcomed yet another visitor to the parlour where mourners were gathering. He'd been a mere stranger to them just days before entering their world at its most fragile moment. He'd assessed the situation and, without hesitation, took command of it. He'd automatically taken it upon himself to handle the details of the funeral. And thank God, she considered over the cutting board in the kitchen pretending to busy herself with food preparations. In all reality, she was taking a break from the chaos that had been swirling ever since she'd found her mother—(*Don't think it!*)—*dead-in-the-bed.*

At present, she avoided the gathering crowd in the parlour. She was no good at small talk and had no patience for false condolences, as most didn't even know her mother. They'd come out of some obligation to her father, either from the mill or from church. Either way, he was drinking in his study, so their efforts to pay their respects mainly were for naught, lost on her and never landing with him.

Her father was a mess. She'd passed him sitting alone in his study with whisky in his grip. She couldn't blame him. She'd have loved a pull on her own flask hidden away in her room, but she daren't. Her baby needed her…No, Frank was in good hands, being fussed over and passed around the mourners like a tray of sweets.

It was her father who needed minding. He hadn't been sober since he'd collapsed upon seeing his dead wife—(*Don't!*) Martha Anne shook the image and the plaguing chant from her mind.

She looked up from her thoughts, surprised to see her sister Lizbeth standing at the threshold. Martha Anne almost had to shake her head to process the sight of her. Lizbeth was still in her travelling clothes, and there was a small

162

carpetbag on the floor beside her. How long had she been standing there spying on her? Martha Anne felt a defensiveness rise and had a sharp insult at the ready if need be. But Lizbeth's eyes were full of sorrow and tears. Her long embrace had removed all slings and arrows from Martha Anne's mind. Instead, she felt relief. Thank God. Lizbeth was here, and she would take over, and everything would be made right, but just as these thoughts took hold, a bald man with a giant red beard, wearing a tweed coat and knee-high boots, appeared at the doorway.

'Ah, there you are!' he huffed and settled a suitcase beside the carpetbag Lizbeth had brought.

Lizbeth let go of Martha Anne and turned around, smiling through her tears. She gestured for the fellow to join her side and introduced her sister. 'Martha Anne, this…this is Willie.' She took his elbow. 'He's me…' She paused, searching for the proper adjective.

He put out his hand and grinned. 'Why, I'm Lizzie's betrothed!' He kissed Lizbeth's hand and lifted it to show off the beautiful gold ring with a small diamond setting. 'It took me months to convince her, but she finally agreed just a fortnight ago!'

Despite her grief, in spite of her tears, Lizbeth was glowing, and Martha Anne thought she'd never seen this side of her sister—happy! She managed a smile as she admired the ring, and when she met Lizbeth's eyes, she was able to carry the smile with her. 'You're to be married, then?' she managed.

'In September,' Willie answered, 'and then off to America!'

'Willie!' Lizbeth swiped a playful hand at him. 'I said I wanted to wait to tell them.'

He made a dramatic cringing face, stomped his foot, and pretended to slap his own cheeks. 'Oh, sorry, luv. You're right, you did, and I'm sorry!' He turned to Martha Anne. 'I, well, Martha Anne, I am over the moon about your sister, and when she agreed to come to America w' me, I could hardly contain myself. I shouldn't have said. I've spoken out of turn.'

Lizbeth wrapped an arm around him. 'It's fine, Willie. We'll tell me dad together.'

'Right, will do.' He glanced around the room as if not knowing where his eyes should land. 'Where should I put our luggage?' he finally asked as if relieved to have found himself useful.

Lizbeth looked at Martha Anne, waiting. It wasn't until she realised that she was being given some sort of deference as "mistress of the manor" by her sister that she was being asked where the pair would be sleeping.

'Oh…um…that's really…well…' She stumbled in this new role, suddenly foisted upon her by default and her "dead-in-the-bed" mother. She glanced upward to the many cold empty bedrooms above. She herself had taken to sleeping in the parlour near the fire so she could keep an eye and ear out for her father. Whether he be coming home from the pub or sneaking out to one, she was on alert. Without looking Willie in the eye, she said, 'Up the stairs then,' she waved towards the door. 'All the rooms are empty, so choose whichever you'd like.' She'd leave it up to him and them to decide whether they were going to share a bed or not.

The sisters stood staring at one another after Willie left. The silence was long and becoming awkward when Millie popped in with the baby. 'He's lookin' for 'is mum!' she said to Martha Anne and then noticed Lizbeth. 'Why, Miss Lizbeth, I didn't know you'd arrived,' she said, handing the baby to Martha Anne. 'Oh, luv, I'm so sorry 'bout your mum.' She patted the woman's arm. 'I've got to refill the cold meats. Good to see you, Lizbeth. Your dad will be glad you're here.' And she left. Again, the room went silent, filled only with the noise of Frank making babbling sounds.

He'd nudged them from the invisible wedge that had filled the space between them. Martha Anne shifted the baby on her hip so he could see her sister and she him. He wasn't crying or needing his nappy changed. He was just eagerly looking around the room for something to feast his eyes upon, and when they landed on Lizbeth, he met his auntie's eyes and grinned a wide gummy grin. He jumped his legs against his mother's hips and, suddenly, lurched forward, reaching for Lizbeth, who could do nothing but catch him as he flung himself into her arms.

'Oh my!' she exclaimed and held the boy against her bosom. He placed a tiny hand on Lizbeth's cheek and smoothed it. Lizbeth looked as confused and surprised as Martha Anne felt. She watched as her baby laid his head against her sister's shoulder and sucked his thumb quite contentedly in this otherwise stranger's lap.

'I think 'e likes you,' Martha Anne said.

Lizbeth smiled. 'Most babies don't.'

Martha Anne chose silence over saying aloud what went through her mind: Most people don't, and instead, moved to the hob. 'Would you like a cup of tea?'

Lizbeth, holding the baby, still in her coat, looked around as if she did not know what to do with him or herself.

Martha Anne rounded the table to her sister's rescue. 'Here, let me 'ave 'im.' She carefully laid him in his little bed and placed a whisky-soaked rag in his fist, and he began to gnaw on it. He was just beginning to teethe, and it seemed the one thing that soothed his pain. She turned to her sister. 'Take off your coat and 'ave a seat.' She pulled out a chair.

Lizbeth did as she was told and was grateful for the hot tea Martha Anne had set before her. Then, clearing her throat, she said, 'I 'aven't seen Dad yet. How is 'e?'

Martha Anne shook her head. 'Not good. In the whisky…' she whispered and let the memory of the last time she saw Lizbeth pass between them without either making mention of Martha Anne having been in the whisky…herself. She was grateful that Lizbeth had let it pass.

She'd been good about her own drinking since Frank came. She'd tipped her flask the night she found her mum dead—but who wouldn't't've found some comfort in the bottle after something like that? Since then, though, what with all there was to planning a funeral and burying her mum, she didn't dare, especially with all the arrangements that Mr Chadwick had made on their behalf. She couldn't let him down by getting drunk. One useless drunk in the family chasing the grain into the ground was enough, and her dad had it covered.

Lizbeth interrupted her thoughts. 'How are things at the mill?'

Martha Anne shrugged. 'Dunno. He hired a new man. An accountant. He's been quite helpful and has taken over nearly all Dad's duties since…Well, since all this 'appened,' she said, and spread her arms wide as if the gesture alone was encompassing the entirety of all that had happened in the last five days. She began to tell her sister of how she'd found their mother "dead-in-the-bed" with Frank when, uncontrollably, she started to shake and felt light-headed. Reaching behind for her own chair, she grabbed at nothing as her knees buckled and she slid down onto the slate. When she hit the ground, the sobs exploded from her chest, and the torrent of tears washed her neck. She buried her head in a nest of limbs as she'd crumpled into the collapsing frame of her body.

Lizbeth was on the floor beside her in an instant, grabbing Martha Anne in her arms and pulled her into her lap. Pressing her palm against her sister's hair, she felt the thick bristle-y tufts. Oh, what had she done to that beautiful mane, now all hacked and feathered? 'There, there, lass...' Lizbeth whispered, rocking her sister, petting her, wiping away her sweat and tears to no avail.

Lizbeth leaned over, resting a cheek against Martha Anne's shoulder. She considered the life of her sister these past few years. She was but a child. Only all of fourteen, and was now a motherless child, and a mother with a fatherless child—what a mess.

Willie reappeared at the doorway. Lizbeth saw him assess the scene between the sisters and discreetly closed the door behind him. She heard his good-natured voice greeting someone in the hallway, and she could easily imagine him guiding the guest to a small dram of whisky for them both.

Lizbeth adored him. She'd fallen in love with him the very day she'd met him on the estate grounds. It was in the garden, and he was tending to some early spring blooms when he'd nearly snipped the bottom of her skirt as she'd passed a row of bushes he'd been trimming. His bald pink scalp was glowing in the morning sun and nearly blinded her, but it was his toothy smile beneath the big red beard that made her laugh out loud. And he joined in her whimsy even though he had no idea what had brought on her giggly joy.

It had taken him weeks to invite her out for a bite at the village pub and another two outings before he dared try a kiss, whilst lying on a picnic rug beside a river, finally. Once their lips met, though, nothing had stopped her first kiss from becoming her first tumble with a man. Surprising even herself, Lizbeth found she liked nothing more than feeling Willie inside her. Shortly after that, he'd proposed, and she'd said yes, and yes again to going all the way to America, leaving this bloody cold, damp island behind for good, just like her brother James had so many years ago, now. He was somewhere in sunny Spain, she'd heard.

Both women stood and wiped their tears and faces. They had composed themselves, and each in her own way had attempted some sort of apologies for past hurtful words and deeds, but in the end, they waved them off and clung to one another as orphaned sisters do.

Lizbeth took Martha Anne's hand. 'We will speak again later, but for now, we must both go out there and greet those who've come to pay their respects before we begin the procession.'

Martha Anne nodded and checked on Frank to see that he was peacefully sleeping and followed her sister out the door.

In the hallway, as it happened, they found Willie regaling a young man with a fish tale worth interrupting, Lizbeth thought, as she heard the threads of the familiar Lake District folklore Willie loved spinning.

'Oh! Lizbeth.' Martha Anne paused before the men with her sister. 'This is the gentleman I was telling you about. The one who's been helpin' with the mill and with…well…all these arrangements, too. Mr Chadwick, this is me sister Lizbeth. She's come down from the Lake District.'

Samuel gave a slight bow. 'I have made the acquaintance of your man, William, here.' He gestured to Willie. Taking Lizbeth's hand, he said, 'I am very sorry for your loss, miss. I did not know your mother, but with the many who've come to pay respects, I can only presume she was beloved.'

'Mr Chadwick has been so helpful—' Martha Anne began when he interrupted.

'Please call me "Samuel", miss, I beg of you.' He smiled.

Martha Anne began again. 'Fine, Samuel has been most helpful. Without him, I do not know what I would have done.'

'Is that right?' Lizbeth managed.

'Yes, why, it was Samuel who contacted the undertaker, hired the funeral carriage, called on the coffin maker, and gathered the neighbour women to…to…come to take care of Mum,' Martha Anne managed.

'Well, that was very kind of you, Mr Chadwick. Our family appreciates all your care.'

'I cannot say it was my pleasure as that is the furthest from my thoughts, but I can say that I am glad I was here to help. And if I may, your sister had quite a hand in putting this all together,' he said with a smile in his eyes as he leaned into Lizbeth.

'She did?'

'Indeed. She organised the procession, made the arrangements for prayers at St Mary's in the Baum Chapel. And, of course, writing all the letters to you and family members.'

'Did you hear from Jamie or Alice?' Lizbeth asked, knowing neither had probably even received them yet.

Martha Anne shook her head.

'Of course not,' Lizbeth said. 'How could they know yet?'

Samuel stepped forward, taking Martha Anne's elbow and guiding her away from Lizbeth and Willie.

'I believe we should begin to ready for the parting,' he whispered. 'Would you like me to be in the first carriage with you and your father?'

Martha Anne looked into the drawing room to see that her father was engaged in some sort of lecture to a group of men whose backs were to her, but his hair was ruffled, and his suit disheveled, and he was waving around a whisky glass, sloshing it over his desk.

She looked over to see that Lizbeth was watching her and Samuel, and was saying something to Willie that, Martha Anne could tell, was not favourable to whomever her subject was, be it herself or Samuel, she was not sure.

'Will there be enough room for Lizbeth and Willie in the carriage?'

He shook his head. 'Only Lizbeth, if I come along, I'm afraid. But they can both be in the second carriage.'

She looked back into the study to see that her father had risen and was now reciting convoluted verses from an old Tim Bobbin poem, which he was getting all wrong, but that was beside the point, and she knew she needed Samuel's help to keep her father in line. So rather than provoke a confrontation with Lizbeth, she instead brought her into confidence, pulling her to the study door where their father was about to pour another round for everyone when he saw his daughters peering in and waved the bottle at them.

'Gennelmen! These two beeeUteeful lasses are me girls! Martha Annie anni anndah Lissahbeth! Awe, Lizzie…you've come home!' He made his way through the group of men, grabbed his eldest daughter and hugged her to him. 'Your mum is gone, luv,' he cried. 'She just died…' And he cried in his daughter's arms. The men in the room sidled past them, lowering their eyes so as not to meet either of the daughters as their father embarrassed himself.

Samuel and Willie had taken John to the washroom and cleaned him up for the processional. Given his state, Lizbeth needed no convincing that it would be best for Samuel to ride in the first carriage with Martha Anne and Frank. She and Willie would be right behind them in the second if needed in a pinch.

'I don't like 'im,' Lizbeth said to Willie as their carriage followed behind her father, Martha Anne and that man.

'Who? Who don't you like?' Willie turned from the window.

'That Samuel character.'

'Character? What d'ye mean by that?'

'I dunno. I just don't like 'im. I can't quite put me finger on it.'

'I'd keep that lot to meself, then, if I were you.' Willie said. 'Unless you've proof he's somehow no good. It's not fair to accuse a man of nothing but a feelin', now is it?'

Lizbeth smiled. It's what she loved about Willie, his willingness to give a lad a second, even a third chance, but especially a first chance, and so she said, 'I suppose not.'

'He's been mighty helpful from all what Martha Anne were sayin',' Willie reminded her.

'I know. I know. I should be grateful it's all not in me own lap,' she said. 'Especially since we're leavin' for America. I might have a harder time goin' if I thought Martha Anne were on her own with me dad. And, well, with the babe.'

'Well, see, she won't be on her own. That Samuel seems a right nice chap.'

She was quiet.

'What is it, then?' he asked again.

'You know I believe in "love at first sight". After all, I felt it with you, Willie.'

He grinned and took her hand. 'And me with you, lass.'

'Well, if there can be a "love at first sight", then there's got to be a "hate at first sight" that is equally as valid, don't you think?'

'I suppose. But do you hate him?'

'No, I don't hate him,' she said. 'I just don't like him, and I don't know why.'

'He's not the babe's father, is he?' Willie asked, but his timing was all off.

'No. Of course not.'

'Does he not 'ave a father?' Willie asked.

Lizbeth frowned and shook her head. 'Well, of course, he's got a father. We just don't know who it is.'

'Won't she say?'

'From what me dad and our Alice have written, she won't give him up for nothin'.'

'You'd think she'd want some compensation.' He went back to staring out the window as the horses clopped along at a slow clip. There were children, women, and old men lining the streets as they went by, lowering their hats and heads as the draped coffin passed.

'Unless she doesn't know who it is,' Lizbeth said.

'Now, luv, that's a bit unkind.'

'She had a wild streak, Martha Anne did, before I left 'ome. Told me dad the father were a lad down at the canal. Then told our Alice it were some mill owner's son.'

'She seems to have settled down, eh?' Willie offered. 'She seems a right good mum.'

'That she does,' Lizbeth agreed, surprising herself at how easily that came. If nothing else, Martha Anne had turned out to be a loving mum. Maybe to make up for the one she'd never had or to be sure not to become the one she did have. They were pulling up to St Mary's in the Baum, and Lizbeth decided none of it mattered anyhow. She would be leaving this family, this country, soon enough, and she'd never have to think of either ever again.

The mizzling rain didn't begin until halfway through the burial at the cemetery. John had fallen asleep in the carriage, and they'd decided to leave him there. He'd prayed too loud at the church and made a few inappropriate comments over the priest's words, and so they thought it best to let him sleep it off. Only a few had continued to witness the casket being lowered and the dirt thrust, but Martha Anne was glad to see that they were familiar faces, neighbours and friends. She'd searched the crowd in hope, but there was no Betty Nuppy. She'd wondered if Betty might come, for her dad at least, if not for her. She didn't blame Betty for being mad at her. She'd broken her legs and ruined her shop, after all. But she didn't think it fair or proper for Betty to have banished her dad. They'd been friends since childhood, and if ever John Ashworth needed a friend, it would be now. Betty must still be angry, as she'd surely know of Ellen's passing from the villagers.

Martha Anne hadn't seen Betty since that terrible night over a year ago, now. She wished she could take it all back. Wished she hadn't got pregnant. Wished she hadn't tried to get rid of him. Wished she hadn't gone to Betty's that night. Wished she could tell Betty how truly sorry she was for it all. She wished and wished. *If wishes were horses, then beggars would ride*—she'd heard her dad's voice in her head. It was something he'd often say when she was a child wishing away her life. She never quite grasped its full meaning until today, as she stood in the rain, watching mud pour into the hole that was her mother's grave, covering the casket in brown sludge, and the adage's full meaning hit home.

As the rain picked up, some who had gathered at the graveside began to head towards the road. Lizbeth and Willie had already returned to their carriage, even before the last words were spoken over the casket. But Martha Anne, carrying Frank under her Macintosh, with an umbrella over her head, remained till the end. And it wasn't till the end that she realised the umbrella holder was Samuel standing right behind her. When she turned and saw him, she couldn't help but feel a calm he seemed to cast around himself. He offered his arm, and she was just about to take it when she looked up to see a hooded figure across the graveyard, just on the other side of the stone wall surrounding it. She squinted through the buckets now pouring down, as the hunched person, with a long walking stick turned and very slowly hobbled up the little lane.

'I'll meet you,' she said to Samuel and left him, hurrying across the mushy grass, around headstones, until she coursed to a large iron gate and pushed with all her might before it broke with its rust and let her out into the muddy path. Despite her broken gait, Martha Anne saw the small image disappearing around the bend up ahead. She desperately wanted to race, but with the rain, the mud, and the babe in her coat, she had to settle for a quick but careful foothold up the hill. The woman, she could tell now, had stopped and sat down on a big cornerstone beside the road, despite the rain. They surprised each other as they looked up and into each other's eyes. It was Betty, she could see, and she slowly made her way across the path, as if approaching a cat that might dart if you got too close. But Betty did not dart. Instead, she made room for Martha Anne on the big stone, so she sat, feeling the old woman's small bones through their wet coats. The rain was back to drizzling, and a small bar of sun had broken through the clouds, making a sparkle in the puddle at their feet.

Martha Anne was just about to speak when Betty raised her hand, stopping her.

'Let me see 'im,' Betty said, looking ahead to the pasture above them.

At first, she was confused, but as she felt Frank squirm within her coat, she understood, and unbuckled the Macintosh and pulled wide its flaps revealing the soft brown curls and big brown eyes of his father, and upon seeing Betty, now looking down upon him, Frank grinned wide revealing his father's dimple in his cheek and stretched a hand to grab a strand of the old woman's white hair. Martha Anne lifted him out and set him on her knee where Betty could see the full of him. The rain had stopped, but a big drop from a tree above plopped onto Frank's nose, and he giggled. At this, Betty stretched out her arms, and Martha Anne shifted him over onto her bony old knees. Frank grabbed a wrinkled old knuckle and leaned back against Betty's chest, smiling at his mother. Betty pressed her nose against his ears and armpits and sniffed. She kissed his neck, his cheeks, and his lips. Finally, she closed her eyes and crowned her palms atop his head and mouthed whispered words that Martha Anne did not recognise as those of her language. Betty slipped her arms around Frank's middle and hugged him to her, but Martha Anne saw that her fingers were pressing small spots up Frank's middle from waist to neck, and she seemed to be counting, but again, Martha Anne was unsure of anything that was happening. She got nervous when Betty circled her palms around Frank's neck but then watched as her fingertips floated down the lengths of his arms and legs, and while she did not know what, she knew that Betty was performing an ancient rite upon her son. She could feel through her own skin that it was a ritual that would protect him, and so she pressed her palm against her baby's thigh and closed her own eyes as the Wise Woman completed her blessings.

When Martha Anne looked up, there was a neckless of tiny red coral beads encircling Frank's neck. Red coral she knew had its own ancient protective qualities. Hard to come by, but those who possessed it swore by its magic, alchemy, and nature. When she'd completed the small ceremony over the baby, Betty handed him back to Martha Anne. She tucked Frank back into his wrap in her coat. He was a bit mewly—she could see it was his teeth bothering him by the way he latched onto her knuckle between his pink gums and tried biting her. His teething cry was also quite distinct. It was a dangerous time in the life of an infant—teething time. It was when many babies died, and many believed it was due to the extreme pain of the teeth cutting through the gums that killed them. She'd like to get home and give him his whisky rag, to give him some relief, and so she buckled Frank in her coat and stood. Still, she hadn't said a word and desperately wanted to tell Betty how sorry she was and how much she missed her, but still, Betty would not allow her to speak. She put her finger to her lips and hushed Martha Anne's protestations.

Instead, Betty took the young woman's palm and turned it upright. She traced a line with her own arthritic finger tapping out four times. Martha Anne frowned, and Betty held up three fingers on her left hand and one finger on her right. 'Three boys and a girl more,' she said but did not look up. Instead, she reached into her pocket and pulled out a heavy silver charm attached to a smooth rounded piece of red coral, like the beads around Frank's neck that would protect him from evil spirits. Martha Anne looked closely at the trinket. Silver, she knew was said to be the mirror to the soul. The red coral, she'd studied had many protective qualities, but its colour was acceptance. She turned it over to see a carving in the silver, and she recognised the branch as sage. *Of course,* she thought, *sage is known for cleansing and the granting of wishes.*

She knew that none of these symbols was happenstance. Instead, Betty had chosen each for its mystical and magical quality and whatever message each meaning might convey.

'What is it?' Martha Anne managed.

'It's called a gum stick. It's for the babe. Whilst he is teething. It will help. Go on.' She pointed to the squirming beneath Martha Anne's coat. She opened the flaps and placed the bright smooth red end into his mouth, and he immediately bit down and bit down again. She could feel him relaxing against her.

'There, see,' Betty said. 'It'll help him through it.'

'Betty…please, I've got to say…'

Betty held up her hand. 'No, lass, you don't. And to be honest, I cannot hear what you 'ave to say. So let's leave us this way, shall we?' And she turned and continued her journey up the muddy hill.

As Martha Anne was thinking of following her, she heard the sound of horses coming from the graveyard and followed the path down around the bend to see that Samuel had the coachmen come to find her, and when she neared, he grinned and said, 'Lookin' for a lift, miss?'

He jumped down and helped her into the carriage. Her father was sound asleep in the corner, and Samuel sat next to him, across from her and the baby.

He pointed. 'What's that he got?'

She saw that Frank was turning the trinket over in his tiny fists.

'A gift. From an old friend,' she managed. 'It's called a coral gum stick.' She took it from Frank and held it up for Samuel to see.

173

'May I?'

She gave it to him, and he turned it over in his palm, examining it closely.

'Well, I don't know who your friend is, but they've got a close relationship with the magical, I'd say.'

'I'm sorry?' Martha Anne took the piece from Samuel and gave it back to the baby. 'What do you mean by magic?'

'I mean, in silver, in coral, in sage, there is much meaning, much magical spirit, much mystical protection among the powerful qualities in all three. Whoever gave this to you wants only good for you and Frank. Lucky you.'

***

Before the carriage came to take Lizbeth and Willie back to the Lake District, Martha Anne had sought out her sister and asked that she join her in the parlour for a talk.

'Lizbeth, I'm glad you came. I'm glad we've had the chance to…mend…' was the word she'd chosen, '…old wounds. At least for me,' she clarified, in case she was misreading the situation.

Lizbeth took her younger sister's hands and said, 'For me, as well.'

'I know you're goin' to America, and I'll probably never see you again.' Her voice cracked, and the tears that pricked her eyes surprised her. 'I always thought you would be here to take care of Mum and Dad. I always thought it was you who steadied our ship. I know now it was you who kept Dad from the drink, who paid our bills, took care of the mill accountancy and on and on. Lizbeth, I now know how much we depended on you. Needed you. I thought, maybe, when you came back for the funeral, that maybe you'd stay.'

Lizbeth let go of Martha Anne's hands and took a small step back.

'No! I'm not askin' you to, Lizbeth,' Martha Anne quickly clarified. 'I just wanted to say I'm glad for you. I'm glad you found Willie and he you. I'm glad you're goin' off to America. I'm so happy you've found happiness is what I wanted to say.'

'Thank you, sister,' Lizbeth said, a small lump rising in her throat and her heart. She'd been so centred on her own life that she hadn't thought to imagine what she'd be leaving Martha Anne with, and yet, maybe the full burden of it all is good for her. It's certainly made her a good mother, a responsible daughter, even a kinder sister, she considered.

'I don't blame you for keepin' Frank's father a secret,' she said.

Martha Anne blanched. She was not expecting this.

'But you can't help look at that child and not see his father in him. Those brown eyes, those black curls. All the child's lacking is a Scottish brogue. I admit I was suspect, but seeing the babe has just firmed those suspicions.'

Martha Anne could feel herself begin to shake and held onto the arm of the settee, across from her sister, trying to read Lizbeth's tone along with her words.

'No worries. Your secret is safe with me,' Lizbeth assured as if sensing Martha Anne's fear. 'I respect you. You could've blown it all up, taken away Alice's dreams. But you didn't, and for that, I have respect. It were a kindness.'

Martha Anne frowned. 'Why you tellin' me this, then.'

'Because you're strong, Martha Anne. Stronger than you think, stronger than you know. I knew you were strong-headed, all growin' up, but that strength goes beyond stubbornness. It's your character, your intelligence, your stamina. I see it all in you now as an almost grown woman. You can handle this with Dad. You can handle anything. I know you can. And so I thank you because if I'd seen otherwise, I might be tempted to ask Willie to postpone our trip, but seeing how you've grown, there is no need.'

Martha Anne did not cry, but wanted to. The tears wouldn't come. It was a mixed bag. Her obvious growing up, this strength her sister spoke of, complimented her on, had trapped her further into this current family situation rather than free her from it. Should she laugh or cry, she wondered, and decided to be the person her sister was describing, and got up and put her arms around her sister's neck.

'I hope you have safe passage, and one day, Lizbeth, I'll come to America to see you.'

'That's my girl. That's the way, lass.'

They stood facing one another. Lizbeth smiled and then placed both hands on Martha Anne's shoulders and looked into her eyes. 'I have one more thing to say…' She waited.

'Oh, all reet, I'm listenin',' Martha Anna answered, a bit taken aback by her sister's solemnity.

'Don't be taking up with that Chadwick chap.'

'What d'ye mean?'

175

'I've been watchin' him. He keeps an eye on you like a hawk. I think he fancies you.'

'He's been the best of help in all of this, Lizbeth, is all. I don't know what I would've done without him.'

'Yes, you do. You did. And you will. You don't need him. You can take care of anythin'. I've seen it. And him? I've seen him too, before. He's one of those lads who's got the good looks and the charm, but all the time, scheming about how to make them both work for him. I don't trust him, and neither should you.'

Martha Anne nodded. She wasn't sure why and didn't want to admit it, but she did think that Samuel Chadwick had appeared like a hero out of a fairy tale. A knight in shining armour if she were to be dreamy about it. She'd been less dreamy about anything since Malcolm had gone, since Betty was injured, since the birth of Frank, and since Mum died. This last scrubbed even the latest sweet dreams from her mind and replaced the void with nightmarish images of life in the mill, life in a terrace row house, or God forbid, life in the workhouse.

Chapter Eleven

Millie had confirmed her fears and was quick to find a solution, most recently, when suggesting she marry Samuel. 'Because, luv, life without a 'usband is not easy. Life without a 'usband is not safe. Life without a 'usband, well, lass, it's not a life at all. It's all work and no play, especially wi' a baby. And, considering your situation, your dad's situation, I think it would be good for everyone if you married Samuel and let 'im take over the mill for you and your dad.'

These were her worries these days, as her dad was getting less lucid, not more, no matter her own or Millie's efforts to bring him back to life. The mill, she knew from Samuel, was suffering for it. There was only so much he could do about some of the problems without John's consent, advice, or even desires for its future, as these were hard to pry out of a man drowning in the drink.

She was praying that Samuel would save them. If what Millie said was true—and Martha Anne knew it was—she and Frank could only count on a good life, a safe life, an easier life if she were to marry, and not just anybody, but a man who could keep them in the comfort to which they were accustomed. She liked Samuel, she mused. He was intelligent, kind, and decisive without being controlling. He did make her laugh, and he certainly eased many of her worries. He was not her type, she knew, but he wasn't bad looking, either, with those blue eyes and toothy grin. She wasn't in love with him. That kind of love, she knew, would always be reserved for Malcolm. She also knew that the dream of Malcolm ever returning was also dead among the other killed-off fantasies she'd had churning.

Recently, a letter from Alice arrived announcing another pregnancy and a move to the Highlands where Malcolm had stepped into his father's Lairdship to run the estate. It seemed that Malcolm's mother was bedbound, and his father suffered gout. So they would be taking over the household. Martha Anne had pressed the pages of the letter to her nose and took in a deep breath and a slight scent of Alice. In her mind, she conjured her beautiful sister holding two chubby-cheeked infants on her lap. When she recognised each resembling their father's big dark eyes and curls, the vision snapped, and they all disappeared.

Before tucking the pages back into the envelope, she noticed tiny writing at the bottom of the last page. She saw the diminutive message was also written in Alice's flowery hand. It read: 'And now you'll never have him.' Martha Anne stared for a moment, not exactly understanding the words. But then, of course, she realised her sister's subtle message threaded through her news-worthy composition.

With each nuanced paragraph, Alice was telling her that she knew everything about Malcolm and Martha Anne. Reading back through the letter, Martha Anne noted the repetition of certain words: "marriage", "my devoted husband", "married", "my attentive husband", "family", "babies my fatherly husband", "wifely duties", "my insatiable husband", "my loving husband", "adoring husband", "grateful husband"…written within a stream of information guised as offerings of family contentment, but in all reality, the true message could not be ignored or misunderstood in the small final postscript: 'And now you'll never have him.' Alice knew.

Martha Anne tore the letter into a million little pieces and tossed them into the fire—every one of them. Alice, baby Robby, the unborn one, the Laird and Lady, and Malcolm—yes, finally, Malcolm.

She knew then that she would never see him again, except when she looked into Frank's eyes where his father lived and loved only her.

***

'I think he fancies you,' Millie said as she was pinning up Martha Anne's hair, now grown out, nearly touching her shoulders.

'I dunno, and if 'e does, I dunno if I care.' Martha Anne looked in the mirror and was pleased to see that her hair was finally long enough to hold a pin.

'Well, ever since your mum passed, what's it been now, eight months? He's been around near every day, 'asn't he?'

'Millie, he's been workin' the books, takin' extra time with Dad, tryin' to get him back to the mill, and—'

178

'And bringin' you tea, playin' with Frank, a train ride to the seaside! What sort of business is that?'

'It were Rochdale's Wakes Week. Where'd you expect us to go? Everybody goes to Blackpool, then.'

'No, some rent a charabanc and spend the day at Hollingworth Lake, is all.'

'We were just out lookin' for some sunshine, and he wanted to show Frank the sea, and it were good for Dad,' Martha Anne defended.

'And good for you, eh?'

'Sure, sure, Millie, good for me.' She stood as soon as the last pin was pushed through her hair. 'The sun is good for everyone. What's your point?'

'All the way to Blackpool? Couldn't find sun this side of the Pennines, eh?'

'Not likely to ever find sun this side of the Pennines. Couldn't find the sea this side of them, either,' Martha Anne said.

'Maybe all that's true, but I still say he fancies you.'

'So what if he does? I'm not interested in fancyin' him back. Not interested in fancyin' any man, back. If truth be told.'

'And why not?' She stood back and assessed her tidy-up work on Martha Anne's hair. Millie had stayed on after Ellen passed. It wasn't so much for Martha Anne or Frank even, but for John, as he was a worse bother than a baby. They would get rid of his whisky, but he'd always found more. So she decided to stay and take care of them all. They needed her, and now, with her only daughter off to America, like all the young people it seemed, she knew this family, with all its troubles, needed a rudder to help steer them right. And in Millie's mind, it would do them all good if Martha Anne would see the bigger picture and find a way to marry Samuel Chadwick. This was a thought that did not remain inside but came flying out of her mouth.

'Oh, for God's sakes, Millie. Why do I need to be married to anyone?'

'As I've said, life isn't easy wi'out a 'usband. It's not safe. I just think it would be good for everyone if you married 'im. He's a good lad. Good with your dad, good with Frank, good with the books, and good with the mill.'

'He's pretty much doin' all that good already without having to lose me own life to marryin' him to boot.'

'You wouldn't lose your life. Instead, you'd gain freedom.'

Martha Anne stood at the mirror and pressed a crease down the front of her dress. It was new. She'd had a new wardrobe made since many of her clothes were much tighter since she'd given birth. With Millie's help, they'd sewed many new undergarments, a few simple shifts, shirts, and an everyday skirt, but for certain occasions, such as today, on her way to Manchester with Samuel, she'd commissioned a tailor to make the blue and grey striped frock with a high neck, puffed shoulders, and long sleeves. *Thank the heavens they'd done away with that ridiculous bustle,* she thought, slipping her arms through the holes of the royal blue velvet waistcoat the tailor had also fashioned and pushed the matching velvet-covered buttons through their slots. She smoothed her hands along her middle. Quite handsome, she thought and hung a pair of gold hoop earrings through the piercings in her ears. They'd belonged to her great-aunt or cousin, or grandmother who was said to have been a gypsy, or maybe she just like the idea of a great-relative down the line having been a gypsy.

Millie held up the new long grey tweed coat, and Martha Anne slid both arms into its satin-lined sleeves as Millie hoisted the layered capes onto her shoulders. 'You'll be warm in that, luv,' Millie said and straightened the Capelets. She stood back, satisfied with the tidy young woman before her. 'Oh, there he is,' she said upon hearing Samuel's footfalls below, as Sarah the housemaid had ushered him into the parlour. 'Now, you be nice to Samuel. He's taken a likin' to you, so at least be kind. And stay open, Martha Anne.'

'Oh, Millie, we're off to Manchester for business, not romance.' She made to leave the room but stopped once more at the mirror before she slipped down the stairs. She was a bit nervous about leaving Frank for the whole day, she admitted only to herself, so she asked, 'You're sure you'll be all reet with both Dad and Frank?'

'More all reet with Frank than with John,' Millie said but smiled. 'No worries, we'll be just fine. Enjoy yourself in the big city.'

'We're off to do banking. Not much to enjoy in that,' Martha Anne said but felt just a tad bit of excitement to be going all the way to Manchester by way of train.

'Well, you just remember if Samuel has something else in mind, be open. If he had some investment in the mill—namely you—you wouldn't ever have to go banking again,'

Martha Anne waved a hand above her head, dismissing Millie, who was following her down the stairs.

Samuel had smiled and nodded to Millie, but it was clear he was anxious to get going, and so he stepped outside whilst Martha Anne adjusted her fur-lined hat and pulled on the soft kid gloves she'd also had tailor-made. Before Martha Anne could yank open the door, Millie pulled her aside once more and whispered, 'Marry him. It'd secure everything for you and Frank and your dad, as well. You know I'm right.'

Martha Anne was now annoyed, and she pulled away. 'No, Millie. What I know is that you think you're right, and that seems to bring you great satisfaction whether I agree with you or not.' She turned and left the manor.

***

Samuel didn't mention the time of the bank appointment, and she didn't ask. They were on the train to Piccadilly Station, this much she knew, and she was delighted. The entire time, Samuel sat across from her. He wasn't even attempting to hide the silly grin under his wide moustache and would not take his eyes off her. She, on the other hand, was not only avoiding his stare, but she was drawn to the window where she tried to capture and memorise each passing church steeple, town clock, rows of terrace houses, main streets of villages, stone-faced farmhouses, fields, and flocks of sheep dotting the moors. They all flew by as if being sucked down the track behind her. That's how fast they were travelling.

She'd only ever been to Manchester once before. She'd been a little girl, and they'd gone as a family for Guy Fawkes Day. It was bright and sunny but bitterly cold. She had held onto her brother Jamie, feeling as if to let go that she would be swept away into the sea of people who seemed to be occupying every cobblestone. Her father led them across Acres Field and past St Ann's church. She remembered the streets were a moving mass of heavy woollen coats, hats, mittens, and jumpers. She had been hot even though it was cold. She recalled she was frightened of the burning effigies of the rebel, Guy Fawkes, being carried through the streets, and she shied away from small children begging money for Guy. Jamie had pulled her out of the path of a burning tar barrel that was careening down the hill with a whooping frenzy of young boys chasing it. Her brother lifted her to his shoulders, and they finally

181

came to a halt around a giant pile of wood ready to become a bonfire, along with many other revellers. While they waited for nightfall and the rest of the town to arrive, her dad told them of the "Gun Powder Plot" when Guy Fawkes tried but failed to blow up the House of Lords. And as he would, without care, her father began reciting a poem aloud for those gathered around him, and he turned to the crowd:

'Don't you Remember,
The Fifth of November,
'T was Gunpowder Treason Day,
I let off my gun,
And made 'em all run.
And stole all their Bonfire away.'

The gathered broke into a cheer, and this had made her mum shake her head, but she was smiling. Others surrounding her dad patted him on the back and let him swig from their flasks. Even her brother Jamie, always at odds with their father, couldn't help swelling with a bit of pride for the man who could remember bits like this, making everyone instantly like John, and he'd become an instant a fast friend to them all.

Samuel leaned forward and gently placed a hand on Martha Anne's shoulder, bringing her back from her happy memory. She could feel the train slowing as the towers and steeples of the shining city were coming into focus. The train came to a halt at Piccadilly. As they waited their turn to disembark, Martha Anne noticed two young men in uniforms, not of England but some other nation that she could see by their insignias. They were speaking in a foreign tongue, looking at her, whispering and laughing, when one pointed at her. She could feel her face go red, but she had no idea why or what they'd said. She didn't know if she was as being complimented or insulted, and she could feel her knees weaken.

Suddenly, Samuel left her side and grabbed the taller of the two by his collar and shoved him hard up against a post. The whole train car got quiet, and Samuel spat some strange sounding guttural words into the man's face. Making him blanch, making him flinch. Both soldiers then switched to English and made many apologies to both Samuel and Martha Anne before they hurriedly disembarked.

'What were that all about?' she asked Samuel as they stood on the platform while he brushed down his suit, straightened his tie, and settled his cap on his head.

'Germans' was all he said.

'What about 'em?' She looked to see the pair in the foreign uniforms hustling down the platform away from them. 'What'd they say?'

'No mind. Not worthy repeatin'.' His tone was flat. He was bothered, she could tell.

'But about me?'

He looked into her eyes, and his face cracked into a grin reserved only for her at that moment. 'It might've been, but it might've been about me own sweet Mum.' His eyes twinkled, and he winked. 'Either way, we can't have foreigners speakin' ill of our English lasses in any language, can we?'

'How d'ya know German?' she asked, curious.

'I spent some time there. Father had relatives, and I would visit,' was his short answer. He took her arm and turned her towards the city, which she saw right away had grown in size, stature and grandeur in its architecture, industry, and energy. The town was humming. She could feel it. She'd never been to London or Edinburgh but couldn't imagine either being more awe-inspiring than Manchester. There were people on foot, riding horses, driving carts, businessmen in bowlers. A small boy driving a small buggy was nearly run over by a drover in a lorry pulled by two oxen. There were many riding those new bicycles. Martha Anne was shocked to see a red-haired woman wearing men's trousers riding one and carrying a giant bouquet in her basket.

They briskly walked as Samuel seemed to have a destination in mind, and she found herself being guided by his gentle but directing hand on her elbow. He was steering her in a certain direction and out of harms' way from each oncoming human, animal, or wheelbarrow.

They walked along Peter Street, where there were shiny new buildings already up and others being built. They paused at the corner near the Free Trade Hall before crossing, and Samuel pointed. 'There was St Peter's Fields. It was the site of the Peterloo Massacre,' he said.

She squinted towards the open square. 'A massacre? You mean where people were killed?'

He nodded. 'Fifteen, to be precise. Hundreds more injured. Working men, women, and even children were gathered for a peaceful protest when it happened.'

'When was that?'

'1819.'

'Mad George?' she asked and could see both surprise and delight on Samuel's face for her reference as he pulled his pipe from his pocket and struck a match.

'His reign, but he was already declared insane by then. So it was George IV who ordered the armed cavalry to charge into the crowd.'

'What were they protesting?'

He blew smoke above her head and nodded. 'They didn't have any representatives in Parliament. Had to do with these Corn Laws that put tariffs on grains and made food too expensive for the poor. Many people were starvin', and there was no one from the north in Parliament. So this chap, Henry Hunt, comes to give a speech for the rights of the people when the local authorities charged the crowd. Hundreds were injured by sabre, trampling, and bludgeoning. It were gruesome.'

Martha Anne let out a gasp. 'Oh no. But why?'

Samuel shrugged. 'Government never wants workin' men to have rights. Shut 'em up before you let 'em rile up, I suppose.'

She glanced over at him as he stared across the road as if he too were seeing the battle between the rich and the poor, right there in the bloody square. He was smart, she knew that, but he was also knowledgeable about many things: history, languages, art, and of course, numbers. A lot like her dad. She smiled at her own thought and then rolled her eyes at her realisation. Of course, that's why she liked him—he reminded her of her dad. She thought this but did not say it aloud. Instead, she turned to listen as he pointed to other historical and architectural spots and feats.

Before they stepped off the curb, Martha Anne placed a hand on Samuel's arm, making him pause in his stride. 'Samuel, while I am enjoying the sightseeing, I really must ask, where is our appointment?'

'Come on.' He nodded and grasped her hand. Before they'd gone halfway down the block, they stopped midpoint, and Samuel turned and faced the sizeable, pillared building across the street in front of them. He let go of Martha Anne's hand, spread his arms wide, and said, 'Here!'

She squinted as the sun was peeping from behind the massive block of sandstone that seemed to go one for miles. There were sweeping arches. She counted balconied windows and storied steps leading from left and right to its gaping doors. A stream of well-dressed patrons filed up the stairs and filtered into the venue. She couldn't quite make out the statue at its centre, a figure leaning on a pedestal, carved of dark grey marble. Maybe Shakespeare, she guessed. She had to crane her neck and step back to see the very top where curved in giant silver lettering was the word "ROYALE" and above each pillar carved into the stone, the word "Theatre".

'What's this?' She frowned, looking confused.

'It's the Theatre Royale!'

'So?'

'So…we're goin' to see a play!'

'What? In the middle of the day? We've come all this way to see a play in the middle of a workday?'

He kept grinning, but it was hard to keep the smile from slipping, as he was having difficulty understanding her questions and tone. He thought she would be delighted, but it appeared she was angry,' he couldn't be sure. 'I saw the flyers…and well…Millie said you liked the theatre—'

'Millie said?' This time she backed away from him. 'Millie shouldn't be sayin' nowt about me to you or anybody.'

She turned around to see if she could remember how to get back to Piccadilly, but the station had been swallowed up in the bustle of the city, and the tall buildings fenced off her line of sight. It was as if the passage they'd travelled to get here had never been or had disappeared as soon as they'd passed through.

She turned back to him. 'I need to get home. I have work. I have Frank. I have Dad!' She felt a panic set in, and tears pricked at the corners of her eyes. She squeezed them tight. She didn't know why she was so upset, but she felt as if she'd been tricked. She thought they were coming to Manchester on some sort of bank business. Did she recall Samuel mentioning a bank? She didn't think so now. Why did she think this? She wondered, trying to recall his invitation to come along. She smacked the side of her head with her gloved fist. Argh, she rumbled in her throat but was not sure it hadn't escaped. Madness.

She was trying to think back to that day when Samuel had invited her to Manchester. She admitted she hadn't been paying much attention. Frank was teething, she was fretting, and Dad had stumbled home. Yes, she remembered now. She'd agreed to the trip in a desperate attempt to get the baby upstairs and to leave her drunken father in Samuel's care. It had been weeks ago. In the jumble of time since she'd got it in her head that the journey to Manchester was purely business. A visit to a bank. She was sure. No. She was not sure. Maybe she wanted to believe they were banking so that she wouldn't believe she had said yes to such a lark.

Her heart was pounding. The clinking noise of hooves and clogs on cobbles, men yelling, carts, prams, bikes, carriages, wagons all rolling and rambling by, animals grunting, as were some people, and the metal on metal sounds of workmen pounding in the next nail, spike, or dowel joining walls and floors into place all made Martha Anne feel a rising within that made her want to flee. She looked up and down the street as if searching for help from some nearby stranger for an imaginary assault that was only happening in her mind. She twirled in a circle, sweating now in the chill air. She felt alone on the street but was not, and she began to run back the way they'd come. She bumped into an old man, tripped on a loose dog, and nearly toppled a babe in its pram. She was now hysterical, tears blurring all vision, and her lungs were bursting by the time she felt hands upon her shoulders.

Samuel pulled her out of the street, off the sidewalk, and into a ginnel where the sun could not reach. It was cold but dark and quiet. By then, she'd collapsed into his arms, choking and sobbing as if she would never, could never stop.

He crouched beside her and pulled her into his lap. Stroking her hair, he whispered, 'There, there…' Resting his head back against the brick wall where he leaned, he took deep breaths, trying to regain his own steady rhythm. He pulled a handkerchief from his pocket and handed it to her, but she was curled into a tight fist in his arms and did not take it. When he made a clumsy attempt to dab her eyes, he instead dabbed first her chin, then mouth, nose, and smeared the snotty cloth across her eyes. He noticed that her sobs became jerky, and she rose to a sitting position, taking the hanky from him.

She leaned back against the brick beside him, and when he looked over, he saw she was laughing. She was laughing as hard as she'd been crying, and the tears were still flowing, but she was definitely laughing, and he started laughing, and for no good reason since just minutes before, he was terrified that she'd lost her mind.

She folded the hanky and wiped her eyes, her cheeks, and even her neck before she blew hard into it. Then, taking deep sighing breaths, her laughter subsided into giggles, into whimpers, into long deep sighs, and she leaned against him. He, too, had calmed, and his breaths were matching hers. He finally spoke.

'You're laughin'?'

'Yes, I'm laughin'! You wiped me own snot into me own eyes is what ye done!'

He let out one last guffaw and then relaxed, while Martha Anne blew her nose again, and once more.

'You all reet?' he asked.

She shook her head. 'Apparently not.' She smiled and shrugged. 'Sorry. Dunno what 'appened.'

'You panicked.'

'Seems I did.' She was now feeling embarrassed.

'You've 'ad a lot on your plate, Martha Anne. Just since I've met you.'

She grinned. 'Should've seen me before you met me. I didn't even 'ave a plate as I just kept smashin' 'em. This is the steady me. Oh lord.'

'Can I ask 'ow old you are?' He was careful with his tone.

'Fifteen. Why? How old are you?'

'Twenty-two.'

'Nearly dead,' she said and smiled when he laughed.

They were quiet for a moment, sitting on the cold ground, leaning against one another, warming one another.

It was nice, he thought.

It was easy, she thought.

Surprising him, Martha Anne finally said, 'We should go see that play, Samuel.'

'Yes?' he asked eagerly.

'Yes.'

'We should get married, Martha Anne,' he dared.

'Yes.'

'Yes?'

'Yes.'

Martha Anne rose and attempted to swipe at her backside. 'Me bum's numb!' She giggled. Samuel stood, swiping his own coat, and when they'd both straightened, he looked into her eyes, leaned down and slowly kissed her soft lips. He felt himself aroused and pulled her tightly to him, letting her feel him before releasing her and grinning mischievously.

As they walked hand in hand towards the theatre, Martha Anne traced his kiss along her lips with her tongue. It wasn't a bad kiss, but his moustache had tickled her nose, and she was keenly aware of nearly sneezing right into his mouth. But for that, it would do. He wasn't Malcolm. There was no passion in that kiss. Well, at least not for her. For Samuel, he seemed excited by it. Good for him. At least, one of them would be happy. Since there would never be another Malcolm in her world, at least she and Frank would be settled and safe, just like Millie had said.

They slipped through the theatre's doors, and each were handed a fan-shaped program. They would be seeing "The Merry Wives of Windsor today", and she couldn't help but shake her head.

***

They were married in St Mary in the Baum, where all the Ashworths and Mosses had been married, baptised, and buried for decades and decades before them. Her dad had managed to stay sober long enough for he and Millie to stand up for them. Baby Frank was wearing a new bonnet and gown Samuel had bought for him and had remained amused by his gum stick while the vows were being said. No one else was witness, and there was no reception. Whom would she invite, and who would even come, anyway?

By the time they tied the legal knot, she was already carrying Harry, the first of Samuel Chadwick's babies, giving her three boys and one girl, just as Betty Nuppy had predicted.

Part Three
The Two Mrs Chadwicks

Chapter Twelve

1899

'Frank!' Martha Anne collared her eldest son as he was about to tear out the front of Prince Place to the streets to meet his pals down the terrace lane before school. 'Just a minute!' She managed to wrestle him into a chair at the table beside the fire. 'Now, sit there, and 'ave a piece of bread. I've got drippings.'

He watched as his mother placed the loaf upon her chest, like a fiddle, he considered. She then slid a big knife across the loaf, like a bow slicing across strings, and took off the crust and then two more thick pieces in the same manner. Whenever she did this, he watched in horror, certain she would one day slice off a bosom. Her reasoning, she'd complained, was that there were no clear counters in the small kitchen. 'Me bosom's handy for more'n feedin' babes!' she'd say and laugh, but everyone just prayed she didn't slice too far.

Frank's younger brother, Harry, slid into the chair beside him and piped up, 'Can I have toast an' drippin's, too, Mum?'

'Sure.' She sliced another piece. Then, peering over their heads, she looked down the hallway to the stairwell, cocked her head, listening to silence. Finally, she turned to the boys at the table. 'Where's Cyril?' she asked. Not waiting for an answer, she went to the doorway and called up the stairs, 'Cyril! You'll want breakfast this mornin', so 'urry down!'

As she passed hers and Samuel's bedroom, she looked into the small alcove to see that little Gertie was sitting up, copper-hair all a flutter, and rubbing her eyes. Even though she was well past four years old, she was still the baby, especially being the only girl.

Martha Anne slowed. 'Mornin', luv,' she whispered.

'Mornin', Mummy.' She reached her arms up and wrapped them around her mother's neck. 'I'm still very tired,' she confessed.

Martha Anne squeezed and settled her back in bed. 'Why don't you close your eyes for a bit longer while I get the lads off to school, and then I'll come for you. We'll 'ave tea with toast and drippin's together, eh?'

Gertie lay back against her pillow, put her thumb in her mouth, closed her eyes, and fell back to sleep. If only it were that easy, Martha Anne thought as she placed a kiss on her daughter's sweaty forehead.

In the kitchen, she turned the bread just before it went too dark and poured last night's fat drippings over it. She then placed teacups in front of her two eldest sons. They were just two years apart and had been inseparable since Harry's arrival. They adored each other, and this gave Martha Anne great comfort. As always, Harry's head was tilted, his rusty coloured hair poking in spiky directions, listening intently to something Frank was saying. *Listening for cues and clues*, she always thought of Harry's study of his older brother.

They were as different as night and day. Frank had dark eyes and lashes, his soft curls were nearly black, and he was tall for just nine years old. Topping her by inches nowadays, his grin produced the same dimple as his father's, whom he favoured more than any of Malcolm and Alice's pale squat skinny children, as she'd seen them in a picture posted last Christmas. Frank was also much like Malcolm in his curiosity and passion for those things that interested him. He was always on the go since a crawling babe when she'd have to tie a rope around his middle and a bell around his neck so that she wouldn't lose him in the house.

When he could finally be out on his own, whether she liked it or not, he'd be down Toad Lane or around the canal. Some said he was as easily found in Spotland as in Newhey. 'Once he was out the door, he was off with the lads, out on the moors'—*That could be a poem*, she thought.

On the other hand, Harry was a Lancashire lad, through and through—short, stocky, ruddy in colour, and rugged in constitution. He was also different from both Frank and Samuel in that he was a quiet, contemplative chap. He rarely spoke, but when he did, it made you want to listen to him, as his words were often quite thoughtful. He was careful in his manners and his words, and she could count him as the most loyal soul she'd ever known. Not just to Frank, but to both his brothers and his sister, too. He would defend them all to the end, fight with bare knuckles as he'd already proved at just seven years old. She knew but didn't let on that he carried a small knife in his pocket. As did Frank, but she imagined this son Harry would have no problem using it if he thought any of his beloveds were in a bother. He was quick with a smile, but it was always soft and rarely lingered. His eyes would twinkle at a joke, and he'd giggle, especially if it came from Frank, but there was a deep seriousness inside that quiet boy. And she somehow understood this about him, this profound loyalty that would make him capable of doing all he had to do to keep his family safe.

And then there appeared Cyril in the doorway. He, like Frank, was tall and lanky, all limbs, elbows, and knobs. His hair was thick and chestnut brown like hers, but he had his father's bright blue eyes. He'd come along just ten months after Harry, in the middle of a blizzard. As the midwife couldn't get to her, it was Samuel who'd caught him, wrapped him, and quieted him. Samuel was always the calm in the storm, the steady hand on an oft-near out of control rudder. When he caught Cyril and all his bloody aftermath, he looked down to his newborn son and said, 'Well, lad, we saved on the midwife, but it'll be spent on me new trousers and shoes! He had laughed and grinned at Martha Anne. When he stood with the bloody baby for Martha Anne to see, the wee one let out a fart first and then a giggle. And there they were, parents and babe all covered in blood, sweat, and tears, while Samuel and Martha Anne couldn't stop laughing. And as it made sense, Cyril was not surprisingly the funniest of her lads. He could make her laugh with a joke, a look, or even just a wink. Today, she couldn't help but look twice as he stood with his hair plastered to his skull, dressed in his Sunday best vest, jacket, tie, and cap! And he was carrying a large leather case.'

'And where do you think you're goin' in those funeral clothes?' she asked, staring at him. But she had to turn her back to him because he appeared to have taken a piece of coal to his upper lip and sketched in a bit of a moustache. She gave a quick look over her shoulder to be sure. The rest of his face looked scrubbed, and the black above his lip seemed quite deliberate.

'I've a job today,' he said, straight-faced.

'Well, you better wipe that smudge off your lip first,' Frank said. 'What on earth, Cyril?'

The little boy's eyes plumped with tears, but he managed to blink them back. 'Makes me look older,' he managed and puffed up his chest as best he could.

She composed by busying herself and said, 'Have a seat, then.' She dolloped a bit of porridge on each of their plates and filled a cup for him.

Martha Anne noticed he had Samuel's old briefcase, the one he'd kept under the bed. 'Here, luv, you can't take Dad's business case, sorry. He might need it.'

'It can't be opened. It's locked.' Cyril frowned and slunk into the chair across from his brothers.

Harry smiled and said more kindly than not, 'Look, lad, you need to wipe your face. Looks like a worm layin' there. Even Dad's real moustache isn't that big.'

'Worm?' Frank laughed. 'More like a turd! A cat turd!'

Cyril kicked under the table, missing his brother's leg but landing with a table leg, and the tea and toast went scattering.

'Awe, now look what you've done!' Martha Anne got up, sopped up the tea with a crust of toast, and put it down before Cyril. 'You'll eat a soggy end, then,' she said. Annoyed at all three, but as usual, it was Cyril (or Harry) who took the brunt. Martha Anne would never take it out on Frank. She knew it wasn't fair. She tried not to favour him, but she couldn't help it. She loved all her children, this was sure, but Frank was her only love-child, and maybe a mother shouldn't have one, but he was and always would be her favourite.

Martha Anne's annoyance did not last long when she saw that whatever coal or paint Cyril had used to make his moustache was now smearing, and he was holding back tears, she could tell. This broke her heart for her funniest son, and so she grabbed a towel and wiped the little boy's upper lip clean. 'You don't need a moustache to look older, luv,' she said, drying his tears, as well. 'You're already handsome and mature. They'll see that.'

He took a couple of deep breaths and reached for the soggy crust. His mother swiped it up, tossed it into the soup pot on the hob, and sliced a new piece for him. 'Now, what's this job you're on about?' she asked.

'It's a messenger.' He took a sip of his tea. 'I'm to wait outside "The Clock Face" for a chap to come by and give me a message. Then I run the message to whoever needs to hear it!'

'They pay you for that?' Harry asked.

'A penny a message!'

'What sort of message?' Frank asked.

'Dunno. Me mate, Jerry, told me about it. Went down last week, and it were true. Chap hired us right on the spot. Gave me half a P for me troubles, he said.'

'You not runnin' numbers for no gamblers, are you?'

Cyril was chewing his toast and shrugged. 'Dunno.' Wide eyed, he gave his mother an innocent stare. 'Who cares anyway? I'm just a wee lad, makin' a bit of pocket change.' He winked at her.

'Cheeky bugger you are.' Martha Anne swatted at her son's head. 'Don't come cryin' to me if they arrest you. Make 'em take you to your dad at the mill.'

'If he could be found at the mill, or anywhere else, for that matter,' Frank said with something of a disdainful tone.

'What's that supposed to mean?' Martha Anne turned and stared at him.

As Frank had gotten a bit older, a bit smarter, a bit cheekier, Samuel had become sterner with him, more demanding, less patient, and the pair had clashed on occasion, as fathers and sons will. But of late, Frank's contempt had become more emboldened when speaking of or to Samuel, and this made her nervous.

'Come on.' She slapped the rag on the table. 'What's up your bum?'

The boy shrugged, finished the tea in his cup, and made to rise.

'You've been reet cheeky about your dad—'

'He's not me dad…' Frank's words had come out quietly.

She'd spun around. 'What was that?' She saw the looks on the faces of her other sons, gob-smacked, looking from mother to brother. 'Harry! Cyril! Go on now. Out you go. School bell's ringin'. You'll 'ave to 'urry!'

When Frank got up with his brothers, his mother placed a hand on his shoulder and pushed him back down onto the chair. The lads clattered out of the house, Harry with his cap on sideways and Cyril with his boots on the wrong feet. She shook her head but stopped herself from stopping him. If he didn't figure it out, he deserved the blisters he would get. As soon as they'd run past the window and rounded the corner, she turned back to Frank and then slid into the chair beside him. He was studying his hands, not daring to look up at her. His curls near covered his eyes under the shadows of his dark lashes. God, he looked so much like Malcolm that it raised a lump in her throat.

Martha Anne calmly asked, 'What do you mean your dad's not your dad?'

He shrugged.

'That's a loaded accusation you've made, son. Why would you say that?'

Again, he just scraped away at his nails.

'Frank! Look at me!' She was losing patience with him.

'NO!' He stood. 'You look at me! Look at me brothers! Me sister! Me so-called dad. I favour no one in this 'ouse, not even you, Mum!'

'Oh, Frank, come on now. You look just like your uncle Jamie. That's who you favour. So what's put all this thinkin' into you?'

'It's not just that…' He paced the kitchen. 'I'm cack-handed! Nobody in this family is cack-handed.'

'I'm cack-handed!' Martha Anne waved her left hand.

'I meant anybody else!' He raised his right. 'They make me use this hand in school, and Mum, you know I cannot. I've nowt interests in common with Dad. In fact, we've opposite interests. And he has no interest in me.'

'That's just not true, Frank. You've spun a tale in your 'ead, and I'm not sure why.'

He looked out the window and shoved his hands deep into his pockets. Then, finally, he turned to his mother and took a breath. 'The lads told me.' He held his mother's eyes, which made her want to look away, but she couldn't. 'The lads say that I was a baby when you married Dad. Davey's mum said you…you had me out of wedlock, and nobody knows who me father is, but there were guesses…' He now looked away.

'Guesses? This is what people have to do with their time? Makin' up stories about people they don't even know. Guesses. What sort of guesses?'

'Well, not so much guesses, but speculations,' he said slowly. 'Sarah's mum said you were but a wee lass, and it must've been a bad man to put you in that way.' He moved away from her to the door. He settled the cap on his head. 'Some say it were a schoolteacher who was…inappropriate with you.' He raised a brow and stared at her as if waiting to see her flinch.

'They're reet fawzin' owd bitches,' she said defensively. 'Those mums should keep their gobs' shut.' Martha Anne made to shift blame. She then saw that her son was dismissing her indignation by winding a scarf around his neck. When he was done, he tucked the ends into his vest and looked up at her.

'Things happen that we've nowt to do with, Frank. Out of our control. Those gossips, they think they know the truth, but they don't know the half of it.'

'So, Samuel *is* me father?' the boy asked hopefully.

She'd decided for everyone's sake, especially Frank's, that she had to sever every hopeful thread that might lead back to Malcolm, and so she swallowed hard and then said, 'I had a run-in with a bad man.'

When she'd finished telling him of the incident, his easy birth, her joy despite how he came to her, she cried when she recalled leaving him with her mum and her mum dying, and she ended with how Samuel had rushed in, taken over, and saved the little family as it was spiralling out of control, and for this alone she was grateful to the man.

'But I'm not just grateful for this, Frank.' She looked hard at him, almost but not quite seeing the man that would grow out of that little boy's frame. 'I'm grateful that Samuel was willing to be a father to you, Frank.'

A cloud darkened his brow as it furrowed, and she could tell he was trying to work it all out.

She continued, 'Not many a lass in my situation would have had such luck, and not many a lad in your situation who could hope for such a good stepdad.'

Frank shoved his hands in his pockets now and looked every which way but at his mother.

'Dad treats you no better or worse than Harry or Cyril, and for this, you should be grateful,' she said.

'Can I go now?'

'Sure,' she said. He began to bolt, but Martha Anne stopped him. 'And, Frank, if you're not grateful to Samuel, you should keep your mouth shut about it.'

He left without another word, and she watched him pull up his collar and skulk down the lane, his shoulders hunched up around his ears.

That evening, after her babes were tucked into their beds, dry as hay in a croft beneath the pounding rain outside, she stood at the window, pulled back the sash, and watched, waiting for her husband to come home. It was well past even a late night at the mill or a visit to the pub. Samuel wasn't above having a pint or two, even a whisky now and again, but he wasn't a drinker. She'd never seen him drunk, and considering her own weakness and that of her father, she was glad for his temperance, as it gave her the self-control she'd lost in the past. To be sure, she looked to the clock on the mantel as it chimed midnight, only to see that it was correct, and then back to the dark empty street outside. No lamp light at this end of the row, and only a few dimly lit windows across the way, meaning old Biddy James was walking about from room to room, looking for a cat that had died ten years ago. This Martha Anne knew as she'd helped guide Biddy back home during one of her sleepwalks and had convinced her to find a way to lock herself inside, which she must've done as

Martha Anne had never had to retrieve her again, but did often see her pass by her windows looking for that damn cat.

'Samuel, where are you?' she said aloud to no one, except that Frank was behind her and answered with a question.

'Is he not 'ome, Mum?'

She turned and saw the worry on her boy's face and put out her arm. He came into her fold and under her wing like the little bird he was, not the angry lad he'd been that morning. 'No, he's not.' She smoothed his damp curls away from his forehead. 'Did you see 'im, today?' she asked.

He shook his head. 'No, but Davey said he saw me dad on the Spotland trolley this afternoon.'

'On the trolley?'

'That's what Davey said. He said he waved, but Dad either didn't see him or ignored him.'

'Well, that's odd. Not any mill business in Spotland that I know of, but what do I know?'

'Shall I go down to the Wellfield?' he asked, knowing Samuel would sometimes pop into the Workingmen's club at the end of the row for a pint or two.

'I think it must be closed at midnight, don't you?'

He had to agree. 'Are you worried?'

She smiled. 'Just a wee bit, but I'm sure he'll be home any time now. You go back to bed, luv. I'll be goin' meself.'

He made his way back up the stairs and climbed into bed with his snoring brothers, end to end in the little bed. A big safety pin through Cyril's nightshirt and the bed sheet ensured he did not try to go out the window in his sleep, as he'd almost done not long ago. Thankfully, Harry'd caught him and called to Frank to help pull him back inside just in time. Since then, they'd put him in the middle and pinned him to the bed.

But Martha Anne had not gone to bed, nor had Samuel come home. He must've spent the night at the mill, or perhaps he'd run into her dad, drunk, and helped him back to the manor, and decided to sleep there instead of coming back in the rain. So she'd got the boys off to school and out the door just as the downpour had waned to a drizzle. She was washing up, with Gertie's help, as she'd expected Samuel to be coming down the lane any minute. She waited until she could wait no more and finally got Gertie dressed, and the pair left and headed for the manor house.

When Millie came to the door, she said that John was sleeping off a wild bender from the night before. One of the lads from the mill brought him home just before she'd gone for the evening. She set him up with tea, and when she arrived this morning, he was in his bed soundly sleeping. She brought Martha Anne and Gertie into the kitchen beside the warm hob, and offered her a cuppa, and gave Gertie a little biscuit she'd just taken from the oven.

'So, it weren't Samuel that brought him home?' Martha Anne asked, stirring the spoon in her cup.

'No, no, it was one of the Bury lads. *Walter,* I think. But Samuel did come by earlier, around noon yesterday.'

'What did he come about?'

'Not sure. Said somethin' to do with some papers in John's study that he needed. Said he knew where they were, and he'd get them himself. I guess he must've found them because he left soon after.'

'Did he say where he was goin'?'

'No.' Millie detected the concern in Martha Anne's voice. 'Is somethin' wrong, luv?'

'He didn't come 'ome last night, nor this mornin'. And one of Frank's mates said he saw Samuel on the Spotland trolley, aft-noon.'

'The Spotland trolley? What's he got anythin' to do in Spotland?'

'Dunno. It's not like 'im. Not comin' home without sayin'. But I 'ave to admit, he 'asn't been 'imself these last few weeks, maybe months even.'

'What d'ye mean?'

'I dunno, he's been off, worried, I guess. Seems distracted, and he's been more impatient with the children. Even shoved Gertie from his lap when she'd got a bit of butter on his shirt and made her cry.'

'Oh, dear, but that's just normal bother, isn't it?'

'If it had been any one of the lads, I'd agree with you, but not Gertie. You know 'ow 'e fawns all over 'er as if she were a delicate flower.' She winked at her daughter, who looked up from her plate and pressed her fingers on top of the biscuit crumbs to get each one.

'I'm no delicate flower,' Gertie said. 'I'm an iron sword!'

The women laughed, and Millie raised her eyebrows in surprise. 'And what do ye know about iron swords, lass?'

'Me dad. He knows about a little boy named Arthur who pulled a sword from a stone.'

'Well, he must've been strong!' Millie said.

Gertie nodded her head enthusiastically. 'Stronger than all the knights in the land. They tried and couldn't pull it out.'

'My goodness, that's quite a tale.'

'After he done it, they made 'im king.'

'As they should've,' Millie said and smiled at Martha Anne. 'She's a wee bit like her mum, isn't she? A daddy's girl, eh?'

'That she is,' Martha Anne agreed. There was no one Gertie loved more, or even as much as her dad, and he in turn. After the lads were tucked in proper at night, Samuel would find a story in his big book of fables and sit beside Gertie's bed and read to her. He'd done it since she was a baby, which Martha Anne always thought endearing, but odd, as he'd never read to the lads. When he did this, she, too, would lie in bed in the next room listening along with her daughter. It reminded her of her childhood and the stories her dad would tell, the poems he'd recite, and the history he'd spin as she'd fall asleep listening to him reading of kings and queens, knights and wizards, castles and magical forests, fairies, leprechauns, talking animals, and worlds she would only ever visit in her mind's eye but were as real as if she were smelling the fragrant burst of a rare tropical flower herself.

She shook these thoughts from her mind, as pleasant as they were. She had a real problem now, and it needed attention, not a flight to another happier time of her life. Good lord. 'Millie, can I leave Gertie with you for a bit? I want to head over to the mill, see if Samuel's there.'

'Sure, luv. It's been a while since I've 'ad our Gertie all to meself! So what d'ye say, lass? Will you 'elp me wash up me bakin'?'

The little girl grinned, and said, 'For another biscuit, I will!'

'Cheeky little thing,' Millie said, laughing. 'All reet, then, another biscuit it is!'

'Now, Millie, don't be spoilin' 'er. She'll twist you around her little finger if you're not careful.'

Millie followed her to the door, and as Martha Anne stepped into the street, she turned around when Millie asked, 'Is it just 'is impatience that has you worried, luv? Or is it more?'

Martha Anne looked to the sky where the grey clouds were churning, but the rain had stopped, and the wind had slowed. She squinted back at Millie.

'It's more than moody, more than stress. He's been stayin' up late, worryin' over the mill's books, and when I ask how everything is, he snaps that it's fine and to let him be. A few months ago, he started goin' to so-called business meetings in Bury, Blackburn, Littleborough'

'What business could he 'ave there? The mill's here?'

'He's also been overnight to Manchester, at least twice, and he's been away later and later in the evenings.'

'I hate to ask, but do you think it's a woman?'

'Dunno. I'd almost say yes, without any proof, except for somethin' else.'

'What's that?'

'Last Sat'day, two men came to the house. One was dressed proper in a suit, had on a straw hat, carried a leather case. The other wore a peaky cap, looked a bit rough around the edges. He leaned on me good table in the entry, and I told him to get off, which he did, but the bugger 'ad the nerve to wink at me.'

'So, what about 'em?'

'They went into the kitchen, and Samuel asked me to take Gertie for a walk until they left.'

'And?'

'And I did, and when I got back, they were gone.'

'Did he say anythin' bout them?'

Martha Anne shook her head. 'He was distracted. Distant. In 'is own world. But he was pleasant, kind even, when he 'ad a game with the lads before sleep. But, later, when we went to bed, I asked him about those chaps. All 'e said was it was best that I do not ask questions I didn't want answers to. Then he rolled over and fell asleep.'

Now Millie felt worried. She thought it's one thing for a man to go wandering with other women. They all did. It was forgivable. But this? This was something else. Something she didn't know anything about. It was a men's world problem, and that was why she was glad she wasn't a man. Their problems were always more consequential, and their consequences were always more dire because they always had to fight each other. Every day of their lives, fighting each other for money, land, women, attention, but mostly a kind of power they imagined more important than God. They more often lost than won, and this tallying of losses and wins seemed the crux of every bad faith altercation man had had with each other since Cain killed Abel.

'What you gonna do?' Millie finally asked Martha Anne.

'I'll go to the mill, see what I can find out. Do us a favour and try to wake up Dad. Try to sober 'im up for me, would you? I might need whatever 'elp he can give me when I get back. Tell 'im he's needed. That might make 'im straight for a minute.'

'Be careful, luv,' Millie said, closing the door but leaving the crack as she watched Martha Anne hurry down the lane and across the highway towards the large red brick mill whose smokestacks had stopped chugging in the distance, which Millie thought odd.

***

As Martha Anne got closer, she began pushing through a wave of mill workers coming out of the buildings, not going in. She realised there was an uncanny silence in the air, and she looked up to the stacks to see that they were dormant. What was going on? She hurried on but eventually stopped a group of women to ask why they were leaving.

'Mill's closin',' one woman said but pushed by.

'Sorry, luv. Got to get 'ome,' and her mate added, 'furloughed.'

What on earth? She made her way to Samuel and her dad's shared office, only to find a constable posted at the door.

'Sorry, ma'am. Can't go in there,' he said as she tried to bypass him.

'What d'ye mean? What's goin' on?'

Just then, the door to the office opened, and the man who Martha Anne had seen at her house last week, the one in the straw hat and business suit who'd come with the ruffian, and who had sent Samuel into some sort of bother that night, was standing in front of her.

'Mrs Chadwick!' he exclaimed. 'Good to see you again.'

She frowned. 'I don't think I got your name.' She was thoroughly confused and tried to peer around him to see if Samuel was within.

'It's Thomas, Mark Thomas, and if you wouldn't mind stepping inside, we'd like to speak with you.'

She hesitated. She did not like the looks of this man. She did not like his tone of authority that he did not have here at her dad's mill, and she did not like that he said we'd like to speak to me. After all, who's we? She wanted to taunt, *Got a rat in your pocket?* But her only response, at that moment, was to step across the threshold and into the office chamber. What she saw within was nothing short of startling. There were two other men within. Strangers. Except she recognised the ruffian who'd leaned on her good table, and he was lifting files and papers from cabinets and drawers and piling them on her father's desk. Another man, bald as an egg, dressed in a business suit, with spectacles balanced at the end of his nose, was seated at Samuel's desk where every drawer was gaping open, and the man wearing glasses was scrutinising papers and writing down notes in a small black binder.

She turned back to Thomas. 'What's goin' on?'

He offered her a chair, but she did not want to sit. She did not want to look up at this arrogant man. She stood her ground, waiting for his answer, but he offered a question instead.

'Mrs Chadwick, do you know where your husband is?'

This stopped her. This was her question. This was what she'd come by for—for answers. This was her morning's quest, and now it seemed that she was not the only one looking for Samuel. He seemed to sense her surprise, or perhaps her weakening, and so he pulled a small stool from the corner and set it next to the proffered chair and gestured that they both sit, and she did.

'Who are you, Mr Thomas? And why are you 'ere? Why is the mill shut? Why are you goin' through me dad's files? And why are you lookin' for me 'usband?'

'Mrs Chadwick.' His voice softened, and his demeanour had become less stern. 'I can see that you know nothing of what is happening here.' His accent was clipped, quite proper, educated. Londoner, she surmised, as he certainly wasn't lanky. She just stared at him as he stated the obvious, waiting for him to tell her all that she did not know.

'Per'aps you could get reet to it, Mr Thomas, as you're correct,' she said through clenched teeth as she gripped the edge of the chair, trying with all her might not to leap to her feet and start screaming. Instead, she said, 'I've not a clue what in bloody 'ell is goin' on, except I've got a sodden father back at 'ome, four babes under ten, a shut mill, strangers goin' through me dad's stuff and a missin' 'usband, so the quicker you get to the point 'ere, the quicker we'll all be in the know.'

He pulled a small white card from his pocket and handed it to her. 'I represent the Flannery Cotton Textile Mill, over in Preston.' He hesitated but could see the impatience on her face and quickly got to the point to which she insisted. 'Mrs Chadwick, Flannery has taken over Moss Mill. Moss had been operating under the weight of many hundreds of pounds in debt.' He paused to let that sink in. 'When your father couldn't pay the bills, the mill went into foreclosure, and there'd been a lien on it. Mr Ashworth and Mr Chadwick had been working with one of the banks, but despite the mill doing fairly well, they could not pay off the lien in time, and so Flannery did, and here we are.'

'A lien?'

'Yes, ma'am, a lien is when—'

'I know what a lien is, Mr Thomas. I may look like an uneducated charwoman, but I assure you I am not,' she said with great aplomb but did not feel it.

'I assure you, Mrs Chadwick, I did not mean to insult. I am sure this is a blow.'

She slumped back in her chair, all bravado wilting. 'I don't understand. Neither Dad nor Samuel ever mentioned a word. How long did you say this was goin' on?'

'I don't know how long it took for the mill to run red, but the lien has been about six months.' He decided to keep quiet while this digested. 'There's something…more, something else, Mrs Chadwick.'

Her eyes narrowed, and her heart quickened as she could feel something even worse coming, but what could be worse than her dad losing the family business, and with Samuel's help? Samuel was supposed to save the mill, not lose it. What on earth? She could barely wrap her mind around it.

'What more,' she finally managed.

'It appears…well, it seems…'

'Get on w' it,' she demanded as his caution just made it all worse.

'It seems that your husband, that Mr Chadwick, has been skimming off the top for quite a while.'

'What d'ye mean "skimming off the top"?'

'Embezzlement, Mrs Chadwick. We believe your husband has been embezzling from Moss Mills for over five years.'

This now was the blow. Samuel was not layin' about with some trollop, as would've been her preference if truth were told. No, this was worse than a straying husband. This…this would be their undoing. This now was the moment of reckoning. This explained more about the last few months than she could wrap her mind around. This was why her husband did not come home. This explains why he'd been spending nights away. This is why Davey saw Samuel on the Spotland trolley just yesterday. This, she knew, was why she would never see her husband again. She looked into Mr Thomas' eyes, and she could see certain compassion, pity maybe, and this nudged tears and tightened her throat, and she looked around the office not knowing what to say, what to do, where even to settle her eyes, and so they wandered back to Mr Thomas.

In the smallest voice, she asked, 'What's to become of us?'

***

They'd lost everything, including Moss Manor. The morning she walked the three long miles with her dad to the Dearnley Workhouse was bitter cold. She could see their breaths in the air as they chugged along Halifax Road, neither saying much. There'd already been so much apology, regret, accusations, excuses, insults, and forgiveness spoken, yelled, screamed, spat, cried and whispered between them in the days since the mill's takeover and Samuel's disappearance that it was only just their company to keep them warm, and she was okay with this turn as there was no other.

John's dive into the bottle had finally tipped him, and there was nowhere to go, nowhere to live. Both Martha Anne and Millie had offered him room, but he turned them both down. He deserved the workhouse, he'd confided through tears, and would hear of nothing more.

As it turned out, Mr Thomas wasn't a bad sort as he was just doing his job. She'd gotten John straightened up long enough to meet with Mr Thomas, who took pity on the pair. It seemed that Samuel had duped them both equally, so he'd given John some time to get his affairs in order. He'd allowed him to sell off furnishings and turned a blind eye when John pocketed his late wife's gold jewellery, even though all the returns should've gone back to the mill. He'd done something else kind—he had offered Martha Anne a job at the new mill and allowed her and the children to remain at 1 Prince Street. She took him up on both.

Her dad slowed and paused against a stone wall. Taking deep breaths and bending over, she could hear the years of cotton lung taking its toll as he coughed up a bit of phlegm and spit into a handkerchief. Before he put it away, she thought she saw a splash of bright red on the white cloth and recalled her mother's dying breaths were accompanied by left red spittle on her lips.

'You *all reet,* Dad?'

He nodded, then gestured with his handkerchief, wiping his chin and tucking it back in his pocket. 'I'm winded, but I'll be fine. I think it's just around the bend, up ahead, Martha Anne. So why don't you turn back here, and I'll be off on me own, luv?'

'No, Dad. I'm goin' with you. I'll turn back when I 'ave to, and not a step sooner.'

As the massive red brick building appeared before them, its centre a clock tower, and surrounded by a quadrangle of buildings, she was taken aback by the size of it. The two stood, taking it in for a good bit before looking at one another.

'It's like a village inside a village,' she said.

'It's reet big, isn't it?'

'Are ye sure about this, Dad?' She could feel her throat constrict, tears prick, and she wanted to take her father's hand and pull him away from the far-reaching prison, bring him home to her tiny lot, let him sleep on the couch and putter around, but she knew, dammit, she knew it would never be like that…No, he'd sleep on the couch, all reet, pissed, wreaking, and ready to do it again the next night and the next, and she knew for the sake of her children, she could not have that in the house.

Instead of answering, upon seeing her tears, John, in proper form, grinned and tipped his cap to her and began:

'Hush-a-bye baby, on the treetop,
When you grow old, your wages will stop,
When you have spent the little you made,
First to the Poorhouse and then to the grave.'

She fell into his arms and wept. He held her until he could bear it no more, kissed the top of her head, tilted her chin to look into her eyes, and said, 'You always were and always will be my "Gifted Girl".'

And with that, he turned and headed through the gates of Dearnley. She watched until he disappeared beyond the checkpoint when she could see him no more. And it was no more, as he'd died just three weeks later, right there in the poorhouse, not a shilling left for a headstone. So down into the pauper's grave he went, and there was nowt she could do about it.

***

It was just a few days beyond her father's passing when she'd felt like things could maybe get to some new normal when a small miracle happened. She'd been clearing out Samuel's things when she came upon the leather case that Cyril had found beneath the bed and needed for his business venture. As he'd declared, the case was locked, and she'd made him put it back, but now that Samuel was gone and nothing was stopping her from doing it, she took a knife and sawed through the leather strap attached to the little lock. Pulling back the flap, she opened the case, but it appeared empty. She reached in, and at the bottom, she felt something and pulled out a white envelope. There was no writing on it, but within was a packet of pound notes. Twenty-five of them, she counted. These, she'd decided, were needed for a rainy day. Then she laughed, thinking that in Lancashire, a rainy day could be today, tomorrow, and the next six months. She checked the time to see it would be a few hours before the children returned from school, and so she made her way to Millie's house.

'Martha Anne!' Millie said, smiling. Millie hadn't seen the younger woman since the manor house had been sold and was delighted to see Gertie by her side. She leaned down to hug the little girl. 'Come in, come in.' She opened the door wide. 'Can I get you a cuppa?'

'No, no, thanks, Millie. We can't stay.' She did not move from the vestibule into Millie's house but instead remained at the door. 'I've come with a favour to ask, though.'

'Sure, luv, anythin'. What is it?'

Martha Anne handed the packet of money to Millie. 'I need you to keep this for me.'

Millie peeked into the packet and looked surprised.

'I found it in a satchel Samuel kept under the bed. I need you to keep it safe for me.'

'What you on about?'

'Honestly, Millie, I've been known to like the drink as much as me dad, so I'm givin' you this to hold onto for me. So I don't spend it on whisky. I may need it someday, and I know I can trust you to 'ang onto it for me. For me babes.'

'Where'd it come from?' Millie asked, looking at the packet.

'It were locked in Samuel's satchel. Under our bed.'

'Do you think you were meant to find it?'

'Do you mean do I think Samuel left it for us on purpose?'

'Yeah, I guess that's what I mean.'

'If so, we're worth shite to 'im, aren't we? Twenty-five pounds is all we're worth. I'd rather think he forgot the money than to think he actually thought about how little we meant to 'im.'

'I understand, luv.' She went to give the woman a hug, but Martha Anne would not indulge in that embrace or any from now on.

'I've got to get 'ome. Now, Millie, don't you dare give me that packet if I'm pissed, if I can't tell you what I want it for, and only use it for me children if I wind tits up before they're grown.'

Millie laughed. 'All reet, then. I'll keep it safe till you need it or know what you want it for, is that it?'

She walked out to the street. 'That's it!' she called and waved.

When she got home, there was a basket on her doorstep. Inside were vegetables, herbs, teas, powders, pastes, tinctures, and scents of every sort she could smell. Martha Anne looked around to see that she was alone on the lane. She rummaged through the basket, but there was no card, no name, nowt to say who'd delivered it but she knew the gift-giver, and hugged the basket to her chest. She pushed her nose close to its contents, took a big breath and closed her eyes.

'Thank you, Betty,' she whispered into the fragrant lot of flowery remedies in her arms.

Chapter Thirteen

1902

'And there I were, left w' four little ones, all on me own,' Martha Anne said to the stranger standing to her right at the bar. He was an older gentleman with a thick head of white hair and trimmed moustache, and he was nodding sympathetically as the young woman spun her tale of woe. She'd been a beauty once as he could see past the hardness around her mouth and the wary look about her eyes. Lines fanned her temples and crossed her brow. Each told of a life that had been especially difficult despite or perhaps because of her fading beauty. She couldn't have been more than twenty-five, and he suspected she'd not even reached that age.

She lifted her pint glass and tipped it to empty. She eyed the gentleman over its top. Then, she set it down on the bar and made to feel around her apron, coming up empty as well.

'Would you do me another, luv?' she asked her companion. 'I've drained me pint, and 'aven't a ha'penny in me pouch for another.'

The gentleman gestured to the barkeep to bring them each another.

'Awe, thanks, luv. I surely don't want to go 'ome now. Not to that one.'

'No?' the man asked, his eyebrows shooting up with his question. He wasn't terribly interested in her story, but he liked her voice and was content to hear her talk.

'No, 'e's a bad lot, this Fred. But I were desperate when we met, I admit. What were I s'posed to do? No 'usband. Laid off at the mill. Then, me middle one, Cyril, 'e run out in front of a mule cart, and the wheel went right over 'im. Broke three ribs, from what the doc could tell. Course, that set me back, one thing after another, and then I met this chap who had a sympathetic ear, ha! Too bad 'is backhand weren't more sympathetic,' she said, and touched the bruise beneath her eye.' She took a small sip of the lager, wanting to make it last, wanting to get slowly drunk instead of pissed right away. 'I told 'im right off that I 'ad a whole passel of wee ones and not a lot of patience for any of 'em, bein' a single mum, alone and all. That's the only reason I took up w' 'im. Fred, that is, and that's the only reason I don't want to go 'ome now.'

There was a tap on her shoulder, and she turned to see a woman about her age, maybe a bit older, dark hair piled high atop her head, much rouge on her cheeks, red lips, and eyes rimmed black. She looked vaguely familiar to Martha Anne, but she couldn't quite place her.

'Tiny Teacher, is that you?' the woman asked.

Hearing the woman's voice and her childhood nickname (given by the ladies down at the canal), she knew right away it was her old friend, Dolly. She was the lass who'd given Martha Anne the scarf she had around her neck just now. Martha Anne smoothed it between her fingers. Dolly was also the one who'd given her a good smack when Martha Anne had attempted to follow Dolly around the corner with a chap who was about to pay a hefty sum for having his wanker yanked. Martha Anne recalled the sting of that slap, but also the protectiveness in it and that of the other older lasses who'd kept her safe from the wolfish canal men who'd eyed her, even before her bosom had blossomed. Those ladies of the night made sure she was safe from the louts, and they also taught her how to smoke cutties, drink whisky, and pick the pockets of market shoppers. Before she left them for Malcolm, they'd each been like a mother hen to her and were successful in their mission because not once had she'd gone 'round the corner' with a leering chap.

'Dolly? Is that you?' Martha Anne asked but knew it was and tried squinting to blur away the lines around Dolly's mouth, across her brow, and the V between her eyes to see the younger version of the woman. The one, many years ago, when she'd sung "God Save the Queen" with in front of the fire at the Flying Horse one cold winter's night while all in the pub had swayed and lifted their glasses to Her Majesty.

After they had finished their merriment, that long ago snowy night, Martha Anne and Dolly had climbed the hundred and twenty-four steps (they'd counted) to St Chad's, the parish church at the top of the hill. They'd stopped to rest, and each turned their faces to the sky to feel the cold flakes of snow falling lightly and melting upon their cheeks. It was refreshing, she recalled, and she felt less pissed than she had at the bottom of the steps. She looked over and saw that Dolly had stuck out her tongue and was catching flakes.

'Come with me!' Martha Anne had grabbed Dolly's hand and ran around the long church that cast dark shadows across the whitening landscape. Graves and headstones suddenly surrounded them. Martha Anne dropped Dolly's hand and appeared to be hopscotching from one marker to another in search of something, or someone, and then, as if remembering, she scurried to the back corner of the courtyard where an iron fence surrounded a solitary grave. She climbed the rail with its sabre blade-tips pointing skyward and hung on peering over the top, looking down on the rectangular raised tombstone.

Dolly caught up and was out of breath when she demanded, 'What the bloody 'ell are we doin' 'ere?'

'It's the grave of Tim Bobbin, the famous Lancashire poet. He's a favourite of me dad's.'

'Let's go. It's spooky 'ere.'

'He wrote his own epitaph, did you know?' Martha Anne reached through the bars, attempting to wipe the snow from the cold stone.

'I don't even know who 'e is, nor do I care,' Dolly said, cinching her collar around her neck and backing away from the drunk girl hanging on the tomb of a dead poet.

'They say 'e wrote it just minutes before 'e died.'

'Wasn't that 'andy,' Dolly said, moving through the snow, away from Martha Anne, away from the gravestones, towards the road that would take her home.

'You can't see it for the snow, but it reads, "Jack-of-all-trades…left to lie in the dark". Don't you think that's sad?'

Martha Anne turned to discover that Dolly had disappeared in between the falling snowflakes and into the darkness beyond the graveyard's wall. She herself had remained to repeat a line or two from the poems her dad would recite, but if truth be told, she was drunk and cold—ha! She was a poet, after all. She laughed, climbed down from the fence rail, and ran across the graveyard as if she were being chased by a ghost.

That, if she recalled correctly, was the very last time she'd seen Dolly. Long before Malcolm, before Frank, before she near killed Betty Nuppy, before her mum died, before her dad went to the workhouse to die, before a husband had abandoned her, and before she'd taken up with a loser who liked to take a swing or two at her when he didn't have anything else to do.

'It tis I, Dolly, yes.' The woman smiled, revealing a missing tooth at the front. 'Been a long time, 'asn't it? Last I remember, you was just a lass. Now look at you, all grown up. How've ye been?'

Martha Anne shifted and turned her back on the gentleman who'd just bought her lager and leaned against the bar, fixing her gaze on Dolly. 'I'm all reet, thanks. And you?'

'Can't complain. I've a good job cleanin' the rooms, upstairs at the hotel, 'ere. But I'm just gettin' off, so I thought I'd come down for a nightcap before goin' 'ome. Can I buy you another?' She pointed to Martha Anne's near-empty glass and gestured to the barkeep for a refill and a whisky for herself.

Dolly pointed to Martha Anne's eye where a fading purple bruise had yellowed, and she said low, 'Now, you say you're all reet, but that shiner would tell me another story. What's up w' you, Martha Anne? You didn't give yourself that black eye,' the woman said sympathetically.

Martha Anne made a lame attempt at pulling her hair over the bruise, but to no avail, and so she gave up and drained her mug.

'Yer right, Dolly. I didn't give meself this eye, and I'm not proud to say I'll be leavin' here in just a few to go back 'ome to the brute who gave it to me.' Martha Anne now sipped from her refreshed beer.

'Awe, lass, I 'ate to 'ear that, and you such a lovely girl, 'ow'd you come by him?'

'Well, as I was just tellin' me friend here...' She thumbed over her shoulder to the gentleman who'd bought her previous round, and she turned a bit towards him. 'What's your name again, mate?'

'It's Charlie,' he said and raised his glass towards Dolly. 'Duckworth— Charlie Duckworth.'

'Charlie, that's it!' Martha Anne patted his shoulder with one hand and Dolly's with the other. 'And this is me old friend, Dolly. We 'adn't seen each other in forever, isn't that right, Dolly?'

''Tis, must be ten, fifteen years, don'tcha guess?'

'I was just tellin' Charlie 'ere, that I like to stay out at the pub, coz if 'e comes home pissed, and I'm there, 'e likes to bat me round, but if he gets 'ome ahead of me, 'e mostly passes out, and I can slip in without rousin' 'im.'

'Have you married 'im?' Dolly asked, settling back on the barstool, readying for a good story. She noticed that Martha Anne had once again turned her back on Charlie, and he had carefully left his seat and joined a group of men watching a couple of lads playin' darts.

'Oh, no.' Martha Anne shook her head. 'I am married, but not to this one. No, me 'usband, he's called Samuel, and he just up and disappeared one night. Left me with four babes. I was in a situation. No money, rent due, me little girl got the cough, and three boys with bottomless pits for stomachs.' She smiled warmly, even though her tone was harsh. 'That's when I took up with this other one. I was in a jam. His name's Fred,' she said and gladly took the lager from the barkeep.

'Not Fred Collingwood?' Dolly asked.

'Yeah, you know 'im?'

'Ooh, 'e's trouble, Martha Anne. You need to get away from 'im.'

'Tell me. But I've got twin boys from 'im. They're just a couple months old, so can't afford to leave.'

'By the looks of ye, ye can't afford to stay.'

Martha Anne took a long draught on this next glass and felt warm through and through. She was glad to see Dolly. It reminded her of better days when she didn't have six babies and a wife-beater waiting for her at home. She was happy to have a mate to be out with for the night. The little ones would be asleep, and Gertie, a proper little mum, would care for the babies if they awoke. Martha Anne just needed out of the house for a bit.

'When I first met Fred, he was funny, generous with a joke and a pint or two, and he started comin' around. Next thing I know, I'm pregnant, and 'e moves in, which I didn't fight one bit as his paycheck were bigger than mine, but then Alf and Norman came, then Fred got laid off, and that's when he started smackin' me around.'

'He's got a wife, you know,' Dolly casually said as if she were revealing the ownership of a dog or a cat he had. 'Her name's Olive. Lives in Oldham. She booted him. That's after she 'eard about you.' Dolly put her hand in the air. 'Swear on me grave, I didn't know you was you…What I mean is, I didn't know Fred had left Olive for you. I just heard he'd moved in with someone else.'

'How do you know all this?'

'Ah, I've known Olive since we were lasses, lived in the same terrace. She met Fred when they were workin' at the mill together. He was a bad lot from the start. He was violent to the kids and Olive. I told her back then to get rid of him, but she wouldn't listen. She has two by him as well, you know.'

'He's married, eh? He never said.' Martha Anne was feeling panic or anger or resentment—she wasn't sure what it was—but with the drink going to her head, she finally let out a laugh and said, 'Oh well, who am I to judge, eh?'

Dolly laughed. 'What's good for the goose is good for the gander!' She looked around to see the pub emptying, and only a few old men left behind. She nudged Martha Anne. 'What you say we get out of here? Go up to Toad Lane, see if the Clock's open?'

They stumbled out of the Flying Horse and into another and then another until they were right pissed and got tossed out of the Clock Face after they'd got into a brawl with some other ladies of the night, and all of them landed on their arses on the road outside, when Dolly pulled Martha Anne out of a pile of bruised and drunken whores and said, 'Come on, let's get outta 'ere before the coppers come.'

They somehow made their way to the Wellfield Working Men's Club at the opposite end of Prince Street to Martha Anne's home. Without knowing, Dolly lived just a couple of rows over on Percy Street, and each was equally surprised to learn this of the other, as they'd never once met up, even though they seemed to fancy the Wellfield Men's Club, which let in women despite its name.

When Jack, the barkeep, saw them coming in, arms around shoulders, holding each other up, he cocked his chin to his son, tending to the end of the bar, who looked up to see the two pissed women swaggering into the room. They were disheveled, loud, uproariously shouting greetings to the room, words so slurred no one could understand them, but as good lanky lads will all the patrons lifted their pints to the pair, who took it as a sign to head to the bar.

Before they made it to the empty spot before him, Jack pulled his son aside and said in his ear, 'Go fetch the Chadwick lads, tell them their mum is here, tell them she's pissed, and they need to come to get her.'

His boy was out the door just as Dolly slapped her hand on the smooth mahogany and shouted, 'Barkeep!'

'There 'e is.' Martha Anne pointed to Jack and managed, with some difficulty, to get up on the barstool in front of him. 'How are you, luv?' she asked him. 'Still married? Don't make me sad, now, you 'andsome chap...'

She leaned over towards him but rested her head on her arm, only to be startled upright when Dolly called out to the room, 'Who's gonna be the gent to buy me and me lady friend here a nice strong whisky?' She looked around and saw the exchanged glances between some of the younger chaps and teased further, 'Who knows what might be the prize "round the corner" with me, or me lovely pal 'ere, Martha!'

Someone called out, 'Whisky for a wank-job, is it?'

And the room exploded with laughter.

'You up first, luv?' Dolly persisted and did not let his insults offend her but as encouragement, instead. She moved away from the bar and to the lad who thought himself funny just minutes ago, but when the drunk woman grabbed between his legs, he first turned red and sputtered, but upon seeing all eyes upon his stiffening manhood, he pushed her away and spit.

'Oh, now, dearie, no need for that,' Dolly said, straightening up. 'Nowt to be ashamed of.' She pointed, and pairs of eyes followed her direction to the darkening spot bleeding through the crotch of his britches where he'd shot his wad within minutes of Dolly's fondling attention. 'All the virgin boys let go *pre-ma-toorly*'—she drew this out—'the first time they have their wanker yanked. You're not alone,' she said slyly as she swayed a bit.

'You cunt!' the boy yelled, as those around him pointed, sniggered, and laughed outright.

'Another round!' someone shouted. 'To the lad's manhood risin'!'

'Cheers to a good hard spindle!'

'Cheers to a canon goin' off on its own!'

And with each jest, the room erupted in laughter until the humiliated lad pulled his coat around himself and fled into the night. And that would've been the end of it, except the lad apparently had a lass with him, and she was none too happy with Dolly's antics. She was possibly equally as drunk as Dolly and took a swing at her, only to have Dolly duck and miss, and so she took another swipe at her. Upon seeing this, Martha Anne rushed from the bar and ran at the woman. The three drunkards were throwing punches, pulling piles of hair, kicking shins, biting ears and noses. But it was Dolly who'd taken a wide swing and connected with Martha Anne's chin, lifting her off her feet, spinning her around, and landing her like a ragdoll, flopped against the wall. That was when the Chadwick lads came through the door and saw their mother. The oldest, Frank, grabbed Martha Anne under the arms and pulled her around, heading for the door. He directed his brothers, Harry on one side and Cyril on the other, to grab each of their mum's arms and pull. And pull they did with all their might, they pulled her out the door and onto the cobble street where they dragged her up past the darkened terrace houses, her clogs sparking on the cobblestones.

They stopped for breath, and while Frank checked their mother's pulse, Harry, in his most serious and curious voice, asked, 'Do you think if we ran as fast as we could, her clogs would spark enough to catch her feet afire?'

Frank stood, satisfied his mother was still alive and smacked his brother upside the head. 'Don't be stupid.'

But Cyril laughed. 'We could 'ave a go of it, Frank. She won't know.' He pointed to his mother, now snoring on the sidewalk.

'Awe, shite!' Frank pointed. 'She's pissin' 'erself,' They looked to the stream coming from her skirt.

'See there, Frank! If we run and her feet catch on fire, the pee will put it out.' He couldn't help but laugh, bending over, attempting to catch his breath. 'Am I reet, 'arry?'

Harry smiled but shook his head. 'Come on, let's get 'er 'ome before Fred gets there. Otherwise, there's bound to be 'ell to pay.'

They'd washed up Martha Anne as best they could. It wasn't the first time this kind of thing had happened with their mum, and it wouldn't be the last. They'd managed to get her into the bed long before the man of the house arrived just shy of daylight, also drunk as a lord. The lads had taken turns staying up in case Fred came home looking for a fight and tried to take it out on their mother. But he hadn't. Instead, he'd stumbled into the bed, next to Martha Anne, with his boots on. As the knocker-upper went by, all three lads climbed the stairs to their bed and fell to sleep on either side of each other. Before his eyes closed, Harry slid his hand into the pillow that was his and his alone and felt the long-handled knife. He'd recently acquired it in a swap for his old penknife and a ball of twine he'd been winding for a whole year, but it was worth it. This knife was the only protection or defence he needed—sliding his fingers along its carved handle—if that monster ever decided to hurt their mum or any of them again.

Chapter Fourteen

1904

'Mum! Mum!' Gertie shouted as she shoved the door open and dashed inside to find her mother. 'Mum! They've got the lads!'

Martha Anne came around the kitchen table to see her daughter, hair flying about her head, frock hanging off one shoulder, eyes wide, and missing two teeth. She saw that the girl had on a pair of her brother's old clogs, and these were barely staying on her feet.

'Oh, Gertie, now what is it?' She saw out the open door behind her daughter a commotion of the neighbours' children, all chattering and pointing and coming towards the front gate.

'They've nabbed both Cyril and 'arry!'

'Oh, good lord.' Martha Anne wiped her hands on her apron and went to the entrance to see her younger sons, each held by the scruff of his neck by two constables who were rapping one or the other across the head with a baton as the boys tried to wriggle away. She closed the door behind her and went to the gate, where she shooed away the children and gave each nosy neighbour a look that would wither Wolfsbane, sending them a bit further along the row, but not so far as to be out of earshot of the bother that was coming down the lane.

Martha Anne crossed her arms and waited for the constables to deposit her sons at her gate, which they did, throwing the lads against the wall where they landed on their bums and where their mother told them to stay put.

'What's up your copper arses now, Constables? Do you not 'ave anythin' better to do than to chase little boys round? Are there no real criminals out there?'

'Mrs Chadwick,' the larger of the two men began, taking a deep breath as if he'd just swam the sea. His face was bright red, and he was sweating profusely. 'Your lads are real criminals, madam! They've been caught runnin' numbers again, and not for the first time!'

'Well, you mustn't be doin' your jobs very well at all, sir! Can't catch grown-up criminals, can't keep little lads from becomin' criminals. I think we need new coppers to actually stop old crooks if you ask me,' she said, more to the gathered crowd than the constables now wiping their faces and eyeing the group of women and children, who were nodding and murmuring their support for new coppers (and old crooks). While neighbours had mostly flooded Prince Street to see what spectacle those rapscallion Chadwick lads had gotten themselves into this time. They also did not like the authorities who came around to harass good workin' people, so any chance to harass back was eagerly taken.

She stood with her chin up, but her heart was pounding. The last thing she needed or could afford were either of these two lads in trouble with the law. It wasn't the first time. It'd started with Cyril running messages, he'd said. Then he dragged Harry into it. And she'd been turning a blind eye since they were both adding shillings to the jar in the cupboard. With Frank now doing an apprenticeship at the abattoir, there would be enough money to give Fred Collingwood the boot sooner than later if she ever got up the nerve. If Dolly was right about anything that horrible night at the pub, it was that Fred Collingwood was no good, and this row with police over her lads would surely be trouble for them all. She was more afraid of Fred than she was of any copper.

'Where's your 'usband, missus?'

'Ha! Your guess is as good as mine, but when you find 'im, tell 'im his children are starvin'.'

'What about the bloke who lives 'ere, wi'ya?' The other one had a pencil out and seemed prepared to take some sort of statement.

'What about 'im?' Martha Anne asked.

'Is 'e the father of this rotten lot?' He gestured with his pencil to Harry and Cyril.

Harry got brave and stood up, yelling, 'He's not our dad!'

Cyril joined him and shouted, 'That's right! He's not our dad!'

The larger of the two officers seemed to be in charge, so Martha Anne pulled him aside. 'Can I 'ave a word?' she asked.

He stepped aside as she'd asked and took a handkerchief out of his pocket and wiped his brow. 'What can we do for you, missus? It's a right bother, 'avin' to sort out these lads of yours every other day. I don't expect they're bad lads, just a bit cheeky, and missus, if I might be frank, they are breakin' the law.'

She nodded and let out a great sigh. 'I know.' She put up her hand. 'I know. You don't 'ave to tell me what path they're on. I can see it already, as little as they are. But can I ask a favour? I'll promise anything, but please don't let this mess get back to the bloke who lives 'ere.' She pulled up her sleeves to show the constable the purple bruises up and down her arms. 'I can show you more, but I'd 'ave to charge you.'

She grinned, trying out the joke, which fell flat.

'What I'm sayin' is, if he finds out about the lads, I'm bound for more of this, and as they've been getting older, Fred's been goin' after the babes.' She looked at him, most sincere, something she need not dig deep for, something right there—her life—no lies, no exaggerations. She was begging that he not unleash that monster upon her and her babies. 'Just give me a week or two. I'm savin' up. I'll be able to boot him out and pay better attention to the lads.' She was trying not to beg, but she couldn't help the circumstances. 'I'll send the lads around to the station. Maybe they can clean up or somethin'. Just, please, can we not make this anymore public than it is?'

He called over to his partner, and together they conceded that the lads could come around the station in the morning, and they'd find something for them to do.

Then, the boss of the pair gave Martha Anne a card with his name on it: Constable Billy Smith. 'If you or them lads ever get in trouble, you come callin' for me, all reet?'

She read the card and slipped into her shift. She nodded. 'Thanks. Thanks so much. I promise I'll do me best to get them on the straight and narrow...'

He lifted a brow and gave her a minute.

On cue, she said, 'And meself, as well.'

She talked with the lads, and when Frank came home from the abattoir, she'd told him what happened and that no one, not one of them, was to whisper a word of it to Fred when he got home. She told them seriously that she wanted them to keep quiet and let her handle it.

They'd gathered around the table in the kitchen, where there was a fire in the hearth and soup on the hob. They were all waiting on tenterhooks for Fred to come through the door, home from the mill. It was dark outside. The rain battered the windows, and black clouds gathered and hung above the River

Roche and the town centre. Then, finally, the door flew open, and a gust of wind whipped through the house, making candles in each room flicker. By the looks of him, the same black clouds had gathered above Fred's brow as he shrugged off his wet Macintosh and boots, leaving them to puddle near the door. He glared at them all as they stood around the kitchen table.

The twins in their baskets were already asleep upstairs, but the others, those not properly belonging to Fred, were standing beside the table, tummies rumbling, as they'd been waiting for him to come home so they could eat. Martha Anne had once made the mistake of not waiting on Fred to serve the children, and she'd wound up with a bloody lip and broken nose. She wasn't about to make that mistake again. More importantly, her beloved children wouldn't let her make that mistake again and would not eat nor leave their places until Fred came home and settled himself in one of the two chairs at either end of the table. His was closest to the fire, and Harry and Frank flanked his sides while Cyril and Gertie stood by their mother.

Martha Anne leapt up and poured a healthy ladle full of soup and placed it before Fred, along with a piece of crusty bread and butter. She then spooned out smaller helpings for the children, according to age, and herself last.

So far, he'd not said a word, and she'd hoped that his foul mood was merely his usual miserable mood and not one incited by the events of the day.

She was almost calmed until he'd grabbed Harry by the forelock and yanked his head next to his own. He spat in the boy's face. 'Lit'l bird says you been runnin' numbers for bookies, these days.' He shook the boy causing him to cough on the soup he'd just swallowed. Then, Fred reached across Frank's bowl, knocking it, spilling his supper over its brim, and he grabbed Cyril by his similar brow. Then he crashed the boys' heads together and flung them backward, sending Cyril bouncing against the wall and nearly landing Harry in the fire. The soup was everywhere, and poor Gertie's little hand was scalded as it splashed from her bowl.

Martha Anne jumped to get a wet rag for her daughter when Fred grabbed her by the back of the neck, slamming her up against the wall.

'And where the bloody fuck do you think you're goin'?' Then he spat in her face.

She pushed at him and tried to turn her head, but he'd clapped her chin between his thumb and forefinger, squeezing against her cheeks, her teeth, she tasted blood. Gertie's crying from the pain of her burn had turned to a scream as she watched Martha Anne struggle against him. She locked eyes with her daughter's, now growing big as she became more frightened.

Martha Anne felt Fred's free hand begin to pull at her skirt. He was jamming his hardness against her thigh, trying to spread her legs with his feet. He was working at his own belt now. She panicked, realising what he was about to do to her in front of the children. They were all yelling now. Frank and Cyril grabbed Fred's arms, but he was strong, and he flicked them off like flies. She pushed his hands away, and he shoved against her harder.

'Be still, you fucking cunt.' His words full of whisky and evil, he slammed her head back against the stone wall and pressed his hand tightly over her mouth and nose. She couldn't breathe, and she bit down on the flesh of his palm. He yanked his hand away, only to slap her with his bloody print. He then wrapped both hands around her throat and began to squeeze.

Then, just as she was about to pass out, he instantaneously released her, and his body dropped to the floor. *Poof*! Just like that. Except it wasn't just like that. It wasn't even *Poof*!

Just behind where Fred had stood was Harry directly in front of her, holding the dry end of a burning log he'd plucked from the fire. By the looks of it, he'd clocked Fred over the head with its flaming end. Her boy's eyes were big and round, and he was frozen in his spot. It was as if he didn't know what he'd done. He dropped the log onto Fred's chest, sending the man straight up on his haunches, but not quickly enough to avoid Frank kicking him back down. Then, startling them all, their baby sister, their little "Gert the Squirt", as the brothers called her, reached for the big pot of boiling soup on the hob and pulled it over. Hot liquid poured down onto Fred Collingwood's head, face, and neck, and he screeched in agony, covering his face with his hands, blistered by the burning log he'd caught when Harry dropped it.

By the time he'd risen from the floor, Martha Anne, Frank, and Harry had formed a barrier between Fred and the little ones. She saw that Harry was wielding a knife nearly as long as his arm when she looked down.

'Get out!' he yelled at Fred.

'GET OUT!' Frank shouted.

'GET OUT! Get OUT! Get out!' They all chanted as they watched as Fred Collingwood, face scalded, head bleeding, hands blackened with burns, rose to his feet, stumbled to the door, stepped into his boots, and fled out into the rain with his Mac tenting over his head.

Cyril had run from the family huddle to his mother's bedroom and came out with a pile of Collingwood's things in his arms. He ran into the pouring rain, into the street, running after Fred despite his family's protestations. They watched as Cyril caught up to Collingwood, threw the bundle at the older man's feet, shouted something, and came running home, laughing all the way. When he entered the house, he was soaked through, but his grin was broad.

'What's so funny?' Martha Anne asked as she took a warm towel to her son's wet head and draped his soft nightshirt in front of the fire. 'You could've caught your death of cold runnin' out there like that. What'd you say to 'im?'

Cyril giggled. 'I told 'im I were sorry I couldn't find his balls anywhere, but 'ere were the rest of 'is stuff.' He grinned. 'Then I ran.'

They were all glad Collingwood had gone, and for good, it seemed. Martha Anne had heard through the village gossipmongers that he was back with his wife, Olive, and their children. It was also said that she had taken pity on him, as he was severely bruised, burned, and bloody when he'd arrived on her doorstep. It was said he'd quit the drink and had been humbled when it was revealed a mere lad and his little sister were responsible for the scarring on his face and the burns on his hands. In her honest heart, Martha Anne prayed every night for the little family, as she wouldn't wish Fred Collingwood on the devil himself.

Money was tight, though. She thanked the lord and her sober self for having entrusted Millie with the money she'd found in Samuel's satchel those many years ago. The drink had got her on more occasions than she liked to admit, and if she'd had her drunken way, that money would be gone by now. It wasn't. She did ask Millie to pay one month's rent for her, just once. The rest was in a secret hiding place chosen by Millie.

Martha Anne had been laid off at the mill so had some spotty charwoman jobs, but not many could afford to have their houses cleaned these days, so work was on and off. She admitted to turning two blind eyes to Harry and Cyril's doings. They swore they'd knocked off the numbers running, but at the end of a Friday night, there was always a bit more sterling in the jar each week. If it hadn't been for Frank's job at the abattoir, they'd been in deep straights.

Today, she'd left the twins with Gertie and was walking into town to see about the market's job prospects. As she came to the end of Prince Street, she saw a line of men, mill workers. She could tell by their clothing. They were rounding the corner and heading to a large window at the side of the end terrace house. She watched the exchanges of money and small wrapped packages go between as the line moved quickly. As she got nearer, she saw a small sign that read:

'Sophia Wright's Original Cornish Pasties, One Farthing Each.'

When the last of the workmen had left for the mill, Martha Anne walked up to the window, and to her surprise, inside, she saw Mary and Sophia Halkyard, and a little lass, about Harry's age, all bustling about the well-lit kitchen. She rapped on the window for their attention, and when Sophia saw her there, she smiled and raised her finger. Instead of coming to the window, Sophia went out the door and greeted Martha Anne with a gentle smile.

'Is that you, Martha Anne?' Sophia asked.

''Tis me, in all me glory,' she said, self-consciously pushing against the flyaway strands of hair escaping from her kerchief. She gestured to the signage next to the window. 'This you? Sophia Wright now, is it?'

The young woman nodded, though her smile seemed to fail her at that moment. 'I were married to Thomas Wright. He were killed in a mill accident, just two months gone now.' Her eyes teared up as she remained heartbroken at having lost him and wondered if she would ever stop crying at the very mention of his name.

'Oh, I'm so sorry, luv,' Martha Anne said.

Sophia took a deep breath and offered, 'Would you like to come in for a cuppa?'

Martha Anne looked to the cosiness of the lighted kitchen. 'Oh, I dunno. I don't want to cause a bother,' she said but did not mean it.

'No bother at all!' Sophia said, regaining a certain cheeriness as she led the way down the hall to the warm kitchen. Here, Mary Halkyard, Sophia's mother, was wiping off a counter, and the little girl—Mabel, she was called— had settled four cups and saucers on the table.

Not having seen one another since that awful night at Betty Nuppy's, when Martha Anne had been banished from the cottage, Sophia and Mary seemed forgiving of those circumstances and were just glad to see her. They'd not asked about her father, her marriage, or Collingwood, as they (like everyone else) already knew of all of that, as nothing was ever hidden in tiny villages, especially for those making bad decisions and drawing attention to themselves as she'd done. And she'd been grateful to them for the forgiveness. She was trying. Really, she was. She hadn't taken a drink since Fred left, and she was keeping a tight rein on the lads, making sure they were home and tucked in at night. If they weren't, she'd lock them out. One night out in the cold and rain was enough to stop their shenanigans—she hoped at least. She was happy to talk about her children, just like a real mum would.

She learned that little Mabel Wright was in school with her Harry, or at least when he came to school. She'd inadvertently revealed his truancy, but Martha Anne let it slide, as the little girl also said that Harry had stepped in and defended her against some bullies not long ago.

'He's a kind lad, your Harry is. He walked Mabel home that day, right to the doorstep, makin' sure she were safe,' Sophia added. 'Mum, here, even invited him in for tea, and she don't invite anyone in for tea! He acted like a fine little gentleman, your lad did. You should be proud of him.'

'Oh, I am,' Martha Anne said. 'Of all me lads, I am.'

As catching up talk wound down, Martha Anne's original curiosity about the pasty shop Sophia was running finally came about.

'How'd you come to do this? The pasty shop idea?'

Sophia smiled and nodded. 'I'm pretty proud of meself, I admit. When Thomas died, I got a bit of money, and even though Mabel went into the mill, I knew we wouldn't be able to manage unless I went back in too,' she coughed then and said, 'I've got the cotton lung, and I didn't want to go back in. So me and Mum put our heads together and came up with the idea to make and sell pasties from the house. I mean, the mill's right there. They march to and from right here. Got permission from the landlord to cut the hole and put the window in the side of the house, and then I invested some of what was left into stocking me kitchen with ingredients and cookware made for vast lots of food. The pasties are not only the easiest and cheapest food to make, but they're a favourite of every workman in the mill.'

'What a reet smart idea! How'd the landlord take to you cuttin' out the side of his buildin'?'

'He was all reet with it once I skinned his palm with a tenner. He said I'd have to put it back if I ever move. I said fine considerin' that's not ever goin' to 'appen.'

'Can I ask how much it set you back?'

Sophia looked hesitantly at her mother.

'Oh, I'm not gonna copy you at the other end, luv. I'm no cook, of pasties or otherwise, but you 'ave given me an idea.'

'What's that?' Sophia asked.

'Well, I'm reet good at washin' up, and I've got a big tub and plenty of coal for me fire. So if I did the same, with the window, I mean, I could take in laundry instead of goin' out and doin' it. The lads at the mill could drop it off and pick it up.'

'That's brilliant, Martha Anne!' Sophia clapped her hands. 'And if you need any help gettin' started, you just ask. It cost me eight pounds to put the window in, but I made it back the first month. You should do the same with laundry!'

***

Martha Anne had gone to Millie to see how much money was left in her savings and was relieved to find there was still over twenty pounds. She was quite chuffed that Millie thought the idea of starting a laundry was cracking! And Martha Anne was grateful when Millie'd offered to accompany her to the landlord to make the case. As Sophia had said, it took some convincing and some palm-skinning, but Mr Burk was a decent fella, said he remembered her father, John, fondly, and wished her the best of luck with her adventure. However, he did stipulate that she had to put it back to the way it was before she moved out, if ever.

Since there was already a window in the side of the house, she'd hired Roy Bench, a joiner, who enlarged it. She'd had her own dolly tub and stick for her own family's clothing, but they wouldn't due if she were to do bigger and more efficient loads. So she took another portion of the savings and bought a used mangler: a washing tub and roller press in one. The lads had had to move the table out of the kitchen, which they were none too happy about, and made their feelings known with a good deal of moaning and worrying about where'd they'd eat their tea. She also purchased a pulley, line, wood pegs and had the lads rig up a clothesline out the back. And lastly, she had Gertie help set up four drying racks, one in each room. They'd all had a laugh at the sign Sophia and Mary Halkyard had hired out for her, reading:

Martha the Mangler's Ideal Laundry Services

Drop off Mondays/Pick up Fridays

Wet Wash: Ha'penny per item. Hand Wash: Penny per item
Bag Wash: Shilling per Bag
Press: Ha'penny per item. Iron: Penny per item

Roy Bench set the sign proper, right above the window. Then, that evening, the night before she would open her new business, she stood with all six of her children outside in front of the window, under the sign.

They stared up at the glow from the lamps within, which made it seem a cosy business, somehow. They were all quiet for a moment. Even the babes, Norman on her own hip, Alf on Gertie's, each seemed to recognise the solemnity of the moment. The hope of the moment. And she, in her mind, saw the reality of the moment and swallowed hard, pushing the tears and fears away.

She'd not had a drink in months, and she was determined never to have another as long as she lived (at least she'd make a go of it). Yet, looking down upon each of her (momentarily) angelic children, she could see her hopes, dreams, and fears reflected in each of their upturned faces. Like her, they too were drawn to the hope-filled warm glow of the window, and the scrolling promises scribed out on the fancy sign. But, unlike her, the lads and Gertie were spared the daunting realisation that they were all depending on her and this window, alone, to keep them alive, healthy, and safe from this moment to the next and the next. And if she had to admit it, even if only to herself, she was scared shite-less.

She felt an arm on her shoulder and looked over to see Frank had come and stood beside her. He was now officially just a bit taller than she and had fuzz growing under his nose. He'd recently had to cut off his lovely curls, for the work in the abattoir wouldn't allow them, but he was still beautiful.

He squeezed her arm and whispered, 'You done good, Mum.'

'Thanks, luv. We'll see, eh?' She smiled as she leaned against her eldest son.

Not to be outdone, Gertie chimed in, 'It's brilliant, Mum!'

''Tis, Mum! You're gonna be rich!' The ever-enterprising Cyril predicted.

She ruffled his hair. 'And you? Will you keep me books?'

'Why sure. I'd be a reet smart numbers man, don'tcha know.' Cyril puffed his chest out a bit.

'He'll rob you blind,' Frank said. 'Steal your money and leave you desolate, just like 'is father did us.'

'Won't!' Cyril shouted and took a swing at his brother.

'Hey now, that's enough. We're 'avin' a reet pretty moment. Let's not bring ugly into it,' she scolded.

She looked at Harry and noticed he was reticent, even for him, not joining in the little celebration nor adding to it.

'What 'bout, you, 'arry? What d'ye think?'

He looked at his mother. She was smiling in a way she hadn't smiled in years. She looked young, suddenly, and he imagined the pretty girl she must've been. She was happy, and deep down, he hoped the whole thing worked out for her. He really did. He'd do all he could to help, they all would, and with any luck, it'd be a grand success. But he just couldn't entirely trust his mother's short-lived sobriety or the short-lived peace and security it often promised, only to be dashed away in disappointment—or even celebration—after that first whisky or whatever his mum could get her hands on. And that's when the good of the good day would wash away with every sip she took. Sure, she was doing well now, he considered. She hadn't had a drink since Collingwood left, but everybody seems to forget all the drinks she'd had while with him and all the bad things they suffered because of him.

Up until then, when they finally ousted the lout, Harry and his brothers were having to fetch their mother from the pubs, weekly—and sometimes nightly—when she was either too drunk to find her way home or was brawling with somebody, woman or man, didn't matter, who'd looked at her wrong and caused her to throw the first insult or the first punch.

On those missions to get their mother, Harry'd been ashamed as he and the lads would enter the pub where all eyes would turn and stare at them as they pushed or dragged her out. It was better when she'd be waiting in a ginnel where she'd either crawled or been tossed by the publican, where they didn't have to suffer the scrutiny of the whole village. He and the lads would carry, pull, or drag her home, sparking her clogs on the cobbles along the way. As if signalling all of Prince Street, the neighbours would peer out their windows to watch the Chadwick Family walk of shame.

It was one more reason he quit going to school, all those whispers, pointing fingers, sly looks, and a word or two always landed like punches from the bullies who knew of or heard of his mother: "fishwife", "whore", "pissed owd cow", "drunk cunt"…he'd gotten into many a scuffle with the bloke who'd dared an insult at his mother because too many hit home.

And, so, now, his mother wanted to be a laundress, to turn their already cramped quarters into a steaming laundry. It was the most demanding job next to the mill, but there she was, Martha Anne Ashworth Chadwick, the Drunk of Prince Street, and she would make a go of a laundry business. He wished her well, he really did, and would reserve judgement but not caution, as he could never fully trust anything his mother said, did, or, he supposed, tried. She was dragging them all along on this new venture, whether they wanted to be a part of it or not.

He chewed his lip for a few seconds and finally allowed, 'I think if anybody could try to make a go of this sort of business, Mum, you can.' And with that, he turned and went into the house.

It wasn't exactly a compliment. Martha Anne considered her son's words that night after she'd finally got all of them to bed. He appeared doubtful of her decision to try her hand at a business. She considered Harry's response, and then, worse, she decided it wasn't the business he doubted at all. She saw it in his eyes. It was she he doubted. It was that he doubted she could run a business, quit the drink, and keep them all safe. That's what she saw in his eyes, and it broke her heart to think her son did not trust her. But, then again, why should he? She hadn't been the most reliable mum on the block, she admitted. She'd show him, she decided. She wouldn't let the whisky win this time.

She lay down with Gertie on one side, already making little purring sounds, like a sleeping kitten. She hugged the little girl and wrapped an arm to cradle Alf, who was on her other side. He was teething and could not settle with his brother in the crib. She liked feeling her little ones sandwiching her, and she began to drift off, thinking about all that she'd hoped to happen tomorrow with her new laundry business.

It was five lonely hours later when she'd stuck her head out the window to see the deserted street. Not one mill worker who'd passed her window had stopped, most had barely noticed, and only one seemed to slow as he squinted, and she could see he was trying to make out the sign. Finally, she heard a rapping on the window, only to be disappointed to see Mary Halkyard with a few pasties in her apron.

'Ello, luv. Came by to see 'ow the openin' went.'

'Come in.' Martha Anne opened the side door, inviting her new friend into the house. 'Tea?' she asked but didn't wait to put the kettle on.

'I've brought enough pasties for the lads and Gertie,' she said, referring to what everyone called the Chadwick Clan. 'We had a dozen left over. We can't eat all those, and to be honest, we're sick of 'em. So I'm makin' tripe n' onions with some crusty bread and butter tonight.'

Martha Anne laughed. 'Yeah, that's what we're 'avin', w'out the tripe or the onions!'

'Oh, lass, would you like me to bring you some.' Mary had taken a bit of a motherly shine to Martha Anne, seeing how hard she tried to keep her family going.

Martha Anne poured them each a cup of tea and waved away Mary's offer. 'Oh, no. Thanks, though. The one good thing we've got goin' is Frank workin' at the abattoir. He brings home lamb bones, ham, tripe, and some nice sides when 'e can get 'em. We're not starvin'…yet,' she said as she looked at the silent mangler, the dolly pot waiting to heat, the drying racks empty, and wondered if she'd made the biggest mistake of her life. She shook her head and giggled. No, that was Collingwood, and Chadwick, and…yes…Malcolm, but these were thoughts she pushed away.

Suddenly, Mary stood up and placed her hands on her hips. She took Martha Anne's hand, 'Come wi' me,' she tugged, and the women went outside and rounded the corner and stared up at the sign above the window.

The sign was a particular dark grey with black lettering and was hidden away in the shadows of the roofline. 'Which way do the lads come to and from the mill, lass?' Mary asked, and Martha Anne pointed towards the southern entrance of the mill. 'And then they turn and pass your sunny front door, around this corner?'

Martha Anne nodded. 'Most of 'em, comin' and goin'. Of course, some go down the side streets, but Prince, as you know, is well travelled.'

''Tis true, and that's your problem right there. You're not facin' the sunny side of Prince Street, down 'ere, not the way me own window shines up at the other end. So no one knows you're 'ere, around this shady corner till it's too late, till they've already passed by and missed you altogether. Would I be reet?'

'Yes, yes, that's exactly what 'appened. They just marched on by w'out a second look.'

'Not only that, I'm afraid that sign up there is hidden away in the shadows. What if...' Mary said, walking back around the corner to the sunny front door of Martha Anne's home, 'what if we bring the sign over 'ere, to the door? Passers-by will see it. You should paint it white and leave the letters black,' she also decided. 'Then, have the lads and Gertie make flyers w' a grand opening date. They can slide them under the doors all up and down Prince Street.'

It was a grand idea, Martha Anne thought.

'And last, do you 'ave any samples?' Mary asked.

'Samples? I'm not a pasty shop. What sort of samples does a washerwoman 'ave?'

Mary seemed to ponder this for quite some time. Her brow knitted together as she stared at the sign and trying really hard to catch an idea as it flew back and forth.

'Bags,' she said quietly.

'What d'ye mean bags?'

Mary tapped her fingertips together in a miniature clap and pointed up to the sign. 'Look, you're advertising a bagwash. Why not make a load of tote bags? In a certain signature colour! If I recall, Sophia mentioned you were quite the artist back in the day. You could paint a...what do they call those...' She seemed to be searching her fingers for the word, ' brand!' she shouted, seemingly proud of herself. 'Yes, you could print your name or design on each, like "Martha the Mangler's Bagwash"!'

Upon hearing this, Martha Anne barely stifled the laugh that erupted at this idea for a logo. She couldn't wait to tell Millie of this most apparent gaff of a name for anyone's business she'd ever heard. Unless, of course, she were some dark lady of the evening. She did laugh now, and Mary seemed to get the joke she did not mean to tell.

Mary laughed and said, 'Well, maybe we'll leave the bagwash out, and leave it: "Martha the Mangler's Ideal Laundry" with a picture of a cat. Can you paint a cat?'

'A cat? Why a cat?' Martha Anne asked. 'Cat's got nothin' to do with laundry. I don't even own a cat.'

'Oh, I don't know. I like cats. Most people like cats. If you put a cat on the bag, people will want you to do their laundry.'

'I'm not doin' a cat, but I do think it's not a bad idea, this makin' special shop bags for me customers to bring to and fro.'

And that's how it went, just as Mary had suggested and predicted. Martha Anne, Sophia, and Mary set to work sewing blue and white striped bags that could hold a week's worth of dirty clothes. She cut a stencil with the logo "Martha's Ideal Laundry" (as she wasn't fond of "Martha the Mangler"), and with the help of Gertie, late into the night, they'd painted the red letters on each bag and offered the first five customers a free one, and for all other comers just a farthing for each with their first bagwash.

It wasn't long before Martha Anne, Gertie, and Cyril were all working with their sleeves rolled up, wet washing, pressing, and even ironing, but that was something the little ones weren't allowed to do as burning a shirt wasn't the least of Martha Anne's worries as burning themselves was just as likely. So she set them to the simpler tasks of hanging the clothes to dry on the line in the back with smaller items like undergarments, socks, and handkerchiefs draped over the drying racks, and late at night, all four of the older children helped fold and package the ironing and stuffing the wet washes neatly into the striped bags. And for every pound she'd make, she'd give a shilling back to Millie to hold onto for safe-keeping.

***

It was a bitter winter's day, in the worst of the bleakest month of the year, February, and Martha Anne realised with all that had gone on in the past nearly nine months she hadn't had a drink, hadn't gone to the pub, hadn't stayed out, got pissed, or embarrassed her lads for almost a year, and she was proud of herself for that. She thought even Harry might be a bit proud of her as he'd often, over the last few months, pitched in to help the little ones with the hanging and folding, as the rains and snow made it impossible to use the clothesline outside. Harry would bring it in and string it right up the stairwell, just high enough above each step for the little ones to reach it easily. Martha Anne also noticed with this contraption that the heat from the dolly pot water and the mangler went right up the stairs and dried the clothes even quicker than out the back. So business was such that Martha Anne had several regular customers, and she could start counting on weekly amounts of money coming in and what was going out. Even though he was but a boy, Cyril was quite good with the numbers, and together, they would sit and keep the accounting books. She was starting to see how much she needed to make to keep her in coal, soap, and starch. A few of the businessmen in town and one of the deacons from the parish church had heard of her prowess in the laundry and had been sending their wives over on Mondays with their business, especially for church and funeral shirts.

One afternoon, she and Cyril were inside working the numbers by the fire, as it was Saturday, so they were free of laundry for the next two days. She'd been counting the high amount of soap when she tutted, and her son looked worriedly at her. 'What is it, Mum? Did I get a number wrong?'

'No, no…not wrong,' she said as she shook her head. 'It's just that the soap is so costly. I think we should go with some chamber lye from now on. It'll be much cheaper.'

He nodded in that serious businessman's way he had about him at only just ten. 'All reet, then, where do we get this chamber lye?' He tapped his pencil.

'Why, under the beds,' she said with a certain tone, unfamiliar to the boy.

He frowned now and put his pencil down. 'What d'ye mean "under the beds"? There's nothin' but mouse dung and chamber-pots…' He said this last bit slowly as its meaning was dawning on him. 'You don't mean…' His eyes grew big, and he appeared horrified. 'Not…not…pee?'

The look on his face tickled her such that she burst out laughing, 'I do, me luv! I do mean pee. I've been reading about it. Urine, they say, gets the worst out—stains, grease, dirt. So we just take our chamber pots every mornin' and pour the pee over the worst of the lots. No one will be the wiser!' She winked.

'No! Mum! I'll be the wiser! And I can't think about our neighbours walkin' around Prince Street in clothes we've washed with our own piss!' He now stood and was pacing the room.

'But, Cyril, think of the savings! Look how many of us there are here. Why, we could even get two more pots and fill them up all day long, don't you think?'

He was now pulling on his ear, the habit he had when he was either in a bother or lying, and tonight, she was tickled to know it was the first, and she couldn't stop her teasing. 'Look,' she ran a finger under a line in the accounts, 'see here? Soap is costing us a shilling a week!'

He stopped to face her, 'No, Mum. I can't let you do this. If word got out, well, our whole bloody mangling business would be doomed,' he said so seriously she could not hold back any longer and burst out laughing, which turned his worry to confusion.

'Oh, luv, I'm just pullin' yer leg, although they did use to use chamber lye quite regular when I were a girl—not so much anymore.'

'Well, that's a good—' His words were cut off by the sound of the front door opening, and both Gertie and Harry came rushing into the warmth of the kitchen. Unfortunately, the cold they'd let in was accompanied by the two fighting over something, and with all their fast-flying words, she could not understand what either was saying.

'Settle down, both of you, and take a breath. What's got you in a bother?'

Gertie started, 'It were 'im, I didn't know it were 'im, but Mr Burk said it were 'im, tell 'er, 'Arry!'

Her older brother gave her a dark look and began to unwind the scarf from his neck. 'Shut up, Gertie, just shut up.'

'Harry! That's no way to talk to your sister. What's she on about?'

'It were 'im! It were Dad!' the little girl now shouted into the void left by her brother, who looked like he was about to slap her.

'Dad? Who's Dad?' Martha Anne asked.

'Ours!' Gertie said, 'look! He gave me a penny!' and she held out her palm, showing her mother the shiny copper coin.

Martha Anne carefully lifted the penny from her daughter's hand and looked out the window to the empty street where the snow was blowing by. She looked at Harry. 'Son, what's she goin' on about?'

He jammed his fists into his pocket and looked everywhere but at his mother. 'It's what Gertie said. This bloke came walkin' down Prince Street. He stopped me and asked if I were 'arry Chadwick, and 'ow old were I? Then Gertie come over, and he asked if she were called Gertie, and said he 'ad somethin' for 'er, and gave her that penny.'

'Anythin' else?'

'He asked 'ow's your mum? And then asked after Cyril. He tried to give me a penny, but I told 'im I didn't want it.'

'And then?'

And then he walked back the way he came.

'Harry, was it your dad?' Martha Anne asked quietly. 'Was it Samuel?'

He shrugged. 'Dunno. Can't say it looked like 'im. I don't really remember 'im, and this chap didn't 'ave a moustache, which is about all I can remember of 'im.'

'Why d'ya think it was your dad, Gertie?'

'Mr Burk were outside his door, watchin' us, and when the chap left, he told 'arry.'

'Told 'arry what?' She looked at her son.

'Mr Burk come over after the man left and asked if I knew who he were, and I said I didn't. Mr Burk said, "*That were ye dad*".' Harry slipped into a nearby chair and asked, 'Can I get some tea, Mum?'

Later, Martha Anne popped around to Millie's, leaving the lads and Gertie in charge of the twins. The wind had waned, but the snowflakes were still swirling as she pulled her shawl over her head and closed it tightly at her throat. By the time she got to Millie's just two terraces over, she was wet and cold, and Millie gave her a dry pair of socks that she'd just warmed by the fire.

'And so, you think it were 'im? Samuel?' Millie asked as she poured the tea.

Martha Anne shrugged. 'Dunno what to think. Mr Burk wouldn't've lied to the children. I went to ask 'im, but he'd gone to the pub, and…well…I'm keepin' away, lately.'

'Good on you, lass.' Millie patted her shoulder. 'It is a mystery, though, 'im showin' up out of the blue like that. What's it been? Six years?'

'Nearly seven. Never 'eard a word. Why now?'

'Maybe he was curious. Wanted to see the lads and Gertie?'

'Well, good riddance to bad rubbish is what I 'ave to say about it. Leavin' me alone with all of them kids, 'e's lucky I didn't catch 'im out there in the road. I'd be takin' more'n a penny off 'im, I would!' And both women laughed. 'I don't miss that lout one minute, Millie. I know it's been hard. Collingwood was a bad mistake. I can admit it. And I can admit I've not been me best self these last years, but I'm doin' all reet now. I 'ope 'e stays away. Last thing I want in me life is another lyin', cheatin', stupid man.'

Chapter Fifteen

THE ROCHDALE OBSERVER, WEDNESDAY, FEBRUARY 13, 1904

SLAUGHTERHOUSE TRAGEDY
ROCHDALE YOUTH FATALLY WOUNDED
FELLOW WORKMAN IN CUSTODY
INQUEST ADJOURNED
COURT PROCEEDINGS TO-DAY

***

Martha Anne stood on the doorstep, bracing against the cold as she'd settled her wash sign offering a special on bag loads of bedclothes. Business slowed in the winter as many weren't inclined to strip their beds till spring. She would rather do them in the winter when it wasn't so hot outside and in. She watched Frank head down the lane with his mate, Eddie-Reddy, they called him. She liked him, she did. He was a good mate to Frank. They'd lived just across the row from the Reddingtons since the lads were in short pants. Eddie was just a couple of years older than Frank. They'd been friends in school, played in the streets, sat on the same doorstep in the evenings dreaming about escaping this godforsaken place.

Thanks to Frank, who'd given him the nickname when they were lads, Edward Reddington didn't have a chance being anything but Eddie-Reddy. Eddie wasn't the only one Frank had rechristened. She'd recently been surprised to learn that Frank had stopped using his surname Ashworth and now went by Chadwick. Since Frank and Samuel were not close, especially at the end, she was curious about this decision by her son.

'Frank, are you goin' by Chadwick?' she'd asked. 'Not Ashworth?'

He'd shrugged. 'I dunno. Yeah, I suppose I am now.'

'Why, though? I never thought you liked 'im—Samuel, I mean.'

Again with a shrug, he said, 'He was the only father I ever 'ad, for starters.'

'That it?' She somehow felt annoyed by this but could not explain why.

Then he said, 'Everybody else in this 'ouse goes by Chadwick—you, the lads and Gertie, and even Norman and Alf. So, if they're to be Chadwicks, then I must be one as well. We're a family.'

Martha Anne smiled and shook her head as she watched Frank and Eddie punch and push at each other—their usual good morning greetings. They were grinning and talking, and she could see but not hear them teasing one another. *Probably over some girl,* she thought. It was like this nearly every morning with this pair unless it was raining. On those days, they'd hunch their shoulders and lean into each other as they'd head out to Dearden's Pass, near Toad Lane to the Bond Slaughterhouse, where they worked together. She'd hoped they'd marry sisters so they'd never have to part company. She looked across the street and saw Bertha Reddington, Eddie's mum, also watching the lads as they rounded the corner. She was a kind woman, a widow. The solo-mums had become friends over the years. Eddie was Bertie's youngest. He'd stayed in Rochdale and took good care of his mum whilst his brothers and sisters all went away.

Martha Anne waved and stepped out to the gate as Bertie did the same at her own. Neither crossed the cobbles, each stayed on her side of the street, but they were only yards apart.

It was Bertie who blurted, 'Did you hear our Eddie's news, Martha Anne?'

'Good news, I hope!'

''Tis! He's got engaged to Sara!'

Martha Anne could not help but grin. Sara Jackson was the loveliest lass in the lane, and she and Eddie had been courting for years. 'Oh, that is the best news! Congratulations, Bertie. You're to 'ave a daughter!'

Bertie smiled, and Martha Anne could see she was a bit weepy, and so she crossed the road and wrapped her arms around her friend. 'Those better be 'appy tears, luv.' She squeezed and released. Stepping away, she let Bertie compose herself as she blew into a handkerchief she had pulled from her sleeve. She blotted tears and swiped her cheeks. 'It's just that Bob would be so proud of Eddie, and he'd be tickled if he knew that Sara was to join our family.'

'Bob was always proud of Eddie, and I'm sure he is tickled by it all. Sittin' up there w' me dad, smokin' their pipes and sippin' their whisky.' She smiled at Bertie. 'Eddie's a good lad, always 'as been. He deserves this. We're all proud of 'im. A good friend he's been to me Frank all these years.'

'And Frank to 'im. They've been like brothers, they 'ave,' Bertie said, dabbing her eyes.

'Funny that, all of them brothers Frank's got at 'ome, and it's Eddie he picks for one.' She laughed.

Bertie leaned over and said in a loud whisper, 'I'm not supposed to say, but Eddie's goin' to ask Frank to be his best man!'

'Awe, that's just lovely,' Martha Anne said and felt a shiver of wind fly up her skirt. 'I won't say a word.' She tightened her grip on her shawl. 'I'll let you get back, then. It's frigid today, it is. I've got a load of wash I've got to get finished.'

'Have a good one, Martha Anne,' Bertie said, turning for home.

Inside, Martha Anne started the fire under the dolly pot, and when she looked at the pile of laundry on the sideboard. She was both relieved and worried that there wasn't much to do today. She'd make a lovely tea, and she'd have Bertie and Eddie come around and bring Sara if she was available. They'd celebrate the happy news. She was looking forward to the lads coming home from work tonight.

***

It was Eddie who'd started working at the abattoir first. He was an apprentice butcher, a right respected legger. He could dress the cleanest cuts from the hindquarters of a lamb in no time and with little effort. Eddie was tall and muscular, and his long limbs seemed perfect for the job. Frank, on the other hand, was shorter than Eddie and wiry. He was hired on at Eddie's recommendation. Initially, they'd had very different jobs. Frank's was to bring in the sheep, stick them, lift the lambs onto the cradles, and help the butchers with legging. Frank had caught on quickly, and soon, he had his own cradle and was legging sheep without much help, side by side with Eddie.

The morning had started as usual, Frank thought back on it. He and Eddie had met up at the corner and talked and smoked cutties all the way to work. He'd been elated when Eddie asked him to be his best man and was happy his mate had finally decided to take the plunge with Sara, whom, Frank had told Eddie, 'You better marry 'er, mate, or you'll lose her to a more handsome bloke!' This got a laugh from them both, as Eddie was a good-looking fellow. Square chin, deep-set eyes, thick head of black hair. There might not be a more handsome fella in all of Lancashire if the truth be told. There also might not be a more quick-tempered one, either, Frank knew.

It was later in the day when Frank saw Eddie coming out of Mr Bond's office. He noticed that his friend's mood seemed to have darkened. Eddie's brow furrowed as if he was bothered by something, but when Frank asked if there was anything wrong, Eddie turned his back on him and told him to mind his own business.

He marched to his cradle in long storming strides as if he were looking to fight it. There was a new lamb there where the apprentice had laid it, but it was not in the position Eddie liked. Its deadweight made it hard for him to turn quickly, and he began to wrestle it with great aggravated flourishes and huffing frustrations.

Frank also had a new lamb on his cradle, to the right of the open abattoir's door, while Eddie's cradle was on the left. Despite the cold beyond the door, inside the butchery was hot and noisy with the animals' bleating, the carcasses dripping, hanging from iron chains and hooks, splattering blood into the red rivers running through the troughs. Most butchers were set at the back of the cavernous structure with ceilings so high that it was hard to see them in the pitch of their darkness where swallows and bats flew. It was a cacophonous echo chamber of many soft and loud sounds.

Just outside the door, Frank noticed a group of men waiting to go into the store to make their sales and purchases. He saw a Mr Burrell, a wholesale butcher he'd met a few times, with a farm in Newhey, and when the gentleman caught his eye, he nodded and smiled. And Frank waved. He'd been hoping that one day, he'd work for Mr Burrell on his farm instead of here in the bloody hell-hole that was the slaughterhouse.

Frank bent over the sheep in his cradle. It was a prize, he had to admit, with haunches that would make a beautiful cut. He took out his knife, and before he could make his first incision, from behind, Eddie had suddenly appeared, yelling something Frank could not quite make out, but he'd been grabbed by the shoulder and spun around.

'What the 'ell, Eddie?' Frank yelled over the din of the room.

'That's me lamb!' Eddie pointed to the thick-legged beast lying on Frank's station.

''Tis not!' Frank shouted. 'I stuck it. I put it 'ere. It's mine.'

Without warning, Eddie grabbed Frank around the neck, put him in a chokehold, then threw him to the ground. Frank got up and took a swing, connecting with Eddie's jaw, and then Eddie punched Frank in the eye. In one quick instance, Eddie ran at Frank, grabbed him around the middle, lifting him off his feet, and then suddenly, like two deflating balloons, he dropped Frank like he was a piece of burning coal. When Eddie slid down against the wall, Frank watched a bloom of red blossom around Eddie's chest, his white apron turning crimson.

'NO!' Frank yelled, running to his friend. He looked down to see his work knife still in his hand and knew it had pushed through Eddie's chest when he'd been lifted. Hurrying from the store, Mr Bond, Mr Burrell, and a few of the other butchers rushed to the lads. 'NO! Eddie, No!' Frank cried out and knelt beside Eddie, watching as the blood drained from his heart and the life from his eyes.

Frank felt Mr Burrell's hand on his shoulder. 'Come away, son,' he said gently, tugging on the boy now shaking uncontrollably.

He looked at the older man. 'I didn't...I don't...I don't know what 'appened...It were an accident. I forgot I 'ad the knife...I wouldn't've ever hurt him.' His eyes filled with tears. 'Eddie's me best mate. I didn't mean it. We weren't even fightin' yet.'

'I know, son. I saw. I saw what happened.'

Mr Burrell had watched as Eddie, much taller and broader than the Chadwick chap, had left his cradle and strode across the room, yelling something Burrell couldn't quite make out. He watched Reddington grab Frank in a chokehold around the neck and throw him on the floor. When Frank got free, and after a couple of swings had been swung by each, Burrell watched in horror as Eddie ran at Frank, grabbed him around the middle, lifted him in the air and then suddenly released him, dropping him. Eddie had pin-wheeled backward against the wall and slid down, exposing his middle where blood was spreading.

When the ambulance came and took a barely breathing Eddie away, Frank was sobbing beside a window where his boss, Mr Bond, found him. He put his hand on the young man's shoulder. Frank turned around and fell into Mr Bond's arms. The older man did not let go. He imagined his own son in this sort of predicament. At least, his son would have a father to turn to, though.

But, unfortunately, as far as he knew of this young Chadwick lad, there was no father in the picture.

'All reet now, son.' Mr Bond had settled Frank on a bench, handed him a handkerchief, and told him the police were on the way. 'You'll need to pull yourself together, lad. Get it all out now, as the police will want to ask you questions, and you'll want to answer them calmly.'

'Yes, sir,' Frank whispered.

'I've retained a solicitor on your behalf, a Mr Hayes. He specialises in criminal law.'

'A solicitor?' Frank now looked at the older man, his eyes narrowing. 'What will I need a solicitor for?' He stood and fidgeted in his pockets for nothing.

'Sit down, son,' Mr Bond said and explained that there would be an inquiry, that he, Frank, might be charged with an offence, and that he might have to spend some time in jail.

'Jail?' Frank now pacing like a caged animal. 'Jail? Why will I have to go to jail? I've done nowt!'

'Now, now, Frank. Calm down a bit. I don't believe you'll have anything to worry over. Three eyewitnesses saw all that happened and are willing to testify as witnesses on your behalf.'

The young man was inconsolable. Before being taken away by police (no handcuffs were needed), Frank turned to Mr Bond and asked, 'Could someone fetch me mum? I need me mum.'

***

Eddie had died on the way to hospital. It was Bertie who'd told her. It was Bertie who'd come to the door, alone, without Eddie or Sara, and when Martha Anne looked to the empty street to see if the pair, along with Frank, were following, they weren't.

'Come in, Bertie! Are the lads to follow? Is Sara coming along as well?' Martha Anne headed to the parlour where Cyril and Harry had cleared away the washing and set up the table where they'd all gather for a celebration tea, she'd explained to them. Then she sent them up the stairs to help their sister put the babies to sleep and wash up for company.

She noticed that Bertie had not followed her into the parlour but stood silently weeping at the door. Martha Anne turned and ran back to Bertie. 'What is it, luv? What's 'appened?' She peered back out the window to see two constables heading towards her gate. 'Oh, lord, Bertie, what's gone on?' But the woman could not speak. She just fell into Martha Anne's arms and sobbed.

Martha Anne had shuttered the shop, pulled down the blinds, and sat in the dark waiting. She was waiting for the time to pass, waiting for the gawkers outside her doorstep to pass, and waiting for a judge to decide the fate of her beloved firstborn. Unfortunately, it would be the weekend before she'd find relief in any of it, as the trial was Monday.

She'd been able to see him, her Frank. They were treating him kindly. After all, he was but a boy and a distraught one at that. When she'd entered his cell, he threw himself into her arms, buried his head in her bosom and cried out, 'No, Ma…Nooo, not me Eddie, not me best mate, me brother, me only true friend. It were a mistake, Ma…an accident…and now he's gone.' The boy collapsed to the cold floor, dragging her down with him, and there they sat, he with his head in her lap, she stroking his still soft baby curls, shorn like the sheep he'd been legging…

'Shh…There, there. It'll be all reet, luv…' Martha Anne whispered over and over, trying to reassure them both, but neither could be comforted by these words.

Since then, not only had each of the lads and Gertie gone and sat with their older brother, but God love her, Bertie Reddington went and held Frank as he cried and apologised and swore and begged forgiveness—for God's forgiveness, for her forgiveness, and for Eddie's forgiveness. He told her he'd never be able to forgive himself. He'd never be right with himself again. And Bertie Reddington had held the boy who'd taken her beloved son from her and whispered, 'Shh…There, there. It'll be all reet, luv…' over and over trying to reassure them both, but neither Frank nor Bertie were comforted by these words, either.

The knock on the door came quite early on Saturday morning. The sun was barely on the edge of the sky but promised to be a bright one today. She'd have preferred sleeping the entire day away, but five hungry bellies would be grumbling anytime now, and so she got up. The last three days of waiting had nearly sent her around the bend or at least nearly around the corner to the Wellfield. Lord, she wanted a drink. When she closed her eyes, she could near feel the whisky warm its way to her belly, numb her brow, and slowly wash away the worry her life had turned into in just a few sad days. But she hadn't gone to the pub, she hadn't any in the house, and she hadn't even considered buying any to bring home. She wouldn't, she swore. She couldn't, she hoped. So far, she'd kept her word to herself, and when that did not feel enough, she looked to her Harry, her wary one, the one who kept her in check. Somehow, it was Harry she never wanted to disappoint, and so she was determined not to undo all the good that'd been done this last year. Last night, she did steal a cutty out of Frank's pouch and saved it till the children were asleep. Then she went outside into the cold, stood under the stars, and smoked it right down to the nub.

Martha Anne tried peering out the window to see who would be knocking at this time, and then the thought of Frank alone in a jail cell came to mind, and her heart sped up. She quickly draped her shawl around her shoulders and hurried to the door. When she opened it and saw the slight figure before her, all the world stopped, all the sounds stopped, all the movements at the periphery stopped, and she held her breath high in her throat as tears plumbed and fell over her lashes, her lips trembling.

She could barely say only just the one word, 'Betty…'

'Come 'ere, luv,' the old woman said, opening her arms and taking in the girl she'd loved like her own. Bless her heart, Betty thought as she felt the bones beneath the flesh. Martha Anne had gotten so very thin. She was still a handsome lass, less so as the cheer that once brought beauty to her face had left, replaced with taught lines, a mouth that had lost its smile and eyes that could not meet hers but had hardened on alert. The laundress work was rough on a body, and in Betty's opinion, beneath the likes of someone as smart as Martha Anne Ashworth. *Ah, John, why did you leave her…?* She mused as she watched the younger woman bustling about her home.

Having settled near the fire, taking the kettle from the hob, pouring the tea, and buttering the toast, the two women sat side by side on the small settee. The children were exceptionally quiet, not a one rousing, not even the twins. It was still well before dawn, though, so there was time before they would be. After the kind of catching up one would imagine at this juncture, Martha Anne was at a loss for words and found herself staring into the fire as Betty tutted and shook her head. She felt herself sliding back into herself but was drawn back into reality when Betty's words struck her out of her morbid meditation.

'I'm sorry, you want me to what?' Martha Anne asked.

'Maybe just once or twice a week, to start, as we get sorted.'

'Get what sorted?'

'The cottage, of course, like you'd done when you were little.'

'You want me to come back to work for you?' Martha Anne was incredulous.

'Yes, that's what I've been sayin'. I do. And I want you to bring that little one. What's her name? Gertrude?'

Martha Anne smiled and nodded. 'Yes, yes, that would be Gertie. She's called Gertie.'

'She should learn the ways of the herbs, as well. Don't you agree?'

'I'm…I'm not…this is such a surprise, and in the middle of all that's goin' on with our Frank…' She reached a hand and took Betty's. 'And there's the laundry.'

'Oh, you've got to stop that nonsense. It'll kill you, and you've got too many babes to raise to keep that up. Look at ye! Rail thin, rough hands. You're lookin' older me!' She cackled. 'Well, maybe not that old, but you and I both know you can't keep this up.'

Martha Anne smiled and squeezed Betty's hand. 'Can I think on it? Talk about it when all this business with Frank has passed?'

Betty nodded and then said, 'That's the other bit I'm comin' about.' She sipped her tea.

'What other bit?'

'I've come to take the twins.'

'What?!'

'For the time bein', and the girl—Gertie. I'll take them 'ome w' me. Give you a rest. You're goin' to need it for that court proceeding on Monday. So give me the little ones, and you try to get some sleep. You can come to get them when it's all over, eh?'

And so that was that. Martha Anne squinted into the sunshine as she watched Harry pushing the pram carrying the twins, keeping pace with Betty. The old woman was intent on Gertie as she danced around Betty, chattering away. As Betty was nodding along, Gertie was given to make up stories and seemed to be spinning a right long one. She'd sent Harry with them to help settle into the cottage. He was her most reliable. He kept his head with the twins, whereas Cyril liked to tease them, Frank ignored them, and while Gertie mothered them, she could not manage them on her own.

When she returned to the house, she smelled sausage cooking. Peeking around the doorway, she saw Cyril at the hob, a towel slung over his shoulder, and the kettle was whistling. He poured the water into the mugs and joined his mother, who seemed frozen in the vestibule.

He turned her into the parlour and patted the stuffed chair beside the fire. 'Here, Mum. Come sit.'

'What's all this?' she asked, doing as she was told. Cyril lifted her feet and pulled the hassock under them. 'Oh, my,' she muttered. He placed a heavy throw across her knees, removed her boots and slid fire-warmed socks onto her cold feet. He looked up from his squat and grinned as his mum said, 'I must be the Queen of England come back. May she rest in peace.'

Stirring the fire, brightening the room, he disappeared, and within a few minutes, he returned with a tray. There were biscuits, different cheeses, some dried meat, Yorkshire pudding, and coffee steaming in a mug. He set them on a side table and pulled a chair up to the fire. 'There now,' he said, as he put bits on a plate and passed it over to her. 'Eat up!' He leaned forward as if to watch her do just that.

'Cyril, luv, this is all so much. Where did you get all this food?'

'It were in a basket. Betty Nuppy left it. She said I should put your feet up by the fire, fix you a plate, and make sure that you had a rest.'

She smiled. 'Well, so far, you've followed her directions just reet.'

He smiled back and stared at her, nodding, encouraging her to eat. Each time she took a bite of this and a bite of that, he nodded again.

She was beginning to feel studied. 'Are you goin' to sit there and watch me?' she asked.

'I'm just makin' sure.'

She passed him the plate he'd made. 'Here, 'ave some. I can't eat all this,' she said, and he took it from her, pinching a bite here and there. 'Coffee's good,' she said as she closed her hands around the warm mug and sipped the hot liquid. She didn't often drink coffee. It was a rarity, as it was an expense, but she was happy to have it. It took the edge off wanting a whisky somehow.

They both must've dozed as she'd awakened to find the fire low and Cyril asleep in the chair across from her. She looked out the window to see it was going dark. Harry, she noticed, hadn't returned home. This no longer worried her as he'd been spending a good bit of time down at Sophia Halkyard's Pasty Shop. Sophia had been paying him to do small jobs, something his own mother couldn't do. Martha Anne didn't object since he'd drop a penny in the jar every now and again. But she mostly didn't object because working at the pasty shop meant one less mouth to feed in the scheme of it all. She also thought he fancied Sophia's girl, Mabel. He couldn't go wrong with that one, Martha Anne thought. That Mabel was a busy lass. She worked hard for the shop. She did charity work, and she was devoted to the church. In addition, Mabel was a talented and avid knitter and had gifted all the children mittens last Christmas and a lovely scarf for Harry. She wasn't the prettiest lass in town, and she had a bit of a quick temper and a sharp tongue, but she got things done, that's for sure. At least, Harry would keep warm in her jumpers and caps. And he would know exactly where he stood at all times with Mabel. Martha Anne thought Harry could do with someone taking charge like that, as he more often than not seemed just to go along.

She made her way to the back of the house as she needed to relieve herself. The coffee had gone right through her, she realised. Her back was aching, and she looked to her hands to see the raw redness of her daily laundry labours. Cracked and peeling, there wasn't a salve strong enough to heal the bloody edges of her cuticles. She thought of Betty's offer of a job. She had to admit it would be easier than the laundry, a business that was keeping them in coal and flour, but not enough for the boots, coats, and socks each of her children needed. She'd like to think about it. She'd like to be around Betty, bring Gertie, show her the old ways of herbs and medicinal plants. She wondered if Betty could afford to pay her enough to give up the laundry. Or maybe she'd do both. As quickly as these considerations entered her mind, she shoved them aside, knowing the only thoughts she could manage now were those of Frank and the upcoming trial.

As she returned to the house, she looked to the sky to see the moon was full. It was a big yellow ball hanging suspended in the black curtain of night. She hoped that Frank could see it, too, and know that she was praying for him.

***

Many who'd stood in a queue since the early morning occupied every available seat in the well of the court and the public gallery. Martha Anne, along with Harry and Cyril, Millie, and Bertie Reddington, had been allowed through the back entrance of the court and were seated just behind Frank, who was dressed in a dark jacket, waistcoat, and trousers. These were given to him by Mr Bond, himself, who sat next to Frank. There was much commotion as the audience settled. Martha Anne could barely take it all in, marvelling at the murals above on ceilings seemingly miles away.

There were giant flags of different Orders flying overhead and ornate paintings in gilded frames, tapestries, and knightly shields along the walls. The long mahogany benches ran horizontally across the court, and above there were gangs and gangs of gawkers, Martha Anne thought as she saw them whispering and pointing, laughing, and shaking their heads. These were not friends or even acquaintances that she knew, or her lads and Gertie knew. These were the gossipmongers with pathetic lives out for a lark. For a lark! Her baby boy might be sent to prison, and they were here to cheer that on. She hated them. She seethed within, not knowing where to place her terror, her fear, her…

She stopped the interior rambling and squinted up into the gallery. He was looking right at her. She was sure it was him beneath the brim of his dark hat. Harry was right, he no longer had a moustache, but there wasn't a doubt in her mind that she was looking into the eyes of Samuel Chadwick.

As the chamber doors opened and the magistrate arrived, he turned away and disappeared through the crowd behind him. Martha Anne stood with the rest as the charges against Frank were read to the court.

Most of the rest was a blur. The evidence, Mr Hayes, Frank's solicitor, would show that there'd been a quarrel, that blows were exchanged between the accused and the deceased, that the prisoner had a knife in his hand at the time of the scuffle, and that this knife had caused the death of Edward Reddington when it pierced his heart. Several eyewitnesses had seen the brawl, had watched Eddie lift Frank off his feet, saw the knife enter Eddie's heart as he'd done so, and watched the blood and life seep out of the lad as he lay dying. Many of these and other witnesses testified to Frank's position, to his horror upon seeing what had happened to his friend, they spoke of how distraught he'd been, how he'd rushed to try to help Eddie, and how he'd told all who surrounded him that it was an accident. Each of the witnesses, including Mr Bond, who promised Frank his job when he returned, claimed it was an accident.

It wasn't until Frank had stood in the witness box, raised his hand to swear an oath to tell his truth that she could see he was terrified, and he appeared on the verge of tears. But then she watched as he glanced to Mr Bond, nodded, and took a deep breath. In the proceedings, each solicitor establishing the facts of the case provided by the witnesses, Mr Hayes did something unusual. He asked Frank to come down to the floor of the court. He then invited the witness, Mr Burrell, to join them. Mr Burrell had testified that he'd seen nearly the entire altercation. Mr Hayes then asked Mr Burrell to demonstrate upon Mr Chadwick the actions of Mr Reddington as he recalled them. Mr Burrell was nearly the same height as Eddie, which made the scene all the more realistic. Frank bent forward as he'd been at his cradle that day. Mr Burrell approached Frank roughly, grabbed him around the neck in a chokehold, and threw him to the floor. The crowded court gave a collective gasp. Bertie grasped Martha Anne's hand, and the mothers held onto one another.

Frank returned to the witness box, and Mr Hayes asked Frank if he would like to give his version of events.

Frank looked to the audience and found his mother's face. She gave him a low nod of encouragement. She wouldn't let go of his gaze, and so he relinquished hers. He began, turning to the judge.

'You see, we 'ad a bit of a bother, me and Eddie. I were dressin' a reet good lamb, and Eddie wanted to dress me lamb.' He paused and took a breath. 'When I told him no, he knocked me to the ground, just like Mr Burrell demonstrated. When I got up, I hit 'im in the jaw, and he hit me here.' He pointed to his eye where the once purple bruise was now a yellowish-green. 'I didn't know we were going to fight. I didn't want to fight. I…didn't know I still 'ad me knife in me 'and. Then, suddenly, Eddie closes in and grabs me. I were off me feet. Next thing…I were on me backside, on the ground…and Eddie…he were…' Frank gave a great sob and put his head into his hands. Mr Hayes came over to him, put his hand on Frank's shoulder.

'Do you want to take a break, lad?'

Frank shook his head and wiped his eyes with the heels of his palms. 'No, no…Eddie, he were across the floor, and all I could see were the blood coming through his apron…' He looked around the hushed gallery as all eyes were upon him, all ears tuned to him. 'At first, I didn't know what 'ad 'appened, and then I saw me knife in me 'and.' Frank fidgeted with the cuffs of his suit coat, looking down.

Finally, he shook his head, and as if he were trying to figure something out, he looked back to the court and said, 'Eddie were me best mate...' His lip quivered, and his eyes filled, but he continued. 'We saw each other every day since I were five year old. I were to be his best man...' His voice cracked. 'It were an accident...' He sobbed, then caught his breath. 'I...I wish it'd been me. It'd be easier to be dead than to have to live wi' this the rest of me life.'

He found his mother's face, once again. Tears were streaming down her broad cheeks. She smiled at him. His brow furrowed as if he were confused and seeking the answer. He cocked his head like he did as a boy with a question. Now his tears flowed freely, he shrugged and shook his head. Then said, quietly, 'It were all over a lamb, Mum.'

THE ROCHDALE OBSERVER, MONDAY, FEBRUARY 18, 1904

SLAUGHTERHOUSE TRAGEDY
THE ACCUSED ACQUITTED
AN EYEWITNESS STORY
FATAL SCUFFLE DEMONSTRATED IN COURT
'AN ACCIDENT'

Chapter Sixteen

A cold wind began whipping up as Martha Anne, with the twins and Gertie in tow, arrived home after retrieving the children from Betty Nuppy. She'd set out that morning to fetch them with the intention of being back by noon, but after a short visit of tea and chit-chat, Betty had got right down to her own business. She offered Martha Anne the right proper job of clearing out and cleaning up the shop, learning to make the healing potions, and selling them throughout the villages.

Betty had made her case. 'After all, you've enough lads to run errands and take a load to market in me wagon with me pony.' She coughed and sipped her tea. 'It could be a family enterprise.' She raised her hand to her heart. 'I admit I 'aven't a lot in silver, but I 'ave everything you need: vegetables, chickens, eggs, fibres, and medicine for the lot of 'em.' She waved her hanky towards the children. She looked to Martha Anne and saw she was calculating costs in her mind.

'Landlord's raised the rent, again. I've a need for coal and such. It'll depend on 'ow much silver.' It was now Martha Anne who sipped her tea whilst looking Betty in the eye. She knew the old woman too well. She was a penny-pincher. Betty had more silver lining her pockets than she'd ever let on, and so Martha Anne held her tongue and waited for the haggling to begin.

Betty was no fool, and she was sly about getting what she wanted, and what she wanted was for Martha Anne to work for her. And so she'd made inquiries and learned just what Martha Anne's laundry income and living expenses were, added a few shillings to the top end to sweeten the deal and made sure Martha Anne didn't have to think twice. And by the end, she didn't. She'd only had to think once. She'd agreed to their terms starting the following week when Martha Anne would formally shutter her laundry business for good. She'd sell the mangler and all but a few drying racks, keep her dolly pot, and she might, if things got tight, take in a delicate item or two for her favourite customers. Keep her options open.

After the trial was over, Frank was acquitted, and he had taken a job at Burrell's farm near Manchester. Mr Bond had also offered him his position at the slaughterhouse, but he wanted to get away from Rochdale and all the bad memories that haunted him. She couldn't blame him. He packed up, kissed his mother on the top of her head, and she stood on her threshold watching as he stopped by Bertie Reddington's door. She saw him say a few words, hat in hand, and then Bertie hugged him. He turned on his heels and was off down the lane. Bertie waved to Martha Anne and she in return, but each went inside without a small chat across the street.

Two days later, Frank had sent a note assuring her he was fine. He was bedding in Burrell's hay barn, where it was warm and dry, and eating well. Also, he would only be able to come home on some Sundays, as it was a long walk from there to here and back.

His going had gutted her nearly as much as his father's leaving, gone now almost fifteen years. Even so, one less mouth to feed was one less mouth to feed. Harry'd been spending most days down at Sophia Halkyard's pasty shop. Spending some nights, even. Except for that one week in May when an angry Sophia had chased Harry down the row with a broom. Martha Anne didn't know what happened, and she didn't ask. He must've rectified himself as he was back down there nearly full time since.

She wasn't surprised to find the house empty, fires out or low. She ushered the children through the door, called out for Cyril, although she already knew he wasn't home. He had his own sketchy jobs going on here and there, he'd say coyly. She thought he was still running numbers, but she didn't ask. He put pennies into the jar, and that was all that mattered. She would, though, offer him the job of driving Betty's wagon, making deliveries and doing errands. She thought he'd like it, actually, and maybe it'd keep him out of a bother with the constables.

She and Gertie had got the twins down and were frying sausages when there was a knock at the door. Gertie moved to answer it, but Martha Anne stopped her, as it was going on dusk, and she didn't want the little girl to open it to a stranger.

'No, you stay 'ere and mind the sausages. Cut some bread, too,' she said, passing by her daughter to the front door.

At the gate, she saw a small wagon hitched to an old mule. A woman stood in front of it, holding the hands of two children. Martha Anne stepped outside and closed the door behind her.

'Can I 'elp you?' she asked.

The woman broached, pulling the little ones along. As she came closer, Martha Anne could see that she was far along with child. 'Here!' She thrust a newspaper into Martha Anne's hands. It was the copy of the "Rochdale Observer" folded to the details of Frank's trial.

'I found…it. I found it in 'is coat pocket. He said 'e were a distant cousin.' She tapped the page, directing Martha Anne's eyes to it. 'He said this Frank Chadwick were 'is cousin.'

There were several small black-inked stars along the margins. Martha Anne skimmed some of the familiar lines that gave details about Frank, the lads, and Gertie. And listed Martha Anne as "Mrs Samuel Chadwick". So she looked from the newspaper and into the face of the very young woman.

'I didn't ever hear 'im mention any cousins in Rochdale before. He said 'e were from Cumbria. And then…and then…' The woman stumbled over her own words. 'And then I started countin' them stars in the margins and seein' 'ow each one was along a line with…"names". Your name, the names of Chadwick children, and "his" name…"Samuel".'

So this is where he'd been all these years. Then, finally, Martha Anne began to understand. Making himself a whole new family with this poor young girl who was obviously, sadly, in love with the scoundrel. He'd been caught out.

'And…and…when I asked 'im more about it, 'e says he's only just curious about the trial of this distant cousin.' She gulped air and twisted the edge of her little one's dress in a desperate attempt to calm herself. 'I tried to believe 'im. I tried not to care, but it were plaguin' me. Keepin' me up at night, and so I told me sister Eugenia, and Eugenia starts gettin' the same curiosity as me, and she goes to her friend Violet, and Violet tells her she's got family in Rochdale, and they said…' She stopped and bent to pick up the little girl who was whimpering. She pressed her cheek against the little lass's face. 'They said that it were rumoured that Samuel Chadwick—my Samuel—had stolen money from his mill job and left a wife and little ones, disappeared, and nobody knew where he were…'

'Until now,' Martha Anne whispered.

'Until now,' the woman agreed.

She was but a girl, really. Quite pretty, thin with shiny auburn hair, her eyes a bright green, and her cheeks pink in the wind. She seemed to thrive in the cold as each gust pushed at her as if it strengthened her rather than weakened her. But it was fear that made taught the lines around her mouth and across her forehead.

'Is this you?' She dabbed a finger at the paper again. 'Are you Martha Anne Chadwick? Mrs Samuel Chadwick? Like it says 'ere?' She pointed again to the paper in Martha Anne's hand.

'I am,' Martha Anne said, somewhat hesitantly. 'And you are?'

'I am Rachel Chadwick. Mrs Samuel Chadwick,' the girl said, lip trembling, and she burst into tears.

***

Rachel had been newly hired as a housemaid at The Spindles. This was a large Victorian manor house belonging to Mr and Mrs Albert Stansfield, the local mill owner and his wife. The large castle-like home was located on Station Road in Micklehurst, not far from the mill itself. Sadly, the large house was void of children and full of empty rooms, and so the Stansfields let out these spares to their bachelor workers and their help. Both Rachel and her sister Eugenia worked and lived at The Spindles, and each hoped to meet a young man who would make them his wife.

She'd spied Samuel Chadwick on the very first day of her employment. He was quite handsome with his rugged good looks and twinkly blue eyes. He was dressed in a white shirt with suspenders clipped to tan trousers. He wore a cap low over his brow and was clean-shaven, which appealed to her. He carried a large duffle bag slung over his shoulder and looked at the numbers on each room door. Rachel knew he'd be stopping at the last on the left, but she did not direct him. Instead, she studied his tight wiry form and the grey at his temples. She could see he was much older than she, but he'd given her a long look and a slow grin, and she felt his boyish flirtations immediately.

From that moment on, she could not seem to get him out of her mind, nor be able to help but to run into him…often. And when she did, he was charming. He would ask about her health, her sister, her family. He'd compliment her hair or eyes or hands. She'd promised Eugenia that she was not planning to ambush him outside his room nor happen upon him as he was coming or going out the front door. She truly did not mean to slide by him on the back staircase nearly every evening. And with each apology, smile, brush, whisper against her cheek, into her ear, with each heated allure, she felt herself wanting him, falling in love with him. He'd given her a mystery novel, "The Woman in White" by Wilkie Collins, with the promise of a Sunday outing where they'd wandered the moors with a picnic basket and blanket and where they'd made love for the first time.

Was it any wonder that these encounters became less surprising, more planned, and no longer grabbed moments along staircases and back hallways, but in Samuel's room in the dark of the night where they would devour each other in Samuel's bed at The Spindles?

***

'It were no surprise to either of us when I found meself was with a babe,' Rachel said, now seated at Martha Anne's kitchen table, with a little one on her lap. 'Samuel, right away, insisted we 'make an honest woman of me' were his very words. He never mentioned he were already married, never mind kids.'

'Don't imagine he would.'

'He told me he'd been to Africa, Spain, and Germany. That he'd worked in London, and then Manchester, never mentioned Rochdale.'

'Never mentioned Africa or Spain to me, but did mention Germany as I once heard him speak it. So where did you say you're from, lass?'

'Mossley. After we were married, we moved out of The Spindles and onto Tabley Street.'

'Yorkshire?' Martha Anne laughed. 'Just over the line? That's how far away he got? What's he do?'

'He worked as a packer at the mill. It were a good life, a happy life. I love 'im.' The young woman sniffed and wiped her nose as she told her story.

'Why didn't you believe 'im? I mean, about a distant cousin?' Martha Anne asked. 'Why'd you come lookin'?'

Tears welled in the girl's eyes, and her face became red. Anger seemed to replace the grief she'd been feeling just minutes before. She took a deep breath to calm herself.

'Before any of this came about, Samuel had been acting a bit peculiar. He'd pretend to go to work but not showin' up. He were gettin' notices about it. He tore 'em up and told me not to worry. And I didn't because the pay packets weren't gettin' any smaller, so what did I know?'

Martha Anne stared at her, wondering if she was expecting an answer.

'Nowt! I knew nowt!'

'There now,' was all Martha Anne could think to say.

'Then I see he's got a notice. They fired 'im! But 'e doesn't tell me. He's goin' off to work every day, like always…wi' out a care in the world, bringin' sweets 'ome for me babes, a bit of a bob for me. He's been lovely. Lovelier than ever if I 'ad to admit.'

'Well, that's good then, yes?'

Rachel let her cup fall to its saucer with a clatter, and she began apologising. Martha Anne noticed her hands were shaking.

'Here, luv, what is it?' Martha Anne asked, but the young woman could not seem to find the words, and when she did, they came out in one long-winded sentence.

'You'd think I could just forget it, go along with his charade. Pretend everything is all reet. Lately, though, I noticed his things 'ave started to go missin'. Not right away, but over time, a pair of shoes, a shirt, his good razor replaced with an old one. And I'm startin' to think he's readyin' to leave me— us.'

Martha Anne tutted and shook her head. 'Well, it's not beyond him, I can tell you that, but I don't remember him packin' up. I just remember him gone. Maybe he's just gettin' a new wardrobe, goin' to look for jobs, eh?' she said hopefully.

Rachel shook her head and let loose a new round of tears. 'If he leaves, I'll be left alone with three babies and no husband. Then what will I do?' She looked up at Martha Anne, tears brimming, fear embedded as the realisation of her situation was unfolding before her.

Sadly, Martha Anne shook her head but did not bring up the irony, as the girl recounted nearly her own story.

There I were, left alone with four babes…

***

'I dunno,' Martha Anne said, answering Betty's question regarding the young Mrs Chadwick's intentions towards her. 'I felt bad for her. She seems to really love him. It's been a couple of rotten blows in a row. Findin' out your 'usband's got a first and legal wife, but four children he abandoned along wi' her.'

'He's a scoundrel, 'e is,' Betty tutted and shook her head. 'That part about 'im goin' off to a job 'e didn't 'ave, that sounds like your Samuel, the way 'e robbed your dad.'

'Not my Samuel anymore, is 'e?'

Betty shrugged. 'Technically, 'e is. Legally, 'e is. If 'e died tomorrow, not only would ye be responsible for 'is burial, you'd get whatever pension or severance or savings he had. You, Mrs Chadwick, not her. She's been livin' a sham marriage. Poor thing never knew what 'appened.'

Martha Anne said, 'She asked would I give him a divorce, and I couldn't 'elp but laugh. I told her she could 'ave him, but only he could divorce me, and that would cost a pretty penny and a King's decree.'

'So, 'ow'd you leave it wi' her?' Betty asked.

Martha Anne shrugged and began moving crates from the morning's deliveries to the bench table in the middle of the shop. 'Weren't much to leave. I told her I were sorry she were in such a spot, an' that I had no interest in Samuel Chadwick. I said I hoped she'd find some peace. She hugged me, actually. And said she were sorry to bring such news. Then she climbed up into her wagon wi' her babes and went back to Yorkshire, I imagine.'

'He's a rotter,' Betty said.

'That he is.'

'Good riddance to bad rubbish, as me ol' granny used to say…' Betty laughed.

It had been a long hard work week. Both Cyril and Gertie had taken Betty's wagon and pony and made all the deliveries around Milnrow and Newhey, down to the city centre, up Toad Lane to the market, and out along the canal where many lived too far away and couldn't get to Betty's shop. Their orders were long-standing and consistent. Betty insisted on teaching Martha Anne how to make the poultices and potions, the healing powders, drops, balms, and rubs that kept the farm and factory families of Rochdale and her surrounding villages healthy. Cyril did a fine job handling the pony, and he and Gertie together made quick work of the drop-offs and pickups. Life was settling into a rhythm, Martha Anne considered one morning, as she waved to a customer from behind the shop counter. The place was spruced up, and Martha Anne was making it her own, as Betty more and more retreated to the back rooms where she made potions or read articles or, lately, took naps they both pretended she didn't take.

Betty had been coughing up blood for some time now. She'd hidden it well, but this morning, Martha Anne caught a glimpse of the red bloom on the white handkerchief in Betty's hand. She looked into the older woman's eyes, and her own filled with tears.

'It's all reet, luv,' Betty assured. 'I'm in no pain. But time is short, and we've much work to do. That's why I brought you 'ere. No one can learn as quickly as you. You're smart, lass. You always 'ave been. So, this is what we must do, now.' She took Martha Anne's hand and squeezed as the young woman's lip trembled, and tears flowed. 'Come on, luv. Take a breath, suck it up. Everybody dies someday.'

Chapter Seventeen

February 1905

The little boy was bundled in a coat and scarf with a heavy wool hat on his head. His face was red, chapped by the cold and wind. He jumped down from the donkey's back, hitched it to the post in front of Betty's shop and came trotting up the path. Both Martha Anne and Betty watched him through the window. His eyes darted from one door to the next, trying to decide which of the three to enter.

'Do you know him?' Martha Anne asked Betty.

'Don't recognise him. Couldn't be more than six or seven by the size of him, can he?'

'He's a little one. He reminds me of someone, like one of me lad's friends, but I can't quite place him.'

The bell chimed as the little lad pushed open the door, letting a sweep of cold air fill the room. He closed it quickly behind him. His eyes were big, and he stood staring at the two women when finally, his sights set on Martha Anne.

'Mrs Chadwick? Is that you?'

It was then she recognised him. He was the little boy who'd come along with his mother, Rachel, those few months ago. What was his name? Ah, yes, 'Stanley?' she asked, as she recalled.

'Yes, it's me, Stanley Chadwick.'

'Why, lad, you're far from home all on your own. And you're freezin'.' She grabbed his little red hands in her own, put them to her lips and blew warm air on them. 'Here, let's get some hot tea into you.'

Despite his chattering teeth and shivering limbs, he said, 'No time, ma'am, no disrespect. But me mum sent me.'

Martha Anne poured the tea despite his protestations. She set the cup in front of him. 'You can drink and talk at the same time,' she said. 'But not another word until you've warmed a bit.'

The boy did as he was told, and when his shivering had subsided, he said, 'It's about me dad.'

'What about him?' Martha Anne threw a sideways glance towards Betty.

'He's bleedin'. Bad.'

'Bleedin'?! From where?'

The boy put his hand to his own throat and sliced across his neck. 'From his neck.'

'But how?'

'Dunno. Mum just said to fetch you home as fast as I can. Would you like to ride on me donkey, ma'am?'

They'd left the donkey in Betty's croft and hitched the pony to the cart. Martha Anne urged the little mare to its top speeds when it was safe. She prayed it could pull them up the little hill to the other side of the moors where they would wend their way down to Mossley and Tabley Street.

When they'd finally reached their destination, the sun had gone down, and dusk was beginning to fall. She'd let the little boy take the pony to his donkey's shed, and she promised him a penny if he'd wipe her down and warm her up.

She lugged her large medicine bag up the steps and knocked on the door. When no one came, she tried the handle and let herself in. Sitting beside the fire wrapped in a blanket was the little girl she'd met when Rachel had come along with Stanley.

'Hello, Hilda.' Martha Anne crouched down and said in a soft voice. 'Your mum's sent for me. I've got me special medicine bag here.' She lifted the satchel for the girl to see.

She had her thumb in her mouth, and she was twirling a skein of hair around her finger. She just stared at Martha Anne.

'Can you tell me where your mummy and daddy are?'

The girl pointed to the stairs behind Martha Anne.

The room was hot and smelled of copper. The air tasted metallic against the back of her throat. The fire roared, and the windowpanes dripped sweat. The first that caught her eye was Rachel pressed up against the wall, her eyes large, hair a ruffled mess. She had blood on her apron, her hands, even smeared across the bridge of her nose, and she was staring at seemingly nothing. Martha Anne followed her gaze to where her husband, Samuel, was propped up in the bed against a pile of pillows. He was holding a towel to his neck, and his nightshirt was drenched a rich blood-red wine. She saw that his face was grey, and it took some effort for him to lift his head off the pillow to address her, and when he did, he managed a grin. His words, while animated and clear, came winded and short of breath.

'Ah, there you are, Martha Anne. Good…good to see…you. I knew…you'd come.' He reached for her hand, but she did not extend it. She saw a bloody penknife lying on the blanket beside but not in his free hand.

She looked from him to Rachel and back again. 'What in bloody 'ell 'appened here?'

After some silence, he finally said, 'I dunno. I…was…I…tried…I dunno,' he stammered. 'Martha Anne, can we speak later? Could you fix me up?'

Turning her back on him, she gestured to Rachel to step outside the door.

'He's bleedin' good in there,' Martha Anne said. 'What 'appened?'

'It's like he said. I come up the stairs, and there he were bleedin' all over everythin'. I asked, "What have ye done?" And he just said 'e didn't know.'

'That all? That doesn't make sense.' Martha Anne pulled Rachel closer. 'Look, if you want me 'elp, you're goin' to have to tell me the truth. I can't 'elp you if you're lyin'.'

This seemed to give the younger woman pause.

In low tones and whispers, Rachel began, 'This mornin', I'm in me kitchen when there's a knock on me back door. There's never a knock on me back door, and so it startled me. Samuel was off to work, and the babes were playin' on the floor by the hob. I wiped off me 'ands, and tried to see through the window, but I couldn't, and so I opened the door, and there were a girl—*a girl!*—standin' there with her belly fuller than mine. She tells me 'er name is Helen and she's to be married to Samuel this week. She came around to fetch 'im because she needed some money. And by the way, she 'ad the nerve to ask me, *Who are you?*'

'And so, she attacked him?'

'No, no, I sent her away. I told her 'e didn't live here anymore. I told her I 'adn't seen him for days, and I told her I was Mrs Chadwick "number two".'

'So, you attacked him?'

Rachel shook her head slowly. 'No…I don't think I did. I came into the room, and there he were bleedin' from the neck, and when I asked him what had 'appened, he said he didn't know, just like 'e told you.'

There was a sound on the other side of the door, and Martha Anne frowned at Rachel. 'So, you're tellin' me that after this…this…girl who's with

Samuel's child came by, told you all about it, and he decides to cut his own throat?'

Rachel nodded quickly. 'That's what I'm sayin'.'

'So what do you want me to do about it?'

Rachel looked towards the bedroom door, heard Samuel moaning, and shrugged her shoulders in response to Martha Anne's question.

Martha Anne re-entered the bedroom to find the towel Samuel had around his throat had fallen off, and the wound, which was a good two inches long and an inch deep, was now just weeping blood. She opened her bag of medicines at the foot of his bed. He looked up at her and smiled.

'Awe…thanks…thanks…luv. You're a good soul. How are me lads and Gertie?'

As he spoke, his voice a whisper, Martha Anne's movements became slower, and she felt her heart begin to pound. She looked down at him, and asked, 'Which lads are you askin' for?' As he began to recite their names, small bubbles of blood popped at his throat, and she could see that the cut ran a bit deeper than she first thought and was agitated when he spoke, as blood oozed faster with every word. She sat down on the bed and slowly rolled out some gauze, cutting it with a pair of scissors, all the while asking Samuel about his own family. The names of his new children, his new wife, his new job, and each time he answered, the gape in his neck seemed to stretch and open wider. Now the sticky red flow was thick and seeped into the collar of his nightshirt and the blanket that was covering him.

She held up the gauze to see that it was ragged at one end and said, 'Oh, this won't do. How can I wrap your wound if I can't cut a straight line?' She hopped off the bed, jostling him, and hearing him moan made her hop back on the bed.

'Oh, sorry 'bout that. Did you know Cyril got run over by a wagon?' And she jostled the bed again, this time making him wince.

She cut another piece of gauze and then another, none as perfect as she'd like, but when she finally had the right one, she noticed Samuel's eyes had closed. She gave him a little slap to wake him up.

'Our 'arry's doin' all reet. Got 'imself a job workin' at a pasty shop. Looks like he's sweet on a girl.' Martha Anne lifted the heavy bag and thrust it across his legs, dropping it on his lap, forcing him to sit up, and this sent a fountain of blood spouting from his neck.

'Ooh, you'll want to try to clamp your hand over that spray, there,' she said as he slapped a palm across his throat.

'Now, Samuel, tell me the truth, did you slit your own throat, or did that little lass finally have her fill of you and your seed-spreadin' ways?'

He opened his eyes and pleaded with her. 'Please, Martha…please 'elp me…'

All the while holding the gauze and the paste she'd applied to it just above his throat. 'Did you know our Frank is workin' on a farm now?' she asked.

He reached out and attempted to grab her wrist, pulling at it. 'Help me, Martha Anne.' His voice came raspy, gurgled, and it was then she saw the spittle of blood on his lips, his tongue, and he coughed up a lump of bright red phlegm.

'Did you slit your own throat, or did she do it for all of us?' Martha Anne asked.

'I dunno…' His voice was but a whisper.

Martha Anne wondered softly, 'How can I help you, Samuel? Shall I leave you the way you left me? Shall we make sure you don't leave yet another and another with babes to raise alone wi'out you? How many more of us might there be scattered around the north?'

And yet, she was the only true Mrs Chadwick.

She noticed, at that point, that his breathing had slowed, each cough bringing up bloody spittle, and so she settled the gauze on her lap and waited.

When she was sure he was dead, she applied the bandage and the poultices to his neck. She'd gotten her own hands bloodied, and she went down the stairs where Rachel and her children waited. She shook her head and told Rachel to send for the doctor and the constable, as Samuel left the world by his own hand, and that would have to be looked into.

'I'll wait 'ere wi' you, so you won't be alone when they come to ask questions,' Martha Anne said, as the girl sat sobbing with her head in her hands. 'Sadly, our answers will be the same when asked. We don't know why he done himself in, and neither did he, but that's the story we've got, isn't it? And so that's the story we'll tell.'

***

After his death, Martha Anne was free. She was a free and clear widow. Respectable. No longer a wife scorned and left. No, now she was the head of the household! A merry widow! She liked to sing out and then laugh. In every way, she felt free. And Betty had been right, Samuel had left a pension, and it was hers. It was small, for sure, but she felt no regret when she split it in two and sent half to Rachel Chadwick and her babes over in Mossley. She'd never heard from or seen her again after that horrible night, when they each, covered in blood, sat with the doctor and constable and told the same and only story they knew about Samuel's death. And she felt all right about it. They each had their own reconciling to do, and it was better if they'd figured it out on their own. For their children's sake, if nothing else.

'Mummy?' Gertie asked, bringing Martha Anne out of her contemplations as they made their way to Betty Nuppy's shop. 'Do you think Auntie Betty will let me make the lavender balms today?' the little girl asked but did not wait for an answer as she spied her little brothers jumping in a trickle of a stream, and she ran to catch up with them.

It was a beautiful spring day. The sun was high in the blue sky, and there was nary a cloud in sight. Enough of a breeze to cut down on the smoke from the chimneys so she could see all the way across the moors as they rounded up Betty Nuppy Lane. The birds were chirping, bees buzzing by, and sheep and cows could be heard lowing in the fields. Flowers in bloom wafted fragrances through the air, and it was so warm that she took off her jumper and placed it in the pram, which was not filled with twins but extra shoes, shirts, nappies, and blankets for their walk home later. She watched as Gertie stomped her foot and splashed the lads, and their lilting giggles were bouncing and echoing along the lane.

She was immediately concerned when she rounded the bend and saw that not only was the door to the shop closed, but the croft doors were still shut, and the animals inside were making loud noises. She left the pram at the gate. She told Gertie to take the twins and open the croft to let the animals out into the fields. When they'd disappeared into the squat building at the edge of the garden, she turned and walked towards the cottage.

Martha Anne lifted the latch and entered the darkened shop. It was cold as the fire in the corner was out. She was shaking as she'd stepped up into the house where the cold and the dark had settled in overnight. Quietly making her way to Betty's room at the back, she could feel the emptiness of the cottage, all the while knowing the old woman was still there. Opening the door, she pushed into the small cavern to see the fire had been out for a long time. Candles snuffed to the wicks. And there, in the bed with her singular long white plait draped down her chest, hands clasped together, eyes closed, lay her most beloved amid a most peaceful dream. There was a small, sweet smile turning up at the edges of her mouth, and all the lines that had once etched her face had smoothed to a baby's newness.

Martha Anne draped herself across her friend, wrapped her arms around her small bony remains, and wept.

***

It wasn't long after the funeral when Martha Anne had been sent an official letter by a local solicitor, a Mr Allen Pindar Walrath, Esquire, asking her to come to his office in the city centre to settle the affairs of one Miss Elizabeth Nell Nuppy of Nuppy Lane, Newhey, Lancashire, England. Martha Anne had brought Cyril along as he was the one with a head for numbers and details of complicated issues. They'd both dressed up in their Sunday best, and Cyril drove them in Betty's pony cart.

The matter was not complicated at all, however. Betty had left everything to Martha Anne. The little farm, cottage, croft, and the entirety of the shop. There were a few papers to sign, but in the end, it had taken them only a few minutes to manage it all. And so, she treated herself and Cyril to tea at the Flying Horse. Only now she did not sit at the bar, nor have a whisky, but instead, she and her son in their finest, feeling like the lord and lady of the manor, treated themselves to a fancy meal where soups, joints, entrees, and sweets were on the menu, and they had one of each, then promised not to tell the others. They did stop at the Chippy on the way home and brought back enough to feed the King's Guard if they happened by.

Frank and Harry had come home to help with the move from Prince Street to Nuppy Lane. They'd only had two loads in the little wagon to bring. That evening, they'd sat around the kitchen, telling stories and remembering together. The twins sat by the fire with kittens on their laps and were stuffed sleepy with their celebration tea of lamb stew and thick crusty bread. Cyril played the fool, told the jokes, and even recited a bawdy tune that had his older brothers sputtering and coughing. She watched Gertie settled between Frank and Harry as she worshipped them both, sitting like a princess between her knights in shining armour. Martha Anne could see that both Frank and Harry were well on their own paths. Both talked excitedly about signing up with the 6th Lancashire Fusiliers, and she knew once they'd gone, they belonged not for her keeping but for God's.

That night, with all her babes tucked in, warmed by the fire in the hearth, this might be, perhaps, the last time they'd all sleep under the same roof. She stepped outside and stood under the black star-studded sky. The moon was but a sliver, shining over the Pennines. The rushing sound of a nearby stream splashed above the crickets and a tawny owl, and in the distance, she could hear the bells of St Chad's, she was sure. The air was crisp, and she could smell wood smoke from neighbouring hearths.

Just as she was about to go back inside, she was startled by a chubby little robin, who had lighted on the fence rail near her hand. It was unusual that she was out at night. She had a wad of straw in his beak, and she was looking intently at Martha Anne.

Betty had once told her that robins were a sign of good luck, new beginnings, and rebirth. Then the bird flew above her head, up into the eaves of the cottage, just above the door, where there was a nest, and the chirping of babies could be heard.

END

Incorrigible Rogue Book Club Discussion Questions

1. In England, the 1824 Vagrancy Act was aimed at the punishment of "idle and disorderly persons," "rogues," and "vagabonds." It defined an "incorrigible rogue" as a homeless person who violently resisted arrest or escaped confinement (this law wasn't actually taken off the books until 2013). How, if at all, did being charged as an 'incorrigible rogue' change the trajectory of Martha Anne's life?

2. How does the author want us to feel about Martha Anne?

3. Was Martha Anne's life was reactive rather than responsive? Was she a survivor who was "dealt a bad hand in life" or did she get the life she deserved?

4. Whose actions were the most consequential for Martha Anne – Malcolm's or Samuel's?

5. How would you describe Martha Anne's relationship with Malcolm? Was it love? Did she believe Malcolm would choose her over Alice?

6. How did the "women of the night" contribute to the development of Martha Anne?

7. Who are the heroes in Martha Anne's life? Is she a hero in anyone's life?

8. What do you think happened to Martha Anne's creativity? Did it manifest itself in other ways? Or was it lost to other priorities?

9. Were you surprised...
...how easily Martha Anne betrayed Alice?
...that Martha Anne and Lizbeth reconciled?

10. How important was family to Martha Anne?

11. How did the lack of mothering affect Martha Anne's development as a person (or did it)?

12. How did the birth of Frank affect Martha Anne? Do you think she was a good mother? What is your definition of a "good mother"?

Note: Be sure everyone has read the [Author's Note/Q&A] before asking these questions.

13. Were you surprised to learn Martha Anne was a real person? Did it change your opinion of her?

14. The author talks about "redeeming" Martha Anne. Did she succeed?

Interview with *Incorrigible Rogue* author Cynn Chadwick by free-lance editor Anne-Marie Dany

A-M: What was your inspiration for writing this book?

Cynn: All my life, I'd heard about my great grandmother, Martha Ann Ashworth; she was born in Lancashire, Rochdale England in the 19th century. She'd been known to me through family stories as: a fishwife, a drunkard, a whore, and a brawler. There were stories of a husband who fled her, a man who beat her, sons who dragged her from fights in pubs, and yet, something didn't ring true as she'd lived long and kept her family close. I made the journey to England to do some research about her, and while there, I realized that I'd somehow been called (100 years later) to redeem her of these charges, or to try to understand how they'd been leveled against her in the first place.

A-M: Wow, Martha Ann was a real person! You say you wanted to redeem her through this book. Do you feel you succeeded?

Cynn: I had to really think about this one. Even though the notion of "redeeming" Martha Anne has been with me since the beginning of writing this story, I looked up the actual definition of redemption: "to compensate for the fault of something", and so I'm not sure that is exactly what I have done. I think, rather than redemption, I have given her a chance to tell her side of her story. Because the family histories had painted her to be so awful, I'd hoped I'd be able to lift her to some other station through this story. Instead, in some ways, it's not so much a "compensation for a fault" but rather an explanation for many of the bad behaviors and the wrong decisions she'd made through her early years. There are no stories of later heroics, no stories of turning her life around, no stories of a sudden epiphany in which she makes up for all she'd put her children through, but...maybe there's a certain comfort in knowing, or at least believing, that many of the disasters of her life were beyond her control, and she was mostly re-acting to it all. Have I succeeded in redeeming her?

Maybe not for anyone but myself. If nothing else, I do believe I've succeeded in opening up a seemingly one-dimensional life to the possibilities that her awful reputation was only part of the story, and perhaps she was not as simple, as horrid, as these stories had let us believe.

A-M: What was your process for writing this book? For example, did you have family stories you knew you wanted to include, so you wrote those sections and then figured out how to connect them?

Cynn: There were a number of anecdotal stories I'd heard about Martha Ann my whole life. They were like punctuation points with lots of blank space in between:

She'd "got herself pregnant..." "Her husband Samuel fled her" "Her lads (sons) would drag her home from the pub, sparking her clogs on the cobbles" she'd become a notable: "drunk, fishwife, whore, brawler..."

Made me wonder how she got to these stations of life? What forces were behind these stories? What had happened to her? Who had harmed her? Ignored her? Used her? The adult me had gone looking for answers. I wondered who she'd been in-between these shitty moments of her life. What kind of girl had she been? What sort of circumstances had led to and from her choices or lack thereof? And it was these curiosities that made me want to fill in those spaces in her in-between.

A-M: It sounds like you did a lot of research. Do you see yourself writing another book based on that research, perhaps focusing on the lives and perspectives of one (or more) of the other characters?

Cynn: I did not anticipate the amount of research I had to do. All novelists do research to some degree or another, but my admiration for the historical novelist grew miles for having written this book. In addition to being ignorant of the history, I was ignorant of the place, as an American. It was especially challenging trying to get everything right in terms of language, dialect, attitudes, and the very specific culture of The North of England. In order to ground myself in place, I chose to go to UK for 2 weeks in the bleakest month of February. I wanted to feel what it must've been like to have lived during such a bleak time at the turn of the 19th Century. And, it was bleak: cold, gray, windy, rainy, snowy, and sleeting serving up exactly what I was looking for, slipping on cobblestones, sliding in mud, getting soaked to the skin...and reminding myself as I soaked in the hot shower at my hotel that she did not go home to this.

I am very interested in continuing to explore writing historical fiction. I have an inkling to write, perhaps, about a character like Betty Nuppy. While Betty was a real person, an herbalist, her character is actually more based on Rochdale's own "wise woman" called Nell Racker who was described as "Wild-haired and witch-like" and lived and practiced in Rochdale. She was suspected to be a witch, and perhaps an abortionist. She was born in 1846 and lived till 1933...and there are pictures of her. I am also interested in the story of a family who now resides in the little graveyard behind my house, and that research might be easier to obtain, so we'll see...

A-M: If you could go back in time and talk to Martha Anne when she was still a child, what would you want to say to her?

Cynn: Wow, this is a great but really hard question to answer. I'd want to tell her that her creativity, her smarts, and her curiosity were enough; that they could see her through. I'd want to encourage her to rely on those gifts instead of on the men who were going to disappoint, use, and abandon her. I'd want to tell her that so much of what she would go through was not her fault, and I'd want to let her know how much I felt her fear and frustration and anger...and, I wished there'd been more joy.